I saw something flash past my nose, but it missed, and I hit Mr. Shanghai in the back of the head as he went by.

At first, I thought he was just wearing brass knuckles, but it also looked like a blade. As it turned out, it was both. An Ophidian Shuriken is a razor-sharp, four-pointed, steel star about the diameter of a hockey puck. It can be thrown, but it usually isn't. There are three finger holes in its center, and the bottom point swivels out of the way so it can be gripped in a man's palm with the remaining three points protruding outward. The ordinary gangbanger usually cuts himself before he gets to the main event, but in the right hands, an OS slices wide, deep, and frequent, and unleashes so much blood the opponent usually flees in terror. I've also seen eyes punctured and one driven through a carotid. It's an ugly weapon with ugly results.

I hit the floor rolling, but before I could get my feet under me, one of Quan's bodyguards threw himself on my back and knocked my wind to Schenectady. While I was deciding if I was going to die, the other clown kicked me in the side of the head . . .

D0802668

By Neil Russell

Rail Black Novels
WILDCASE
CITY OF WAR

Nonfiction
CAN I STILL KISS YOU? ANSWERING YOUR
CHILDREN'S QUESTIONS ABOUT CANCER

NEIL
RUSSELL

WILDCASE

A RAIL BLACK NOVEL

HARPER

An Imprint of HarperCollins*Publishers*

HARPER

An Imprint of HarperCollins*Publishers*
10 East 53rd Street
New York, New York 10022-5299

Copyright © 2011 by Neil Russell
ISBN 978-0-06-172173-1

First Harper paperback printing: March 2011

HarperCollins ® and Harper ® are registered trademarks of Harper-Collins Publishers.

Printed in the United States of America

Visit Harper paperbacks on the World Wide Web at www.harpercollins.com

10 9 8 7 6 5 4 3 2 1

*This book is dedicated to America's
and Great Britain's special operations teams,
and especially to the brave members of Delta Force.
I have been fortunate to be able to call
many of you friends.
May God bless you and your families
and guide you on your missions.
Our children sleep in peace tonight
because of your sacrifice.*

My sister can play aces full. It's what you do with two small pair that separates the artists from the shoe clerks.

AN UNKNOWN GAMBLER

1

Ashes and Badges

Just coming out of the Cajon Pass, a goddamn stop sign came hurtling out of the darkness and whanged across my hood. At the speed I was traveling, it sounded like a manhole cover, not to mention the divot it dug. Somewhere a Rolls-Royce paint salesman smiled.

The road to Vegas is always busy. Even in the middle of the night. And when the high desert winds are blowing, it's deadly. Dodging fishtailing big rigs in blinding sand is as much fun as lights-out in a Turkish prison. The only thing that could make it worse is if you've had one too many and haven't slept since the day before yesterday. As the actress once said, "Who do I have to fuck to get off this picture?"

LAPD Deputy Chief Yale Maywood had suggested I follow him in my car because he didn't know when he'd be able to free up somebody to run me back to town. That gave the attitude-infused cop chauffeuring him the opportunity to make it as difficult as possible. Dancing steel and machine-gun-velocity debris screamed, "Slow down, asshole!" but he kept banging along at ninety, and I had to do the same to keep the city-issue Crown Vic in sight. Eventually, traffic began to thin, making the unmarked sedan a little easier to see, and the right-to-left hurricane steadied enough that I didn't have to keep jerking the steering wheel a quarter turn into it.

My day hadn't started any better . . .

Woody Allen likes to say, "I'm not afraid of dying; I just don't want to be there when it happens." Having been close a few times, I'm with Woody. Unfortunately, when it comes to people I care about, too often I've drawn the short straw. This time it was Bert Rixon.

We stood on the aft deck of my yacht, the *Sanrevelle,* and looked into the clear, noontime sky, the gusting breeze threatening to blow into something bigger. I'd double-checked the coordinates with the Neptune Society before we'd left Newport Beach, so I knew we were in the right place. Hopefully, they'd given the air charter the same information. Under normal circumstances, I'd have asked my own pilot, Eddie Buffalo, and his usual right-seater, Jody Miller, to do the ash drop in Jody's Stearman, but Eddie was in New Orleans handling some business for his mother, and Jody was showing off his plane at a Wisconsin air show.

Bert had picked this spot himself, halfway between Catalina and San Nicolas Islands. It was where he'd been fishing when Brittany had finally agreed to marry him. At the time, he'd been battling a twenty-pound barracuda, so he'd been a little distracted and hadn't quite caught what she said until she reached over the transom and cut his line with his brand-new Microtech knife, which she then proceeded to drop. That's Brittany's trademark. If she's on a boat, she's going to lose something over the side. Glassware, bracelets, hats, who knows how many shoes, and one time, two pieces of a sectional sofa—but since she'd been trying to throw them at Bert, they may not count.

The proposal and lost knife had been eight years ago. She'd been twenty-three, and fresh off the Laker Girls roster with a torn labrum, her place taken by a nineteen-year-old centerfold who wasn't likely to surrender it after Brittany rehabbed. Bert Rixon was a newly minted triple centimillionaire, not yet out of his thirties, who'd sold his cutting-edge prosthesis business to a private equity firm, then pissed them off to the point that they barred him from the offices.

The ALS diagnosis had come last year, and the doctor had given Bert eighteen months. He'd been an optimist. It took nine. The last two . . . well, some things are better left unsaid.

Now, all five-three of the Widow Rixon was huddled against me, and even though the sun was warm, I felt her trembling. Rhonda Champion stood at the railing with her new husband, Oscar, a reality show producer who was minting money on one of the chick networks with something called *Let's Go Buy a Purse*. Somehow, I kept forgetting to TiVo it. Rhonda and I had once been involved, and it didn't end smoothly. She does interior design, mostly on yachts, which is how she met Oscar, and he went head over heels for her, something you wish for everyone.

There were a dozen others on deck, craning their necks, looking for the plane, most fellow boaters from the Dolphin Bay Yacht Club. As usual, the majority were wearing my sunglasses. When you own a boat, you keep extra shades around, and I'd found this little company, Zeal, that had smart designs and grasped the concept that people come with different face shapes. I ordered an assortment to keep in a tray in the salon. Only now, when guests arrive, the first thing they do is put their own glasses in their pockets and grab mine. The day somebody returns a pair, a gong's going to go off, and a duck will come down and hand them a check for ten grand.

Mallory, my very British houseman and best friend, was on the fly bridge, keeping the Benetti from bumping around too much in the chop. At 102 feet, it's more boat than I need; more even than I wanted. It was custom-built for one of the NBA's premiere big men who liked the same colors I do—red and black—but suddenly found himself playing in Europe for a tenth of his former salary. When you're my size and find a doorway that doesn't leave knots on your fore-head, you buy it. If it's surrounded by a beautiful piece of machinery, so much the better.

My watch said 12:21, more correctly Bert's watch. A black and gold Rolex with a little too much going on with the dial for my taste. Normally, I don't wear jewelry of any kind, but the week before he died, Bert handed it to me with tears in his eyes. He tried to say something, but his throat muscles had lost their ability to make words, so I put it on and thanked him. My plan was to toss it in a drawer when I got home, but Bert had had the Rolex's bracelet replaced with a simple, black alligator strap, which I found unusually comfortable. I left it on, and now, as I felt Brittany's fingers brush over it, I was glad I had.

I heard the plane before I saw it. The pilot was coming right out of the sun, so we had to wait until he banked to get a glimpse. I'd asked him to make a low pass over the *Sanrevelle* first, and he took me literally. He couldn't have been more than ten feet over the deck when he went by, and that close, even a single-engine Cessna looks large. I could see the two men inside. They were young and clearly happy to be flying on a travel-poster day. I couldn't blame them.

The prop wash combined with the wind blew some expensive hair around, and I heard an agonized female voice cry out, "What the fuck?" which would have amused Bert no end. Then the Cessna climbed back to a thousand feet and made another approach. I heard the engine slow and saw an arm extend out the passenger side. The sun caught the ashes as they spread. They looked like tiny pieces of silver . . . drifting . . . swirling . . . And then it was over. The pilot kicked the plane back to speed and turned toward the mainland. Brittany buried her face in my jacket.

"Rail . . . Rail Black . . . you come out here *right now*!"

The words were alcohol-slurred and the voice familiar. I was in the *Sanrevelle*'s salon with Emilio, the yacht club chef, and his significant other, Tenelle, sous chef at the Montage, trying to wrangle an invitation for dinner. I ignored the interruption the first time, but it got louder, and profanity was added, so I excused myself and threaded my way through the crowd just as the Brazilian band came back from a break.

Bert had planned the party, all the way down to who couldn't come—a longer list than those who could—but it was an uneasy fun we were having. Every person aboard had cared deeply about him, even when he was being an asshole, and the small talk was manufactured and the dancing halfhearted. Then Brittany had gotten too drunk too fast and made something of a scene with one of the musicians. She was in my bed now, sleeping it off, and I didn't expect to hear from her until well into tomorrow. But it takes the edge off a memorial when the widow does a lap dance on the drummer.

As I stepped onto the aft deck, Rhonda was swaying uneasily and holding a bottle of champagne in one hand and a glass in the other. The Santa Ana winds had kicked up strong and driven everybody else inside. While her hair blew wildly, and her dress fought against modesty, she took a slug of Brut, then tried to refill the glass and missed. "Well, fuck it anyway if you won't hold still," she said and threw the offending vessel over the side. If she was intending to hit water, she missed by 180 degrees, and I heard glass shatter on the concrete dock.

She was now drinking from the bottle, and based on the two staggering steps she took backward as she raised it, this wasn't going to be her first empty. The problem was that, unlike Brittany, Rhonda could pound it all night and not pass out. She either got passionate or belligerent, and sometimes both. I looked around for Oscar, but she set me straight. "Cocksucker left. Said I could fuck my way home." She grinned crookedly. "I told him I didn't have to cause I was just gonna fuck you and stay. After all, you're no stranger to this pussy, are you?"

Wonderful. Just wonderful. So much for grabbing a couple

of beers and some bonito fishing with the new husband. "How about I get somebody at the club to run you home, Rhonda? Maybe you can get there in time for makeup sex."

"I can have all the makeup sex I want without going a step past that big-ass mattress of yours. Now, come here, Mr. Black." She was loud enough now that pretty much everyone was drifting in our direction to see what the commotion was.

She advanced toward me, unsteady, but undaunted. With her free hand, she reached over her head and unclipped the back of her little black dress. There was no graceful way to handle this, so as she fumbled with the zipper, I plucked the champagne bottle out of her hand and swept her up in my right arm. She threw her head back and shouted at the stars. "I'm gonna ride you until I can't walk."

Taking a couple of long strides, I cleared her feet over the transom and dropped her, leveraging her far enough out so she wouldn't hit the ship on the way down. It was a good fifteen-foot plunge. Time enough for her to get off a, "You motherfucker!" before the splash.

I was suddenly very tired, and as the crowd began meandering back inside, I made my way along the railing to the pilothouse. Mallory was seated in one of the captain's chairs, holding court with a couple of good-looking women whose husbands were talking navigation equipment.

"I'm going to walk up to the club and get a room," I said. "Tomorrow, I want to run down to Dana Point for a couple of hours; then we can head back to Beverly Hills."

"What about Mrs. Rixon? Will she be okay alone?"

"I'll ask her if she wants to go with us, but my guess is, she'll pass. She needs to find her way through this, and her support network is right here."

I saw Mallory's eyes drift beyond me and through the windshield. I turned. Two young men in suits were coming down the pier. They might as well have had signs around their necks. A couple of very junior plainclothesmen, hoping someday to make detective, but now just equal parts grandstand and nervousness. I stepped outside, and they looked up but kept walking until they got to the portable wooden staircase that led up to my deck. I watched them pick their way past a young couple locked in a heavy embrace, and a few seconds later, they were standing in front of me.

"You Black?" one of them said out of the corner of his mouth. I think he was trying to sound like Lenny Briscoe, but when you're a fast twenty-four with a pimple on your nose and chewing gum, it doesn't have the same impact.

"It's gotta be him," his partner said. "They said he's bigger than hell."

"Either of you ever been on a boat before?" I asked.

The question seemed to confuse them, so I waited until Mr. Wrigley came up with an answer. "My old man used to go fishing up at Big Bear. Had a little aluminum job. Why?"

I looked at his partner. "You?"

He shook his head no.

"Well, the first thing you do is ask permission to come aboard. The second, you don't scuff up my deck with leather soles."

They both involuntarily looked at their feet. The one guy mumbled, "Sorry," but Gum Boy wasn't on the same page. He flashed his badge and gave me a stare he must have practiced in the mirror. There are two things that really frost my ass. One is post office clerks going on break when there's a line, and the other is the I'm-a-cop-and-you're-not attitude of about 10 percent of every force in America. The ones who look at a soccer mom with a carload of six-year-olds, and say, "I know she's dirty, she just hasn't made a mistake yet."

When you see it, you can make book that, growing up, the guy was a bully. He also isn't going to heal. For the doubters, drop by a cop convention. It'll take less time than it took to park your car to find the go-ahead-make-my-day crowd. They'll be hanging together, grabbing their nuts in front of women, and talking loud. Even other cops don't want to be around them.

I looked at the badge, then at its owner. "You're thirty

miles outside your jurisdiction, Junior." Then I turned and went back into the pilothouse.

It took about ten seconds for him to follow me, but I reached out and closed the door in his face. While the two couples watched in silence, I turned my back on the glass and told Mallory that Rhonda was going to need some dry clothes and a ride home. A couple of moments later, I heard the cops walking back along the deck, then saw them striding up the pier, the jerk waving his arms and talking loudly to his partner while the wind whipped their hair and suit coats.

Five minutes later, a middle-aged, uniformed officer wearing all the brass in the world came down the same way. I knew him. Yale Maywood. A good man, a legendary cop. I stepped back on deck, and he stopped just below.

"Evening, Yale."

"Sorry about the false start," he said. "Thin recruiting class. We gotta pay bounties just to fill the ranks."

"That one's gonna be a problem his whole career. Along about the fifth lawsuit, the ACLU'll send you a plaque."

"Three more fuckin' years, I'm fishin' in the Ozarks."

"What can I do for you, Chief?"

"Like you to take a ride with me."

"Can it wait till morning?"

"If it could, I'd be fightin' my Lab for a spot on the sofa." I hesitated, and he added, "Chuck Brando's dead. Lucille too."

2

Voodoo and Victorville

As the dark desert stretched out in front of me, I turned my thoughts to LAPD Homicide Capt. Charles Scott Brando, whose forty-second birthday party I had recently attended.

Every year, my foundation gives a chunk of money to Blue Rescue. Whenever a cop or firefighter in LA County dies in the line of duty, BR pays off their mortgage. And if they're renting, they buy the life partner a house. No publicity, no bows. It just happens. I can't think of a better way to send people off to do a life-or-death job than for them to know that if it all goes to shit, their loved ones will have a roof.

Chuck was on the board. My attorney, Jake Praxis, Hollywood's gift to the Bone Crusher Hall of Fame, introduced us. Somebody had written a best seller about one of Chuck's cases, and Paramount was pretending they never heard of him. That's correct. If you do something noteworthy, and a story is published about it, it can be made into a movie without your getting paid. The writer gets a check, but not necessarily the guy who lived it. Producers don't even have to tell you go to piss up a rope, but they like to anyway.

To avoid a hassle, the studio usually offers you a nickel, and if you don't get weepy over their generosity, they tell the screenwriter to change your name or ethnicity or composite you, and bingo, legally, you're not depicted anymore. If the story's big enough, and you're so entwined in it that even the Hollywood sharks can't figure out how to separate you from events, they simply work from news stories, official documents and interviews and turn you into a cardboard figure. And good luck with a lawsuit over cardboard. That is, unless you can make noise. But it has to be the right kind of noise.

Life story rights and technical advisor services are the mother's milk of movies based on real events, but you can count on one hand the number of attorneys you want representing you in this rarefied air. For my money, you can count them on one finger, Jake Praxis, but that doesn't keep every real estate and tax clown with a bar number from regularly getting civilians screwed six ways from Sunday. A wise man once said, "Everybody's got two businesses: their own and show business." A doctor sees something he doesn't understand, he calls in a specialist. Lawyers? Take a look at the Senate.

With Chuck, Paramount's position was basically, there are a million cops out there who can tell us which gun goes with a brown suit, and we already own the book. If you don't like what you see on-screen, take a number. And while you're at it, go fuck yourself.

So Jake dusted off another of Chuck's cases, sobered up our mutual friend, the spottily employed, but brilliant screenwriter, Richie Catcavage, and while Paramount was giving everybody the finger, Jake got a script in three weeks and a greenlight from Warners two days later. The picture was called *Voodoo Tax,* which is cop talk for a senior officer shaking down a crooked underling. As in, "Pay up, motherfucker, or some bad voodoo is gonna come take your pension away."

The execs at the mountain logo heard about it when a photo of Chuck shaking hands with the star who was going to play him hit the front page of *Daily Variety,* and like good studio folks everywhere, the hard talk got in line behind seven-figure incomes and instant tables at the Ivy. And presto! Chuck had *two* movies, and Paramount sprinted to pay twice what Jake had originally asked. To quote Mr. Praxis, who stole the line from Frank Yablans, "The biggest sin in life is to have leverage and not use it."

When *Voodoo Tax* got nominated for an Oscar, Chuck bought a laptop and started writing his own books. Five best sellers later, he was the richest cop since Wambaugh and playing golf at Riviera. Since he'd joined the Blue Rescue board, Chuck had become our go-to guy. His celebrity status helped raise funds, but he was also a rock for survivors. People revered him, and not without reason. He was as fine a man as any I had ever met, and he and his wife, Lucille, were inseparable. I guess they still were.

Not too long ago, Victorville was a wide spot in the road where you filled up with cheap gas before running the last two and a half hours to Sin City. Now, it's the fastest-growing city in California. Affordable housing eighty miles city hall to city hall has also made it a refuge for LA civil servants, including lots and lots of cops. If you're a home invasion specialist with a death wish, move to Victorville.

We stayed on the freeway through town, got off at the second exit north, and headed into the desert along Quarry Road. The immediate and total darkness coupled with the occasional sand whorl swallowed my headlights. About five miles in, my escort turned right onto an unpaved road and, off in the distance, I could see the flashing red and blue lights that marked our destination.

Chuck Brando had used his movie money to buy seventy acres along a stream fed by an underground spring. Over the last several thousand years, the stream had cut a deep enough ravine that Chuck periodically had to chase rock climbers off his property. He told me that every now and then, he caught a good-sized trout down there, but what he really cared about was the two-hundred-yard swatch of thick woods that the water nourished along the sides. "I call it

Oregon without the rain," he'd said. But as I approached it tonight, Oregon looked like a gale-whipped Vincent Price flick.

Ahead, I saw several LAPD squad cars and crime scene vehicles scattered around a long, low main house and a pair of Los Angeles County ambulances parked nose to nose across the front walk. There was a corral on the right, where two horses poked their heads over the fence, watching the goings-on and, a little farther along, several ATVs and a backhoe parked in a neat line near a whitewashed shed. When I got out of my car, the wind was still stiff but easing, and Yale Maywood was waiting for me on the porch. I didn't see his plainclothes detail anywhere.

The deputy chief was wearing a surgical cap, mask, booties and latex gloves. He handed me a set. When I was dressed, he said, "I'm told it's a little raw in there," and opened a jar of Vicks. We dabbed VapoRub on our masks, and went inside.

A dozen men and women, similarly attired, were efficiently going about their business. The place had been trashed. Broken light fixtures. Random chunks of plaster pounded out of walls. Food stuck to the ceiling. A cigarette had burned itself out on the coffee table, reducing a magazine to ashes, but remarkably, it hadn't spread. This wasn't a systematic search by professionals looking for valuables, but frenzied, like somebody on drugs . . . or kids.

Yale read my mind. "That's what I thought too, but wait."

We threaded our way past the CSI people and turned left down a long hallway. It had been hot in the living room, but as we walked, I could feel the temperature going up. Each room we passed was a mess, and on the laundry room floor lay a dead beagle, not more than a year old. It didn't have any marks on it, so I guessed its neck had been broken. Whoever had done this had been filled with, not just violence, but cruelty.

The master bedroom was starkly illuminated with large, law enforcement spotlights, raising the heat index even higher, and as we approached, I saw camera flashes. Nothing, however, could have prepared me for what was inside.

Chuck, a handy guy with a welding torch, had constructed an overhead bed frame out of wrist-thick, tempered steel that Lucille had draped with lightweight, ivory muslin. At the foot of the bed, the fabric had been torn down, and Chuck, naked, his hands cuffed behind him, was strung up by his ankles. At least, I assumed it was Chuck, because his welding equipment was also in the room, and it had been used liberally on the body, which was swollen grotesquely, indicating that it had been hanging there a while.

Despite the Vicks, the smell was overpowering. You can get familiar with the putrefaction of death, but you never get used to it. I felt bile rising in the back of my throat and took a few short, shallow breaths. Yale was a little green too but stepped toward the corpse. As he did, some foul-smelling gas escaped through its mouth, and the change in pressure caused the body to slowly turn forty-five degrees to face us. Whatever the animal who did this was after, there would have been no satisfaction in defacing a corpse, so Chuck had lived through most of it. The thought caused me to shudder involuntarily.

Yale pointed to a spot on the white comforter where there were two dirty marks like somebody had knelt there while he worked or perhaps where an accomplice had positioned himself to ask questions. Here was the only blood I could see. Large dried spots the size of silver dollars had been sprayed around near the body's head, then a small puddle had formed between the two depressions.

"Looks like Chuck got his teeth into somebody," I said.

"Chief, you might want to see this," said a diminutive female technician squatting on the other side of the bed.

Yale and I bent over her and looked. On the carpet was a piece of white fabric, about three inches long, soaked in blood. Using a pair of tweezers, she carefully unfolded the material revealing what looked like a chunk of jerky. Chuck had indeed bitten one of his killers, right through his shirt.

Yale stood up. "Somebody left here with a permanent reminder."

I needed some air and said so. Outside, the wind had calmed a little, so we dropped one side of our masks and stood on the porch, letting the hot breeze cleanse the stench in our nostrils.

"I didn't see his wife."

Deputy Chief Maywood shook his head. "We'll take ATVs to where she is, but first I want to go over a couple of things."

"Like why you brought me out here?"

"It was my idea. When I suggested it, the chief almost had to be restrained."

I wasn't surprised. I'd filed a lawsuit against the department last year, and it hadn't left me on very good terms with Yale's boss. It had only been a ploy to get some homicide people off the dime, but because I'm a quasi-celebrity, basically for no other reason than having a lot of money, the media ran it up everybody's ass for a few weeks.

I said, "He's a big boy. Tell him to get over it."

Yale grunted. "He's a hothead, but once he got a grip, he agreed." He stopped, shifted his weight a couple of times, then spit it out. "Rail, we need a favor. We want you to keep Jake Praxis on a short leash on this."

I don't know what I'd been anticipating, but this wasn't it. "You find somebody Jake listens to, let me know. But why would he get involved anyway? Looks like one of Chuck's old collars came back to settle a score. Or somebody didn't like the way he was portrayed in a novel. You'll have a short list in twenty-four hours. At least, that's what all the books say you guys do."

He looked uncomfortable. "We're not going to tell anybody. At least not right away. This gets out, no matter how it happened, it starts the clock on a whole lot of shit we don't need."

He must have seen the look on my face. "We've got a little time. Chuck didn't have any family, and far as we know, Lucille's people are all in China . . ."

I'd had enough and cut him off, "What are you talking about? Not tell anybody? Jesus Christ, Yale, you want eye-balls on this. You want tips." I paused. "Unless you already know who did it."

"We don't, but Chuck was handling something sensitive. Other lives might be at stake. That's why we need you to intervene with Praxis. If that fuckin' lawyer you guys are so in love with starts making noise, it . . ." He stopped. "Look, I can't get into it. I need you to trust me."

He was making absolutely no sense. Cops don't cover up murders. Especially when it's another cop who's dead. "I think you picked the wrong guy. You should have brought Jake out here himself."

"I suggested that, but the chief said you were the right guy."

"Meaning there are more ways to fuck with a civilian than a member of the bar."

"You said it, I didn't."

"Then there's that messy business that as an officer of the court, Jake would be obligated to report a crime—including the ones you're committing."

"You want to stand around moralizing, I'll catch a nap and come back when you've blown yourself out."

Police chiefs aren't cops, they're politicians. That goes double for deputy chiefs. My father used to say that we ought to take *politician* out of the dictionary and replace it with "coconut." That anybody willing to be called a coconut for a chance to serve his community is exactly the kind of civil servant we want. The older I get, the more I agree.

"Coconut," I said.

"What's that supposed to mean?"

"Private observation." I changed the subject. "So what about the locals? And the San Berdoo D.A.? This is on their doorstep."

He jerked his head toward the house. "They've each had a guy in there, so they're covered . . . and cooperating. And they don't know any more than I've told you."

I watched a tumbleweed blow across the front yard. "If you want me to even try, you better give me something with a little more heft to it, because what I've got now won't even slow Jake down."

"Let's go see Lucille."

3

White Napkins and Red Roofs

More crime scene floods outlined one end of the structure. We'd run a couple of miles over a fairly rough piece of desert with the wind at our backs, and now the sand smoothed out like it had been graded. I couldn't quite make out what we were coming up on, then I recognized the shape. A Pullman railroad car. Probably from the thirties. Painted a shiny, dark green with fancy, gold script above the row of windows. . .

New Orleans and San Francisco Railway

And in bold letters below the glass . . .

THE LADY LUCILLE

We parked next to two ATVs on the right, away from the yellow tape at the car's other end. A pair of LAPD Ford Explorers sat a few yards away. Through the Pullman's rectangular, curtained windows, I could see a brass lamps sitting on white-clothed tables. The *Lady Lucille* was a restored dining car, and, from the looks of her, first-class.

"Chuck bought it for Lucille," Yale said, answering my unspoken question. "Usually, it's guys who have a train jones, but Lucille wouldn't fly and got hooked on railroads. Was a walking history book on the subject. Once Chuck had some cash, he surprised her. Spent a goddamn fortune finding just what he wanted and having it rebuilt." He pointed to the track. "This siding's one of the reasons he bought the land. Practically the whole department came out the day it rolled in from Chicago. Never saw anybody so happy as that lady."

"I noticed a couple of horses on my way in."

"You know anything about Arabians?"

"That they're expensive."

"'Bout all you need. Except that sometimes people don't take care of their animals, and the ASPCA don't have a pot to piss in."

"So Lucille did horse rescues."

"To quote Chuck: 'It'd be cheaper to take in lonely 747s.' I figure since Lucille couldn't have kids, she compensated. My wife would say I don't know shit about women."

There was a uniformed officer at the foot of the steps. "We need to suit up?" Yale asked.

The officer shook his head. "No, Chief, they've already vacuumed and dusted for prints. But if I was you, I'd sure use some Vicks."

He didn't have to tell me twice. I took the jar from Yale and dabbed a healthy dollop under each nostril. We mounted the steps and entered.

The workmanship inside was beautiful. Mahogany and brass with thick, dark green carpeting. Two rows of green leather booths ran its length, and the starched tablecloths looked even more formal than they had from outside.

A sound system was thumping away with something I'd heard before but couldn't place. It wasn't abrasively loud, but it was jarring, and the guy singing pulled you right into the song.

"'Red Right Hand' by Nick Cave," said Maywood. "An Aussie. My kids used to play it when they wanted to creep out their mother. Didn't do much for me either. It was on when she was found. Endless loop. Either part of some ritual or somebody messing with us. I told them to leave it on until we can get a tech in here to see how the system was programmed. Maybe pick up a print."

I gave up trying to figure out murderers after my parents were killed by a guy my father made rich. "It will have been burned off something. You might want to check the source code."

He looked at me like a turd on his arch supports. "No shit, why didn't I think of that?"

The ceremonial dressing-down of a civilian out of the way, he got back to business. "Lucille used this place for an office. Quite a businesswoman. Had their money invested all over the place. Not like Chuck. Long as he had ten bucks for a pastrami sandwich and a cup of Joe, he didn't give a shit if he slept in his truck."

Most of the CSI people were at the other end. A few more stood between us and the tables, and as one shifted, I saw the back of a woman's head and a bare right shoulder in one of the booths. Lucille had coal black hair, and I recognized the Pleshette cut. I also noticed a phone and a stack of papers. She'd apparently been working.

"Any idea how long she's been here, Phil?" Yale asked a lanky, older man in a brown suit and Hush Puppies.

"Not ready to make that assessment yet, Chief. But I'd say forty to fifty hours give or take."

"What's the give, and what's the take?"

"I gotta check the weather service's hourly temperatures for the last few days. The air conditioner's running, and the thermostat's set to sixty-eight, but just to be sure, I'm gonna need a chart and a calculator."

"Don't jack me off, Phil. If it's sixty-eight now, it's probably been sixty-eight the whole time. Give me your best guess."

Phil shifted his weight, squinted, and stroked his chin in the practiced way they teach at functionary school while you're thinking up a way to dodge going on the record.

"Phil, give me a fuckin' time. Now."

"Tuesday afternoon," he finally drawled. "Between three and four. But that's not when they started working on her." He shook his head. "That was about five hours earlier."

He stepped aside giving me a full view, and I saw what he meant. One of the table napkins had been rolled into a kerchief and tied at the back of her neck. A wooden spoon had then been slotted through the knot so the noose could be tightened and loosened to alternate suffocation with breathing. The technique probably goes back as far as human conflict, but it was perfected by Torquemada.

The instructors at Delta Force's interrogation school had put each of us through one round, just to give us the feel of it, and I still remember how glad I was when it was over. Done by an expert, the subject can be taken into unconsciousness and back indefinitely. It's a gruesome way to extract information, requiring a steady hand and a dulled sense of empathy, but it's almost one hundred percent effective. Given a choice, you'd run to be waterboarded.

Yale walked beyond the table, and I moved to the body's front. In some ways, this was worse than Chuck. At least he was a cop. Violence was in the job description. Healthy, handsome ladies in their thirties aren't supposed to die. And they certainly aren't supposed to die this way.

The USC cheerleader Lucille had been was still evident, and her trillion-cut diamond earrings of a couple of carats each were still in place, so any lingering idea of robbery was put to rest. She had always drawn admiring looks from men—me among them—which made her current nakedness all the more disconcerting. But when I finally registered what my eyes were seeing, I had to force my analytical brain back into service.

Her delicate Hong-Kong-born face, though now corpse gray, had been kept from becoming death-distorted by the low temperature, but that was where natural stopped. The baseball-sized head of a jade tiger had been jammed into her mouth, mashing her lips and breaking teeth. The animal's watchful expression now stared at me directly beneath the horror in Lucille's wide-open eyes. Its positioning was obviously deliberate and meant to convey a message, but as I searched my mental archives for something that made sense, I came up empty.

Yale wasn't doing much better. "They described it to me on the phone, but . . ."

Phil pointed to the corner we had passed on our way in. A two-foot shelf jutted out from the wall, and the headless body of a crouching tiger sat on it like a ruin in a museum. I'm not a jade expert, but I know pieces that size are expensive. Probably at least $25,000.

"Damn thing must weigh ten pounds," Phil said. "They had to beat hell out of it on the doorjamb to get the head off, so as slick as they were with everything else, it seems like an afterthought."

Maybe, but it was more interesting that it had been put back on the shelf.

I returned to Lucille. Her wrists had been taped behind her, and on the table next to an open *Wall Street Journal* were several bloody single-edge razor blades and a folded square of stained, medium grit sandpaper. Some sadist had cut multiple striations down each of her breasts then ground down her nipples with sandpaper until they weren't much more than brown circles. Large droplets of dried blood from the procedures had spattered the tablecloth, run down her bare stomach and pooled in her lap.

Her sliced, raw flesh had also been painted with a greenish brown liquid that had blistered the skin. Near the blades and sandpaper were two unlabeled, pharmaceutical bottles, their brush tops off and lying to the side. Through the clear glass, I could see the contents of one was bright red, the other the same dark color as the residue on Lucille's breasts. I leaned down and inhaled from the red one. The unmistakable metallic smell of blood was undercut by something slightly sweet that I didn't recognize. When I did the same to the other bottle, even cut by the Vicks, the fumes caused me to jerk my head away. "What the hell is that?" I asked.

"Don't rightly know," answered Phil. "Sulfuric acid probably, but until I get it to the lab, I gotta take the Fifth. Looks like our boy brushed the cuts with this stuff to bring her around after the choking. The other bottle . . . your guess is as good as mine. It's none of my business, but from the looks of it, Lucille was just as stubborn as her husband."

I knelt and looked under the table. More blood had run down Lucille's legs and onto the floor. Her ankles had been taped to the stainless steel, center support pole, and straining against it had caused her bare feet to swell to twice their normal size. She was also wearing panties, which for some reason, I thought odd. As I stood up again, I noticed the shredded leather backrest where her bound hands had frantically torn at the only thing they could reach.

What in the hell could this woman have possibly known that somebody would go to this much trouble to find out? It was coldhearted to be thinking about the torturer's inconvenience, but she and Chuck were beyond insult. The kind of questioning they had undergone takes time, and even a psychopath knows that the longer he's on the scene, the more likely it is somebody will stumble in.

I stood and looked at Phil. "What's your guess on cause of death?"

Phil looked at Yale for an okay and got it. "She didn't lose enough blood to kill her, and the usual signs of asphyxiation aren't there, meaning the tiger head went in after she was already gone. I'm gonna guess heart. But I might find a needle mark when I get her on the tray, so put a maybe on it."

"Semen?" Sometimes, a professional will have a fetish and take time to indulge himself. The panties and welder's torch on Chuck argued against it, but I needed to ask.

"Nope. Guys mighta taken a piss or two up front, but that's all. Didn't leave anything in the shitter, but we'll pull the tank and check for cigarette butts and whatever."

"How many?"

"We got several sets of ATV tracks, but the wind's pretty much ruined them. No vehicle, though, and Lucille didn't hoof it out here."

"So somebody drove hers back to the house."

"That would be my guess. Way I hear it is that Chuck's got a slew of them and always kept two right out front for running around the property. Killers probably doubled up on the way out and came back singleton. Why bring more if two will do."

Phil knew his stuff. Two was my bet too. Somebody to do the heavy lifting while the pro asked the questions. "How about other blood?" I was thinking about the bite Chuck had taken out of one of his assailants. Maybe if they hadn't been able to get what they wanted out of him, they'd come out here, grasping at straws.

He shook his head. "Other than what's obviously Lucille's, none."

That meant Lucille had been done first, making it all the more incomprehensible. But it did account for the trashing at the house and probably the dead puppy. They hadn't gotten what they came for. I turned to Yale. "Who found them?"

"One of our guys. Mike Lombardo. He'd been calling and not getting an answer, so he came out."

"Drove eighty miles rather than have a local cop take a look?"

Yale looked at Phil, who got the message and walked to the other end of the car. When he was out of earshot, the deputy chief lowered his voice. "I told you Chuck was in the middle of something sensitive."

"Sensitive enough to get him killed."

"It's possible."

"'Possible' isn't any more than you gave me earlier. So far that cage you want Jake Praxis in doesn't have any sides. You're going to have to open up, Yale."

"Can't do. We're appealing to you as a citizen."

"I live in Beverly Hills. The LAPD thinks we're assholes."

He didn't think that was funny, so I told him I didn't like

being dragged way the hell out in the middle of nowhere to have my stomach turned, then strong-armed into a bullshit assignment a priest couldn't make good on.

He was silent for long moment, like he was trying to figure out a way to tell me something without telling me. But as clever as cops are about sucking information out of a brick, when it comes to dispensing it, they've got one eye on the code of silence and the other on their pension. Eventually, Yale shook his head, turned and walked out. Before I followed, I took another long look at Lucille. I thought I saw a tear in the corner of one eye, but it could have been my imagination.

Yale was standing by the ATVs, double pumping a Camel Ultra Light. He offered the pack, but I declined. "Don't blame you. Like smokin' a tampon. Fuckin' Surgeon General."

I noticed that his hands weren't steady. Dead friends notwithstanding, he'd been around enough bodies. His emotions should have had calluses on top of calluses. It didn't take a genius to know he wanted to say something but couldn't get started.

Normally, I sit people out. Sooner or later, most open up. They just need to get to it in their own way. But with a cop, unless you've been his partner for seven lifetimes, that can take forever. They're also born with a case of big dick, so prodding them only causes them to dig in deeper. The only way to speed up the process is to have them in a vise, and even then, a cop will drag his feet until every option expires. Sometimes, internal affairs people must just scratch their heads.

I didn't have anything that would scare a deputy chief anyway, and I sensed Maywood was really trying. So I took a stab in the dark. "I don't believe I'm taking this tour because of Jake Praxis."

"Why do you say that?"

His answer should have been to tell me to believe anything I liked and, while I was at it, to go fuck myself. He knew that too. He was letting me pull something loose.

"Because the chief wouldn't put his cold, calculating ass in anybody's hands. Not mine, not Jake's and especially not yours." Yale's cigarette had burned down to his fingertips. He dropped it and lit another, but this time he broke off the filter. "I think you and the chief are up to your neck in shit, and you're dancing without choreography. Only you're not very good at it." I took the pack of Camels from him and lit one for myself.

As I blew smoke toward the stars, he said, "You remember Lefty Delano?"

"The SWAT guy who got dropped by another sniper?"

"Two ex-Marines a thousand yards apart, staring at each other through their scopes. Know what Lefty's last words were? 'Motherfucker's got seven grand worth of McMillan, and I'm sittin' here with a peashooter some budget director was able to slip past City Council. Color me dead.'"

We smoked and watched the silent, blinking lights of a jet at thirty thousand feet.

Finally, I said, "Even a McMillan can't aim itself."

Yale turned to face me. He suddenly looked very tired. "Couple of weeks ago, Lucille comes to see me. Never been alone with the woman in my life, but there we were, huddled in a back booth of the Biltmore bar like we're getting ready for a nooner. She's completely at ease. Got both her hands on mine and looking me right in the eyes. I got no idea what's going on. All I can think about is she's going to ask me to get a room, and I ain't about to do that to Chuck. Then again, she's an eyeful."

"You've got quite an opinion of yourself."

I'd caught him off guard, and he laughed. "Hey, I'm a cop." But it seemed to loosen him up a little. "She asks me to make her a promise. I'm so relieved I'm not going to have to sweat the hard decision, I say, sure, anything. She leans real close and almost whispers, 'There's a chance something could happen. Something bad. Soon. If it does, I need to know you'll keep it from going public until . . .' Then she just stops."

He shook out another Camel. "So I'm waiting for the rest, and I can see her turning it over. You know how it is with a woman who's trying to protect somebody. Like if she says it, it's going to happen for sure."

I did know. She'd worked up her courage, worn just the right outfit and practiced her lines. Then at the critical moment, she saw it in her mind and suddenly realized she wasn't talking about a maybe. "I won't insult you by asking if you pressed, but did she say anything about Chuck knowing she was there?"

"She was real clear it was all her. Then she just got up and left."

"So when this mess went down, you started asking yourself if there was anything you could have done. And, of course, there was plenty—not the least of which was watch the house instead of just having Lombardo call once in a while. Then, you had to lay the whole thing out for the chief. That must have been one mother of a walk down the hall. And sensitive as his royal highness is, he's thinking about his own butt hanging out there, and he unloads—hard."

I waited for a reaction, but he just kept smoking. So I continued, "But the chief's boxed in because if it comes out that one of his guys—a deputy chief, no less—knew this was a possibility and sat on his hands, he might as well walk over to the *Times* and grab his ankles. But maybe, if he authorizes some kind of investigation—top secret, like the lady asked—he can buy enough time to get fitted for an asbestos suit. How am I doing?"

"The detective exam's coming up. You should maybe look into it."

"And I'm going to make the leap that if Chuck was working on something sensitive, it wasn't for the department. At least not officially."

I'm always uncomfortable when I catch somebody bullshitting me. Usually, a lot more uncomfortable than the bullshitter. This time, though, Yale Maywood was suffering enough for the both of us.

So there it was. He was carrying the guilt of the ages. His pension was probably safe, but the day he hit the door, his picture was coming off the wall. And that was almost as bad. "There any more layers on this cake?"

He glanced at me nervously, and I got a sick feeling in the pit of my stomach. "One. Lucille said that if anything happened, I was to tell you. That you'd know exactly what to do. That's the biggest reason I dropped the ball. I figured I was just last in a line of people who knew more than I did."

He was still talking, but I didn't hear him. Me? What did he mean, tell me? I'd only been in the same room with Lucille Brando a few times. And those were social events. I saw Chuck only marginally more often. At board meetings and for a couple of lunches. We'd played Hold 'Em at some director's house after Chuck's first picture came out, but that was it. Secrets that can get people dead I don't usually forget.

"And, of course, you didn't tell the chief this last part," I said. It wasn't a question, and he didn't answer.

Two lab guys came out of the Pullman. One of them lit a joint and passed it to his friend. I don't do drugs, but if there's a job where a little weed should be part of the gear, these guys had it.

"So how long's the chief going to hold his water?" I asked.

"I'd say until the first time somebody asks him a question."

On my way back to the freeway, I almost ran off the road twice. If I tried to make it home in my current sleep-deprived condition, I'd be able to personally ask Chuck and Lucille what happened. As soon as I hit the city limits of Victorville, I saw a sign for a Red Roof Inn, which, in my punchy state, got me laughing about a hotel owner named Red Roof. Real funny stuff when you're out on your feet. My eyes were so blurry I had to feel my way into the parking lot.

The young, African-American clerk in a smart-looking navy blue jacket glanced up when she heard me coming. I knew the look. She was about to ask if I was a Laker. I was wrong. She knew exactly who I was, and my Platinum Card confirmed it.

"You're the guy who got shot last year, aren't you? It was like the only thing on TV for a couple of weeks."

Jesus, why couldn't I have gotten some dim bulb with her head in a magazine? I didn't say anything.

"You're a billionaire or something, right? What're you doing in Victorville?"

Her name tag read ZENDA COLE. I gave her my best smile. "Actually, Ms. Cole, at the risk of sounding like a jerk, I just did a couple of Vegas all-nighters, and I shouldn't have been on the road this long."

She smiled. "Made that drive sleepy a few times myself. No fun. No fun at all. Glad you're all healed up." And from that moment on, she couldn't have been more accommodating. I was checked in and directed to a room in thirty seconds.

I may have undressed first, or maybe I pulled off my clothes in my sleep. Either way, it was the most wonderful mattress I've ever fallen into. My compliments to Mr. Roof.

Omelets and Saints

When I awoke, I thought I was in Rio. It was probably the cheap painting of Corcovado on the wall, but it could have been the dream about the machete fight with the guy wearing a smiling piranha T-shirt. That had actually happened in Prague, but somewhere in my reptilian brain, it had gotten turned into Brazil and tended to show up when I was beyond exhausted.

I stood under the hot shower until my skin wrinkled, then dressed. Since everything I'd come in with was on my back, I was good to go. I noticed the clock. It was 4:45. I'd slept twelve hours. All I wanted now was a twenty-four-hour breakfast menu.

I opened the door and stepped out. Half a second later, somebody stuck a pump shotgun under my chin, and a voice yelled, "On your belly! Hands on the back of your head!"

I had a snappy comeback, but a rifle butt to my kidneys sent it packing. I went down on both knees and felt a pair of cuffs being jammed onto my wrists. Remembering Chuck Brando, it wasn't a comforting thought.

FBI Special Agent in Charge Francesca Huston sat across

from me. I knew her name because she'd pushed one of her business cards along the laminated table between us. We were in one of those buses like country music stars use, only this one was dressed out like an office, and there weren't any windows. I heard the engine, probably to keep the air-conditioning blowing, but all it was putting out was a luke-warm breeze.

The contents of my wallet were spread neatly on the table, facing her. So were my registration, cell phone, Thomas Guide, and two coupons from Burger King that had been in my Rolls's factory-installed safe. The way I see it, any thief who has to resort to that kind of B&E probably isn't eating regularly.

"You're welcome to everything but my free Whoppers," I said. She didn't think I was funny, but the thumping pain in my lower back might have hindered my delivery.

"What are you doing in Victorville, Mr. Black?"

"I heard you might be in town. Okay to just call you, 'sir'?"

Despite my winning personality, she looked at me without any warmth at all. "When you finish playing the lounge, we'll get down to business."

"I'll make you a deal. You take these cuffs off, and we'll find ourselves a Denny's and talk. Otherwise, one of those cards is for a guy named Praxis. He's my attorney."

"I'm familiar with Mr. Praxis. We're not doing a film deal. And if you're thinking about pulling another stunt like you did last year with the LAPD, the FBI doesn't blink."

First Chuck and Lucille. Now the FBI. And I don't like even little surprises.

"I repeat. What are you doing in Victorville? And don't tell me you're on your way home from Vegas. That might have worked on Ms. Cole, but we've had you under surveillance since you arrived at the Brando ranch."

She gave me her best Michael Madsen stare, and for the first time, I noticed that her eyes were ice blue and as mesmerizing as any I'd ever seen. But I didn't think she wanted to hear that, so I said nothing. Then more nothing.

It was a Bob's Big Boy not Denny's, but all I cared about was that the cook could conjure up a four-egg omelet with lots of tomatoes and onions and a double order of sausage. SAC Huston stuck to coffee. Her militia waited out front.

"Why were you at the Brandos?" she asked.

"I hope that doesn't mean we're skipping the Victorville question. I've been working really hard on an answer."

She didn't handle her coffee cup like somebody who had a cannon under her jacket, and her nails and makeup were perfect—and expensive. I couldn't be sure her hair had come in the color it was now—an almost platinum blonde—but the Louise Brooks cut nicely accented the exceptional length of her neck. That wasn't accidental. Beautiful women with a particularly remarkable feature know how to showcase it. I also caught a hint of something citrusy in the air. It would have been difficult to describe her as anything but striking; however, I was going to reserve final judgment until I saw her smile—which so far she gave no hint of knowing how to do.

"I knew an Audrey Huston once, but she had bad teeth and smoked cigars. Glad to see somebody is balancing out the line."

The chill in her eyes got considerably colder. "If this is the charm offensive, wait'll I fasten my seat belt."

I had a good comeback, but I desperately wanted my omelet. So I went with, "I was invited."

She looked at me like she'd stepped in something unpleasant in her Jimmy Choos. "Of course, you were invited. You arrived with a deputy chief. What I want to know is why."

I thought it over. Whatever was going on, this wasn't your classic turf war. Bluster, handcuffs, and my sore back aside, the Feds were on the outside looking in, which meant one of three things: no jurisdiction, no invitation or the Brando murders had suddenly intersected something else they were working.

The first two didn't count. Since 9/11, all anybody has to do is whisper, "National Security," and God couldn't keep the FBI out of an investigation. So Huston and her heavily armed crew were bumping up against the LAPD, and Maywood didn't have a clue they were there. More interesting was that the FBI was a step behind whatever was going on—possibly even several steps.

In life, like poker, silence is usually the best answer. And when it comes to law enforcement—especially the Feds—it's the one thing the manual has no answer for. Well, there's an answer, but you need to be someplace besides a booth at Bob's Big Boy to trot it out.

So Francesca Huston sat and watched me eat, which I did slowly and with joy. When I finished, I casually called for the check and paid it. She insisted on giving me two bucks for her coffee, which I left, along with five of my own. Then I stood up.

"Where do you think you're going?" she asked.

"Unless I'm under arrest for ingesting too much cholesterol, home."

"We're not finished." But there was uncertainty mixed with the attitude.

"Ms. Huston, no offense to you or the picture of J. Edgar under your pillow, but we were finished when your drill team got badge heavy at the hotel. I just waited until I had a full stomach to tell you."

I started toward the door, half-expecting a couple of JCPenney suits to come charging in and pistol-whip me. Instead, I heard her voice. "What kind?"

I turned. "What kind of what?"

"Audrey's cigars," she said. "The thin, elegant ones or something she bummed off a longshoreman?" It wasn't exactly Don Rickles, but at least she was trying. She gestured at her empty cup and smiled, kind of. It was forced, but even so, it was better than I expected.

"Audrey *was* a longshoreman," I said.

The wind of the previous night was gone, leaving behind as intense a sunset as I'd seen for some time. As I drove into it,

I replayed my conversation with Huston, which, because she wasn't interested in telling me anything, and I didn't know anything, could be best defined as tango with two people trying to lead. She asked the same questions every way she could think of, and I countered with my own until we pretty much ran out of language. Adding to the futility was that she kept slipping into hard-ass, and I couldn't tell if it was contrived or real, though I had a pretty good idea.

One of the few things she did let go of was that it hadn't been her idea to rough me up. "Agent Curtis insisted you were too big to take a chance with," she said.

Considering there had been six of them—all armed—and they had me by surprise, I wasn't buying it. My look must have said so too.

She cleared her throat. "He also thinks people always talk more readily after a hard takedown. I'm of the opinion that's just plain male-stupid, but sometimes a supervisor has to give her subordinates a little leeway."

"Did anyone happen to mention it was illegal?"

"You want to file a complaint?" she asked. "I've got some forms in the bus."

Feds. Gotta love them. Just then another agent, a square-jawed guy with a brush cut, came in and handed her a folder. I caught his eye and was pretty sure it was Curtis. "Sorry to mess with your theory," I said.

His face took on the color of a tornado sky, so I'd guessed right. He started to answer, but Francesca shook her head, and he took a deep breath and walked away. She spent a couple of moments perusing the file, then looked at me with narrowed eyes. "A Forbes 400 member *and* a decorated army veteran. Beverly Hills address but with a D.C. number to call if anybody has a question. Care to elaborate?"

I didn't.

The waitress had been rolling her eyes and huffing every time she passed because we were clogging up her station. I felt the same way and stood up.

My interrogator looked at me. "I had a husband once," she

said, the corners of her mouth twisted into ugly commas. "He was sleeping with half the wives at our tennis club, but all the son of a bitch ever did was just smile and lie."

"I haven't told you anything, so I haven't lied. And I'll do a little more smiling when I get a couple of Advil in me."

On my way out, I passed a white Malibu with Curtis and another agent in the front seat. I bent down and leaned in the driver's side window. There wasn't a lot of room between us, and our faces almost touched. "Next time you're in Quantico for some refresher training, Curt-baby, give me a call. I'll fly in and show you how I'd have made *you* talk." I waited for a response, but none came, so I crossed the parking lot and made my way back down the road toward the Red Roof Inn and my car.

I gave it a thorough going-over, and because you can't open anything on a Rolls-Royce without a special set of tools, I'd have noticed any tampering. As expected, the safe—it's in the trunk—was ajar, but they'd used an expert. No scratches. I put my coupons back and closed it.

It was possible the storm troopers were finished with me, but I never underestimate a federal officer with a purse. It's difficult to put a bug with any range in a cell phone, but once you have a phone's signature, it might as well be a homing beacon. At the very least, Huston would be grabbing my numbers, so I decided to amuse myself. I hit 411 and asked for the White House. The real one. You can do that, it's listed.

When the operator answered, I said, "Tell the president Bonks called. Got delayed by the Feds. A hard-ass named Huston." Then I clicked off.

Bonks was my grandmother's Corgi. He never met anybody he liked, so it was a safe bet he wouldn't have liked Francesca either. My number is blocked, but the White House switchboard never gets a message wrong. The Secret Service would check Bonks against its known threat list, and sooner or later, just to close the loop, somebody would run down SAC Huston. Bureaucracies being what they are, she wouldn't tell them she knew I'd called, and they wouldn't tell her what I'd said, just ask her enough questions for lightning to shoot out of her eyes. It was the least I could do for her—and for Bonks, whose teeth marks are still in my shins.

I did the same at the CIA, and just for good measure, Antonin Scalia. I don't know why I picked him, but I'd seen a recent interview on *60 Minutes,* and he had a sense of humor. Also, he might have let me sue Bonks.

I pulled off at the next exit and into a truck stop. One of my companies buys blocks of phone numbers in various countries for employee use. I maintain a dozen or so, all registered on the Isle of Man, where privacy is embroidered on the flag.

After I bought the Rolls, Nino Scucci, a friend and a Michelangelo with leather, opened a seam in the passenger seat backrest and built me a pocket where I keep a few grand, a credit card, and an extra cell phone. I used a razor knife from the emergency kit to pop the seam and extract the clean phone. Then I walked my old one and its accessories over to a stocky Hispanic trucker leaning on his cab, knocking back a Red Bull. The lettering on his door read LUIS SANCHEZ INTERNATIONAL FREIGHT, and he was hooked up to a full load of pigs.

"Luis?" I said, and he nodded. "How would you like to talk for free until the end of the month?"

He looked at the phone. "What's the catch, man?"

"No catch. Some people are tracking me. Nothing dangerous, just a pain in the ass."

He smiled broadly. "No shit, man?"

"No shit. How far you going with the pigs?"

"All the way. Tapachula."

Couldn't have been better. On a clear day, you can see Guatemala. He took the cell and was already dialing when I pulled away. Adios, Francesca.

Back in the Rolls, I plugged in the new phone to charge and dialed. Three rings later, a sandpaper voice picked up, "Praxis."

"We missed you at Bert's sendoff."

"I'd apologize if I'd intended to be there. I thought I made it clear I don't do funerals."

"Yours is going to be like Harry Cohn's. The town'll turn out just to make sure."

"Great Limey Standups. Still no entries."

"You're the second person today who's had that opinion. Before I forget, tell Stella to send out an e-mail to the usual suspects. They should go to the next phone number on my list. Former one's vacationing in Chiapas."

I heard him talking to someone, probably Stella. "Okay, what else?"

"We need to talk. Preferably tonight."

"I'm going to a screening. CAA."

"I won't be back in the city until later. And frankly, I'd rather have a root canal."

"You pompous cocksucker. Like that crowd of yours is such a prize. How about Benny Joe Willis? He still on track to shoot up a school bus?"

Benny Joe's a former government photo analyst with a JFK assassination obsession. He and Jake have some kind of history neither will talk about. I said, "I admit I know some oddballs, but unlike most of your clients, if the first-person singular disappeared from the language, they'd still be able to get up in the morning."

He ignored me. "There's a reception for the director afterward. He's an old friend of yours. I'll leave your name at the door."

"Who's the friend?"

"Dallas Bronston."

"I thought he punched out the president of Fox and got blacklisted."

"You have to be toes up to get out of this business. Went to Europe and made some bullshit picture about a lady bullfighter. Won a bunch of swish festivals. Now there's a bidding war."

"And you represent him, of course."

"You wouldn't want the guy floundering around with second-best." He hung up without saying good-bye.

I had one more call to make. Another cop. One I really liked. He'd been lazy once, but who hasn't. The phone rang a long time, and when he answered, he sounded half-asleep and none too pleased at the interruption.

"Sergeant Manarca?"

"It's Lieutenant Manarca now. Who's this?"

"Rail Black."

"My accountant says I can't loan you any more money."

Dion Manarca is all-LA. According to him, clear back to Balboa. With somebody else, that might be a little awkward because he's Italian, but if you stand at a bar long enough, pretty soon, he'll grab a napkin and start drawing maps and lines connecting El Cid and the Castilian Knights to Venetian noblemen. Even if it's bullshit, it's a great story, and I learned a long time ago that life is a lot more interesting if you let people have their personal histories.

"I wake you?"

"What time is it?"

"Coming up on seven."

"Stakeout. Thirty goddamn hours. What can I do for you, Rockefeller?"

"I spent a little time with one of your coworkers last night. Yale Maywood."

"A deputy chief working at night? Must have been a mirage. You get to that level, you're tucked in at nine thirty, home or away."

"We drove out to Victorville together." I waited, but there was silence.

Finally, he said, "You're pickin' at a thread, except I ain't wearin' a sweater."

That was exactly what I wanted to hear. "You know where CAA is?"

"Creative Artists? Century City, why?"

"There's a get-together this evening. Can you swing by around eleven? Maybe dressed in something that doesn't scream, *You have the right to remain silent*?"

"How about white ostrich Tony Llamas and my new leather sport coat?"

"Careful, somebody might try to sign you."

"I hate that parking structure."

"The agency valet will be full of VIPs. Park at the Hyatt and walk across. I'll hang by the door. Eleven, okay?"

I hit Beverly Hills just before eight and, in the lengthening shadows, slipped my Ray-Bans above the visor. Coming across Sunset, there'd been a major commotion at the Bel Air East Gate that had tacked on an extra fifteen minutes. Half a dozen LAPD black and whites had converged on a taxi with its trunk so packed with luggage the lid had to be bungee-corded. The turbaned driver was standing in the middle of the street yelling at the cops, and his passengers, three businessmen probably on their way to LAX, were out and yelling too. The empathy extended toward these unfortunate folks by my fellow motorists was indeed heartwarming.

Dove Way is in the hills north of Sunset, and as I wound my way up, I was reminded again why I live there. Yes, the houses are large and the neighbors wealthy, but there are few cities as dynamic as LA where you can reside in complete serenity ten minutes from the action. My part of Beverly Hills doesn't appear on cop shows. For two reasons: You can't see much from the street, and it's not a crowd that rents their places out for an ego boost. The people up here either own the studios or don't care about show business. Aggressively don't care.

My place is a rambling, white stucco hacienda built in the heyday of Hollywood by Howard Hughes's attorney, Joe Stinson. Supposedly, H.H. lived in the guesthouse off and on when he was dodging process servers and phantoms. That keeps my address on the street-corner tourist maps, but even if you manage to thread your way up, you can't see anything but the gate. It's so secluded that if you were to arrive blindfolded, once on the property, you wouldn't know there was anybody within miles.

None of this prevents the occasional agoraphobe worshipper from leaving a note for Howard or a bouquet of the favorite flower of some actresses he was rumored to have bedded. I know it's February 8 when I see ivory roses for Lana Turner or October 16 when it's Linda Darnell's yellow tulips. I always wish the girls a happy birthday.

Stinson designed the place himself and oversaw every detail of its construction down to a private, soundproofed elevator between the master bedroom and underground garage. He was as eccentric as Howard, apparently puttering around in bare feet, rolled-up brown slacks, white shirt with St. Christopher cuff links, brown fedora and an FDR cigarette holder clamped between his teeth.

Many of my houseguests and my valet, Mallory, claim to have seen him wandering the grounds or sitting at the iron picnic table on the far edge of the yard, using a yellow pencil stub to make notes on the stock page of the August 3, 1954, edition of the *Los Angeles Examiner*. Why that particular paper, I have no idea, and even though I'm not in the visual loop, I've smelled cigarette smoke from time to time where there shouldn't be any. I tracked down a copy of the paper which now resides permanently on the table in the foyer. So far, no investment tips.

As I entered the lighted, limestone drive, a gray Jaguar sedan was parked near the Apollo fountain. It wasn't familiar, and Mallory, who usually comes out to meet me, was nowhere in sight. I parked behind the Jag and went in. I heard voices in the living room and rounded the corner just as my houseman was serving Booth's Gin Rickeys to two men dressed in expensive, vested suits.

I knew the younger one, R. Beaumont Stephenson, a ramrod-straight, sandy-haired gentleman in his forties. Beau, as he is known, had been named the U.K.'s Consul-

General in Los Angeles last year, and I had attended his welcoming dinner. He came quickly to his feet. "Mr. Black, so wonderful to see you again. Please forgive our calling on you without an appointment. Mallory has been a most gracious host."

The other gentleman stood as well, though it took a moment for him to get his feet under him. He was in his seventies, and somewhat infirm, but there was a keenness in his cobalt eyes and a real warmth to his smile.

"Mr. Black," the Consul-General went on. "This is a colleague of mine from London, Lord Anthony Rittenhouse."

I shook both men's hands. "Lord Rittenhouse," I said, "my father used to speak about you . . . warmly, I might add."

His smile got wider. "James and I did tear things up a bit when we were young. Back before he owned all those newspapers and had to learn to stay off his own front pages." He allowed himself a chuckle. "From what I heard, you had some wild moments of your own."

"Most of them I'd like to forget." I urged both men to sit and took a wingback chair across from them.

"Would you like something, Mr. Black?" Mallory asked.

"Not right now, Mallory, thanks. But tomorrow, run the Rolls down to Nino and have him stitch up the seat. It'll need a new phone as well."

"Certainly, sir." And he departed.

"I'm sure you've been told you look just like your father," Lord Rittenhouse said. "A little taller, possibly, but as I age, everyone looks bigger."

I looked at the man my father had called the finest sailor he'd ever known. His family lineage ran back to Charles II, and the Rittenhouse seventeenth-century ancestral home, Lyonesse, was only a few miles from my own Derbyshire residence, Strathmoor Hall.

"What can I do for you, Lord Rittenhouse?"

"Actually, Mr. Black, I'm here to do something for you. You see, you've been selected to be knighted by Her Majesty. The Most Distinguished Order of Saint Michael and

Saint George. Will you give me leave to carry back your acceptance?"

I don't know what I was anticipating, but this was so far off my radar that I was speechless. My father's lordship had died with him in a Himalayan avalanche, and as both a British and American citizen, the idea of one day being titled myself never crossed my mind. Not only had I had served in the United States Army, I've never made any bones—publicly or privately—about my love for my adopted country.

I finally managed to get out, "I'm sorry, Lord Rittenhouse, I'm simply floored. Whatever did I do to be considered for such an honor?"

"As it was explained to me, it is for brave and exemplary service to the Crown. I'm afraid that's all I know."

I had assisted a past prime minister in a delicate matter, but my success had been more from name and social position than courage or cunning. It certainly hadn't warranted notice by the queen. Whatever had prompted this was a mystery.

I stood and walked to the front window. The home's previous owner had spent the GNP of a small country on landscaping and lighting. Tonight, it was as beautiful as ever, but the deep, desperate loneliness that I try to keep locked away now hovered over it like a shroud. My father, mother, wife and unborn child were all dead—no, all murdered—and what should have been a moment of joy and sharing had suddenly become one of solitary heartbreak.

Beau Stephenson's voice came from behind me. "Mr. Black? Is anything the matter?"

I didn't trust myself to turn around.

5

Bold Kings and MacBeth

In the unseasonably hot Asian sun, two British warships eased into the turquoise water of the narrow rain forest gorge jutting east from the Pearl River. From the deck of the seventy-two-gun HMS Wellesley, *Capt. Jeremiah Blaine, sweat running down his face, watched as crewmen lashed to the high masts used swords to hack away the thick, barbed limbs that threatened the sails. Thirty yards behind, the HMS* Furious *followed, its gun crews standing nervously along the rails, searching the dense foliage for any sign of danger.*

Two miles farther to the rear, still in open water, loomed the breathtaking spectacle of the rest of the British fleet. Forty more warships constituting the greatest concentration of sea power ever assembled. Aboard the largest, Adm. William Trask, Commander of the Fleet, anxiously watched the scout vessels through a long, brass telescope.

Never one to enter an arena softly, Captain Blaine nodded

to his aide, who gave a command, and a conductor's baton rapped against a thin, wooden podium. A moment later, on the foredeck, the Royal Marine band, attired in their best red regalia, launched into a lively rendition of "The Bold King's Hussars." The captain allowed himself a small smile as the crash of cymbals sent a flock of large birds flapping skyward and startled a family of golden monkeys into hysterical screams.

Moments later, the world erupted in fire. Hundreds of pieces of artillery and heavy mortars camouflaged along the high banks rained shells down on the helpless ships, ripping apart decking and tearing through flesh. Amid screams and shouts, men sprinted to their battle stations, but there was little cover. Then, suddenly, the main mast of the Furious splintered, groaned and toppled, taking sailors and cannon into the river with it.

A few of the ships' big guns returned fire; but in the narrows, they could not elevate high enough, and their shells fell harmlessly short. Marine riflemen fired wild fusillades, but with no visible target, they did little but move leaves. And then, a tumultuous wave of spin shells shaped like children's pinwheels dropped onto both ships' decks and fragmented into thousands of pieces of hot lead that chewed up what remained of the resistance.

Just as quickly as it had begun, the onslaught ended, and an eerie quiet descended. The two ships, now with no one at their helms, drifted aimlessly in the gorge, ablaze. Captain Blaine, bleeding, his jacket torn, one arm hanging at his side, lay amid the burning remains of the Wellesley. His eye caught the band conductor's baton, lying on the deck, still gripped by a severed, white-gloved hand.

The cave was close enough to the edge of the ridge that Maj. Ethan Jellicoe and Lt. Freddie MacBeth could see the campfires dotting the valley below. Dressed in khaki, their heads and faces wrapped in green silk scarves, the two British soldiers lay watching through binoculars.

Far below, two hundred Chinese soldiers were passing opium pipes among themselves, sending clouds of smoke wafting upward. Lieutenant MacBeth sniffed the air. "If you don't mind my saying so, Major, this opium business is nasty going."

Jellicoe shook his head in agreement. " 'Tis indeed, Freddie. The Chinks don't give two shits if we steal the whole goddamn country. Just as long as they don't have to pay for their yen-shee. By Christ, I do miss India. It's bloody, dusty hot, but at least a man can get a cold glass of gin. You see any artillery, Freddie?"

"None, Major."

"Aye, and none along the river either. Just the paths to get it in and out."

"Those cliffs are almost straight up, and we counted 138 emplacements. It's a safe bet those blokes down there didn't do it. So how?"

"Don't rightly know, Freddie, but we've got to find out before the fleet can move upriver. Admiral Trask won't risk any more surprises like yesterday."

Jellicoe eased a silver flask out of his pack and opened it. He took a long swig and offered it to Lieutenant MacBeth, who declined. "Then get some sleep, lad. They're waiting for something, so we'll wait right along with them. Maybe we'll be able to give the admiral an early Christmas present."

"When should I relieve you?"

"Not the least bit tired tonight, Freddie." He held up his flask. "And got my best girl along. Pretty as a Dover sunset, and never a harsh word."

Lieutenant MacBeth shouldered his rifle and pack and started out. Jellicoe's voice stopped him. "Why not sleep under the roof tonight? Looks like rain, and those buggers down there are too chandooed to do much patrolling."

"You're probably right, sir, but regulations . . ."

"I know, the deadly bed is the obvious bed. Just don't go more than a hundred yards. And don't snore."

As the lieutenant crawled away, there was a low rumble of thunder and a flash of lightning. And the rain came.

At daybreak, the storm had passed. Morning birds called out as Lieutenant MacBeth picked his way through the still-wet underbrush. Though he did his best to move quietly, the mud made loud sucking sounds under his boots. Shortly, the cave came into view, and he froze. Jellicoe's rifle was stuck bayonet first into the ground, and the early sun glinted off the silver flask, balanced delicately atop its butt. There was, however, no sign of its owner.

MacBeth dropped and belly-crawled to the edge of the cliff. Nothing could have prepared him for the sight below. Extending to the distant horizon was an undulating line of thousands of men, women and children, most carrying a cannon barrel, a ramrod or a shell. It was a convoy of unfathomable proportions, urged along by fierce, whip-wielding men on horseback, its perimeter patrolled by large, long-haired dogs.

But as awe-inspiring as this procession of humanity was, it was eclipsed by the tigers. Using his binoculars, he tried to count them, but still they came. A hundred cages, perhaps more, each sagging on four long poles slung over the shoulders of six men—twenty-four bearers to a cage—while inside, the great, striped beasts with fearsome yellow eyes, paced and growled and sometimes reached out a plate-sized paw to swipe at a passing back.

"My sweet Lord," MacBeth whispered. Ten years earlier, as a schoolboy, he had been among the first visitors at the London Zoo, and he remembered standing at the big cats exhibition until his father had to pull him away. Again, he felt the exhilaration of seeing something so wild, so close, and he tried to imagine what it must like to hunt one.

After a while, he trained his binoculars on the dogs. They were not like the dogs he had grown up with in England.

These massive black and tan animals had heads like bears and full manes, and they snarled and bit at anyone who deviated from the columns, even, from time to time, challenging the tigers. Suddenly, something familiar caught his eye. Major Jellicoe, badly beaten, staggered under the weight of a cannon wheel tied across his shoulders, his hands secured to its spokes. As strong as he was, it was clear he would not last long.

As the convoy passed, the Chinese soldiers rose and joined it, many showing the effects of a drug hangover. Nearby, astride a magnificent black stallion, sat a figure whose stature and ornamentation set him apart. Gold-helmeted and with regal red silk billowing beneath his chain mail breastplate, the warlord surveyed the spectacle with the easy calm of accustomed command. His men all had carbines slung across their backs, but he wore only a wide sword in a scabbard that reached below his boot and a dagger tucked near his heart.

As he watched, a bearer, lurching along under an ammunition case nearly as large as he was, stumbled and fell. Two men with their own loads broke from the line, and with the dogs converging on them, retrieved the man's cargo and rushed back into formation, leaving their fallen comrade to his fate.

Calmly, the warlord drew his sword, a horrible, steel instrument shaped like a longboat hull, and brought it hard across the throat of the armed rider closest to the disruption. As the man's severed head dangled down his back, held only by his spinal cord, his horse bolted, crushing several people and initiating fresh chaos.

Aboard the fleet flagship, Freddie, still caked with mud, stood with Admiral Trask and his commanders at the map table. Trask regarded the young lieutenant. "Tigers you say? What the bloody hell are they doing with tigers?"

"The Orientals believe they possess mysterious powers, sir. They grind their bones for medicine and make potions

from their organs. And only the most revered families are permitted to display their skins."

One of the generals spoke, "I'm told the beasts can increase a man's . . . how shall I put it . . . prowess."

Freddie turned to him. "That is correct, sir. They soak the penis in alcohol, then consume it."

"My God, what heathens."

"Perhaps not," said another. "From the damn number of them, it seems to be working." The officers laughed.

"You don't think these bearers will fight?" Trask asked Freddie.

"They're forced labor, sir. Probably raided from villages. Even if they wanted to resist, they're unarmed and undernourished."

"And the warlord?"

"He's in the tiger business. Somebody paid him dearly to move those weapons, not to do mercenary work. The government has no interest in enriching these rogue operators any more than necessary."

"May I ask how you know all this?"

"University of Edinburgh, sir. China studies. Thought I might join the foreign office once my tour is over."

The admiral poured himself a glass of brandy. "How many men do you think one would need to put an end to this narrows problem?"

"Thirty would be ideal, but properly planned, it could be done with twenty. Plus half a dozen sharpshooters to take care of the dogs."

A general scoffed, "Against two hundred trained soldiers? Impossible."

Freddie answered calmly. "I believe most of them will run when the shooting starts. Opium doesn't increase one's sense of mission."

The admiral regarded his officers. "Anyone have an objection to the lieutenant's commanding this operation?"

The doubting general frowned. "It's a job for a major at the very least, Admiral. Tactics and all, you know."

"Is that a military assessment or Royal Academy non-sense? Besides, it seems the last major didn't fare particularly well."

The general's face reddened, but he made no reply. Trask nodded at MacBeth. "Select the men you need. But take the thirty. We must get the fleet upriver."

"Yes, sir."

When he had gone, Trask looked at the assembled officers. "MacBeth's Tigers. It has a certain ring to it. Use it in the report. And if he's successful, I want a place made for him on my staff."

6

Matadors and Ambulances

There are three major agencies in Hollywood: Creative Artists, ICM and William Morris Endeavor. Each will tell you it has global reach, and to an extent, they all do. However, their real power base is a compass rose beginning with Disney in the north, extending to Sony in the south, then Paramount east and Fox west. Within these few dozen square miles lie a trillion dollars' worth of entertainment, sports and news assets, along with the writing and visual talent to sway the world. Yet, for the most part, unlike the second-stringers who live in New York and a few local ideologues, the real power brokers are timid about wielding it.

CAA used to occupy an I. M. Pei masterpiece at the corner of Santa Monica and Wilshire Boulevards in the heart of Beverly Hills. William Morris was a couple of hundred yards down the street, and ICM just a few blocks farther. Today, CAA and ICM have relocated, but only to Century City, a single mile west. This continued closeness is not by accident. They like to keep an eye on each other.

I knew Michael Ovitz, one of the five founding partners of CAA and by far the most ambitious. I liked him. Not in a let's-grab-a-beer way, but because he was transparently ruthless—even with the people he depended on to watch his back. And that recklessness and lack of pretense made him interesting. He overdid the Sun Tzu and cloak-and-dagger crap, but in less than a decade he took a startup to the top of the planet's most competitive industry. Most of the grousing is done by the same kind of crowd that made jokes about Napoleon—at his funeral.

Ovitz and I met when I engaged him to manage the sale of Black Group, Ltd.'s only Hollywood holding, a small television advertising company with one very large client. In the end, he didn't actually do the transaction in a traditional M&A sense, but he generated the heat that raised the price beyond my—or anyone else's—most optimistic projections. As was to be expected, this caused considerable teeth grinding among those who had begged me to steer clear of him.

The brain trust that runs CAA today is not as visible or as well-known. They are, however, more than worthy heirs, and it has been said that the coldness of their new quarters equals that of some of the hearts that work there. Not being in that business, I can't speak to cold hearts, but Jake has clients all over town, and he says that if he had to pick one agency to negotiate with St. Peter for his eternity, CAA would not only get him into Paradise, but a three-picture deal with first-dollar participation.

One of the nicer things about going out in LA is that if you're neat and clean, you're acceptable. You don't have to dig deep in your closet if you don't want to. After Beau Stephenson and Lord Rittenhouse had left, I showered and washed off several layers of FBI. Then, dressed in an open-necked blue-and-white pin-striped shirt under a camel cashmere sport coat, a favorite pair of Levis and white deck shoes, I headed for Avenue of the Stars in my Dodge Ram.

I half expected the valet to blanch at the sight of a pickup amid the German and Italian steel, but the guy taking cars eyeballed me and decided that, even if I wasn't somebody he recognized, I was too big to hassle.

Because of its hole-in-the-middle configuration, the CAA building has been unflatteringly nicknamed the Death Star—as in *Star Wars*. Detractors say that's unfair to Death Stars, but I kind of like the place. Admittedly, it's not I. M. Pei, but they're making deals, not design history.

The reception was in full swing. The soaring atrium with its pastel-lighted panels flanking open walkways was crowded with the beautiful, the powerful and the hungry—and more than a few who were all three. Jake had left my name at the door, but it wasn't necessary. No one at CAA misses anything, and I was immediately surrounded by two of the managing partners and several Armani-clad underlings. Star power is important, but money drives the machine.

I smiled, shook hands, promised to have lunch, then broke away to find my lawyer. He was standing with a young lady dressed in a red, black and gold matador outfit, minus the *montera*. Some women spend all day getting ready to make an impression, and some roll out of bed with their hair mussed and take your breath away. Marisol Graciela Rivera-Marquez could have been wearing a nun's habit, and it wouldn't have made any difference. When she turned, I stopped dead in my tracks.

If you've ever looked into a woman's eyes and felt yourself being hopelessly pulled into another reality, this was one of those moments. I was suddenly completely lost. She was so delicate, so finely featured, that she seemed surreal, like a three-dimensional mirage. Her raven hair was pulled back tightly into a chignon with gold chain woven into it, the two loose ends hanging down her back. And the makeup brush had only touched her flawless, pale copper skin.

Jake introduced us. Holding on to her hand and feeling its warmth extend up my arm, I stumbled for something re-markably brilliant to say, and came up with, "Was it chal-lenging to play a matador?"

Her look was one of bemused dignity. "Mr. Black, I *am* a matador."

Never one to miss an opportunity to add to someone's discomfort, Jake intoned in his best Charlton Heston, "The picture's a documentary, Rail."

I was saved by Dallas Bronston returning with a couple of flutes of champagne. Since I'd last seen him, he'd given his hair plugs the gift of Hollywood Orange #6, sometimes called orangutan's ass. As a director, though, he should have known better than to stand under a green ceiling light. He gave a flute to Marisol, then shook my hand. "Rail, long time. I see you've met my wife."

I felt the wind go out of me, then Marisol said, in her featherlight, high-Spanish accent, "Dallas, please stop telling people that." She turned back to me. "He thinks it is good for promoting the picture, but he already has a wife."

I smiled and was rewarded with a better one in return. Something was going on in her too, and I didn't think I was imagining it. I glanced at Dallas, and he didn't seem to be thinking about promoting pictures.

Jake, as lawyers always do, killed the moment. "You said you wanted to talk about something."

I looked at my watch—10:55. "There's somebody else coming, and he should hear it at the same time. Be right back."

A number of people had drifted onto the plaza to smoke and talk. Earpieced security men, muscles bulging inside dark designer suits, meandered on the perimeter, alert for intruders. A photographer and his assistant were taking unobtrusive candids that would find their way onto the next day's tabloid shows. CAA and the other heavy hitters around town have long ago mastered the art of stiff-arming the paparazzi, so even though there was the occasional long-range flash, the LAPD had them penned up blocks away.

I wandered out toward the valet and looked across the street at the Century Plaza Hotel, where Reagan declined the vice presidency from Ford, then four years later turned its penthouse into the White House West. Even from fifty yards away, I could identify Lieutenant Manarca's slightly bowlegged walk coming down the hotel drive, and I watched as he ducked traffic running across one of the widest boulevards in Los Angeles.

There were a couple of pedestrians on my side of the street, and I lost sight of the detective for a couple of seconds as his path intersected theirs. When he came back into view, he was clutching his neck with both hands and staggering up the half horseshoe of grass toward me.

I grabbed one of the security men and ran. Before I got to him, I saw the blood running between Manarca's hands and down the front of his shirt. While the security guy got on his walkie-talkie, I raced down the sidewalk in the direction the pedestrians had gone. At the corner of Constellation, I looked right and saw the two rear doors of a dark Denali slam shut and the SUV peel away. All I caught of the plate were the first two letters, KS.

When I got back to the fallen detective, a crowd had formed, and a doctor who happened to be at the party was applying pressure in the right place to stem the blood flow. Manarca's eyes were wide open, and he tried to say something, but the only sound he managed was a stomach-turning gurgle. The gaping knife wound ran almost ear to ear but had not gone deep enough to bleed him out.

Jake pushed through to us and knelt beside me. "What happened?"

I heard sirens in the distance and turned to him. "I know you don't like listening to anybody, but this time you have to. This probably doesn't have anything to do with us, but until we're sure, you can't go home. You can't even take your car out of here."

He surprised me and nodded. "Then where?"

"We'll figure it out in the ambulance."

He looked down at Manarca and shook his head. "Jesus Christ."

At first, the EMS crew wasn't going to let us go with them, but Manarca countered with his shield and some hand gestures, and they backed off. Now, as we roared toward UCLA Trauma Center, I got a chance to talk to the doctor who had probably saved the detective's life. Hadley Carson was a pediatric neurosurgeon at Children's Hospital of Orange County who had just begun dating an actress on a well-known network show. The CAA reception had been his first Hollywood event.

"Welcome to the dark side," said Jake. "Next come the jackals looking for your life story rights."

Manarca held up two fingers, indicating the number of attackers, and I nodded. "They left in a Yukon Denali. Mean anything?"

He shook his head, and Dr. Carson almost shouted for him to lie still.

With a physician in attendance, both EMS guys were in the front, the one in the passenger seat holding Manarca's ID and talking on a cell phone. "Like I told you, he's a cop. Manarca. LAPD. The doc is Carson. From Newport Beach." The guy turned and leaned over the partition. "They want your names too."

I could read his name tag. V. CONWAY. "I'm Conway," I said.

"And I'm his brother," said Jake.

Conway gave me a twisted grin, shook his head and turned back to his phone. "They're busy. You can ask them when we get there."

When we hit the outer edge of UCLA, there were dozens of agitating blue lights a couple of hundred yards ahead. Exactly what you'd expect with a cop down, but it wasn't going to do any of us any good being tied up for hours answering questions. I gestured to Manarca that we were getting out. He blinked in acknowledgment.

"Stop," I shouted to the driver.

"No way, man. We're almost there."

I reached out and opened the back door. We had just swung into a turn, and the momentum wrenched the handle out of my hand. The door flew open and slammed into the vehicle's side.

The driver got all over his brakes. "What the fuck?"

Jake and I were already out and walking quickly back the way we'd come. Suddenly, a BMW sedan loomed out of the darkness, flashing its lights. It stopped.

I looked in the open passenger-side window. The driver was wearing a matador's outfit. "You sure you're not a lawyer." I smiled.

"I do not understand," Marisol Rivera-Marquez said. "I just thought you might need a ride back."

Jake and I got in.

"What will Mr. Bronston say?"

"He will say nothing, or I will go back to Spain, and he can promote his movie by himself."

7

Pizza in White Silk

As it happened, one of Jake's clients, some music guy I'd never heard of named D. D. Shoulders, was making an early appearance in the speedball section of Forest Lawn, and while the estate was being settled, his Malibu place was vacant. We sat in front of a closed Baskin-Robbins in an empty strip center while a Realtor drove over from Calabasas with a couple of remotes and the alarm code. While we waited, I dialed the Beverly Hills PD and got a Sergeant Fordham on the line. He recognized me right away. "What can we do for you, Mr. Black?"

"I've been called out of town for a few days, and I was wondering if you could rotate some off-duty uniforms to babysit my place. Maybe park a black and white outside the gates. I'll be generous."

"Everybody here knows you, Mr. Black. No problem. You expecting trouble?"

"Couple of anonymous phone calls," I said casually. "Probably nothing, but Mallory's there by himself."

There isn't much overt crime in Beverly Hills, but because of the high-profile and economic status of many of its residents, there's always unseen danger. Threats from angry exes, disaffected business partners and the occasional deranged groupie are commonplace. Then there are the professional criminals who spend years in San Quentin dreaming about scoring something more valuable from a celebrity than his autograph. Even if they get caught, taking down a mansion that makes national news ratchets up their status during their next stretch.

Like most major departments, the BHPD cross-trains with the Feds, but they spend extra time with the Secret Service and receive regular briefings from the intelligence agencies. As a result, they operate as proactively as a presidential detail.

"I'll alert the appropriate people," Sergeant Fordham said. "And if Mallory's gonna be cooking, there'll be guys putting in for vacation days to get the gig."

"He likes showing off. Just don't anyone ask him for a well-done steak . . . at least not while they're standing near a hot grill."

Then I called Mallory and told him to be on the lookout for some hungry guests. Like the professional he is, he didn't ask why. My last call was to UCLA, where the receptionist connected me to an LAPD Public Information Officer. "Unless you're a family member, I'm unable to provide any details regarding Detective Manarca," she said.

"I'm not the press, I just want to know his condition."

"I'm sorry."

"I was with him when his throat was cut."

I could picture the young officer checking the phone screen, but even if the call hadn't been routed through the switchboard, my number is blocked. For a long moment, the silence on the other end was deafening. "May I have your name, sir?"

"Is Yale Maywood there?"

"No, Commander DiMartino is in charge. Why don't I put you through to him."

I didn't know DiMartino, and I didn't think introducing myself over the phone was destined to do anything except raise both our blood pressures. "Thanks, I'll pass," I said. The PIO started to say something else, but I hung up.

I redialed UCLA reception and asked for the surgery scheduling office. There, a polite voice told me that Detective Manarca would be taken into Theatre 3 in approximately ninety minutes. He was being prepped now.

"Good news," I said to my companions. "He made it . . . so far."

As Marisol wheeled the BMW through the eight-foot steel gates, vanity spots popped on and illuminated the courtyard of a long, low beach-modern place. It was fronted by a massive, gold tile waterfall that would have been impressive anyway, but flanked by life-sized, exquisitely painted, nude statues of two of the most famous female vocalists on the planet, the lily was gilded beyond even my fertile imagination.

"And I always thought they were *both* blondes," said Marisol.

Our headlights picked up a couple of raccoons getting a drink beside the leg of the Texas-haired semi-brunette, but neither seemed fazed by the interruption. Our driver swung right and into an open garage, where she parked between a red '46 Pontiac Woodie and a max-stretched yellow chopper that looked impossible to ride.

The house, mostly glass and mostly overdone, was in the Colony, the oldest and most secluded section of Malibu, where the lots are locked between the PCH and the high-tide line. Inside, the flocked foil walls were decorated with the framed gold and platinum platters record companies hand out instead of royalties, and nearly every flat surface was festooned with overly exaggerated, erotic statuary that you had to be careful not to take out with an elbow.

Until the thirties, the entire—and uninhabited—twenty-seven miles of Malibu coast was owned by a Massachusetts insurance prick named Rindge, who maintained a private, tommy-gun-toting security force to run picnickers and shell-gathers back to Encino. After Rindge died, his widow, May, got into financial trouble and, desperate for cash, rented some of her precious land to movie stars to build secluded getaways. But by the early forties, May was dead, and the speculators had swooped in—one of them, a young millionaire named J. Paul Getty, who snapped up the sixty-four acres that would later become home to his first museum.

Today, an oceanfront lot with a teardown will run you $10 million—minimum. Fire and flood insurance? Well, if you need backstopping, you can't afford to live there.

Marisol said she was going to take a walk on the beach and disappeared. I took a seat on the longest leather sofa I'd ever seen, which faced a wall of floor-to-ceiling windows. Presently, I saw her, now shoeless, pad out to the lapping waves and head down the beach, kicking water like a schoolgirl. I admired the easy way she walked and the swing of her hips until she was swallowed by the dark.

Jake had been prowling around the kitchen and come up with a bottle of 12-Star Metaxa and two anisette glasses. He joined me on the sofa, and we sipped some Greek sweetness while I brought him up to speed.

When I finished, he thought for a long moment. "Chuck and Lucille were good people. Never met anybody kinder—except when it came to business. He ever tell you she wouldn't let him sign the Paramount deal until the studio agreed to contribute the same amount to Blue Rescue? She was so damned mad about what they'd put her husband through, she didn't care if they walked."

"Chuck never mentioned it."

Jake smiled. "When I dropped that bomb on the production chief, I had to step away from the phone. 'Blue Rescue? What the fuck's that? Some kinda save-the-oceans bullshit?' After he heard it was for dead cops, he came clear out of his lifts. 'Dead cops! You're kiddin' me, right? You know I gotta go to the board for shit like that!'"

In a way, it wasn't a funny story, but after the last couple of days, I was looking for any laugh I could find. "But the guy finally went along."

"Not right away. He was in full studio stall. So I told him, no problem, I knew people on the board, and I'd take it up it with them myself. And while I was at it, I'd ask what they thought about that frog director he'd just paid seven mil. The one who told *Dateline* that if Americans had any class at all, we'd move our war dead out of Normandy." Jake paused and took a pull on his Metaxa, obviously enjoying the memory. "Son of a bitch had a check on my desk before the receiver got cold."

Vintage Jake. That's why I like him . . . and also why I stay away from the movie business.

"And you don't believe this FBI chick, Huston, was bullshitting you?"

"I've thought about it, and the answer is no. To a Fed, seppuku comes easier than sharing, and she was as cool as an academy handbook. Not even a hint why she and a small army were picking sand out of their teeth in Victorville. But when it came to Chuck and Lucille, even her hair twitched. She was going to have to report something, and she didn't have a starting place."

"That's why you caught the Upside-Your-Head Express. And it wasn't a subordinate who got carried away. That was her call all the way."

I didn't know whether that added to or detracted from my opinion of SAC Huston, but while I was thinking about it, Marisol reappeared on the beach, her matador pants wet to the knees. She smiled, waved and headed toward the house. A couple of minutes later, I heard a shower come on.

Jake refilled our glasses. "So Maywood and the chief decided they had no choice but to call in the cavalry. You."

I nodded. "Even so, I had to pull it out of Yale."

"Cops," said Jake. "Sometimes they're so busy being clever, they miss the butler with the candlestick. But don't give them any marks for coming clean. They knew that once you found out Chuck and Lucille were dead, you'd get involved. It's what you do—help friends. What brought them out of the closet was that they couldn't take the chance you'd stumble around and knock over the good crystal . . . or maybe use that media empire of yours to make noise. So they tried buying you off by letting you see a little of the crime scene, then told you nothing."

"The cop half-Monty."

"Probably less. Think about it."

When it hit me, I was irritated. My only excuse was that no matter how many violent deaths you've seen—and my list is unpleasantly long—unless you deal with man's inhumanity every day, it takes time for the shock to dissipate and the narrowing of focus to subside. The Dallas Cowboys Cheerleaders could have been holding auditions in another part of the Brando house—or on the other side of Lucille's train car—and I might not have noticed.

"By the time you got the tour, every piece of paper, every check stub, probably even the cars were gone, am I right?"

"Goddamn it."

"Not your fault," Jake said, but it didn't help.

"They couldn't have known I'd call Manarca. And I was on a clean phone, so somebody had *him* tapped."

Jake wasn't even mildly surprised. "Probably for being comped a Snickers. It's one of my biggest hard-ons. Internal affairs has a budget, so they have to make cases. Doesn't matter if they've got a department full of choirboys. There's no glory in shoving it up the ass of some patrolman, and if you mess with the brass, you end up working the men's room at LAX. So they're always on detectives. Especially the creative thinkers. I ever retire, I'm gonna work pro bono just representing gold shields against IA."

He drained his glass. "I appreciate the opportunity to see Malibu by moonlight, but I think it's a long shot slicing up your friend had anything to do with Chuck and Lucille."

"Long shot, I'll give you. But cops don't usually set out to kill one of their own."

Jake stared at me, hard. "Really? Those the rules in Rail World? Give me a break. Whatever Manarca's into, gold-plated asses are probably on the line. When you wandered in, it gave them an opportunity to do some spring cleaning. But it was either a hurry-up job, so they missed, or a very skillful cutter."

"The implication being it was a message."

"There's an old saying: You hear hoofbeats, think horses, not zebras. Got doubts? Ask the guy who got sliced."

I intended to.

Jake took the yellow chopper and went home. But first, he called a security team to meet him in Santa Monica and escort him the rest of the way. He lives in one of those gray stone, faux-embassy palaces on Sunset that tour guides make their living pointing out. It has a fancy architectural pedigree and is filled with priceless Western art, but the only thing that matters to the gawkers is that some half-famous starlet once chased a lover down to the wrought-iron gates and emptied a .38 into him.

The joke at the time was that all you needed to know about who was in the right was that the victim was a producer. Jake got a jury to agree and ended up with the house as his fee. But as Richie Catcavage once observed, "It's always bittersweet for Jake when an asshole dies. The air's a little fresher, but it kills off a whole line of billing."

Jake said he'd move into his pool house for a few days because it was easier to lock down, and he could come and go through the back. That was definitely going to cut into his sex life because even rich, powerful and with one of the best plastic surgeons in LA, he freely admits that driving a date up that long driveway increases his batting average several hundred points.

He also said he didn't think Chuck and Lucille's investments were anything but conventional, but he'd take a closer look. And he'd call a former federal prosecutor he knew and see if he could rustle up a profile on SAC Huston. Something that might indicate what she was working on.

I knew that wasn't going to bear fruit, but I didn't tell him.

I had a different plan. I also needed to go back to the Brandos with a clear head and fresh eyes.

The Metaxa hadn't settled comfortably, and I suddenly realized I hadn't had eaten since Denny's. As I was sorting through a stack of menus next to the kitchen phone, Marisol came up behind me.

"I heard Jake leave. I hope it wasn't something I said."

I caught the faint aroma of tangerines, which seemed perfect for her and turned. She was barefoot, and her hair was still damp, and somewhere she'd dug up a pair of gold-monogrammed, white silk pajamas that would have been loose on Charles Barkley. Apparently, D. D. hadn't missed any dessert carts. She'd rolled up the sleeves and cuffs and double-wrapped a red terry-cloth bathrobe belt around her waist to keep everything in place, but there was still way too much fabric and way too little girl.

"Very Michelin Man, don't you think?" she said, turning to model.

"You look dazzling. Hungry?"

"What are my choices?"

"At this hour, pizza or pizza."

"Garlic . . . but only if you're going to eat it too."

"You're on. How about some chopped tomatoes?"

"Excellent. There's a fair-sized wine collection downstairs. I'll see if I can come up with just the right *rojo*."

She trotted off in a wave of rustling silk, and I picked up the phone. I was actually a little surprised to find a dial tone. Malibu has a Johnnie's, which, for my money, is the best pizza in LA, but as soon as the guy answered, he had attitude. "This the Shoulders place?" he snarled.

"There a problem?"

"About four hundred and seventy bucks worth. You're off service."

"Mr. Shoulders is dead."

"Yeah, I heard. So's his address."

I'm not a Luddite, but don't get me started on caller ID.

But it was either principle or my growling stomach. "You take American Express?"

"At sixty bucks a slice, you better keep eating."

Marisol had her mouth full and a tiny piece of tomato on her chin. She looked terrific. She raised a glass of Bosconia Gran Reserve. "To Johnnie's," she said. "May their ovens last a thousand years."

We clicked glasses and sipped. I took a napkin and wiped away the tomato, then bent forward and kissed her forehead, then her lips. It was like putting a match to gasoline.

Only one other time in my life had this happened. And I thought that when I buried her, I'd buried it as well. I knew we'd both felt electricity at the CAA reception, and but this was beyond attraction. This was explosive and, in a way I can't describe, painful. I wanted her like no woman I had wanted since my wife's death, and I felt her body shudder all the way down. I'm not so sure mine didn't do the same.

I don't know where her wineglass went, but we suddenly became such a part of one another that if she had been stuck with a pin, I would have jumped. I was so much bigger than she was that I completely enveloped her, and somewhere in the back of my mind I worried that she might be too fragile. But if that were the case, she gave no indication.

She unwound the folds she had put into D. D. Shoulders's sleep attire, and her torrid Mediterranean skin came against mine. I realized that somehow I had also gotten undressed, and now she drove her mouth against mine so hard I tasted blood. She arched her back violently, thrusting her pelvis against my stomach. I felt her wetness . . . then her hand . . . guiding me into her.

And then, suddenly, I felt a burning in my eyes. The kind men aren't supposed to feel. And I pushed her away. I hadn't thought about it; it just happened. I saw the shock on her face and looked away. I stood up. I don't know who was more surprised, but I do remember how cold the air suddenly got.

"Why?" she choked out.

I didn't have an answer. In truth, I did, but there weren't words for it. At least none that would have made any sense. But I couldn't continue. I wasn't ready for this kind of intensity, this kind of loss of control. And if I let myself go . . . gave in to the moment . . . it would change everything. And I would lose her. As certainly as I had lost Sanrevelle. Differently, perhaps, but just as absolutely. This was not a moment of passion that ends with a romp and a cigarette. This was the emotional edge. Where peril lived, and the abyss awaited. And like a wary tightrope walker, I had made the fatal mistake: I had looked down.

I heard her get up and go downstairs. I dressed and was looking out the window when she came back up, wearing her wet matador pants and jacket and carrying the rest of her outfit, including her shoes. I turned around, but I didn't recognize her. Her face had changed.

"In my country, a lady does not do what I have just done. It was wrong, and now I have paid for it. I should thank you for being so much stronger. Please do not see me out. I couldn't bear any more shame."

And then she was gone. I turned back to the window. A pair of pelicans cruised low across the sand, then turned and headed out to sea. As they disappeared into the darkness, I heard a car start. It sounded like a BMW, and the driver was having difficulty getting it into gear.

8

Two Latins and a Tango

DECEMBER 16, 1944
SOUTH CHINA SEA
FIFTY-EIGHT MILES SOUTHWEST OF HONG KONG

Ensign Fabian Cañada let the neck strap catch his binoculars and continued scanning the darkening horizon without them. He'd always had better night vision than anybody he knew, which had served him well hunting coyotes in the San Gabriels and later, as a rookie patrolman, walking a beat in downtown LA. But even superior eyesight couldn't see something that wasn't there.

For twenty-three hours, the Casablanca-class aircraft carrier, USS Resurrection Bay, *had been making lazy, twenty-mile loops at dead slow off the Chinese coast, and there was still no sign of the pair of seventeen-foot speedboats, four sailors and eight Marines they had put in the water just after sundown the previous day. Now, as last light again faded, and the massive flattop became invisible against the moonless sky, they had no choice but to run dark yet another night in the event a Japanese patrol entered the area.* Or worse, the landing party had been captured and compromised.

Captain Hackin hadn't sugar-coated it. "I don't give a shit if you see somebody flashing our call sign or hear your mother yelling Lou Gehrig's shoe size, until we can see again, you don't answer a goddamn thing. Got it? We're so far up the devil's ass, King Kong couldn't reach us with a fistfuck."

So it looked like for the next several hours, the only chance a returning boat had of finding home was by colliding with it. But despite the danger, Hackin had reaffirmed that they would hold their position until 0730, a full half hour past sunrise. Then, boats or no boats, they would have to haul ass. With no destroyer escort and their Hellcats and Corsairs tied down tight, they were a tiger without claws, and they had already pressed their luck to the extreme.

Casablanca-class carriers or CVEs weren't designed to be tip-of-the-spear strike vessels to begin with. Sardonically referred to as "Combustible, Vulnerable and Expendable," they were hastily built, lightly armored and undergunned. They might have been called warships, but they weren't much more than a five-hundred-foot runway strapped to the Staten Island Ferry.

When the *Bay* wasn't shuttling men and machines to forward bases or running shakedown cruises for new personnel, her job was to lie an hour's flight time off the main fleet and replenish the attack carriers with aircraft and pilots lost in battle. This trip, she also carried 850 hollow-eyed Marines who had seen the horrors of Tarawa and Guadalcanal and would soon be called upon to make their next blood donation on a sprit of volcanic rock most of them would have been hard-pressed to spell . . . Iwo Jima.

As a result of her ever-changing missions, everything about the *Bay* was transitory—and crowded. Paint peeled, homesick graffiti covered the walls of the heads, and, from engine room to flight deck, a thick cobweb of hammocks draped her superstructure. With few recreation choices, gambling ran rampant, and you were likely to encounter men shooting craps or a session of High, Low, Jack and the Game anywhere there was space to squat. The spit-and-polish navy of recruiting posters was half a globe and a hundred thousand lifetimes away. This was what world war looked like three gut-grinding years in.

It wasn't much better for the officers. Fabian had grown weary of rotating a smelly bunk with two other ensigns, so he now slept most nights on one of the starboard artillery batteries. The guns' steel shielding deflected all but the strongest winds, and the ocean brushing the hull forty feet below drowned out the endless sounds of sixteen hundred sweaty, uncomfortable men jammed into too small a space. His reward for braving the occasional downpour was a modicum of privacy and a few private hours under a canopy of a billion South Pacific stars.

A yeoman with a fresh pair of eyes arrived on the bridge to relieve him, and Fabian stepped into the pilothouse. Blackout screens covered the outside glass, and the skin of the duty officers and enlisted personnel took on a jaundiced hue under the dim, yellow lights. Fabian lit a Chesterfield and inhaled deeply.

From across the room, a voice called out. "Hey, Cañada, I need you to win a bet for me." It was Commander Bennett, the ship's executive officer. "I say the LAPD doesn't give a shit if a guy can't find his ass with both hands, they hire pretty boys like you 'cause the movie bosses don't want their million-dollar stars I busted by horse-faces. Am I right?"

"That's part of it," Fabian shot back. "We also gotta service actresses who need their itch scratched. That's why they issue us two sets of cuffs—one regular, one mink."

Guys laughed, and a magazine came flying in his direction.

"Hey, Fabe, take a look at this, will ya?" Lt. Luca LaPaglia, late of the Bronx, was hunched over the chart table. Despite having enlisted all the way back in 1941, Pags was still struggling to master basic navigation. In his defense,

*he'd been an aviator until shattering a vertebra during a
hard landing at Guam, but as far as the surface navy was
concerned, a pilot couldn't find his dick unless you painted
an arrow on his chest. Pags had people's respect for pulling
strings to get sea duty rather than fly a desk at Pearl, but it
was a running joke that if you were hungry, you didn't try to
follow him to chow.*

"What is it?"

*Pags was looking at a well-worn book filled with columns
of numbers.* "The tide tables don't match the position com-
putation. I think somebody fucked up."

At that, Bennett yelled out, "Hey, Flyboy, careful you
don't drop a nut doin' math. Some of them figures go all the
way up to three digits."

Pags ignored him, "See what I mean, Fabe. The only way
you get this fix is if you're readin' across the wrong line."

*Fabian ran his finger along the page Pags was indicating,
then did a quick mental check.* "Christ, it looks like some
tired motherfucker started with the wrong basis, so everything afterward was off."

*The other officers hurried to the table, their earlier levity
replaced by looks of concern. After a moment, Bennett put
his finger on two sets of initials penciled next to the solu-
tion.* "And some other tired motherfucker just okayed it."

Pags looked at his fellow officers. "You know what this
means."

"Yeah," *said Bennett,* "somebody's gonna get court-
martialed."

Fabian face was grim. "It also means we were out of position when we put those boats in the water, and we're even
farther out now." *He took a deep breath.* "Somebody needs
to wake the captain?"

*As two sailors adjusted his life vest, and he strapped on
the Colt .45 he hadn't fired since basic training, Fabian
couldn't see the captain's launch riding the light chop four
stories below. He only knew it was there because Pags had*

to keep gunning the engine so it wouldn't stall. Only a select few—not including Fabian—knew why the Bay *and two destroyers had broken off from fleet formation five days ago and begun steaming northwest. Then, sometime during the third night, the destroyers had dropped away, and at daybreak, the* Bay *was alone.*

As the ultimate projection of American power, aircraft carriers are the centerpiece of all naval strategy, and the first tenet of any mission is to protect them. They never operate alone—ever. They are far too precious and vulnerable. So everyone aboard knew that whatever was happening was beyond dangerous. Not surprisingly, betting pools had sprung up in every department about their ultimate destination. And none of the favorites was comforting.

An hour earlier, Captain Hackin and the unsmiling Marine commanding officer, Col. A. K. Jackson, had brought Fabian and Pags into the information loop. Months before, two stateside newspapers had broken the story of the massive airlift taking place from bases in India as they supplied Chiang Kai-shek's forces in China. However, the New York Times *and* Chicago Tribune *were specifically not circulated to combat units, so no one aboard the* Bay *had heard of it.*

The two junior officers now learned that army and civilian pilots had been "Flying the Hump"—the Himalayas— since April, 1942, keeping Chiang in the war and holding down thousands of Japanese troops that might otherwise be thrown against the Allies. Between the horrific mountain weather and the Zeros that preyed on the slow, unescorted transports, the Hump was as deadly a piece of airspace as existed, and hundreds of aircraft had been lost.

The Bay *was being diverted to pick up seven pilots who had survived going down and managed to evade capture. A network of missionaries had rescued them, consolidated them and gotten word out that eventually reached Washington.*

With the Japanese on the run everywhere, there was no

military imperative for risking critical assets to collect a handful of men. But at the White House, the opportunity to deliver the war-weary American public a Christmas feel-good story was too good to pass up. So with no advance planning and no verifiable intelligence, a medical team had been dispatched aboard a submarine, the USS Parrotfish, *to collect them. The sub, however, had missed three position checks and was presumed lost. So in the time-honored tradition of bureaucracies everywhere, stupidity gave way to insanity, and someone—without consulting the navy— substituted the* Resurrection Bay.

"So how do we find these pilots?" Pags asked.

"Just get there. If they're alive, somebody will find you," said Hackin. "A guy they call Big Jim Rackmann is running the operation, and they tell me he's one tough son of a bitch."

Pags raised an eyebrow. "There you go, a bad-ass missionary."

"No offense, sir," said Fabian, "but this has all the makings of a cluster fuck."

Hackin's silence was agreement enough. Having your ship shot out from under you in battle was every captain's nightmare, but at least it was honorable. Losing one on a bullshit mission in some godforsaken stretch of water, likely without firing a round, was the dignity equivalent of having your wife leave you for another woman.

He looked at his two men, lingering on Fabian. "You want to reconsider, Cañada, you won't get an argument. I never could figure out what a detective was doing out here anyway. I thought cops got automatic deferments."

Fabian smiled. "The recruiter said I'd be able to work on my tan."

It wasn't a particularly funny line, but everyone welcomed the laugh.

The captain turned to Pags. "What about you, Lieutenant? You got a problem taking orders from an ensign?"

"Hell, Captain, who cares about rank? I'm not worth a good goddamn unless I'm drivin' somethin' fast, and I *wouldn't miss scarin' the hell out of LA's Finest here for anything less than a case of beer and a hooker. Make that two hookers and a suite at the Royal Hawaiian."*

"We'll sit an extra hour. You're not back by then . . . I'm sorry."

Colonel Jackson regarded the two officers. "Gentlemen, if you have to make tough choices about who to bring back, I assure you my men won't cause any problems."

Pags looked at Jackson. "Shit, Colonel, don't say that. The major leadin' them owes me two hundred bucks."

Now, as the sailor holding the bowline threw the loose end to Fabian, and the launch accelerated away from the carrier, Pags shouted over the unmuffled inboard. "Hey, partner, aren't you proud of me for catchin' that fuckin' mistake? I'm really gettin' this navigation shit down."

"Well, Magellan, there's a whole continent out there somewhere, let's see if you can hit it."

As it turned out, what they hit was a lot smaller.

Shortly after their departure, an easterly breeze kicked up a layer of fog that blocked the stars and reduced an already impossibly dark night to a thick, wet gauze with zero visibility. They could barely see each other, but to cut power meant precious time off a schedule that didn't have any slack. So with Fabian fighting to see even an inch ahead and Pags grinning like a sixteen-year-old at a burlesque show, they kept the throttle full open.

The gargantuan, ghostly hull draped with steel cables loomed up out of the mist and penetrated both men's consciousness at almost exactly the same time. Fabian braced himself for the collision while Pags jammed the engine into reverse and threw the rudder full to port. The launch, a wooden, twenty-five-foot Chris-Craft hardtop, scraped along the mammoth vessel's side with a sickening, grinding sound, and Fabian waited for one of the cables to rip it open like a cardboard box. Miraculously, none did, and moments later, they came to a full stop.

*They held their breath, waiting for the inevitable shouts
and lights, but silence once again descended around them.
Fabian craned his neck and squinted, but whatever was up
there was swathed in the impenetrable fog.*

*"Fuckin'-A," Pags shouted, "that's what you get when
you ride with Mr. Lucky. Eight jillion boats in China, and
I hit the empty one." He brought the engine up again, and
as they neared the large ship's bow, they passed under an
anchor chain. The white lettering beneath the hawsehole
could be read through the gloom. USS* Tango.

*Fabian felt a chill run down his spine. He'd seen this ship
at Midway. An Andromeda class attack cargo ship heading
out as they were heading in. He especially remembered her
skipper, standing on the bridge barking orders wearing a
baseball cap and ratty denim shirt with the sleeves torn off.
That, plus the guy's full red beard weren't like any captain
Fabian had seen before, and he'd asked Bennett about it.*

*"If somebody tried to put me on a fuckin' AKA, I'd shoot
myself," Bennett had said. "The only thing 'attack' about
them is the attack of the runs the crew gets when they weigh
anchor. Just enough guns to piss off the Japs. The brass
knows it too, so they cut them some slack. But you gotta
admire that red-haired motherfucker for taking it to the
limit."*

*At nearly five hundred feet and equal part cranes,
booms and gantries—with a single deck cannon and a few
.20-caliber machine guns thrown in—Andromedas usually
looked like a construction zone in a bad neighborhood. Tonight, though, this one was a cadaver.*

"What the fuck?" said Pags. "It's one of ours."

*"I think that's past tense. Looks like she's a sub barrier
now with probably forty or fifty mines strung underneath.
That's what those cables are. Lucky for us, nobody anticipated a crazy wop and his half-wit sidekick ramming into
her side."*

"I owe it all to clean living and a fast outfield."

Pags pushed the launch back up to the maximum. Fabian

turned and looked back at the Tango. She was invisible again, but he thought for a moment he saw a faint pinprick of light. And then it was gone.

Ten minutes later, Pags elbowed him. "Look, even the goddamn fog is givin' us a break." He was right. Several faint glows could be seen through the mist, then more, until the shore and hills of the Pearl River were dotted with lights. And finally, lanterns, thousands of them, strung along the decks of houseboats, junks, trawlers, gently dancing in the breeze. From somewhere, music drifted across the water as clearly as if they'd been listening to a radio.

Fabian took in the scene. "Well, against all odds, we're right where we're supposed to be."

"I'll take that as a thanks. Whatever happened to blackouts?"

"The war's lost, so the party's on."

"Boy, what I wouldn't give for a couple of hours ashore. Think about it. Guys as handsome as us with a pocketful of Uncle Sammy Bucks and big, stiff American dicks."

"You still got a tent in your pants on the way back, I'll drop you off. In the meantime, keep an eye out for anything Japanese. They'll be the ones trying to kill us."

Off the starboard side, Fabian saw a whirlpool, small but nonetheless disconcerting. "Hackin said the river's unpredictable. Sandbars where there shouldn't be. We're shallow enough to ride over almost anything, but let's not take the chance."

Pags backed the throttles down halfway, then crossed his hands behind his head and sat back. The water was mostly calm, the ride smooth. "I been meanin' to ask you, partner, what kinda name is Cañada anyway?"

"It's not really CAN-ah-dah, it's supposed to be Can-YAH-dah. There's a tilde over the N, and the accent's on the second syllable. My grandfather got tired of fighting an uphill battle. Me, I'm an asshole. I stuck with the original. I like to make people uncomfortable."

"Shit, we're livin' the same story. There's no hard G

in LaPaglia, but try tellin' that to the navy. What'd your grandpop do?"

"Started with a donkey cart picking up scrap metal. Now, Canada Salvage's got plants up and down the coast. People think we're from Montreal. My grandfather just smiles. Might not have happened the other way."

"Scrap metal? Where I come from, you gotta be a Jew to be in that racket. But you're some kinda spic, right?"

"The best kind. Mexican."

"And a cop instead of workin' for the family. That spells outcast."

Fabian's smile was tight. "Outcast doesn't begin to cover it. You?"

"Luca Sr. owns a shithouse full of nightclubs. A real stud around Manhattan. Day I was born, he started groomin' me to take over. Then I discovered jazz, and there went servin' booze. Played piano behind Sinatra once, but the old man got me blackballed at the mob joints, expectin' me to come crawlin' back. Didn't happen. Went to Harlem and jammed with the best. After this shit's over, I'm headin' west. Gonna try the movies. Music's the only thing I was ever really good at."

"Don't forget navigation. You play Armstrong? I can't get enough of his stuff."

"You kiddin'? I do an 'All of Me' that'll get you laid standin' at the bar."

Half an hour later, the harbor was behind them, and they were once again enveloped in darkness. The banks of the river were invisible again, but with the fog gone, the stars reflected off the water and turned it into a lighted highway.

9

White Coats and Fat Cats

Driving toward Westwood in D. D. Shoulders's red Woodie to see Manarca, I didn't feel any better, but I didn't feel any worse either. I dialed Mallory. "How are things with Beverly Hills Finest?"

"There's a USC game on, and they're into the Mid's."

Having Mallory around is like living with the *Robb Report*. Only instead of six-hundred-thousand-dollar watches and million-dollar Phaetons, he's a shamus of food. One of his finds is a pasta sauce there are no words for. Mid's. I put it on anything that lies still.

There aren't any words for the price either. Diamonds are cheaper. Mallory heats up big bowls of the stuff and sets them out with loaves of Italian bread. Tear off a hunk and have at it. Nobody ever complains there isn't any guacamole.

I could picture my kitchen. What's enough food for a cop? Just a little more than he ever gets. "I suppose it's too much to hope that you held some back for the guy who pays the rent," I said.

"Since he's the same guy who put my life in danger, he doesn't get as much consideration as the guys with the guns." Then he added, "A Mr. Bronston called. Said something about a bullfighter going back to Spain and studios canceling bids. When I asked him to be more forthcoming, he yelled, 'Here's forthcoming, motherfucker . . . I'm going to kill your boss.' "

"He calls back, tell him to take a number behind Francesca Huston."

"I won't ask."

There are two groups that put sweat on the upper lips of law enforcement. One might think that would include defense attorneys, but most cops don't even break stride dancing through a cross-examination. Judges are another matter. They know that no investigation or prosecution ever goes by the book, and the only reason we're not knee deep in felons is because corners get cut and bullshit gets canonized. But every now and then, some Baron in Black gets bored or pissed or has a moment of constitutional conscience, stops the band and starts asking real questions. And you can lie to your boss, your wife, your girlfriend, internal affairs, even your priest, but fuck with a judge, and you better have a very rich aunt and a retirement cabin on Machu Picchu.

The second group is doctors. Cops are taught early on that when a white coat shows up—get the hell out of the way. Half the departments in America are sitting on more litigation liability than their towns are worth, and nothing gets a jury's mouth watering like a cop fumbling out an explanation about why the guy in the wheelchair won't be enjoying lap dances anymore because John Law slowed down the medics.

I don't give money to large institutions. But I do help individuals, and over the years, Dr. Austin Stillwell hasn't been bashful about asking. As Chief of Surgery at UCLA, where they treat anybody who shows up, he sees more than his share of horror stories. I'm glad to have been able to ease a few. So when he and I arrived at Manarca's room, the uniform on duty didn't blink. He actually held the door.

The curtains around the first bed were pulled. Somebody was behind them, which I thought was strange considering the security, but if they were short of beds, the hospital would do what they had to do, and the cops would just have to adjust. Manarca was next to the window. His skin was a little wan, and there were tubes and wires running off in all directions, but aside from a couple of whorls of gauze around his throat, he didn't look too much the worse for wear. He gave me the finger, which is always a good sign.

Our positions had been reversed when we first met, and I remembered how much I hated being down. People used to being on the move make difficult patients. Manarca got the doc's attention and emphatically pointed toward the other side of the bed.

Stillwell shook his head no. "He wants the catheter out," he said to me. Turning back to the detective, he offered some encouragement. "Tomorrow, maybe."

I promised to stay only a few minutes, and Stillwell left. I pulled a metal chair next to the bed and sat. "When you're up to it, I'll let you take a poke at me for dragging you out to Century City."

Manarca held up two fingers.

"You got it, two pokes. Any idea who cut you?"

He hesitated, then gestured to a pad and pen on the nightstand. I handed them to him, and he scribbled a few lines. Most cops can't read their own notes when they get cold, but Manarca wrote in a swirling, elegant script that was almost feminine.

> *Stepped in some shit. Been talkin' to the grand jury.*
> *Sooner or later, it was gonna get out.*

"Anything I can do to help?"
He shook his head no and took the pad back.

> *Insider's game. My fault all the way.*

Jake had been right, it was a cop thing. Fortunately for Dion, whoever he was ratting out didn't want to have to answer for a body too, so they sent a wakeup call first.

But that wasn't why I was there. Starting at the Brando house, I gave the detective a summary, leaving out my session with Ms. Huston. When I finished, he stared out the window.

"You and Chuck have any dealings?" I asked.

About six months ago, we crossed on a case.
Custody fight turned into a homicide.
The usual shit: lose in court, shoot your old lady.
It was my ticket, but Chuck showed up in the middle.

"He tell you why?"

He was on my perp for poppin' somebody else.
Seemed odd cause the guy was a fuckin' accountant.
Not the usual DNA for a multiple.

"What happened to him?"

Checked into a hotel in Chinatown,
drank a bottle of Beam and ate a .357,
which Chinks usually don't do.
Mostly they're fliers. Sometimes pills.

"The guy was Chinese?"

Yep. Chuck's stiff was the business partner.
A hit set up to look like a home invasion.
But there was a snitch. He never said who.
I figure once the guy was dead Chuck just closed his mess out.

I took back some of my earlier applause. Even if Jake were right about the attack on Manarca not being related to the ones on Chuck and Lucille, the two were connected by more than a badge. And there was another home invasion involved. Until I knew if it fit, I'd keep it to myself.

Manarca's writing was getting difficult to read. He was

tired. I started to put the pad back on the table, but he grabbed it.

If Maywood's involved,
somebody's gonna get it in the ass.

"Why? Was he in on the Chinatown case?"
Manarca let out a snort of disgust and wrote angrily.

No, he's a fuckin' chief, that's why.
Brass never plays team ball.
Talk to Fat Cat.

"Who's Fat Cat?"
"That would be me. Saleapaga. LA Sheriff's Department. Homicide."
I turned. Hugo "Fat Cat" Saleapaga was coming through the curtains encircling the other bed. Only slightly shorter than me but considerably wider, he looked more like a bear than a cat. I also noticed that as big as he was, he moved easily, like an athlete.
Fat Cat's skin was dark chestnut, his features Polynesian, and he was expensively dressed in a dove gray suit that took up several bolts of Italian wool. The suit was set off by a pair of smartly shined, tan alligator shoes. Add in a yellow and orange silk tie against a white-on-white shirt, and he wasn't trying to hide his candle.
"Hard to get any shut-eye around here, what with Dion moanin' all night and now you jabberin' away about sand-paperin' titties." A broad, noncop smile lit up his face. He extended his hand, and I took it.
"Rail Black," I said.
"I know," he said, nodding at Manarca. "Slick Speechless here ran some things by me when that Corsican thing went down. Bothered him there were so many unanswered questions . . . leastways on his part." He looked at me with a pair of coal black eyes that didn't match the warmth of his grin.

I don't know what he was expecting, but if it wasn't silence, he was disappointed.

After we'd played a little I-can-keep-from-blinking-longer-than-you, Manarca rattled an IV, and we used it as an excuse to disengage. The detective's eyelids were getting heavy, and a nurse came in and gave us hard looks while she rearranged his wires and took his temperature. Smart enough to know not to mess with ladies wearing white panty hose, I suggested to Fat Cat that we take our conversation elsewhere. On our way out, Manarca gave me a thumbs-up, which I assumed meant he didn't have any secrets from his friend.

At the coffee stand on the first floor, Fat Cat got himself some kind of latte that took a paragraph to order, and I grabbed a cold bottle of lemonade.

It was a four-star Southern California day, and we wandered outside.

"You two meet on a case?" I asked Fat Cat.

"Not the kind you're thinkin' of. We go back. You ever hear him tell how he's related to Balboa?"

"Couple of times, but I'm still not clear."

"Me neither, but that's his specialty. Tellin' stories and stickin' to them. Little prick saved my life with that fast mouth of his."

We moseyed over to a marble bench under a couple of maple trees and sat.

"Came here when I was eleven. Me and my mother. Samoa to Honolulu to LA, courtesy of the DEA. My old man, David Saleapaga, headed a narco unit in Hawaii and was the first to find the Medellin Cartel movin' shit through the South Pacific. Once he started bustin' up their operation, he had the life expectancy of a gnat. We found out later Escobar had made him a *Ciento,* which meant a hundred grand dead. Double, if you kidnapped him or a member of his family. So some long-forgotten uncle named George took us in because the Justice Department promised him a check every month.

"The Manarcas lived across the street. Dion was a couple

years older and the leader of the neighborhood cool guys. He took me under his wing."

The bench we were occupying was on the edge of a parking lot, and we both noticed a shirtless teenager with a shaved head and too many tattoos walking through the cars, looking in windows. You didn't have to be a cop to figure it out. Fat Cat held up his shield and whistled. The guy looked, sneered and took his time disappearing.

Saleapaga shook his head. "Back in the day, I'da run like hell."

"Me too. Every kid had two gears: standard-issue Jesus Fucking Christ and cop-speed."

He laughed. "Dion always had to wait for the rest of us. Man, was he fast."

"Where'd Fat Cat come from?"

"One day, these guys come around askin' for my mother, Nita. Four motherfuckers in suits. Sayin' they're from Immigration, but they got Colombian accents, and they're drivin' a Mercedes with Florida plates, so I'm bettin' no. Uncle George tells them she gets home at seven. By this time, money or no money, he didn't give a shit. We'd been cloggin' up his house for two years, and he couldn't wait to see us gone.

"I was gettin' to be a handsome dude too, and George's hot-lookin' daughter, Lola, couldn't hang around me enough. Probably had as much to do with her old man turnin' Valachi as findin' the bathroom locked when he wanted to take a dump."

He took a long pull on his coffee. "There was this guy in the neighborhood. Gus. Hunted everything. Duck, deer. Went to Montana once for some kinda goddamn sheep. We'd all scoot over when he got back from a trip. See some blood. Maybe score a hunk of meat nobody's old lady would cook.

"One day, Gus comes home with this big-footed kitten. Said he found it in the desert . . . next to its dead mother. Swore he didn't shoot her, but since nobody was askin', why even bring it up unless you had? Little thing was cute, though. Claws sharp as shit, but if you held it in a towel, you could cart it around.

"Couple of months go by, and it's gettin' big. Gus said it was a feral mix, but everybody knew it was a fuckin' cougar."

"And he had it in the house?"

"Yep, which was startin' to be a problem. Tearin' up the furniture, drapes. Then it grabbed the Thanksgiving turkey and held the family off while it ate it—raw. That was the end for the wife. So Gus offers twenty bucks to anybody'll take it off his hands."

"And naturally, that's you guys."

He smiled, remembering. "We kept it in an old widow-lady's garage. She never went out there. It was like our club-house. And for some reason, I was the only one could handle that goddamn cat. Scratched me up pretty good, but never bit me.

"So the day the Florida dudes show up, Dion sends some-body to intercept my mom at the bus stop. Tells her my dad's gonna be callin' her at her girlfriend's house. He did that sometimes—when he didn't want Uncle George listenin' in on the extension.

"By seven, my uncle's gone. Took Lola and went to the movies. So when the fake INS guys come back, nobody an-swers the door. Us kids are on Dion's front porch, watchin'. We give them a minute, then Dion moseys over and says Nita and her kid blew town. Then he gets real earnest. Tells them she left a suitcase at his house. And he peeked inside. Cash and bars of metal. Like maybe gold. Says since the guys look like cops, they might want it. Doesn't need his family messed up with some drug assholes."

Now I was laughing.

"I had that cougar in the biggest motherfuckin' Samsonite the Salvation Army had, along with half a dozen bricks to give it some heft. Even then, every once in a while, the bag would walk a few feet on its own. Dion gives the signal, and I lug it across the street to the Mercedes. I'm sweatin' big-time, scared shitless. Dion tells the Florida guys it's gotta sit upright, cause if the gold shifts, it might tear the sides out."

"Let me guess, so they load it in the backseat?"

He nodded. "And all the time, I'm prayin' the cat don't go into one of his screams. They got a block before somebody couldn't wait to look at all that gold. Four doors flew open like a half ton of napalm blew. Guys runnin' in all directions. Driver didn't get it in park, so the car rolls over a fire hydrant, and next thing you know, there's water shootin' half a fuckin' mile into space. Goes without sayin', nobody came back."

I was laughing by then too. "What happened to the cat?"

"Saw it jump a fence between some houses . . . headin' toward the railroad yard. Probably why I never get a Christmas card from PETA."

"But you picked up a nickname."

"I wasn't heavy back then, but what the hell. It was better than 'Big Hugo,' which sounds like somethin' you get at Nate & Al's."

We finished our drinks. "I'm not going to ask why Dion picked the LAPD, and you went with the sheriff."

"You know anything about the politics in those days, you don't have to. Shit's over now, and we both done good. How can I help you?"

"What do you know about Yale Maywood?"

"Knocked him on his ass at a weddin' once. Got a three-day suspension, and it was worth it. But you probably want more than that."

"Care to sniff around?"

"For Dion, anything. You got a card?"

One of the officers protecting my house met me in the lower-level garage of the Century City shopping center. The official name has been Westfield Shoppingtown for almost a decade now, but I don't know anyone who would recognize it said that way. In most businesses, people pay a premium for established brands and never fool around with something ingrained in the public consciousness. But it's been my experience that the life-form with the most ego and least common sense is a developer. NFL owners run a close second.

The cop, an off-duty, fresh-faced rookie named Jarman, brought my Dodge Ram and a leather overnight bag Mallory had packed. His face lit up when he saw the Woodie, even though it was coming off the assembly line when his grandfather wasn't much more than a notion in somebody's eye. "Think you can handle this?" I asked.

"Three on the column and a clutch about as subtle as a Jerry Bruckheimer sound track. No problem, Mr. Black. No problem at all."

Even if he couldn't, the owner wasn't going to be doing any complaining, but the kid eased away like he'd done it every day of his life. After bouncing around in the old Poncho, it felt good to be back in the Ram, and as I adjusted the seat to fit me, I put on some Miles Davis for the ride back to the desert.

Before I left, I drove around both levels of the garage a couple of times, but if somebody was shadowing me, they were cleverly disguised as good-looking ladies dressed for a day at Bloomingdale's.

Taxi Drivers and Price Cutters

My plan had been to go straight to the Brando place, but it was nearing 3:30 when I came to the Victorville business district exit. There were a couple of bases I wanted to cover, and I decided to do it sooner rather than wait for morning. I was also hungry, and an In-N-Out Burger sign large enough to direct air traffic had gotten my stomach growling. While I gnawed on a Double-Double—heavy on the grilled onions—and sipped a chocolate shake, I thought about Chuck and Lucille. Pretty soon, what their last hours must have been like took away my appetite, and I dumped the rest of my meal and headed downtown.

An hour of combing the archives of the *Daily Press* for the preceding month didn't reveal anything even mildly out of the ordinary. Neither did a call to the local television station's newsroom, where a high-desert Edward R. Murrow ran down every federal crime in the area going back to a bank robbery in 1972.

Intelligence operators know that if you want to find out what's going on beneath the surface of any town, ask a fireman. They see everything, and unlike cops, they'll talk to you. And I do mean *fireman* not *firefighter*, a designation that matters only to the Cult of the Perpetually Offended, not the men and women who risk their lives running into burning buildings.

LAFD Battalion Chief Anita Watson, who I dated before she was killed trying to rescue of one of her men from an apartment house inferno, once told me that if any of her team ever called her a firefighter, she'd give him a week of desk duty. I'd made that mistake when I first met her. "I didn't grow up wanting to do this so I could change the name of the proudest tradition in public service. All I ever wanted was to be what my daddy was . . . and his daddy. A fireman, plain and simple." Anita is how I got involved with Blue Rescue. I miss her. For her aversion to bullshit and a lot of other reasons.

Lt. Del Brockman at Victorville Station 322 was my kind of guy. Crew cut, perpetual smile on his wide, tanned face and slightly hard of hearing, which he said seemed to get worse when the mayor talked. He invited me into the station's dayroom. where a couple of guys were playing eight ball, and two others were doing their best to disrupt them. "Hey," Brockman called out, "this guy here used to date a chief."

"Fuckin'-A," one of the spectators answered. "Hey, Sweeney, weren't you and Chief Green an item for a while? Until he found out that two-incher of yours couldn't reach his fun zone?"

A burly guy with a tattoo of a snake curling up his forearm fired a cue across the room, which just missed its mark before burying itself in the Naugahyde sofa. From the looks of the sofa, though, it wasn't the first time.

"Enough with the bullshit," said Brockman. "Listen up."

The four men joined us, and I introduced myself. After handshakes, I said, "Sorry to interrupt your downtime. I'm trying to get a line on anything unusual that happened around here in the last couple of weeks. Something that didn't make the papers."

The guys looked at each other, and I suspected what they

were thinking. So I added, "Besides the commotion on the Brando property the other night."

Whatever they'd been told about Chuck and Lucille, it must have come with a warning, because they noticeably relaxed. Brockman looked at the guy with the snake tattoo. "Sweeney, tell him about the taxi."

"Shit, man."

Brockman nodded. "I'd do it, but you were there. If there's any blowback, I'll take responsibility."

Sweeney sighed and went for it. "Two weeks ago Tuesday, a call came in from some lieutenant in homicide. Said they needed a pumper over at the self-storage joint on Route 18. Rent hadn't been paid on one of the big units, and when they opened it up, there was a car inside. Wanted us standin' by in case of a fuel leak."

"A homicide cop for a back rent beef?" I said.

"Didn't make much sense to me either till Smitty, me and Renner got there. There was like thirty badges comparin' ball size. Locals, bunch of sheriff's investigators and a couple of CHP. Biggest pair, though, belong to a broad. A Fed. Real knockout, but with an asshole so tight she could squeeze piss out of a prune pit. It was her show all the way, and nobody was happy about it."

"FBI Agent Huston," I said. "She was alone?"

Sweeney looked at me suspiciously. "Far as I could tell. You know her?"

"We've met, but not dated. Please go on."

He relaxed. "Like Del said, car turned out to be a taxi. Big ass Ford. Pus green with a yellow plastic toplight. It didn't fit in the shed, so somebody unbolted the bumpers and stuffed them in the backseat. Then they piled all kinds of shit on top. Lawn furniture, old blankets."

He stopped and went across to the Coke machine. After he'd guzzled half a can, I said, "So tell me about the body."

He was perspiring heavily now. "I didn't say there was a body."

"Jesus Christ, Sweeney, tell the man the story." It was one

of the guys who hadn't spoken, and his voice had command.

Sweeney took a breath. "He was sittin' in the passenger seat, still belted in. The bugs had got to him pretty good, but even so, you could tell he was an Indian . . . Native American, if that's better for you."

"How'd you know?"

"I didn't, but Smitty's Pechanga on his mother's side, and he took one look and said there ain't no hair on earth like Indian hair."

"Local cab?"

"No, Vegas. Plates were gone, but it was painted on the side. CACTUS TAXI. LAS VEGAS. 24-HOUR SERVICE."

Martinez was pissed. "Hey, asshole, why didn't you tell us about this before? I thought we didn't keep secrets around here."

Brockman stepped in. "Put that on me, Joey. Chief called and asked me to keep a lid on it. I made that an order to Sweeney."

Sweeney was irritated now. "So why are we tellin' this guy?"

"How long they let you slide on the rent in one of those places?" I asked.

Brockman laughed. "That one belongs to the fuckin' Scotsman, Taggart. Law requires thirty days' notice, but that prick wouldn't give ten minutes' grace to a crippled Girl Scout."

"So if somebody paid for a month, he'd have sixty days before anybody opened it," I said.

"To the second," Brockman answered.

I couldn't see anybody thinking they needed more time than that to get lost. The driver had probably been killed just before, so we were looking at a roughly ten-week-old murder.

"Did you stay the whole time?" I asked Sweeney.

He nodded. "To the bitter end. They made us move way back while they hooked up the wrecker, which didn't make much sense if they was worried about fire. And they didn't take the body out, just rolled the whole shebang into a trailer, piled in all the other crap from the shed, and some guy in a suit drove it away."

"Trailer?" said Martinez.

"Feds have an aversion to eyeballs," I said. I looked at Sweeney. "Thanks."

Sweeney was past his heartburn. "Forget it, man."

"Anything else?" asked Brockman.

"I could use a name."

Brockman turned back to Sweeney. "Who was there besides Bender?"

"The usual. Ralphie and Dickman."

"What about Wes?"

"Yep."

Brockman smiled. "Let me make a call." He walked toward the office.

"Who's Wes?" I asked Martinez.

"Wes Crowe. Chief of Detectives. His kid brother runs the Desert Freeze stand over by the highway, and guess what fire lieutenant owns the land under it."

The Crowe place was in the San Bernardino Mountains near Lake Arrowhead, twenty miles south of Victorville. Twenty-one, if you count the extra mile of altitude. That doesn't sound like much until you've driven it. Rumor has it that the only reason people live up there at all is because there's no way they're getting on that road a second time. It's not the cliffs, hairpin turns or missing guardrails that makes them lose their nerve. Not even the unpaved section that periodically slides away. It's the clowns with accelerators and cell phones. Give me a war zone any day.

On the way up, the desert turns from brown to dark gray. I know that indicates something underneath, but don't ask me what. If prospecting had been left to the Black family, the world economy would be based on wood. Del Brockman sat next to me pointing out the local landmarks. Rooster Knob, Slack Jaw Ridge, Punchy's Gulch. Problem was, it all looked the same. Put me on a body of water, and in few minutes, I can tell you what's a hundred feet down and over any horizon. The desert? Forget it. I wouldn't have been any better at leading wagon trains than prospecting.

I'd hoped a phone call would have been enough, but apparently that wasn't the way Wes Crowe worked. So my stomach put its arms around itself and hugged while I hand-fought the unfamiliar road and the jerks tailgating me.

The white, one-story frame house tucked into the Alpine escarpment looked almost new. A brown pickup and a red Volvo sat in the gravel drive. Why people live in a forest in wildfire country escapes me, but since I don't work for Allstate, it's none of my business.

Fifty feet beyond, and a little deeper into the trees, another building in the same style but windowless was set at a right angle to the main house. Across a dirt road opposite it, a half acre of land had been cleared, but the stumps and scattered stacks of firewood remained. In place of the trees was a circle of six forty-foot antennas, anchored with thick cables set into concrete footings. When we parked, I noticed that the towers' tops were strung together with two loops of wire a few feet apart. Somebody was either expecting ET or heavy into shortwave.

Maxine Crowe was blonde, petite and pretty and wearing an expensive white sundress and matching heels. She was coming out as we were heading up the walk. Del looked her up and down admiringly. "Max, you look terrific, but we can't run away tonight. Cheryl's barbequing ribs."

She had a great smile. "Hi, Del. Dinner with the girls."

"So some waiter's about to cut his wrists when you ask for separate checks."

"We'll make it up to him by tipping ten percent." She grinned. "Wes is over in his playhouse. Tell him I should be back by ten, and there's ham in the fridge. Best to Cheryl . . . and her ribs."

She got into the Volvo and roared off. Since Del hadn't introduced us, and she hadn't asked, I surmised that when business came calling, she stayed clear. Probably smart when your husband's a cop.

I'm not sure what I'd conjured up in my mind's eye, but Wes Crowe wasn't it. First, he was almost as wide as he was tall. Probably five-eight, 250. And none of it was loose. More like an Olympic weightlifter who can't find a suit to fit but can bend a rail with his neck. And second, he was Chinese.

An Asian man with an Occidental woman isn't common, even in SoCal, where the American melting pot is well ahead of everywhere else. It's an anomaly there are anecdotal explanations for, but I'm not aware of any empirical data. I do know there's deep-seated anger among some American-born Asian men who grew up watching the Wrigley Twins but are now invisible at singles bars. On the flip side, white or black men with Asian women is ubiquitous and the source of outright hostility in many Asian families—especially the Japanese. I don't know what their position is when the genders are reversed, but my guess is it's not nearly as potent. No surprise.

Wes was as effervescent as his wife. Big smile, big voice, and a big hug for Del who, after escaping, offered, "Maxine said to tell you that she'll be spending the night with me. Oh, and there's ham for dinner."

"I love ham. What was the other part?"

We laughed.

He shook my hand firmly and grinned. "You're probably asking yourself, 'What's a hot-looking dude like this doing with a blonde when he could be dating Asian chicks?'" I already liked the guy; now I liked him more.

We sat in some almost comfortable IKEA chairs with cold bottles of Sam Adams, watched over by hundreds of glowing lights from what was easily half a million in radio equipment. Some playhouse.

"Very impressive," I said, gesturing.

"It was this or broads. Equal craving and couldn't afford both."

My eye caught something on one of the shelves. Another

jade tiger. But where Lucille's had been crouching and watching, this one was up on its hind legs, mouth open, in full attack. I was almost certain, though, it was part of the same collection. I stood and walked to it. "Magnificent piece."

Wes hesitated just long enough to decide which lie to tell. He came up with, "Supposed to bring luck. Maxine picked it up somewhere. Probably fuckin' eBay. I'd like to strangle the cocksucker who invented that goddamn thing."

I'd estimated Lucille's at twenty-five grand. In paintings or sculpture, animals in action brought more. A cop's wife wasn't cruising the net making those kind of impulse buys. I decided to watch Detective Crowe's reaction when I tried to pick it up. He didn't exactly fly out of his chair, but he was almost to me when he realized his mistake. True to form, though, he didn't give it up. "Sorry," he said, "it's just that it's heavier than it looks."

Handling it with both hands, I casually turned it over and, like Lucille's, found no markings. I said nothing, replaced it and went back to my chair. Wes Crowe seemed relieved and changed the subject. "Del said you've got some curiosity about the taxi we found. Why?"

Since he didn't take the long way around, I didn't pull any punches either. "Because Chuck and Lucille were friends of mine, and I think there might be a connection."

Wes's eyes never left mine, confirming he'd been the local cop briefed at the Brando murder scene. Made sense, he was the boss. To firm up that we were working from the same playbook, I added. "That, plus Special Agent in Charge Huston and her pals gave me a stiff case of handcuff burn."

He looked amused. "Really? You guilty of something?"

"Coming out of a Red Roof Inn."

"When was this?"

"Couple of days ago."

He thought about that. "So she's still around. Not surprised. A real piece of work, that one." He looked at Del. "How's this for an opening line to a dozen cops? 'Anybody breathes a word about this, and I'll have his ass for obstructing a federal investigation.' "

Del grinned, "And being the shy, retiring guy you are . . ."

"I told her she had something green between her teeth."

It looked like I'd been SAC Huston's second comedian in two weeks. "Got a decent laugh from the guys, but sort of hampered the early going. She recovered, though, and managed to insult everybody a couple more times before it was over." He leaned forward. "So tell me you're not a reporter."

It didn't seem like a good idea to bullshit him. "I own some media properties, but they keep me as far from the news as possible."

"Reason I made you come all the way up here was so I could look at you when I asked that. Got no interest in dealing with that Huston hump again, even if she is full of shit. I noticed how you carry yourself. You've had some training. My guess is military."

That's why he was a detective. "Correct, but a long time ago."

"Not that long. Okay, fire away."

"How'd she find out about the body in the first place?" I asked.

"Fuckin' owner. Old Man Taggart. Called the FBI before he called us. When I jacked him up about it, he said the Feds routinely send out memos to storage companies. Showed me one. 'Be on the lookout for terrorist shit. Don't touch anything. Just call.' "

"He thought a taxi looked like terrorism?"

"Taggart likes being the center of attention. He'd have called them if it'd been a load of dildos."

"Is Huston local?"

"Nah, Victorville's got no FBI office. There was an 800 hotline on the memo. Probably drove out from LA. She was already there when we showed up."

"By herself."

"Yeah, I thought that was peculiar. Feds are usually in pairs. Sounds like you got to meet the whole family. I'll pass."

"Somebody said the driver was an Indian."

Wes raised an eyebrow. "Who? Smitty the Pechangan? The only thing that clown knows about Indians is that before the tribe started handing out casino checks, he was Irish. The dead guy was Chinese. Yanlin Li."

I sat up a little straighter. "What about the one who rented the storage unit?"

He nodded. "Him too. Taggart just called him a slope, and he had phony ID, but he was on the office security tape."

"No chance he was something else? Korean, maybe?"

Wes Crowe looked at Del like, can you believe this guy? Then he said to me, "I suppose, but asking to pay the fee in Hong Kong dollars sort of argues against it." He paused. "That, and I recognized him."

It looked like I'd earned a spot right next to Smitty. I waited.

"Maxine and I like to run over to Vegas every now and then. She digs the slots, and I'm all over the buffets." Wes patted his waistline. "Where else can you get a lobster and martini breakfast for $6.99? There's this discount electronics place off the Strip. Donnie's. That's where I picked up that Yaesu receiver." He pointed to a rack of black steel boxes. I couldn't tell one from the other but nodded like I knew. "The guy on the security tape was Donnie Two Knives."

"I'm sorry?"

"TV ads. Guy in martial arts gear stands in a parking lot surrounded by flatscreens, computers, all kinds of shit. Couple of big-titted chicks in G-strings hold up a cardboard sign with a price on it. 'Come to Donnie's,' the guy shouts. 'You no like price . . .' And out comes a big-ass Rambo knife, and he whacks the board in half, screaming, 'I cut!'"

Del grinned wider. "Then the girls hold up a lower number, and Donnie screams even louder. 'You still no like . . .' And naturally, he's got a knife in his other hand. Whack! Donnie Two Knives."

I shook my head. "A Chinese Crazy Eddie. Go figure."

"If you're in a bar when he comes on, the joint stops dead.

My wife says men are such simple creatures. Tits, Toys and Touchdowns. If we could suck our own dicks, civilization would end."

Hard to argue with that.

Wes sat back and took a sip of beer. "We all know Asians do Vegas like it's around the corner. Charter 747s. Bring the whole village. I figure that's how Donnie came into the Hong Kong bucks."

"And you told this to Huston?"

"Made her work for it, but yeah. Glad to be rid of the problem—and her."

So out of three dead, two were Chinese. But Donnie Two Knives didn't get Hong Kong currency from a tourist. Nobody travels halfway around the world to buy a TV to ship home when the factory's up the street. And Crowe knew it too, but I wasn't a cop, so he was just doing what cops always do to civilians—giving me a little jerk-off. They can't help it, it's like breathing.

I stared at him so he knew I knew. Finally, he shifted his gaze to Del. "You mind moseying over to the house for a bit. Maybe help yourself to some of that ham."

Del wasn't offended. "Fuck the ham, I'm thinkin' donuts."

When we were alone, Wes the Smile disappeared, replaced by Wes the Snarl. "You're acting like you're way ahead of the desert hick from Victorville. That true?"

"Probably not, but if I am, I'll make sure you get to the party. Chuck and Lucille were a little more than friends. There's also a detective lying over at UCLA with his throat slit because I told him what happened. You know how it is when people you care about get hurt. You go the extra mile."

"Another cop? This is getting more interesting all the time."

"I thought maybe because Chuck and you were both law enforcement . . ."

I'd struck a nerve. "We got so many LA badges living out

here. somebody farts, ten people tell us where it smells. We don't go looking for more help."

Made sense. It's a fraternity, but there are different handshakes. It was also a good bet that some of the big-city boys Barney-Fifed the locals. He hadn't pulled the phrase "desert hick" out of thin air.

His voice got colder. "But where you're really going with this is did Lucille and I know each other? Two Chinks married to Anglos. Did we ever get together and read a little Mao? Or maybe swapfuck our brains out?"

I learned a long time ago you've got to head off that kind of shit before it puts down roots. "Well, since you've got a case of the red ass, why don't we cover it now?"

His muscles tensed, and I wondered how many guns he had hidden in the room. But he relaxed. "Sorry. There was a rumor going around a couple of years ago. Right after the Brandos moved here. Upset Maxine pretty bad."

"So you were friends."

"Not really. Went out to dinner a few times. Nothing that would've raised an eyebrow if we hadn't been . . . mixed. Some people though . . ."

With a British blue-blood father and a Brazilian mother, I knew only too well.

"Chuck thought it was funny. Lucille didn't. And neither did Maxine. So we decided it wasn't worth it. We never made an actual decision. Just moved on. Waved to each other at church, but that was about it."

I changed the subject. "Any idea how Mr. Li died?"

Wes pointed to the back of his head under the skull. "Cerebellum. Somebody jammed an ice pick in there and stirred the contents. Guy probably twitched a little, but not for long." His eyes regained their earlier warmth. "I ain't as smart as the FBI, which that Huston broad pointed out, but I'm bettin' Donnie."

We both laughed, and most of the tension left. "I'm also bettin' he was here to do the Brandos—or at least help. But something . . . or somebody . . . got in the way. Screwed up the timetable." He paused. "No reason to kill people that way unless . . ."

He let it hang, but I knew what he meant. Unless they had something you desperately needed.

"How's that fit with your theory?" he asked.

"Pretty much the same." I also wanted to know what the LAPD told him and the San Bernardino D.A. to keep them out of it, but that might have meant reciprocating in some way, and I didn't want to lie to the guy. So I said, "Not that it matters, but I don't think Huston has a clue."

"There's always a silver lining."

I thanked him and stood up.

We walked out to the pickup, where Del was waiting. "Sure you won't stay for some of that ham?" Wes asked.

He didn't mean it, of course, but it was a nice gesture. "I'll take a rain check. Like to come back someday and watch you tune in Antarctica."

"Anytime."

As I slid into the Ram, I lowered my window. "I don't suppose you happened to check up on Donnie or Cactus Taxi."

Wes looked at me. "And get in the middle of somebody else's investigation? That would be damned unprofessional." He paused. "But maybe one night after one too many brewskis I called Vegas PD. Just to see. Seems Donnie Two Knives has disappeared, and nobody's looking for him or a cab."

"After two months?"

"Hard to believe, ain't it?"

I made a note to stay in touch with Wes Crowe. Three anything but run-of-the-mill homicides had gone down on his turf, and he'd been frozen out. I didn't kid myself I'd just heard everything.

As we rode back to town, I said to Del. "Wes mentioned church. You guys go to the same place?"

He shook his head. "I'm a Member of the Tribe—nonpracticing with a vengeance. Ask my rabbi. Wes and

Maxine belong to that big joint out west of town. Cathedral of the Testaments. Used to be a JCPenney till they built the Wal-Mart. It don't look much like the neighborhood parishes back in Chicago, but they sure do pack 'em in. Drive by on a Sunday, you can hear the prayin' all the way out to the road."

11

Reverends and Warlords

DECEMBER 16, 1944
PEARL RIVER–HONG KONG

Neither Fabian nor Pags knew about the ambush of the British fleet ninety years earlier, but the gods of the Pearl must certainly have smiled as they entered the narrows where the Wellesley *and the* Furious *had given their last full measure. Where the two* Resurrection Bay *speedboats now also lay, burned to the waterline, the bloated bodies of their sailors and Marines bumping against the launch as it eased its way to shore.*

Fabian lowered himself into the waist-deep water and ran the anchor up onto the sand, where he plunged it in a few feet from a dead lance corporal he remembered somebody calling Woody. Pags helped Fabian pull the launch in far enough that it no longer moved with the water, then knelt next to the Marine. He crossed himself and said the Prayer of St. Benedict. Fabian hadn't been to church since he was a kid, but he crossed himself too and stood for a moment in silence. Not that it mattered, but whatever had happened didn't have anything to do with tide tables and bad math.

Fabian estimated they had roughly two hours before the receding tide expanded the beach to the point it would be difficult to refloat the launch. A few dozen yards inland, the sand ended at a jagged, foliage-encrusted cliff face that shot straight up. He squinted along the shoreline in both directions, but they could have been on an abandoned planet in a forgotten galaxy. If the same shit that had killed the first landing party hit the fan again, come morning, he and Pags were going to be just two more dead specks that the gulls wouldn't have to work to find.

Splitting up seemed too risky. They might never find each other again. So Fabian flipped a mental coin and went what their compass said was northeast. Not sure if he'd have the guts to use it, he brought along the flare gun and four flares, two red for signaling, and two white, which cast more light. He considered bringing Woody's rifle too but decided that whatever was out there, a bolt-action Springfield probably wasn't going to be much help.

After they had gone what Fabian estimated was a mile, they'd encountered nothing but more sand, and the cliff seemed even steeper. "Well," said Pags, "we're dead anyway. Might as well shoot a flare and have some fun."

Fabian couldn't argue. He loaded, cocked, and pointe 1 the gun upward at an eighty-degree angle. "You got insurance in case I burn something down?"

"I'm carryin' a couple of rubbers."

"Should cover us." Fabian pulled the trigger, and the gun whooshed, sending a hot, red streak in a long arc toward the unknown. It burned its required seven seconds and fell, still glowing, until they could see it no longer. They listened. Nothing.

"Fuckin'-A, give them a white one."

Fabian did but forgot to close his eyes, and the flare's extraordinary brightness took away his night vision. Blinking to recover, he heard a shout coming from back the way they'd come. He turned and, through the spots, saw a shape. A man on horseback galloping toward them.

"*Goddamn it,*" Pags said, "*we went the wrong way.*"

"*I thought I was riding with Mr. Lucky.*"

"*Hey, I brought the cavalry, didn't I?*"

The Reverend Big Jim Rackmann was a barrel-chested, ruggedly handsome man in his late thirties with a mane of prematurely white hair and a smile that exposed a forest of perfect teeth. Even though his stark white stallion was good-sized, the reverend fit him well. Fabian guessed six-four, maybe 220.

He was dressed in worn cotton dungarees and a home-made white shirt, open to the waist, and his canvas moccasins were exactly like the ones Fabian had seen on Gary Cooper in a recent shipboard newsreel. He didn't know why he remembered that, but he felt good that he did. Apparently, a couple of years at sea hadn't completely dulled his cop's attention to detail. The reverend was also carrying a carbine.

"*Missionary with a gun,*" said Fabian. "*Somebody call Warner Brothers.*"

Rackmann's grin got wider. "*Going quietly was Jesus's job. If I have anything to say about it, dying for my faith will be a last resort.*" *He stuck out his hand.* "*Somebody hung Big Jim on me, but I'm easy.*"

Fabian immediately liked him. He and Pags introduced themselves, then Fabian asked, "*What happened back on the beach?*"

The reverend shook his head. "*Japanese gunboat. Poor souls never had a chance. My folks will make sure they're buried.*"

"*Why are you even here? You couldn't know we'd show.*"

Rackmann gave him a smile. "*Couldn't know? Really, Ensign? Not too long ago, I had a pretty good life riding a motorcycle and writing tickets. You willing to consider there might be a reason I gave that up to thump Bibles in this no-man's-land?*"

"*You're a cop?*" *asked Fabian.*

"Past tense. California Highway Patrol. Mostly Riverside County."

"Nice to meet you. LAPD. Mostly politics."

"This is all fascinating as hell," said Pags. "But where the hell are the pilots?"

"It's a little complicated. You'll need to come with me. I brought extra horses."

Pags wasn't sure he liked that. "I don't think you get it. We're on a short fuse."

Big Jim's smile disappeared, and his eyes bored into the officer. "No, Lieutenant, you're the one who doesn't get it. For the last three days, I've been dodging guys who like to shove glass up your penis, then smash it with a rifle. So why don't you grab a mouthful of shut up, and I'll do my best to get us past the samurai you revved up with those flares. How's that sound?"

He'd made his point, Fabian and Pags fell in behind him. Fifteen minutes later, with Fabian trying to remember how to use his knees to stay tight in a saddle and Pags doing his best not to get bitten by a chestnut mare that had taken an immediate dislike to him, they turned onto a steep trail and entered the dense rain forest. Rackmann was often far ahead, scouting, but even as sure-footed as their mounts were, Fabian always felt better when he caught a glimpse of the missionary. It also occurred to him that the reverend's choice of a white horse and white clothes probably hadn't been an accident.

After the intense darkness, the glow through the trees was almost otherworldly. Then suddenly, they were surrounded by a pack of enormous, long-haired, maned dogs that snarled, sniffed and swirled around the horses. Their mounts started to shy, but the reverend's stallion instinctively moved in front of the two mares, and they calmed.

"Hold your cheeseburgers high," laughed Rackmann.

"What the hell is this?" said Pags, as one of the dogs stood on his hind legs and put his front paws on his saddle.

"Just looking you over," said the reverend. *"But I'd advise against petting."*

Fabian counted twenty-two dogs. *"Had a collie once, and I thought he was big."*

"Tibetan Mastiffs. Largest anywhere, and just for good measure, unpredictable. Keep your hands in full view and don't make eye contact."

Moments later, they broke free of the rain forest, and the officers were riveted by a deep cut in the limestone mountain. The glow had become brighter and now bathed over them like an early dawn, except that it wasn't yet midnight. They followed the dogs through a narrow pass the width of a subway tunnel. Once inside, the cut widened to few hundred feet, and on all sides jagged escarpment rose out of sight, walling out everyone and everything.

They had entered a hidden city. Having no option but to grow vertically, structures hung from the rock as far up as Fabian could see. It wasn't quite Shangri-La, but the homes were neatly painted in bright colors, and cobblestone streets clicked under the horses' hooves.

"Welcome to Hu-Wei," said Big Jim. *"Empire of the Fearsome Tiger."*

Silent women and children now appeared in doorways, watching the procession with expressionless faces. Fabian smiled, but it was not returned. *"They don't seem very happy to see us."*

"Hu-Meng—the Tiger People. Until I arrived, no outsider had ever set foot in here. Most had never seen a white man. Since before Christ was born, they have remained hidden from the rest of world, mostly because they are the most dangerous tribe in China. They've never been conquered— not even by the Khan boys."

"No offense," said Pags, seeing a scrum of pigs tearing at the carcass of something unrecognizable, *"but a million bucks and Madison Avenue couldn't sell me on this place as an empire. As for not being conquered, who the hell'd want it?"*

He still wasn't making points with the reverend. *"In Asia,*

Lieutenant, power flows in many directions. Until this war began, these people held sway over the key trade routes from Russia and India. Every time an invader tried to exterminate them, they only succeeded in hardening their influence. These homes all contain riches their countrymen would not even know to dream about."

"Pardon my French, Parson, but are you trying to tell me some bullshit mountain tribe controls what happens to half a billion Chinese?"

"No, but they control the trade in tigers, and the elite of China and Japan believe supremacy in battle and virility in the bedroom can be ensured by consuming their organs and sleeping under their skins. They also grind the bones into powder and add them to food or steep them in alcohol. Tiger tonic. Supposed to cure anything. Those who can afford it will pay fortunes. But to be sure they're not getting goat parts stuffed into an old carcass, they accept only live animals; then their shamans do the harvesting and preparation themselves. China has some tigers left, but they're a relatively small breed and, because of competition for land, mostly undernourished. Russian and Indian animals are much larger, and therefore much more desirable. For kings with armies, riches can be acquired anywhere. Tigers you get from the Hu-Meng."

"What a fucked-up place."

"And the dogs?" asked Fabian.

"Imagine you must transport cargo worth a thousand times more than gold the distance between San Francisco and New York with no paved roads and cutthroats around every bend. Fifty hardened men with ten dogs are worth a battalion of soldiers. They can move in any direction, attack when least expected and live off the land. And they can round up locals to do the heavy lifting. During the Opium Wars, the Hu-Meng stopped the entire British fleet in its tracks and slaughtered the best armed, most experienced fighters of their day. Quite gruesomely too, legend has it."

"*So why the soft spot for missionaries?*" asked Fabian.

"*We've got no stake in the country's politics. So in return for not proselytizing the tribe and acting as go-betweens with outside parties, they permit us to minister to the villages. Now Zhang wishes to ask a return courtesy.*"

Fabian wasn't sure what favor he was in a position to grant. "*And Zhang, I presume, is the warlord.*"

"*His bloodline runs as far back as the Tiger People themselves, but he's lurching toward a date with extinction, and he knows it. When this war is over, the Americans will go home, and without them, Chiang Kai-shek cannot survive. China will fall to Mao, and his first priority will be to exterminate the warlords. The Hu-Meng bear the distinction of being at the top of that hit list.*"

"*So if no one else has been able to do it, how can Mao?*"

"*By declaring war on the tigers. Superstitions and traditions mean nothing to the Communists. Their soldiers have already raided the Hu-Meng pits and dealt their remaining tigers to the Japanese in exchange for guns. The rest will be hunted to extinction. Once that happens, those who trade in them will become just one more ragged group of hungry peasants, easily tracked, easily killed.*"

"*A pox on both their houses,*" said Pags. "*Where are the men of this burg?*"

"*Most are fighting with the Nationalists. The rest, Zhang's guard, are waiting at the temple.*"

Fabian eyed him. "*You've got the I'm-just-a-humble-missionary spiel down pretty good, Reverend, but you're into politics right up to that big toothy smile of yours. No offense, of course.*"

"*None taken,*" Big Jim said, and rode on.

Still escorted by the mastiffs, they threaded their way through a tight maze of alleyways, where their legs sometimes brushed the buildings, until they broke onto a circular plaza outlined with eight buildings extravagantly inlaid with coral and jade. Even the protruding ends of the roof beams had been intricately carved into animal heads and birds in flight.

But the architecture was quickly overshadowed by the fifteen, shirtless Japanese soldiers, bound to tall wooden posts, their arms jerked upward behind them. Adding to their suffering, a sharpened piece of bamboo had been thrust through each man's waist, left to right—a wound designed not to kill but to inflict terrible pain. The prisoners moaned and cried out, but the men guarding them were unmoved.

Near the largest building sat three olive drab vehicles. A troop transport, a Nissan staff car, and a Japanese ambulance. Fabian tried to imagine how they had gotten them up the mountain.

Rackmann dismounted, and the officers followed him into the most impressive and spacious of the buildings. The interior was candlelit, the air thick and stale, and Fabian stopped to let his eyes adjust. Ahead of him a richly carpeted aisle was flanked by two five-foot-tall, magnificent jade tigers, and beyond, a circle of men surrounded a pair of Japanese Army doctors bent over a low, intricately constructed bed—also of jade. The physicians were speaking anxiously to one another and did not look up.

When Fabian and Pags got close enough, they saw a woman lying on a silk-covered mattress overlain with tiger pelts. She was cradling two tiny infants, at most, a few days old. Even allowing for the poor light, the children looked pale, and their breathing was labored and wheezing.

A large man, dressed in flowing red silk and wearing considerable gold, stepped forward and embraced the reverend. They exchanged a few sentences in quick dialect, then Big Jim turned to the officers, "Zhang says you honor him with your presence, and he apologizes for not offering better hospitality."

Fabian and Pags extended their hands. Zhang shook them while Rackmann continued, "The woman on the bed is Ai, Zhang's wife. Four days ago, she gave birth to two sons and a daughter. Among the Hu-Meng, multiple male births are considered providential. But one boy is already dead, and if neither survives, the family will be thought to have been visited with a curse."

Fabian understood perfectly, "Not good. It might give people ideas."

Big Jim nodded. "The Japanese medical unit was kidnapped and brought here as a last resort, but these doctors are powerless and will soon join their friends outside."

"And Zhang's daughter?" asked Fabian.

"She is of no interest to anyone. This is not a culture that is kind to girls."

"Fuckin' barbarians," spit Pags. "If we weren't responsible for those goddamn pilots, I'd shoot this motherfucker right between his beady eyes."

"How does all this suffering square with a man of God?" Fabian asked.

Big Jim looked at the ensign. "If it comes to it, I'll do everything I can for the girl. Including take her to Hong Kong, which is unlikely to do either of us much good. The Japanese medical team . . . well, they can pray to their emperor."

Fabian knelt by the bed. He carefully examined the infants, touching them lightly, feeling their tiny pulses. All LAPD recruits received instruction in emergency childbirth and common irregularities. But he didn't need special training to diagnose this. The babies were premature, their lungs underdeveloped and filled with fluid. Without immediate, specialized care, they would soon join their brother. In fact, any breath could be their last. The mother knew it too, and her face was heavy with fear.

Fabian brushed the woman's hair from her brow, and she managed a weak smile. He stood. "Okay, Reverend, we're here. What's the favor?"

12

Purple Dogs and High School Reunions

It was getting too late to drive out to the Brandos'. I decided to pass on another night in Victorville, where I didn't know who might be watching, and headed back south on the 15. Three miles outside of Apple Valley, I dropped my speed to fifty, which on that road is the equivalent of being parked, and everything in my rearview mirror passed me, some shooting me the traditional California hello. As far as I could tell, nobody hung back, but just to belt-and-suspender it, as soon as I exited, I pulled onto the shoulder. The few cars that got off in the next few minutes all went by without a look.

The Purple Dog Motel was appropriately nondescript and, from what I could tell, minus dogs of any flavor. When I paid cash and wrote Donnie Two Knives in the register, the nearly comatose clerk didn't look. As I parked in front of Room 146 and opened the door to the worn but reasonably clean unit, the chance that SAC Huston might someday come across the registration lifted my spirits.

I hadn't heard from Jake, and my call to him went straight to voice mail. So I wandered into the bathroom, killed two good-sized spiders, rinsed some black hairs out of the sink and brushed my teeth. Then I cranked up the air-conditioning and lay back on the bed with my cell phone. The Verizon 411 operator efficiently connected me to the LA outpost of the FBI.

"I'm sorry, sir, we don't have an Agent Huston in this office. The Agent in Charge is Ronald Hyatt. Would you like to speak with his secretary?"

"No thanks," I said lightly. "It's not business. Francesca and I went to high school together, and I was just calling to tell her about the reunion. Somebody said she was working out of Los Angeles now, but maybe they got it confused with Las Vegas. Do you have their number?"

It turned out SAC Huston didn't work in Vegas either, but the polite young man on the phone said she'd been there a week earlier. "If any calls come in for her, we're supposed to forward them to Washington. May I have your name and number please?"

Washington. That's why she'd been alone at the crime scene. She jumped a flight, and the rest of the team had to catch up. "Sorry to miss her," I said. "She still as warm and cuddly as ever?"

There was silence on the other end.

"I'm kidding," I said. "We used to call her Luca Brasi. It takes more than a circus to put a smile on that face."

The kid lowered his voice. "Jesus, mister, I could get in trouble for saying this cause everything's recorded, but I didn't think she *could* smile. The whole staff cheered when she left. Some of the agents too."

Miss Huston was truly an asshole with a propeller, leaving a little shit wherever she went. "I'll catch up with her another time," I said, and hung up.

The best time to get something done on the phone is after midnight. Overnight shifts in any business are notoriously bored, tired or busy faxing out their résumés. It was almost eight in California—eleven in the East—but I wanted to make my next call when body clocks are at their most vulnerable.

Doctors term 4:00 a.m. the death hour. No matter how used to being awake we are, in the sixty minutes between four and five, something deep in our primeval being slows the autonomic nervous system to a crawl. It's when hospital patients flatline, and the elderly drift away. At four, flight attendants are trained to take hot coffee to pilots and strike up a conversation. Military commanders recheck their sentries. The death hour is also when a cop might hesitate over a decision that would be instantaneous two hours earlier, and when a long-haul trucker is most likely to find himself straddling eighty thousand pounds of steel, sound asleep.

I found a restaurant with a parking lot full of gardening and construction trucks and *ranchera* music drifting outside. Rosario's turned out to be owned by a handsome Guatemalan lady who supplemented traditional Mexican dishes with Paella Marinera and Chicken Pepian. When I spoke Spanish to her, she immediately treated me like a celebrity and brought so much food I started sharing it with other diners. Eventually, we had all the tables in the place pushed together, and the band cranked it up several notches.

I've got nothing but respect for law-abiding people who risk death seeking a better life. Not so the illegal immigration hustlers who care about nothing but a quick buck and accumulating power. Add to that the disorder and mixed messages fomented by the country's elected officials, and you have a reprehensible brew of anger and tears. But at some point, if one wants to continue to have an America, there has to be a moderating, universally enforced policy, and the first president to articulate one and not crawl under his desk when somebody loud or rich disagrees will get enough support on both sides to make it stick. For a start, I suggest he or she invite Rosario to the White House to cook. It'll get things off on the right foot.

Way too many Pacificos later—and having humiliated myself singing—I managed to break away from my forty newfound friends and head back to the Purple Dog. It was a good bet I had no business driving, but fortunately I limped home without attracting attention, though it did take a while to fumble my key into the door. It was almost 11:00. I set the alarm for 12:30 and fell asleep with Steve McQueen and Ali MacGraw ducking shotgun blasts in the background.

At 1:15, freshly showered and with a cup of horrendous, in-room coffee, I put Verizon back to work and was quickly connected to FBI Headquarters in Washington. Two internal transfers later, I found myself talking to a young lady who sounded like she was in line for a root canal.

"Department 11," she mumbled. "Ms. Luchinski."

So far, no one had called me on the high school reunion story, so I stuck with it. When I finished my spiel, there was silence on the other end. Then Ms. Luchinski burst out laughing. "You want Agent Huston to come to a party? What the hell are you? Nuts? God, I can't wait to tell the rest of the office. Nobody's gonna believe me."

"Well, I haven't seen her in a while. Does she still go by Fantasy Fran?"

The girl laughed again, this time uproariously. "Oh my, God. Fantasy Fran. This is too much. Somebody said she used to be married, but we've got a pool going that nobody's ever seen *that* promised land . . . the money doubles if you can prove it's not platinum. Believe me, you don't want her at your reunion. Take my advice, and forget you called. Enjoy yourselves."

I got conversational. "How's the weather in D.C.?"

"Rained all week. Where are you?"

"Juneau. And it's raining here too."

"Where's Juneau?"

"Alaska."

"Huston's from Alaska?"

It could have been a trap question, but I was betting the graveyard shift didn't have access to a SAC's personnel file. And it didn't sound like Fran-baby did much sharing with the girls in the office."

"Yep, good old Central High. Want me to sing the alma mater?"

"You sound like fun. What's your name?"

I decided to amuse myself. "Curtis."

"We got an agent named Curtis. Pete. I hope you're not related. He's creepy."

"Might be an unhappy cross-dresser. Get somebody to check for panties."

She laughed again. "Boy, are you a welcome break."

"My friends call me Hank."

"Hi, Hank. I'm Roxy. Never been to Alaska. Anywhere really. Except Sarasota once. Almost died from old people smell. What time is it out there?"

"Late. Just got into port. I own a crab boat."

"Wow! Like those guys on Discovery?"

"Just like that."

I think she swooned over the phone. "You guys are so macho. You ever take people on rides?"

"Pretty girls, all the time. You qualify?"

I could hear the smile three thousand miles away. "I don't think I'd disappoint."

"Next time you're in town, come on over. Put you right up in the wheelhouse. Let you steer. Hey, what's Department 11 anyway? Sounds important."

"I don't actually know. I asked once but just got a shitty look." Roxy had lowered her voice, which wouldn't have made any difference to the recording system. I couldn't believe she hadn't been told all calls to the FBI are monitored, but it only takes about an hour for new employees to figure out no one checks tapes unless there's a problem, so that wasn't the reason. I guessed there were other ears nearby.

"Nosy neighbors?"

"Jesus, you can say that again. There's an old broad across the way that might as well put out a newsletter."

"We get a guy like that, we throw him overboard. You were telling me about Department 11."

"All I know is everybody's always closing their doors when they talk—and they travel a lot. I've only been here since Christmas. I wanted to work at the Pentagon. That's where the real men are. Maybe meet a naval aviator like in *Officer and a Gentleman*. Rest of this town is full of Ivy League dorks who took their moms to the prom."

"Who calls there?"

"Mostly people from other FBI offices. But it's weird. We don't get any mail, and there's no Internet. Just some internal system where you can't even play solitaire. Most of the girls read books or do crosswords, but that gets really old, really fast. If I didn't have a car payment, I'd be outta here."

Suddenly, there was a loud thump against the wall of my room that rattled the mirror over the TV. "What was that?" Roxy asked.

"Couple of my guys are having a disagreement. Happens sometimes after we've been at sea a while."

Then a woman screamed, and there was more banging.

"That didn't sound like guys," she said.

"There's a girlfriend involved. I need to call you back. You have a direct line?"

"No, tell the switchboard you want Ext. 664. The Hot Code tonight is Gemstone. It's the only way you can get to a specific phone in this office."

This was why I made calls at four in the morning. In five minutes, I had a friend inside Department 11 and had learned it was code protected. Whatever Huston was in charge of, it wasn't the Ten Most Wanted List.

"And Hank, we're not supposed to take personal calls, so if somebody else answers, hang up, okay?"

Something shattered against the wall next door.

"Wow, they're really going at it," Roxy said. "Good luck. I get off at six."

I hung up and picked up the room phone. No one answered at the front desk. Then next door, a woman began begging for her life.

I went through the cheap door with my shoulder, hit the floor and rolled. I'd assumed the Gestapo insignia on the over-chromed Harley Rocker parked next to my pickup would be consistent with owner's rank in the human race. I was wrong. The guy was big but looked more like Saturday night in Newport Beach than a one-percenter in search of a bar fight. Sandy-haired, clean-cut and with no visible tattoos, his designer jeans and the soft, black leather vest over his shirtless torso said Nordstrom not outlaw. However, the girl he was pounding on probably wasn't making those kind of distinctions.

She had a thick mane of long, curly raven black hair and a pair of unending athletic legs that jutted out of her cutoff jeans and left little to the imagination. She was cowering on the bed, trying to cover her face and head while Vest Boy whaled on her with a wide, leather belt. She alternately moaned and screamed, which should have had the place swarming with cops but didn't. Her white blouse, its tails tied under her ample breasts, was torn, and her forearms sprayed red froth each time the strap hit them.

If the guy noticed my entrance, he didn't care, because he never looked and kept swinging. I got my feet under me, pushed up and went into him. I wanted to take him square on, but he moved slightly, and I felt leather sting my cheek.

My momentum took me past him, and I grabbed his right arm and ducked under the belt's tail as it came around. I fell on my left hip and rolled toward the bathroom, pulling his body across mine. The twin snaps of his radius and ulna followed by his elbow taking his full weight against the floor should have meant the fight was over, but as his face brushed mine, I smelled the unmistakable odor of acetone, which meant he'd either been gargling with fingernail polish remover or smoking meth.

Oblivious to pain, he pulled away from me and crawled into the bathroom, where he armed himself with the toilet tank cover. Bellowing like a rhino, he rushed me, holding the slab of porcelain like a battering ram. It would have crushed several ribs, minimum, but he bumped into the doorframe, and the slight course change gave me a chance to get heavy torque into a flat-handed chop across his windpipe. He went to his knees, clutching his throat with both hands. Picking up the tank cover, I brought it down on his head, shattering it. He slumped to the floor, out.

The girl was still on the bed, now in a fetal position, whimpering. I crossed the room and stepped outside. Except for the faint hum of traffic on the interstate, it was dead quiet. If anyone had heard the commotion, they were ignoring it.

I got the first-aid kit out of the Ram and examined the young lady's wounds. Despite the blood, they weren't serious, and a little gauze and tape took care of them. Her emotional state was another matter. Even though she was conscious, she'd gone limp. At first, I thought she might be in a meth crash, but her pupils were normal and her pulse only slightly elevated.

She wouldn't or couldn't answer even simple questions, so I picked her up and carried her to my room. The bed was turned down, and as I slipped her between the sheets, I saw her eyes flash. She relaxed when I pulled up the covers and stepped away.

I found the guy moaning softly, checked his pockets and came up with the Harley keys and a wallet. My guest was Byron Gilbert Frankel, age twenty-nine, six-three, 220, who lived on Skyline Terrace in Calabasas. An address among multimillion-dollar homes indicated he wasn't a professional badass, and his Screen Actors Guild card cemented it. "Well, Byron," I said. "What say we send you back to the Land of Milk and Pretend?"

I returned to my truck and found a roll of duct tape—probably the most useful tool ever invented—then started the Harley and rode it into the motel room, where I walked it back and forth until I got it between the foot of the bed and the dresser and pointed toward the door. Mr. Frankel's eyes were open, but there was nobody home. I manipulated his broken arm until I awakened the right nerves, and he sat straight up, coughing. His sweat was cold, which probably meant he was in shock, and his jeans suddenly darkened as his bladder emptied.

I grabbed the belt he had been using on the girl and wrapped it tightly around his broken arm, securing it with tape. My makeshift cast wasn't much aesthetically, and if it wasn't removed soon, would cut off the circulation, but that wasn't my problem. I helped Mr. Frankel to his feet and shouldered him to the Harley, warm piss running down his legs and onto the toes of a two-thousand-dollar pair of black and tan Luccheses.

It took a couple of tries to get him to straddle the Softail, but eventually he was aboard, and I could tape his legs to the frame and put a loop around each hand on the grips. I also gave the roll several winds around his thighs, anchoring him firmly to the seat. His head lolled a couple of times while I worked, but I squeezed his bad arm, and he came right back.

When I was sure he was secure, I hit the starter, and he did exactly what I'd hoped—woke up and gunned the throttle. The brain remembers repetitive functions with extreme clarity and can often go about its business even when its owner isn't all there. That's why, once you learn, you can always ride a two-wheeler. And why you can sometimes drive for miles and not recall anything about the trip.

Byron Frankel revved the Rocker a few more times, then popped the clutch and roared out of the room. I walked outside and watched him turn away from town toward the freeway. Eventually, the night air would penetrate his drug haze, and he'd realize that if he tried to stop, the bike was going down. Hopefully, while he was reasoning it out, the CHP would notice he wasn't wearing a helmet and motion him over. Maybe even find his stash jammed somewhere in the expensive steel or tucked into the top of a boot. Too bad there wouldn't be pictures.

I found the young lady's purse and took a final look around. Even if management ignored the broken door and toilet, the blood would bring cops. And in a small town, that meant answering questions until the cows came home. Pass.

I roused Sleeping Beauty and tucked her into the pickup, wrapping her in a blanket I keep in the backseat. She made no protest. After one more walk-through of both rooms to be sure I had everything, I started the Ram and headed toward Victorville.

I considered dropping my passenger at the fire station, but if they'd changed shifts, that meant too many explanations. Besides, she wasn't going to sleep any more soundly there than right where she was. So I watched the city lights go by and headed for Chuck and Lucille's. I glanced at the clock on the dash. Ten minutes to six in Washington. Too late to get back to Roxy.

13

Snakes and Arabians

The sun awakened me. I was parked alongside Chuck and Lucille's gate, facing southeast. My passenger was still out, her seat in the same three-quarter recline I'd put it in when we'd left the Purple Dog. I'd hit an AM/PM minimart on the way, and there were a couple of Italian subs and a picnic-sized bag of Doritos tucked behind my seat.

The Rhodes scholar ahead of me had bought five lottery scratchers, two Red Bulls, a pack of Kools and four Tuxedo condoms. When it was my turn, I asked the clerk in what sequence she figured the guy would be using those, and it broke her up enough that she agreed to sell me her personal thermos for fifty bucks. Now, I grabbed it and poured myself a cup of blazing coffee that, for all its hoopla, Starbucks, still can't beat.

I opened my door and stepped outside. The high-desert morning chill was bracing, and I ambled around loosening up. I actually felt pretty good though I was looking forward to brushing my teeth.

Several miles away, I caught the sun's reflection off a white shape coming in our direction. After a minute or so, the unmistakable colors of FedEx came into focus, and I walked back to the Ram, leaned against the hood and waited.

The driver was really hauling ass, but when he threw out the anchor to turn into the Brando drive, he came to a stop and slid open his door. "Car trouble?"

"Nope, just getting ready to go up to the house when I saw you."

"You staying with the Brandos?"

"Just checking on the place. They're out of town."

He thought about that for a second, and I wasn't sure what was coming. He surprised me by saying, "Shit."

"Beg your pardon?"

"Drove all the way out here for nothing. Standing order for a pickup the fifteenth of the month. Somebody usually calls when they're gonna be away. They didn't happen to leave anything with you, did they?" He held his fingers an inch apart. "FedEx envelope? About that thick?"

I shook my head. "Family emergency. They took off in such hurry they probably forgot. Chuck didn't say anything about it."

"Not Mr. Brando. Mrs. Brando."

My curiosity went up a notch. "Standing order. That usually means something's going to the same place."

He nodded. "Perth, Australia. Parkinson-Lowe Imports."

"Ever see what was inside?"

His eyes narrowed. "No, why?"

"I could look around."

He relaxed. "No, it was always ready when I got here."

"And Lucille gave it to you?"

"Every time but once. I rang the bell, and nobody answered. I could hear a baby crying, so I knocked, and this incredible-looking chick opened the door. Maybe twenty-four. Super hair. Blonde. Little small upstairs for my taste, but still okay. When I got my eyes back in my head, I saw the envelope on a table and pointed. The girl handed it to me, and just then Mrs. Brando came running down the hall. In a robe, hair all wet. I figure she was in the shower. And boy, was she upset."

"At you?"

"No, at the girl. She told her to go back to her room and not to open the door again. But it wasn't like she was pissed. More like afraid."

What was going on? Chuck and Lucille didn't have children, grown or otherwise, and Yale had been clear that their only family wasn't even in the country. "That was the only time you ever saw her? The blonde?"

"Her, yes. But one other time, Mrs. Brando was giving me the envelope, and two different ones walked across the room behind her in nothing but bra and panties. A FedEx guy's dream. Well, half of it, anyway."

"But not the blonde?"

"I was excited, mister, not comatose. One looked like she mighta been Hispanic. The other was almost six feet tall with a serious pair of airbags."

"And no babies."

"Not that I saw. There was a guy, though."

"A guy?"

"Well, I didn't actually see him, but I heard him. And saw his equipment. Some kinda artist. You know, easel and shit."

"What was he painting?"

"No idea. It was facing the other way. But I know Mr. Brando's a famous writer, so I figured it was maybe for one of his books. I don't read much, but if he was painting them girls, that mighta got me motivated."

"If I hear from Chuck or Lucille, I'll ask about the envelope. In the meantime, you don't need to make the run out here again. Somebody'll let you know when they get home. I apologize for the mix-up."

"Forget it, man. Shit happens." He got back in his truck. Before he closed the door, I said, "They ever *receive* anything?"

"Every now and then. But nothing international. I'da remembered. Overseas waybills are green, and I gotta log them separate. Don't get many."

I watched him accelerate back the way he'd come. While I was pondering what he'd said, my passenger got out of the

Ram. She was holding the blanket around her shoulders, and even though she was a little unsteady, her eyes were clear.

"Where the hell are we?"

"A few miles outside Victorville. I've got some business to attend to, then I'll run you into town. Where do you live?"

"Arcadia."

"Santa Anita country."

She nodded. "You're looking at the best damn trainer-in-waiting in all of racing."

"Why the in-waiting?"

"How many women trainers you know? In the meantime, I hot walk, shovel shit and eat a lot of it. But it beats a cubicle at Google."

I liked her already. "Best bet is probably Amtrak. I think Victorville's got a station."

"Where's Byron?"

"Last time I saw him, headed toward Calabasas."

She looked me up and down. "I thought he was big, but Jesus, you're a whole different category. NFL?"

"Usually they guess NBA."

She shook her head. "Big fan. I know all the players."

"Then I better not lie. Nope, not an athlete. Not one who gets paid anyway."

She pulled one of her arms out from under the blanket and stared at her bandages. "Thanks for this . . . and for saving my life."

"Put me on your Christmas card list. You and Byron an item?"

"That son of a bitch," she sneered. "Just met him last night. My daddy used to say if a story starts, 'I was in this bar . . .' it's not gonna have a happy ending."

"Wise man."

"Byron plays a doctor on one of my soaps. So when he put on the moves and asked if I wanted to see his Harley, I was like what are we waiting for. Next thing I know we're in the middle of nowhere, and he's huffing a meth pipe with ten hillbillies in a broken-down Airstream."

"Not your scene?"

"Notice how long I slept? Two beers. But I convinced my cranked-up ride home we'd both be dead if we tried to get back to LA. I figured it was better to sleep with him than end up being hosed off the freeway. I'd known the jerk was gonna Ben-Hur me, I'd have taken my chances with the big rigs."

I took a look at her. Not many women can hold up to morning sunlight, even fewer after a hard night. This one . . . it was difficult to imagine she could look any better. I extended my hand. "Rail Black."

She smiled and took it. "Birdsong Nash."

"Professional name?"

"Worse. New Age mother. Friends call me Birdy . . . with a Y, please. And no offense, but Rail isn't exactly missionary position either."

We both laughed.

"Anybody you want to call?" I asked.

"Nope, it's just me an' my horsies. Besides, Dr. Asshole took my phone at the meth house. Your guess is as good as mine what happened to it."

Actually, my guess was probably better, but I kept that to myself. "Okay, Birdy with a Y, sing out if you change your mind. Let's head up to the house. I've got food if you can stand high cholesterol and no redeeming social value."

"Whatever it is, put me down for a double with extra cheese. In the meantime, I'd kill for a cup of that coffee. Smells like heaven."

A beautiful woman who'll eat comfort food with you—especially when she doesn't think she looks her best—is somebody you want to hang on to. It means a low bullshit quotient. I've never met an eater who was a drama queen. Check it out. Next time you're at Ruth's Chris and see a *Vogue*-type picking at a dry piece of lettuce, notice how many times her date looks at his watch. Been there, taken the aspirin. But a power eater named Birdy Nash I wanted to get to know better.

* * *

There was a law enforcement padlock on the front door but no crime scene signs or tape. If the police were intending to come back, it wasn't evident. While I dug out a tire iron to pry the hasp off the door, Birdy wandered down to the corral, and a pair of good-looking mares trotted over to nuzzle her. I noticed a horse trailer with the ramp down sitting along the fence. Evidently somebody planned to take them. I hoped not this morning.

Inside, the mess was gone, along with most of the furniture, making the holes in the walls even more glaring. On my way to the master bedroom, the odor of peppermint disinfectant met me halfway and turned cloying the closer I got. This room had been professionally stripped as well. Even the wall-to-wall carpeting had been pulled. Empty, it seemed larger than it had the other night, but the vision of Chuck was still there.

I pulled the door closed and went back to the living room. Birdy was just coming inside. "Nice place, but maybe they could add a chair or two and maybe lighten up on the air freshener. What's with the padlock?"

"The people who own it are away. I'm supposed to keep an eye on things, but I lost the key."

"That's the first thing that came to mind when I saw you . . . house sitter."

I changed the subject. "How are the horses?"

"Your friends know their animals. All Arabians are beautiful, but those two are special. Something's bothering them, though."

"How do you mean?"

"Horses are sensitive to their surroundings. Way more than dogs. You're pissed at somebody or have a hangover, they know it and don't like it. But they don't have long memories, so whatever it is with those two, it's current. Hey, any chance I can get a shower."

"Give me a minute." I walked into the other wing of the house, the one I'd been too one-track to notice previously.

Two bedrooms. Identically furnished with a queen bed, baby crib, changing table, and a bookshelf of toddler toys. Nothing had been touched in the first, but in the second, the bed was turned down and the sheets wrinkled. The crib had also been used, and an open box of Huggies sat on the changing table.

The connecting bathroom was large and newly remodeled. Polished nickel fixtures and black marble walls accenting a curved, walk-in glass block shower. A couple of towels lay on the floor, and when I picked them up, they were just slightly damp in the folds. I tossed them in a hamper and found a fresh set under the sink which I put on the counter next to a basket of toiletries. On my way back through, I opened windows in both bedrooms, then gave Birdy the go-ahead.

Anybody searching a house with no time pressure wouldn't have missed a room, let alone two. So the trashing had been staged.

While Birdy showered, I got my Dopp Kit out of the pickup, stripped off my shirt and brushed my teeth twice in the half bath off the living room. I had just lathered up to shave when I heard the scream. As I came out, a naked Birdsong Nash and all that curly hair came sprinting toward me. I braced myself and plucked her up in midstride. She was running so fast, I had to take a step back to keep from going down.

I hadn't noticed before how wide her shoulders were. Hilary-Swank-wide. Something I find extremely attractive.

"Jesus Christ, it was ten feet long!" she yelled.

"What?"

"A snake! In the goddamn shower!"

If you spend time in the desert, you're going to see snakes—sometimes in the house. And considering how much the place had been open recently, it wasn't surprising one had dropped in for a look around. It probably also wasn't anywhere near ten feet, and after Birdy's exhibition, the poor creature was probably more frightened than she was.

But I was enjoying holding almost six feet of warm, wide-shouldered girl, so I put on my gravest face, got her calmed down then led her back to the bathroom. She faltered at the door. "I can't go in there."

The water was still running in the shower. I walked around the glass block wall and looked inside, but rolling steam from the two pounding showerheads cut visibility to almost nothing. Wishing I'd left my shoes on, I kept my eyes on the floor until I could reach the handles and turn everything off. A few seconds later, the steam dissipated, but there was no sign of anything except a bar of soap and a shampoo bottle.

"Where was it?" I called out.

"Under the bench," Birdy yelled from what sounded like the middle of the bedroom. "You mean it got away! Holy shit!" I heard the mattress give as she climbed onto the bed.

A solid, three-inch-thick slab of stainless steel jutted out of the marble wall at sitting height, but there didn't seem to be enough cover for a snake, regardless of size. I got down on my knees and looked under the bench. Nothing. Then suddenly, I felt a slight breeze across my face.

"Birdy, come in here and turn out the light."

"Do I have to?"

"Please."

After a moment, the bathroom plunged into darkness, and I bent again. Now I could see a tiny sliver of daylight where the slab met marble. I felt along the gap, half-expecting a pair of fangs to sink themselves into my hand. Nothing happened, so I ran my fingers over the underside of the bench. I actually had to do it a second time before I found the lever. I pulled it, and the entire section of wall beneath the bench dropped silently away, leaving a man-sized hole into the outside shrubbery.

Three-quarters of the homes in Beverly Hills have an escape portal, including mine. However, it's not something you expect to find in the wilds of the Mojave. I'd also never seen one in a shower. Very creative. I went back to the living room, slipped on my shoes and went outside.

In the side yard, Birdy's snake, a juvenile diamondback a quarter the advertised size, was making its way along the foundation in no particular hurry. More importantly, the redwood bark ground cover around the shrubbery showed signs of human disturbance. Somebody had come out this way in the not-too-distant past. Reading track in a desert climate is inexact, especially after high winds, but I guessed a few days, tops.

I walked to the edge of the ravine where the trees bracketing Chuck's trout stream began. The water below was so thickly hidden by the foliage that I could only hear it. I stopped and let my eyes sweep slowly down the steep slope.

Law enforcement and outdoorsmen are taught to look for certain signs—moss on a tree, footprints, broken branches, predator scat. Those are certainly useful, but special operators—especially those who hunt men—are also interested in what's not there. Missing birds. A hive with no bees. An absence of fish where there should be many. In this case, it was the lack of uniform decay and erosion.

Everywhere I looked, the ground was, as it should have been, awash in the cycle of life and uneven from sliding rock. Rotting logs, molding leaves, tangled vines, loose shale. However, like a serpentine path of stepping-stones, there were also irregular patches of smooth space that were glaring in their emptiness. Raked almost completely bare and each marked by a small, whitewashed rock, the casual observer wouldn't have paid any attention to. But if you knew what you were looking for, you couldn't miss them, and in the dark, someone with a flashlight would have been able to follow them as easily as reflectors along a highway. And since Chuck had gone to this much trouble, he'd probably used luminescent paint as well.

As I picked my way from one trace to another, I created several small avalanches while thorns took nicks out of my bare chest and legs. Sixty yards down, I reached a clearing invisible from where I had begun. Here the trees were as thick as any mountain forest, and I had to remind myself I was in the middle of the Mojave.

I made a methodic, 360-degree visual search of the perimeter and saw nothing. Same result at eye level. Dogs are taught to track the ground. Their physiology doesn't give them any advantages even a few feet above their heads. People who hunt clever killers don't like to publicize it, but there are bodies stashed in trees all over the country. Eventually, insects, elements and time break down connective tissue, clothing disintegrates, and bones fall for animals to drag away. As a result, very few of these victims are ever found. Not a pleasant thought for families of the missing.

I shifted my gaze to the ten-foot level, then twenty, making the same circular sweep. And then I saw it. Halfway up a forty-foot California piñon, a camo-painted metal box was tucked into a confluence of limbs. Its door was open, and a squirrel was sitting inside.

I made a careful search of the area immediately beyond the tree and found an empty plastic carrier for a tubular assault ladder. The fully extended item had been tossed another dozen feet downhill. I retrieved it and climbed.

There were two hooks inside the camo box. One was empty, the other held a black, North Face backpack. I lifted it out, slung it over my shoulder and descended. When I unzipped it, I found standard-issue survival gear: compass, Maglite LED, first-aid kit, MREs, two Mylar emergency blankets, magnesium fire starter and three bottles of Arrowhead water.

Under that, however, standard-issue went out the window. First, money. A large freezer-weight Ziploc contained ten grand in used bills. In a second, a U.S. passport, Social Security card, California driver's license and two birth certificates—all blank—plus a MasterCard in Lucille Brando's name. A third bag held a cell phone and charger and a car key clipped to a Jeep Wrangler fob. And in the final Ziploc, a loaded Smith & Wesson .38-caliber snubnose. Not high tech, but concealable, easy to fire, and you could bury it in mud, and, a month later, it would operate like it had just come out of the box.

It looked like whoever had used the shower escape had left with resources. I tried to imagine the chaos of that night. Knowing Chuck, he'd made the intruders concentrate on him while his houseguest escaped. And based on the FedEx guy, the guest had most likely been a woman.

I took out the phone, turned it on, and got the Verizon logo and a full complement of bars. I checked the call history. None. But there was a single number in speed dial. Area Code 702. Vegas. I hit SEND.

It rang seven times, and I was about to hang up when a male voice answered, "Who's this?" I didn't say anything, and the guy switched to, "*Wai*?"

I speak several languages and understand a few more, but I struggle with everything Asian. However, I recognized the standard Chinese salutation. When I remained silent, the guy disconnected.

A few seconds later, the phone rang. More accurately, it bonged. Like Great Tom, the hour bell at St. Paul's. The LED readout said RESTRICTED. Not necessarily meaningful, but interesting. The best way to disguise your voice is to whisper an octave above your normal speaking voice. I let the phone go five bongs before I connected and breathed, "This is Chuck Brando. Who's calling?"

I could have read *War and Peace* in the interval. Then, I heard him speaking to someone nearby in rapid Chinese. When he got back to me, he was aggressive. "You are definitely not Chuck. Where did you get this phone?"

So he knew Chuck was dead. Interesting *and* meaningful. "How about we meet for coffee and catch up? Maybe we dated the same cheerleader." There was another pause, and I assumed the guy was getting more instructions. While I waited, I heard more chimes, only these didn't remind me of London. Somewhere, a slot machine was paying off.

Finally, he returned. "Fuck you," he said, and was gone. I pressed SEND again. I knew he wasn't going to answer, but I thought I might get his recording. Instead, I got a polite lady robot from Verizon telling me the voice mail on that number had not been activated.

Birdy's voice cut through my thoughts. "Hey, you down there somewhere?"

"On my way up." I turned off the cell and put it back in the pack. Something was nagging at me. I climbed halfway back up the ladder and slowly took in what the woods would give me. Farther down the hill and well right of where I'd been earlier, something scurried along the ground, moving leaves as it went. I traced its path backward. Flies. Lots of them.

The guy was on his face, the back of his black vest stiff with dried blood. Two neat slices in the leather indicated entrance wounds. He was six-five, at least, with long black hair and biceps as thick as my thighs. I didn't relish turning him over, but with the slope, I was able to use the sole of my shoe to get him rolling. A family of rats skittered away, and what they'd been doing to his face wasn't nearly as poetic as eternal sleep.

From what was left, he could have been Asian . . . or Martian. Only the rats knew for sure. But there was no secret what had incapacitated him. His head lolled awkwardly on the downhill, his neck broken. I tried to imagine a young girl with a flashlight in one hand and perhaps a baby in the other, running in terror, trying to follow the markers. Most likely, the guy had tripped early in the chase, and it was possible he passed her as he cartwheeled down the steep grade. She'd have been lucky not to start screaming. Maybe she had.

His chest was ripped away by the two exiting explosions. The girl had definitely had a steady hand. But why shoot him if he was no longer a threat? The best answer was that he had still been alive, perhaps moaning, and once she had the gun from the backpack, she went the extra mile. Hard to blame her.

I searched his pockets and came up empty, but he was wearing a gold bracelet with Chinese characters on it. He also had a death grip on a roll of duct tape. There was some justice in that.

Just beyond him, I saw another of the whitewashed stones, then a second a little farther down. They would lead to where the water could be crossed, then probably to a vehicle hidden on the other side. Now, the shooting made more sense. She might have had to step over him. Maybe he even grabbed her leg.

"Hey, I don't like it up here by myself." Birdy's voice was a little anxious.

I left the body to the residents and went back up the hill.

"I thought I heard a bell," she said when she saw me. "There a church around here?"

I didn't answer.

Birdy had put on a navy blue LAPD T-shirt that covered almost nothing that mattered. Modesty, however, didn't seem to be something that kept her up nights. She came into my arms, and when she pulled back to look in my eyes, I noticed shaving cream on her cheek.

"It's some kind of emergency escape, isn't it? But why put it there?"

"You answered your own question."

She thought about it, then nodded. "Because nobody would guess, right?"

"Right."

She followed me back into the shower and watched while I worked the lever again, and the opening closed. Even though she saw me check that it was tight this time, she said, "You know, I'm still not going to be able to be in here alone."

She turned both showers on full blast and stripped off her T-shirt. While I was deciding my next move, she knelt and unzipped my shorts. I stepped out of them, and she took me in her mouth. I had a lot on my mind, but it suddenly slid to the back burner.

A long time later, and very clean, we headed for the bedroom. We were a lot of man and woman for a queen-size, but we made it work. She had an active mouth, and never a slacker, I joined in. At the moment of no-return, we disengaged and joined together, our stomachs slapping against each another. Seconds later, her X-rated cries sent us over the edge. As we fell into deep, sex sleep, our arms and legs hooked together, I silently thanked a snake.

I awakened an hour later, her warmness still under me. I started to move off, but her tongue found mine, and her hand guided me inside her again. This time we moved so slowly it became a sweet agony, and when we finally dropped into the abyss once more, I felt her muscles hold me in place like I never had felt before. I buried my face in her hair and fell asleep once more.

We sat on a big swing in the shade of the front porch, laughing the laugh of the recently intimate. My sub, along with a couple of Rolling Rocks I found in the fridge, was as fine a meal as I've ever eaten. And Birdy, her arms newly bandaged, matched me bite for bite—except for the Rocks. But I'm pretty sure she sneaked an extra handful of Doritos when I got up to get my second beer.

I liked the way she ate. The food got manhandled, not nudged. And she licked her fingers unapologetically. She had her cutoffs back on but had replaced her bloody blouse with pink Polo a size too small. She said she never went out without a change of clothes in her purse. I complimented her on her foresight while I admired the way Ralph Lauren stretched over its contents. Byron Frankel never came up.

When we finished, Birdy scared up a bag of carrots, and we walked down to the corral, a fifty-foot square enclosure abutting a low red barn with the side doors open so the horses could come and go. Before we got halfway there, two Arabian mares bolted out of the barn and charged toward us, ears up, tails in their trademark high-carriage position. They were an identical dark chestnut, but one's mane and tail were coal black, and the other's a reddish blonde. Magnificent is the word often used to describe fine horses; these were magnificent plus.

Birdy handed me a carrot, and our new friends went after the offerings with the same zest we'd used on our subs. Seconds later, they were trying to get at the bag.

"Looks like we found their sweet spot," I said.

"It's more than that. They're ravenous, and they shouldn't be." Birdy pointed at a long, green metal feed trough inside the fence to our left. It was three-quarters full, but even if it hadn't been, it was bracketed on both ends by stacked bales of high-grade horse hay. Plenty of available calories, but everything looked untouched.

"Let's try something," she said.

I followed her around the outside of the enclosure. The Arabians watched us attentively, but didn't follow. Birdy handed me another carrot, and we held them over the fence directly above the feed. The mares whinnied, pawed the ground and tossed their heads, but they wouldn't come within ten feet of us, not even when I deliberately dropped my carrot in the trough.

I bent and examined the ground beneath the feeder. There were some large, rough-shaped rocks there, which seemed out of place around expensive animals, and the earth bulged ever so slightly for several feet along the inside of the fence.

"Birdy," I said, "I want you to take the horses back inside and stay with them." She won me once again by not asking why.

Panamaxes and Countesses

I walked up the road to the whitewashed shed. The cops had backed Chuck's seven ATVs into a neat, tight row, but somebody had carelessly left a surgical mask dangling from a handlebar. I pushed the memory it evoked back into its cage.

The backhoe was a new John Deere, but the ignition slot was empty. The padlock on the shed door had been cut, and on an inside wall, I discovered two long rows of nails holding a dozen tagless keys. Fortunately, only one was die-stamped JD. I also took a round point shovel and a length of three-quarter-inch chain with a grab hook on each end, both of which I tossed into the Deere's front loader.

Heavy equipment isn't my strong suit. Neither are planes. But I can handle both given a little time and a lot of room. I was proud of myself for not rearranging any of the ATVs but deducted points when I made a stab at widening the corral entrance.

The livestock feeder's legs were set into concrete footings that looked recently poured. I wrapped the chain around the two center struts and attached the hooks to the loader. The green steel pulled away with a sickening, bending sound, and I dragged it to the middle of the enclosure. The hay bales offered even less resistance, then I went to work with the hoe. Five feet down, I struck metal.

I dismounted and took the shovel into the hole. I was standing on what appeared to be a rectangular sheet of tin, and as I threw the rest of the dirt up and out, the smell of decaying flesh wafted over me.

Donnie Two Knives hadn't died in his sleep. Lying on his back, he was still wired to a straight-backed wooden chair, eyes wide, mouth frozen open in a silent scream. I didn't need a pathologist for the cause. Somebody—my bet was Chuck—had left a thin-bladed stiletto protruding from each of Donnie's ears. One should have been enough, but either Donnie hadn't been lucky enough to die after the first, or Chuck's sense of irony had intervened. Either way, they had been inserted at an upward angle until the quillions hit facial bone, leaving a pair of pearl-handled dreadlocks. I saw no other obvious marks, so maybe Chuck had sweet-talked information out of him before administering the coup de deuce—but I doubted it.

Wrapping a handkerchief around my face, I went through the corpse's pockets and came up with a wallet—Donnie's last name was Martin—a wad of cash and a crushed pack of Camels. No car keys and no cell phone. If Donnie had driven in here, Chuck would have needed his keys to get rid of the vehicle, but then they would have gone into the hole. That meant he'd had a driver. The cell phone was easier. Chuck was an experienced homicide cop; he would have burned it.

I tossed the items aside and started to climb out. In the distance, I heard a truck turn from the main road onto the property. Probably the guy coming to collect the horses. Nice timing.

I yelled to Birdy, hoping she was within earshot. She was a step ahead of me. I saw her bolt from the barn on one of the Arabians, riding hard to head the guy off. Despite the situation, I couldn't help but admire the vision of her hair flying, bare legs clamped tight against the horse's flanks, two fistfuls of mane in her hands. She might as well have been glued down. The girl could ride.

I fished my cell phone out of my hip pocket, but as I was trying to remember Yale Maywood's number, it rang. Jake. "Can't talk," I said. "Call you back."

He got out, "It's important," before I hung up and dialed Maywood. The deputy chief picked up on the second ring. "Yeah?"

"Rail."

"You sound stressed."

"Who'd you send to pick up the horses?"

It took him a moment to get on the same page. "Rancher in Riverside. Nat Tappan. Why?"

"He know the score?"

"Fuck no, he's my ex-wife's cousin."

"Then call him and tell him to go home. Come back some other time."

"Now?"

I glanced down the road. Barely a hundred yards from where I stood, Birdy had intercepted Mr. Tappan. They were conversing, but I could tell from the way he was waving his arm out the window, she wasn't going to be able to hold him much longer.

I said to Maywood, "Unless you want to see one helluva headline."

"I'll call you back."

"I'd rather not wait. Doesn't one of those mouth-breathers who drive you around have a phone?"

I heard him grunt something, then some rustling and clicks. Finally, Yale's voice came through my phone as he talked to the rancher. "Nat, that you? Listen, there's been a major screwup. Make it tomorrow, okay? Dinner on me. You pick the place."

I watched as Nat Tappan jerked his arm one last time at Birdy, then made a slow U-turn and headed back the way he'd come. The rubber he burned getting on the old road pretty much summed up what he was thinking.

"He gone?" Yale was talking to me again.

"Yep."

"Then tell me what the fuck you're doing back out there?"

I hung up.

I reburied Donnie and covered my work as best I could with the bales. Even so, my backhoe aesthetics left something to be desired. So to deter the casually curious, I piled the wrecked feeder on top, creating a rickety sculpture that would probably collapse if somebody blinked hard. The Arabians would have to live in the barn until Mr. Tappan got back. Birdy stayed clear until I finished, but I suspect the stench told her all she needed to know.

I helped her get the horses settled, then left her at the house while I took one of the ATVs back out to the *Lady Lucille* for another look around. Before I went inside, I dialed Jake.

"I don't like being hung up on," he said. I ignored him and waited. When he decided that was it for an apology, he got down to business. "I've just been over the Brando assets with Ernie DeHoff, their estate lawyer."

"And?"

"Mostly blue chips and T-Bills. Couple pieces of real estate. On the other side of the ledger, there's a bequest to the Orange Empire Railway Museum, and a bullshit grant to some USC professor named Felton who's traveling the world collecting sperm from Arabians. According to DeHoff, he's creating a DNA database to facilitate breeding. I'm praying that means horses."

"Very droll, Groucho. How much?"

"A hundred grand with a hundred more due next year."

"I don't think locomotives or Arabian sperm have anything to do with this."

"No shit, Sherlock."

There was more on the horizon, but apparently, Jake had to reaffirm my position as supplicant before he got to it. Fucking lawyers.

"A few months ago, Lucille leased a ship. Did it through an offshore shell, Brando Maritime Holdings."

I gazed across the desert landscape. "Chuck had to take Dramamine to watch *Jaws*. Said if The Big One ever turned Victorville into oceanfront, he'd cash out and move a hundred miles farther inland."

"No, schmuck, a ship ship. As in mutinies and stowaways. Container vessel. Old fucker. Built in Stockholm way back in '88 as the *Princess Zenzi*. Captain gashed her side on a breakwater a few years ago, and the insurance company walked away when he blew a .21. She was collecting barnacles in the Philippines until Lucille signed a six-month contract at $20,000 per, then popped for an extra $17,000 to change her name to the *Resurrection Bay II*. A place that actually exists, if you're interested. Middle of nowhere Alaska."

"Lot of money for a name."

"Rush job, I'm told. Right now, the *RBII* is sitting at an old submarine-refueling installation left over from that little dustup with the Japanese back in the forties. Vuku Island. Tonga, if you didn't know. The uninhabited part."

"A container ship in Tonga? I thought their primary exports were shell necklaces and laundered money." Then something clicked in. "Passports," I said.

"Yeah, what about them?"

"Back a bit, they had something called a T.P.P. Tongan Protected Person. For a few grand, you could buy a passport with a citizenship chit attached. All kinds of people grabbed one. Billionaires with tax problems, drug kingpins, even Imelda Marcos. Easy money for the Tongan king until somebody realized they were naturalizing thousands of Hong Kong businessmen and whole Triads. They'd probably still be doing it if they hadn't gotten up one morning and found the Chinese running everything in the country."

"Greedy royals with a room temperature IQ. There's a surprise."

"They killed the scam, but I'm betting it wasn't retroactive."

"I'll see if the Brandos made the cut. You want me to make a run at getting the manifests?"

As slick as Mr. Praxis is, my company has substantial holdings in the Bahamas, and I knew firsthand that their bureaucracy moves like a studio sending out profit participations. "Seems like an errand we can postpone. Can I presume there was an original *Resurrection Bay*?"

"You can. A flattop. Same war as the refueling station. But you might want something more to go on than Wikipedia."

"Where would one find Brando Maritime Holdings?"

"If you happened to be in Miami, you could dash across for lunch."

"Freeport."

"Yep. Had a house on Grand Bahama once. Nice place to fuck with the tax man. Then I met my first hurricane and couldn't get out of there fast enough. Give me the IRS and earthquakes any day."

The Bahamas registration probably didn't mean anything. Ninety percent of oceangoing ships are registered in places where they've never dropped anchor. Flags of convenience are based on financial considerations, not patriotism. "What did DeHoff say happens the day Chuck and Lucille are no longer with us?"

He cleared his throat. "I thought you might already know."

"Take off your cross-examination hat."

"The Brando Trust has a single successor trustee. Rail Sheridan Black. Want his address?"

First Yale Maywood, now this. "We never discussed anything like that."

"So what? They had Super Bowl tickets too. Looks like they left you a mandate and the means. Now, all you need is a mission."

"You think that up all by yourself? If you weren't so thin-skinned, I'd tell you my father's plan to keep lawyers from breeding."

"Sounds like a personal problem. See the chaplain."

He was right. I was angry, and I didn't even know why.

Actually, I did know. I find satisfaction in helping those who need a hand, but I don't like being presumed upon. I took a moment to collect my thoughts. Jake or no Jake, DeHoff wasn't going to release documents without an okay from the Brandos or a death certificate, neither of which was going to be forthcoming anytime soon. "I don't suppose you asked about instructions to go along with the trustee job?"

I could hear him smiling over the phone. "Didn't have to. DeHoff volunteered. One sentence, handwritten by Lucille: 'Rail, I'm so sorry, but it's in your hands now.'"

I know you're not supposed to speak ill of the dead, but I might have muttered something I'd have to apologize for later. Jake started to say something, but I cut him off. "You have a size on this *Resurrection Bay*?"

I heard him shuffling papers. "Panamax mean anything?"

"It means another foot in any direction, and it couldn't get through the Canal. Think three football fields end to end."

"If my life weren't in jeopardy, this wouldn't be even mildly interesting. There's a thirty-million-dollar actor in my lobby who just walked off a picture."

"I'm sure that was Chuck's last thought. 'I hope Jake's got a couple of minutes.'"

There was silence on the other end. He didn't deserve that. "Sorry, Counselor, you done good."

"Just pay your bill for a change." Click.

With the ship's lease, Lucille would also have gotten unlimited Bahamian passenger permits and entry visas, no questions asked. All Brando Maritime's agent had to do was file a short-form request over the Internet, and in seventy-two hours, the documents could be printed out by any consulate. And under international law, once aboard, passengers would be answerable only to the *Resurrection Bay II*'s captain and the government in Freeport.

I didn't know how it fit, but suddenly, Lucille's monthly FedEx pickup to a South Pacific import house moved from curious to very interesting. And gently nagging at the back of my brain was Wes Crowe's antenna farm.

*** * ***

Without the music, the Pullman seemed strangely quiet. The LAPD had been as efficient at clearing it of evidence as they had the house. However, most railroad car furnishings are either built in or bolted down, so it hadn't been stripped bare. Fortunately, someone had left the air-conditioning on, and I welcomed the coolness.

There was nothing visual to indicate that violence had been done, but murder changes the character of a room forever. No amount of time or redecorating can put it back the way it was. Twenty years later, a dog will know instantly. People who deal in death will too.

I slowly walked the car's length, pausing from time to time to allow my other senses time to absorb what my eyes couldn't see. There may be genuine psychics among us, I just haven't met one. What everyone does have to one degree or another is the ability to intuit minute changes in our surroundings. To "feel" a small radius.

Delta and SEAL teams advancing on a target aren't planning their next meal or thinking about getting laid. Every nerve ending is taking in tiny details. Cracks in the walls, the way water runs off a roof, background noise, cooking smells. And especially energy. High or low; positive or negative; anxious or calm?

The engineers at Bragg and Dam Neck can build an exact replica of an objective, and the command structure and intelligence analysts can train and brief you until you're able to execute the mission blindfolded. But as true-to-life as they try to make it, it's never going to be the real thing . . . where one small cue might be the difference between a celebratory cold beer or being dinner for the carrion eaters.

Anyone can learn to be more perceptive. It's about paying attention. If I were running the country's educational system, I would make awareness instruction as mandatory as math—especially for young women. We're terrific at telling our girls they can do or be anything—urging them to take risks. But we're criminally negligent by not warning them about the predators who lie in wait, watching for exactly that profile. To a nation of "liberated," good-news-only parents, the hunters say thank you.

After several minutes, I turned and went back to where I had last seen Lucille and took a seat in the booth directly across the aisle. Her table was bare now, the blood on the seat and floor gone, but I didn't need those things to replay the scene. Whoever had done the face-to-face torturing had probably sat opposite her while his associate knelt in the booth behind and managed the strangulation. That meant Razorblade Man had been in charge, because he would have been monitoring the victim's reaction to having her air cut off—the back and forth between half death and one more excruciating breath.

I wasn't a homicide detective, but I didn't believe the indignities visited on the Brandos would be in the toolbox of very many murderers. They were too organized and too time-consuming. And though I disliked applying the word *professional,* the questioning had been exactly that—mercilessly so. The sexual overtones were also impossible to miss.

I took out my phone. A minute later, Gianatta Sabatini's secretary put me through to her boss. In her day job as head of a Beverly Hills CPA firm, Gianatta is as buttoned up as any Stanford-degreed money manager for the well-to-do is expected to be. What her other clients don't know, however, is that she earns less pushing numbers around a spreadsheet than by writing erotic novels under the nom de plume, Countess Paloma.

Normally, this is the kind of thing that would triple business among Tinseltown's diamond-heeled, but Gina says being identified with seventeen kinds of fellatio would play hell with her treasured membership at the Los Angeles Country Club—a place still iffy about corned beef because it might attract the wrong element. I wouldn't have suspected her secret either if, a few years ago, she hadn't come to me, frantic about a Countess groupie who'd cracked her identity and shown up in her kitchen in the middle of the night.

When she found him, he was eating a bowl of Frosted Flakes and wearing nothing but wingtips and a catcher's mask.

In the black humor of Hollywood, if you don't have a stalker, you're not a player. In truth, if you have any connection to the business at all—even driving the prop truck—you've probably had your very own whacko whose car you're always on the lookout for. The LAPD has a unit devoted to these crazies, and there are tough laws on the California books, but in a litigious world, deterring the obsessed is a legal no-man's-land.

I'd fixed her problem the only way these guys understand, meaning I'd stayed inside the law just enough to avoid San Quentin, yet gotten close enough to the edge that the guy didn't want any part of a next time. It's instructive how quickly you can get through to someone with a pair of handcuffs and a pitching machine. So he'd appreciate the lesson's poetry, I'd let him wear the mask and wingtips.

A grateful Gianatta had torn up my accounting bill for the year. The Countess handled it a little differently, spending the weekend at my place while we worked on ideas for her next book. Despite the autographed copy on my shelf, I won't be reading it. When you drink that much red wine naked, it's better to skip the replay.

"To what do I owe this pleasure?" Gianatta asked. "It certainly can't be the taxes I saved you last quarter."

"I never look. Take off your glasses, I want Paloma."

"Ready when you are. Please talk dirty. And if your current lady is longing for a threesome, I'm free all weekend."

Without giving a name, I described what had been done to Lucille. When I finished, she peppered me for clinical details that, even over the phone to a sex author I'd been intimate with, were uncomfortable.

Finally, she said, "The dead woman's Asian, isn't she?"

Apparently, I'd called the right person. "Chinese," I replied.

"I'd have guessed a little farther east, but it doesn't matter."

"Care to enlighten me?"

"Remember the Japanese Red Army?"

"Before my time, but yes."

"Mine too, but they hold a special place in my cold, dark feminist heart. Before they and their associated degenerates came along, it was pretty much unheard of for a woman to have power in a terrorist network. Mostly, chicks did what they always do, run errands, cook and sweat under smelly men. Then the repressed daughters of Nippon put forth the lovely and demure Fusako Shigenobu who could have taught Himmler a thing or two."

"Sounds familiar," I said. "During the Indian Wars, the worst thing a prisoner could hear was, 'Give him to the women.'"

"Fusako went on the lam early, but her ideas were copied by the United Red Army. In the dead of winter, 1972, twenty of them traipsed into the mountains for a little light purging. A couple of weeks of sexual indignities and creative torture later, twelve were dead, and the rest were in a pitched battle with the cops."

"You're saying this was some kind of ritual?"

"All sex murder is ritual to one degree or another. We just don't usually waste time figuring it out. Was this dame from Taiwan or the Mainland?"

"Hong Kong."

"Interesting. Okay, the crap in one of the bottles is venom. My guess, cobra. The other will be acid and concentrated capsaicin—which is about fifty times hotter than a mouthful of habaneros. First the blades, then the venom. It impedes coagulation, and as a man with your experience knows, unchecked bleeding plays tricks on the psyche."

I did know. Absent severing a major blood vessel—and there are very few of those—it's almost impossible for someone to bleed out. Even on the battlefield, you're more likely to die from shock or infection than loss of blood. But when it's your red stuff running onto the ground, logic runs right along with it, and even pros have to fight down panic. Deep in our prehistoric subconscious, we're imprinted that seeing our blood is a prelude to death. It's why we get a sick feeling in the pits of our stomachs when we visualize a sharp blade cutting us or have to turn our heads when a hypodermic-wielding hematology tech heads our way. It's also why a person who might stupidly challenge a gun backs away from a knife. Few of us ever see a real bullet wound. Everybody knows what it feels like to be cut.

Gianatta continued, "So once your lady had the full visual effect, her torturer painted on the pain agent, which also constricted the capillaries and shut off the flow. Presto, time to get a few questions answered. Only from what you told me, that didn't happen."

"It doesn't appear so."

"Poor thing. Eventually, seeing that much blood becomes so emotionally distressing that the victim actually begs for the acid."

In other words, submission. The essence of interrogation. Choking would have accelerated the process. I said, "The sandpaper seems like overkill."

"That's because disfigurement doesn't get your rocks off."

"I don't follow."

"The killer was a woman. Ten to one her helper was too. And they would have been naked . . . and stopping every now and then to masturbate—or more."

Even though I hadn't considered this combination, my question to Phil had been on the money. There was sex involved, just no semen.

"You still there?" she asked.

"What about the tiger in the mouth?"

"That will be personal. Very personal. Something that meant a great deal to the dead woman."

"Any chance you're wrong?"

"Sure, and I might give up shopping, but I wouldn't count on either."

After I hung up, I stared at Lucille's booth, trying to will myself to see her attackers. Gradually, something pushed its way past the haze. The green leather where she had been sitting was indented. Since we're creatures of habit, that was probably where Lucille always worked, and the seat had taken on her shape. The bench on the other side of the table was firm, new. Chuck probably didn't come out very often, and if he did, he probably did what I was doing, sat across the aisle with his legs out. If I was correct, then the other bench never got used.

But as I stared at it, the half next to the window wasn't entirely pristine. Where the back of the booth met the seat, there was a slight irregularity. I focused on it, then I remembered the dirty knee prints on Chuck's bed. If someone had been kneeling here too, they would have unconsciously pushed their toes into the gap, widening it. Eventually, it would return to its original shape, but for the moment, the twin anomalies were like matching signatures.

But why sit off center from your victim and not make straight-ahead eye contact? I cast my gaze to the carpet on my right. It ran the length of the car and was the same shade of dark green as the leather booths. But only the four-inch borders were solid. The wide center was in a tiny, green and gold checkerboard pattern.

And then I saw it. In the far border was an almost invisible, pointed dent. I got up and knelt next to it. Sure enough, lost in the checkerboard design were two more. I recognized them immediately. Tripod points. The nail-like protrusions that dial down from a camera stand's rubber-tipped feet to anchor it.

I thought back to the crime scene. The floor had been covered with plastic, and because of people moving up and down the aisle, the work lights had been rigged on the dining tables. There had been no tripods. That explained why the questioner had positioned herself to the side. She wanted the camera to have a clear shot.

I stood and redialed Gianatta.

"I must be irresistible," she said.

"You are, but that's not why I'm calling. Might the ladies—or demented fucks—you described earlier want to record the session?"

She didn't answer right away. Then, "I should have thought of that, but yes."

"Why?"

"Probably to get somebody else's attention." She hesitated. "And then for the same reason everybody else does. To enjoy later and maybe sell."

"Sell?"

"The rarer it is, the more your affinity group will pay. Jesus, Rail, I thought you ran a business."

"Sorry, Adam Smith didn't cover snuff films."

"Bullshit, he covered everything. By the way, you've probably already figured it out, but that elevates the tiger's head from simply a message to a piece of theatre."

A light came on. "And if they set it to music, that would probably mean it wasn't their first time."

"A sound track? How very sick . . . and slick. Something appropriate, I trust?"

"Nick Cave. 'Red Right Hand.'"

"Literate too. Inspired by *Paradise Lost*. The vengeful hand of God. How deliciously decadent. Gotta love those gals."

I hung up before I said something that cost me a friend. I looked at my watch. People would just be going to work in Western Australia. I dialed 411 and asked the operator to get me Parkinson-Lowe Imports in Perth. The male Aussie voice that answered was polite and businesslike.

"May I speak with either Mr. Parkinson or Mr. Lowe."

"I'm sorry, sir, this is a virtual office. We only answer telephones and receive mail."

"I see. How do your clients collect their things?"

"Some come in, but mostly we communicate by e-mail. Letters and packages are delivered by our messenger service to whatever address is on file. I've been here four years, and I've never met anyone from Parkinson-Lowe."

"Would you be able to give me their address?"

"I'm sorry, sir, but no. That's one of the reasons people use us."

"Of course it is."

"I can pass along a message, if you like."

I gave him my number and decided to give Parkinson or Lowe or whoever something to think about, "Tell them Lucille Brando called."

"I'm sorry, sir, it sounded like you said Lucille."

"Your ears are fine. And my middle name is 'Just Breathe.'"

15

Sequoias and Sears

I needed time to think, and the ranch was as good a place as any. I asked Birdy if she wanted me to run her into a hotel in Victorville. I didn't catch her answer, but a few hours later, we were showering again.

"I'm not much of a cook," she said while we were toweling each other, "but if I can locate some Ragu, I can get rid of this hole in my stomach." She was right. It had been a long time since the subs and Doritos.

"I've got a couple of calls to make. Think you can handle the shopping and find your way back?"

"Only if you spot me a few bucks. I don't carry cards when I hit the bars. Some crumb grabs my purse, he's welcome to the lint."

I handed her five twenties and the keys to the Ram. "I've got a soft spot for Italian sausage," I said. "Hot or sweet, just lots of it."

"How about the pasta?"

"Anything thicker than vermicelli, I'll send you back."

"Gotta love this man," she said.

* * *

Even when it's necessary, I don't like conning innocent people. I felt especially bad about Roxy Luchinski, a girl in a job she hated who'd ended up with me on the phone. I made a mental note to send her something nice. Maybe a couple of cruise tickets.

The night operator at FBI Headquarters answered with the same clipped efficiency as before. When I asked for Ext. 664, she waited for me to give her the Hot Code. The one I had was now a day old, but if I didn't say anything, I was definitely going nowhere. Maybe they had a grace period for the ADD crowd.

"Gemstone," I said.

There might have been a split second's hesitation, but it could just as easily have been my imagination. Then the phone was ringing.

"Department 11. Ms. Luchinski."

"Hi, Roxy, still raining in our nation's capital?"

"Hank, is that you?"

"Sorry about last night. Had to do some couples counseling, then I got busy with a Coast Guard inspection."

I should have expected what came next. "Maybe when we see each other at the reunion, you can show me your seaworthiness certificate. Where was that again? Juneau?" Francesca Huston's voice hadn't lost any of its charm.

"Hank, why did you lie to me? You seemed so nice." Roxy sounded like she was about to burst into tears.

"Want to tell her your real name, or shall I?" Huston asked. "Refresh my memory. Black or Bonks?"

"I'm sorry, Roxy," I said. "I'm genuinely ashamed." And I meant it. What I wasn't ashamed of was learning that Department 11 had the budget and the personnel to review every incoming call. In penny-pinching times, that put Huston in rarefied air. It also made her vulnerable. The enemy's not always the bad guys, sometimes it's the spotlight.

"You may hang up now, Ms. Luchinski," Huston said. "Security is waiting for you in Conference Room B."

I heard a muffled sob, then a click as Roxy left the call.

Unfortunately, she hadn't taken Vampira with her. "I may cut our dumb broad some slack, but you're on your way to prison, Mr. Black."

These people never stop. No wonder the courts are clogged. "Lighten up, Frank, the only thing I've done is hurt a naïve girl."

"Fuck you with the Frank bullshit, and I can count at least a dozen felonies. In twenty years, you might be working a real crab boat."

"You have Jake Praxis's card. But if I were you, I'd wait till morning. He's a combat-qualified prick after a few bourbons. In the meantime, before you start scaring that poor girl half to death, tell your boss that the first thing we're all going to do tomorrow morning is get on the phone to the California Attorney General—no friend to anybody in your fair city—and explain why he wasn't consulted before you removed evidence from a local crime scene." I was guessing, but her silence told me I'd hit the fat part of the elephant. However, with jerks like Huston, you have to pile on.

"I also found Donnie Two Knives. How you doing in that department?"

The powder keg blew. "Where the fuck are you, Black? I want your ass in front of me NOW!"

"When you get a grip on your manners, we'll talk. Until then, don't call me, I'll be busy dictating my memoirs." I hung up while she was teaching me some new words. Damn, I really did feel bad about Roxy.

I spun through the channels and came up empty on a McQueen picture, but Harvey Keitel was dragging himself around the *City of Industry* with a couple of bullets in him, so I settled in until it was over. Then I called Huston back.

"Goddamn you, Black, you hang up on me again, and . . ."

I hit the END button, counted to a hundred and redialed. She wasn't any less angry, but she was at least trying "Okay, Special Agent in Charge Huston, here's what you're going to do." She got out half a threat before I clicked off again.

This time I gave her two hours. Funny how not talking

to someone shifts the advantage. My father taught me that, and it's far more effective than winning debating points with someone who isn't listening anyway. This time there was nothing but angry breathing.

"You know Sharpley Hartland?"

"The blowhard congressman? Who doesn't?"

All congressmen think they should be senators, and all senators think they should be president. Problem is most couldn't hold a job busing tables at Applebee's. Sharpley Hartland thinks he should be a senator too, but he occupies a seat that's so safe he can skip campaigning altogether and focus on piling up seniority and wreaking vengeance on those who cross him. He's not averse to lining his pockets either. A soothing consolation to not being in the club across the rotunda.

"That would be him," I said. "He's got a daughter, Amanda. Nice girl. Real commitment to redwoods. Started an organization called Love a Sequoia. I'm in favor of sequoias, how about you?"

"Where are you going with this?"

"Last year, I had a group of friends over to meet Amanda. Liked her so much, we shelled out a couple of million to make the down payment on some acreage she was anxious to save. My trust kicked in the balance." I let that sit for a moment. I knew she got it, but I wanted the analyst working that slick FBI recording system to get it too, and you can never tell about analysts. Some of them went to Harvard.

"I was thinking about sending Roxy on a cruise, but after what you've put her through, I think she deserves more than a tan and a week of karaoke. So here's where you come in. As soon as the switchboard opens at the Pentagon, you're going to get on the horn and find Ms. Luchinski a job. Preferably in naval aviation. And I don't want her reporting to anybody below a vice admiral."

"Are you crazy?"

"Then you're going to give her the kind of send-off from

your place you'd want everyone at the reunion to hear about. You know, show her your real, gracious self."

"And if I tell you to pound it up your ass?"

"Then Congressman Hartland is going to get some serious face time with me at his next committee hearing. Subject: you, Mr. Curtis, my sore kidney and whatever else happens to come up. Maybe even Department 11, which I'll bet he's never heard of. And if you doubt my ability to draw a crowd, SAC Huston, call around."

Her bite was gone, but she couldn't help herself. "Hartland's committee deals with agriculture."

"We'll open with Mexican ham, then see where things go." When I didn't hear anything, I knew she'd met Luis and his truck full of porkers. That must have been a fun flight. "And don't jerk me around, Francesca. I've got my own way of checking that Roxy's settled in. And that she's permanent. When I'm satisfied, I'll call back." I paused. "Gemstone," I said. Click.

My next call was to Freddie Rochelle in D.C. He's not a friend; he's not even an acquaintance, both of which imply some kind of human emotion. I don't like Freddie, and he's incapable of liking anyone. I use him only when I absolutely need to, and he bills me with the restraint of Clinton auctioning a pardon.

By business card, he's a lobbyist, but Washington has a class of people that can only exist in a city where they don't manufacture anything but trouble. Freddie's real job is putting people who control vast amounts of wealth together with people who control vast amounts of power and making sure that some of each sticks to him.

The phone in Georgetown rang only twice. "I hope I woke you," I said.

"Oh, my dahhling, dahhling, Rail," Freddie cooed into the phone. "Is that really you? Please tell me you're just around the corner and can dash over for drinks tomorrow. You should see who's coming. Leon, get me the list."

During business hours, Freddie's voice is radio announcer

baritone with the inflection of a politician caressing some-body else's wallet. At the office, he dresses like the Duke of Marlborough meets Ricky Riccardo and chain-smokes Sobranie Black Russians. But it was late, so my guess was a pastel caftan and Virginia Slims.

Leon is Freddie's other half—better half, actually—and they've been together as long as I've known him. I could hear their two ill-behaved dachshunds, AK and 47, yapping and probably tearing hell out of something expensive.

"Tell Leon hello and to stand down. I'm not in town."

"Damn it anyway, I'd love to see you. Are you still with Archer?"

"She's back in Europe. Modeling."

"What a goddamn shame. She was perfect for you and all your macho, gun-toting bullshit."

"Put a sock in it, Freddie, and get out your calculator. This is a business call."

"Is there any other kind?"

The Pentagon part was easy. Freddie knew an adjutant to the CNO, and he'd follow up on Roxy. "She doesn't happen to be into pain, does she?"

"I doubt it."

"Too bad, there're some chicks in the Marine comman-dant's office who like to . . ." He started to detail their pro-clivities, knowing I'd cut him off, and I did. Two minutes in, and I needed another shower.

When I got to the FBI and Department 11, it was a differ-ent matter.

"Christ, I stay as far from that place as possible. Not only don't they have any money, famines are less depressing. And the wardrobes. My God, if you tried to make a Bulgarian street sweeper wear suits that drab, he'd break your neck. I even hate the fucking building."

"So far I haven't heard a no."

"Look, Rail, most secret police slap you in a dungeon, bring in some guy with a toolbox in one hand and his dick in the other. It's unpleasant, but it usually doesn't last more than a week before they put a bullet in your head. The Feds break you financially, then ruin the rest of your life with innuendo. Ever hear of an FBI apology? Fuck no. You think that's because they always get it right or just don't give a shit?"

"Sounds like you had a run-in."

"Two hundred grand in legal for the pleasure of being a good citizen. I got the 'Mr. Rochelle is not a target,' then as soon as I talked, here came 'We're not sure Mr. Rochelle was truthful in his answers, so let's go downstairs and visit the grand jury.' That's the game. 'Come on over for coffee, then bend over while we shove the urn up your ass.'"

"The question on the table is how much?"

"The two hundred they cost me, plus another fifty for having to say FBI again."

"For a couple of sentences of information?"

"If I knew where bin Laden was, I could get 25 mil for a word."

"Okay, but you throw in the Pentagon."

"Not a chance. That's another fifteen. Remember when I loaned you my Bentley, and you promised to park it inside? Well, it had to be repainted."

As usual, Freddie had worn me out. "Send the bill to Jake."

"No. To Mallory. He nags."

"I'd also prefer not to break any laws."

"That's the great thing about D.C. Nobody with a security clearance has pot to piss in, so when they feel their star dimming, they validate their importance by dropping a top secret bomb between jumbo shrimp. You'd be surprised at the things I hear without even asking."

Unfortunately, he was right. Over at Langley, they've figured that out and try to give operatives a lot of support, but the rest of the town is just one cocktail party away from publishing a newsletter. "Tomorrow," I said.

"Then get off my phone. Leon, where's my directory? The zebra one."

* * *

After a soul-satisfying breakfast of warmed-up sausage and angel hair, I drove through the gates of the ranch and turned right, away from the highway. Birdy sat beside me, quietly looking out at the desert. I mentally tipped my hat. People who can occupy a silence go to the top of my list. I enjoy a good story as much as anyone, but I detest the stream of consciousness ramblings many otherwise intelligent people visit on any beating pulse trapped near them. Some of the best times I've had were driving or walking or just sitting with a person I like. It's not wholly a gender issue, but it's disproportionate. In most things, I don't want my women to be men, but on this, I fist-bump Henry Higgins.

The sun was behind us, and its angle caused the quartz crystals in the sand to twinkle like daylight stars. The road wasn't straight, and Chuck's woods gradually receded until it was just a strip of green in the distance. About six miles from the gate, a deep pair of ruts overlaid with ATV tracks intersected the road and headed off to the north. It looked like rough going, but that's why I'd driven the Ram.

I stopped and made Birdy tighten her seat belt until she was cinched flat against the leather, did the same and turned into the ruts. The ravine bent north as well, and we bounced along for half an hour before it was back beside us. I saw a path leading into the woods and turned into it. A short time later, we crossed the gorge on a cattle bridge just barely wide enough for the truck.

Once out of the trees on the other side, the ruts disappeared, and the desert stretched off to the horizon again. I picked up the pace to forty and aimed at an old, corrugated tin barn in the distance. It was rusted a dark caramel, and as we got closer, it seemed to list several degrees.

I parked next to the barn, and we got out. It was deathly quiet, then a sudden loud bang caused Birdy to let out a little yelp and jump. I walked around front and saw the wide metal door swinging in the wind. I propped it open with a broken two-by-four to and went inside.

The front was a mishmash of clutter. Old tarps, broken

machinery and an elaborate stone birdbath cracked in half. All the way in the rear, a late-model, red Jeep Wrangler sat facing the doors. It was buttoned up tight, and about a week's worth of blowing sand covered its exterior. I tried the door, and it swung open.

There was an infant carrier strapped into the passenger seat and two extra blankets in the back. I saw no key in the ignition, so I retrieved the one from the backpack and inserted it. The engine sprang to life on the first try, and the gas gauge read full. I popped the glove compartment. Inside was the pink slip and a current Allstate certificate, both in the name of Lucille Brando, along with an auto club map of Southern California, Arizona and Nevada. I unfolded the map and checked for markings. There were none. I turned the Jeep off and got out.

Birdy had come into the barn, and her curiosity got the best of her. "You knew this was here?"

"No, but logic said it should be."

"I've got no clue what that means, but I've got ways of making you talk."

"And I'll hold you to them." I stepped away from the Wrangler. It was positioned in such a way that there could have been another vehicle parked beside it, but the wind had erased any tracks. What it hadn't erased was the chunk of tin bent away from the barn doorframe. I crossed to it, knelt and examined the jagged metal. Flakes of bright red paint came off on my finger.

One very brave, very scared lady in one hell of a hurry. There was no longer any doubt what Chuck and Lucille's killers had wanted, and they'd gone away empty-handed.

Whatever the original arrangements had been, Chuck would have had a backup plan—one that couldn't be deduced if someone found the second backpack. This woman was running for her life, probably without knowing why, and she was doing all the right things. I liked her without knowing her, and I hoped I'd get a chance to tell her.

Yale Maywood wouldn't be a factor because Chuck

wouldn't have trusted anyone with stars on his collar. Victorville was out—too close. So was Vegas, which was probably the girl's original destination, but in an emergency, Chuck's sphere of influence wouldn't have been strong enough there. However, he did have a network that was both inside and outside the system. One where no one would question anything he asked. Perhaps even die for him. Blue Rescue.

I knew the names of the people we'd helped in the last few years, but I'd never worn a badge, so that disqualified me from ever being confided in. Same with Jake, who hadn't been particularly conscientious about attending meetings anyway. There was someone who could help. Question was, would he?

Capt. Julius Watson of the Los Angles Fire Department hadn't liked me from the moment he met me. Part of it was the usual father antipathy toward any man dating a daughter. The other part was that Anita was a battalion chief with plans to one day run the department, and Julius didn't think being squired around by a rich guy with a low regard for politicians enhanced her chances.

He might have been right, but we never got to find out. Then, when Anita was killed, I had to make a decision about attending the funeral. Either way, I was screwed. He'd see me and be pissed I was there, or not see me and be pissed I had a cold heart. I opted for out-of-sight, maybe out-of-mind, and paid my respects my own way.

She'd been gone three years, and we'd had a dozen Blue Rescue meetings in the interim. I was still waiting for him to look my direction. I had his number in my phone for no other reason than our common charity association. I asked Birdy to wait in the Ram, leaned against the Jeep and hit SEND.

Unlike retired cops who get the cold shoulder when they stop by their old precincts, firemen usually enjoy hanging around with the old guys. Not that Julius was old. Fifty-six, and he was a certifiable hero, still carrying a couple of slugs in his chest courtesy of a firebug who took umbrage at being busted for burning down half the Angeles National Forest. All the same, he had a prick quality about him that probably set active commanders' teeth on edge. At least it would have mine.

When he answered, I heard a bell going off, men running and trucks starting up in whatever station he was gracing with his presence. "Who's this?"

Why try to put lipstick on a pig? "Rail Black, Julius. I need a favor."

"Go fuck yourself."

"Feel better?"

He didn't answer, so I laid it out. "Chuck and Lucille Brando are dead. Murdered. You won't read about it, and you're now one of two dozen who know." I waited.

"Go on."

"There's a girl who has information. I've never seen her, and I don't know her name. She'll be good-looking in an obvious sort of way, and probably not out of her twenties. She's got a kid with her probably. Chinese. Most likely an infant. And unless she's changed cars, she's driving a red Wrangler with its left side scraped up pretty good."

"Tell you what, I'll drive around town on my lunch hour. Buzz you if I see anything."

"Fuck you, Julius. I'm sorry Anita got killed, but I didn't do it. All I'm guilty of is showing her a good time and caring about her. We probably wouldn't have ever been anything but good friends, but who knows? She was a heckuva girl. So, help me or don't, but get the fuck off your high horse."

When he didn't hang up, I went on. "If I'm right, there's a Blue Rescue recipient Chuck was especially close to, and that's where she is. Could go all the way back to when he came on the board, but with a few phone calls, you'll know who it is."

"Anything else?"

"Watch out for an FBI chick named Huston. You'll recognize her by the four-hundred-pound chip on her shoulder."

"You know what you call a Fed on an arson case?"

I didn't know or care, but what the fuck. "What?"

"Retired. Fuck her. I'll be in touch."

As we hit the outskirts of Victorville, Birdy looked at me. "What now, Rail Black?"

"Train station. Send you home to your ponies."

"Where are you going?"

"First to church, then Las Vegas."

"That usually work?"

I laughed but didn't elaborate.

After a moment, she said, "Racing season's over, and I'm off until the end of the month."

"I don't know what I'm going to run into over there."

"Church or Vegas?"

"Both."

"Is that a no?"

"Just a caution."

"Then think about the last thirty-six hours."

She had a point. Plus, a couple is always less conspicuous. Delta learned the hard way that nothing draws attention faster than physically fit guys traveling together. Now, when they fly commercial, each operator is accompanied by a female—military, of course, with clearances. Also attractive and an excellent actress.

I took my eyes off the road long enough to have a moment with her. "Under one condition. If I tell you to do something, you don't even blink. There might not be time for me to explain—or to worry about your feelings."

"Hey, why should you be any different?" She let that sit for a moment, then burst out laughing. "A little joke, General. You have my word. You point, I'll hurl myself on the grenade. But if I'm going to be squired around fancy casinos by a good-looking guy, I need to do some shopping."

"There's a mall at Caesars."

"You must be kidding. Find me a Target."

I smiled and put my hand over hers. "Money's not an issue."

She turned toward me and took my hand in both of hers. "We were pretty good together, weren't we? I mean besides digging holes and feeding horses."

For an answer, I squeezed her hand.

"Well, when we go to bed tonight, if I'm taking off my own clothes, it won't be an obligation."

Somewhere in the back of my brain, a voice called out, *Uh-oh. A special one. You don't need this now, Black. Take her to the train. Take her to the goddamn train!*

So naturally, I said, "I know where there's a Sears."

16

Pierce Arrows and PT Boats

The launch rode low in the water. Built to hold four men comfortably, six without equipment, it limped along with nine, not counting the babies. The pilots took turns holding the fragile infants, who were swaddled in tiger skins, but several of the fliers were in even worse shape.

Pags was back at the wheel. "Jesus Christ, partner, I can't believe you. Why didn't you ask for a couple of fuckin' dogs too?"

"As I recall, it was a certain lieutenant who got all wound up about baby girls. So it came down to both babies and the pilots, or no babies, no pilots and probably our own monogrammed posts in the plaza."

Pags spit over the side. "You know we got no shot at getting back to the carrier in time."

"At least we'll go out breathing fresh air."

Fabian turned to check on the passengers. The pilot holding the baby girl smiled. "Thank you, Ensign. Especially from this little one. I've got two of my own back home, and refusing to take the boy unless you got her was extremely brave."

"Oh, he's quite a sport," Pags shouted over the engine. *"Hey, partner, here comes our old pal."*

With the fog mostly gone, the Tango's outline was now clearly visible. More than two years into his hitch, Fabian was still awed by the sheer size of warships, and this cold, dark piece of steel seemed even larger in its slumber.

And then he saw the light again. It was coming from the top of the bridge, and it swept first one way, then back in a rough sixty-degree arc. Fabian timed an interval. Eleven seconds, start to return. The next, identical. Pags had begun to angle the launch off the AKA's bow, but Fabian gestured for him to change course back toward it.

Pags nearly came out of his skin. *"I'm not gonna fuck around with you, Fabe. We've got a full house here, two sick babies and no time to give."*

"You already said we're not going to make our rendez-vous. Maybe there's a radio on board we can use to contact the Bay. And if that's an American up there . . ."

Pags grunted and jerked the wheel a little too hard, causing the port side to dip perilously close to the water. He quickly corrected and eased back on the power. From somewhere onshore, familiar music wafted across the river.

"Hey, hear that, Piano-Man?" Fabian said. *"'Smoke Gets in your Eyes.' Paul Whiteman. You still got those rubbers?"*

"Goddamn you. Just plain goddamn you."

The hull stairway to the deck wasn't extended, but with Pags holding the launch steady, Fabian was able to stand on the boat's hardtop and reach the bottom tread. As he swung out into space, one of his hands slipped, and he dangled for a moment with only three fingers clutching the sharp steel. After what seemed like forever, he was able to get his other hand back on the step and leverage himself up.

He signaled for Pags to throw him a line and cut the

engine. The lieutenant shook his head no, then reconsidered and complied. He wasn't happy, but they didn't need somebody coming out to investigate. Fabian tied the launch off to the stairs and ascended.

Empty ships are a symphony of sound. Creaking, groaning, cracking and the odd whistle of wind blowing through rigging. Fabian crouched, his .45 drawn, and let the Tango's audio signature imprint on his subconscious. The bridge, rising thirty feet above, was a dark silhouette. If the light was still there, it wasn't visible from his angle.

Hearing nothing out of the ordinary, he moved, staying low against the rail. Normal maintenance had been ignored for some time. The ship smelled stale, and there were patches of mold on her superstructure and seagull shit everywhere. Some of the cables securing the twin, multiple boom cranes were frayed, others were missing, and the smaller derrick near the bow leaned over the side at a precarious angle.

But nothing commanded his attention like the dark, tarpaulin-covered shapes lining every inch of deck. He unsheathed his shark knife and cut the rope securing one so he could lift its corner. The fat whitewall tire and chrome bumper were so unexpected that it took him a second to process. But when he slid the tarp a little further, the Rolls-Royce "Spirit of Ecstasy" hood sculpture was instantly recognizable—even to a guy from the wilds of Pasadena. Fabian uncovered two more. A powder blue Duesenberg and a light cream, 1939 Cord. And he saw that shoved into the spaces around this acre of cars were spare tires, steamer trunks, furniture, and dozens of motorcycles.

Unless somebody thought this would be terrific shrapnel, Fabian's original sub barrier hypothesis was out the window. Nobody hung mines where a nearsighted dolphin might blow their expensive booty to kingdom come. The cables were a charade. The Japanese were doing a final bit of shopping on their way out.

Fabian made his way to one of the deck guns and found the ammo rack full. You don't store shells where salt spray *can get to them, and if there'd been a battle, the rack should have been partially depleted, if not empty. The gun showed no sign of having been fired recently, so the* Tango *had been quietly taken or surrendered.*

When he had completed a careful sweep of the main deck, he made his way to the bridge stairs. Just as he reached them, he heard the launch bump against the hull and a baby cry out. He paused, and both noises stopped.

The first level held the captain's quarters. Papers were strewn about, and there were a few small pieces of debris but no signs of extreme chaos . . . and no bullet holes. He tried the map light over the captain's desk, and it came on. Battery power meant the ship's engines had been run within the last week, but based on the mold and guano, it probably hadn't been her crew running them. He wanted to find the log and determine her last position, but that would have to wait. He turned the light off.

The second level had taken a bit more of a beating. The glass covering the instrument panel for operating the cranes was smashed, and the loudspeaker system had been torn out. He stopped and listened. Above, he heard a low rattle, then a click, then the rattle again to another click. He counted. Eleven seconds.

His .45 locked and loaded, he inched his way up the stairs. The pilothouse windows were dark, but from his crouch, Fabian could see the low sweep of a light on the far side, accompanied by the click, rattle, click. He watched it through several rotations, then, taking a breath, he stood and walked toward it.

A metal caged work light rolled back and forth in the open doorway in rhythm to the gentle rocking of the ship. It clicked when it hit the first jam before beginning its journey to the opposite side. It had apparently fallen from an electrician's stand next to the ship's wheel and turned itself on as it slid the length of its cord to the doorway.

Fabian picked it up and stepped into the pilothouse. The light might have been used to pilot the ship. The shield would have directed illumination where it was needed while keeping ambient glow to a minimum. He hooked the lamp back on its stand, clicked it off and turned.

The rifle butt hit him on the side of the head, but he was lucky. It had been directed between his eyes. He went down, but not out, and was firing the Colt before he hit the floor. The percussion of his shots combined with his muzzle flashes deafened and blinded him, but he was already rolling away when an automatic rifle burst tore through the small room with unimaginable fury.

Fabian crouched against an equipment locker, trying to will his eyes to see through the continuing torrent of white smoke and orange flame. He finally realized that the shooter was already dead, his finger frozen on the trigger. Moments later, the clip ran dry, and the man pitched forward, hitting the wheel with his face on the way down.

The sentry was a Japanese enlisted man whose rank had been torn from his uniform. Fabian guessed he was a criminal reprieved from the stockade and hauled out to the ship to keep the locals away. The mystery of the light solved, Fabian needed to find the radio room, but the blow to his head had staggered him. The shooting might have also been heard ashore.

With blood dripping from his temple, he woozily made his way back to the main deck and stood for a long moment at the rail, recovering his equilibrium and watching for approaching boats. Minutes went by, but the music played on with no sign of an alarm. When he felt steady enough, he went back down the hull stairs and lowered the extension to the launch.

"What the fuck happened?" hissed Pags. Fabian ignored him, and shortly, one of the pilots, a Pittsburgher named Tully, joined him aboard. He examined Fabian's wound and pronounced it superficial. Unfortunately, the favorable diagnosis didn't lessen the ringing in his ears.

"We've got a bigger problem," said Tully. "One of the kids is only breathing about once every three tries."

* * *

The dead man had been bedding down in the executive of-ficer's quarters. He had ample rations and several bottles of sake, which indicated he wasn't due to be relieved anytime soon. His thoughtful superiors had also provided him with a comfort woman—an emaciated, nineteen-year-old Chinese girl named Luli who spoke terrified but excellent English.

After Fabian and Tully convinced her they weren't going to kill her, she led them to the infirmary. Two more pilots then came aboard with the infant in extremis*—Zhang's son. One hooked up an oxygen tank, and the other used scissors and tape to rig a mask to fit him. It was still too large, but they took turns holding it in place.*

Luli told Fabian the dead man was Cpl. Hiroki Sato, and he'd already been aboard when she'd arrived two days ear-lier. She'd been taken at gunpoint from her brothel and put on a Japanese vessel bringing cargo to the Tango.

"What kind of cargo?"

"I don't know. Boxes. Big ones. With Emperor Hirohito's seal on them."

"How do you know?"

"Before they were executed, my parents worked for the Brit-ish trade office. Japanese companies use two seals. One for commercial goods, like silk and rice, and the royal one for dip-lomatic and banking consignments. I saw both many times."

Even with a deck of expensive automobiles, the lone sentry had seemed wrong. If somebody actually thought some poor-ass Hong Kong fishermen were a threat to their Christmas presents, there would have been more security—a lot more. And why a comfort woman? Japanese command-ers didn't worry about the sexual urges of busted corporals. That is, unless his commander needed to be sure this par-ticular corporal remained in place. Finally, there were the functioning engines. Since the deck space was filled, the Tango *was probably going to be sailing soon . . . very soon.*

"I want to see those boxes," said Fabian, "but first, a radio."

Unfortunately, the communications room had been

stripped clean. But where the Japanese had taketh, they had also lefteth. On their way across the deck, Luli pulled back a tarp and showed Fabian a banged-up PT boat, apparently headed home for repair. "I tried to convince Hiroki that we could run, but all he wanted to do was drink sake and pass out on top of me."

Fabian examined the PT as carefully as he could in the dark and found machine gun holes above the waterline, a caved-in port torpedo tube and a slightly bent port screw. Nothing, however, that would interfere with seaworthiness. Climbing aboard, he primed the three Packard V-12s, crossed his fingers and hit the sequential starter. Vroooom! Vroooom! And Vroooom! The fuel gauge jumped to three-quarters. To quote Pags, Fuckin'-A. He quickly shut everything down.

The PT would hold everyone, but handling the sick baby's oxygen tank at speed was going to be difficult if not impossible. But it wasn't just the oxygen. The child needed a hospital—and fast. Fabian could pretend things might work out if they could get him back to the Bay, but in his heart of hearts, he knew that by the time they arrived, the kid would be just as dead as if they threw him in the river. He had a tough decision to make, but he didn't want to think about it yet.

As he climbed out of the PT, he said to Luli, "Okay, show me the boxes, then tell Tully to figure out a way to get this thing in the water."

The forward hold was the deepest part of the ship, and he entered through a narrow emergency hatch that barely accommodated his shoulders. Immediately, the odor of gasoline wafted over him, which was disconcerting but made sense. At this point, gas was harder to come by than whiskey and ten times more expensive. If you were stealing wheeled transportation you were going to have to run it on something.

As Fabian descended the rungs into the seemingly bottomless chasm, he heard rats bruxing below. Rumor had it that you hadn't really seen a rat until you'd seen a Chinese one. He resisted the urge to use the flashlight clipped to his belt for a preview and hoped these were just hitchhikers from San Fran.

When he felt the steel floor under his feet, he glanced up. A few stars were visible through the tiny aperture above, but their piece of sky seemed a long way off. The gas smell was stronger here too, nauseatingly so. It was going to have to be a quick trip.

He hit the switch on his flashlight and let the beam wander. Luli had said "boxes." In a literal sense, she was right, but these were finely engineered black steel cases the length of coffins. And the Emperor's seal wasn't wax or ink, but a dinner-plate-sized circle of gold inlaid into each one's top.

As he made his way among them, Fabian counted. Thirty-one, each on its own wooden skid and braced against shifting at sea with thick pine slats. He ran his fingers along one's seam. It had been fitted so tightly that he could barely feel where the metal came together. There was no latch, and the lid was immovable. He kicked a row of slats away and tried to push it, but it wouldn't budge.

He slid his knife out of its sheath and wedged it into the seam. He had to do it in several places, but pretty soon, there was a rush of air, and the lid gave. It took his full strength to lift it back.

War annuls subtlety. Everything moves too fast or doesn't seem to move at all. Colors disappear or are unpleasantly vivid; sounds are uncomfortably loud. Its partner victims are personal intimacy and private reflection—the building blocks of beauty. In another time, Fabian would have had words for what lay before him. At that moment, six hundred pounds of dead, white Siberian tiger didn't bring any to mind.

A voice interrupted his thoughts. "Jesus Christ, what's that?"

Fabian turned and saw Tully halfway down the ladder. He didn't think it was a question that needed an answer, so he closed the lid. "How's the PT coming?" he asked.

"Once we made space to move some of those goddamn

cars, no problem. The rack was on rollers. Good thing too; son of a bitch must weigh ten tons."

"More like forty."

"Either way, it's gonna make a helluva racket when it hits. Boy, how you standin' that smell?" Tully aimed his flashlight into the far reaches of the hold. "No wonder."

Fabian looked where the beam lingered. Apparently, sealed barrels were as hard to come by as gas. The Japanese had filled anything they could get their hands on—buckets, watering cans, flour barrels, empty bottles—and capped them with rags or ill-fitting pieces of wood.

"How much muscle do you need to finish?" Fabian asked.

"Way it's sitting now, Luli could do it."

"Then get everybody but the sick kid in the launch, pronto. And tell Pags to keep it on the side away from the PT. I don't want the damn thing falling on anybody."

"Will do."

As Tully disappeared up, Fabian took one last look around. Then, on an impulse, he lifted the lid on the case again. Delicately, he cut off one of the big cat's whiskers and carefully folded it into his handkerchief, which he buttoned into his shirt pocket. He wanted to remember, and something told him that, a few years from now, this kind of ugliness might not seem real.

Up top, the wind had picked up, and he could see white-caps forming. Tully came across the deck holding on to his hat. "Everybody's in the launch except Luli. She's with the kid and willing to stay. What do you want to do?"

"Put them in the boat too."

"You sure?"

"No, I'm not sure, but I'm not leaving anybody."

Pags brought the launch around to the *Tango's* bow but was careful not to drift beyond the protection of her starboard side. The water had become much rougher, and his passengers had to make weight adjustments to keep the small craft from tipping.

Fabian watched from deck, and when Pags was in place, he moved quickly back to the hatch leading to the hold. He jerked the tarp off a '32 Pierce Arrow, crouched behind it and rammed the tip of his knife upward into the gas tank. Liquid immediately began dripping onto his wrist. He shifted position and jabbed the knife into the tank again, only this time above where he estimated the fuel level would be. With the change in pressure, the drip became a stream that ran rapidly along the deck toward the hold.

Fabian kicked away pieces of the raised edge of the hatch and watched the gas flow over the lip and into the darkness below. He then opened the Pierce's front door and scooped a handful of liquid onto the front seat. For a moment, he was concerned the wind would blow out his Zippo, but just like the ads, it stayed lit. Seconds later, the interior of the car was on fire.

The PT rocked precariously halfway over the bow rail, her nose rising and falling with the chop. Tully's crew had used a block and tackle to get it that far, then chocked the rack and tied everything off with two thick lines affixed to her stern. The ropes, however, were overmatched and could go at any time.

In the increasingly rough water, the PT was backing up an inch each time the Tango seesawed, and the last thing Fabian could afford was to cut it loose and have it slide backward. He found an eight-foot length of steel bar and shoved it under the boat rack, then pulled it tight over a cleat. It wouldn't hold long, but for the moment, the PT was locked in place. He took a deep breath and cut both ropes with his knife.

Forty tons of mahogany and metal suddenly danced free, pitched up and down a couple of times, then shifted sideways, seemingly trying to walk the rail. Its tension gone, the steel bar dislodged and windmilled at Fabian, head high. He dove away just in time, and the bar hit the starboard rail and clattered along the deck.

With a final loud, scraping sound, the PT pivoted 180 degrees and slid transom first over the side. Fabian got there in time to see a thundering splash and watch it disappear beneath the swells. A moment later, it exploded back to the surface. He leaped onto the rail, gauged the drift and went after it.

Fabian collided with the water at an awkward angle and momentarily lost his breath. While he spit foam and coughed, he found one of the securing ropes and began pulling himself toward the PT. By the time he had the engines started, Pags was already alongside, and people were climbing aboard.

Fabian brought the PT around in a tight arc, but instead of heading toward open water, he aimed the prow directly at the harbor, the three Packards wide open. Pags screamed something unintelligible, but he ignored him. A few minutes later, he throttled back as a large, dark houseboat loomed ahead. Wheeling the PT into a sideways drift, he brought it to a stop almost against the stationary boat's side, his wake rocking the houseboat violently. Lights came on, and a family of Chinese scrambled out.

Fabian yelled, "Hand them the boy!"

The pilot holding the kid froze, but Luli understood. She took the infant from him and reached up. At first, no one on the houseboat reacted. Then Luli shouted something in Chinese, and an older woman stepped forward hesitantly and took the bundle. Fabian jammed the throttles forward and whipped the wheel hard.

The Tango was well aflame, and even from his water-level vantage point, Fabian could see orange plumes shooting from the area where the open hatch would be. It wouldn't be long before the first explosion.

Over the thundering Packards, he heard sirens onshore. As they roared toward the mouth of the river, the first rays of sunlight slashed across the horizon. It was going to be a short ride into an even shorter morning.

17

Air-Conditioning and Martinis

The Cathedral of the Testaments sat at the edge of an empty parking lot half the size of the Rose Bowl. The JCPenney signage over the front door was gone, replaced by an immense marquee flanked on either side by a ten-foot crown of thorns and an even larger Bible, open to the Book of Revelation. And in black, grand-opening-size lettering was the always intriguing

WHERE WERE YOU THE NIGHT JESUS DIED?

"Don't you just love a soft sell?" asked Birdy.

Three cars were nosed into the curb in a no-parking zone inches from the front door. Ten yards farther down, a yellow Mercedes 500 with a wheelchair rack was half-in, half-out of a handicapped space.

Birdy looked at the Mercedes. "Wouldn't it have been closer . . . Oh, never mind."

It was interesting, but some people instinctively follow the rules. I took his lead and parked the Ram in a designated slot. The air was oven-hot, and a waft of thick breeze kicked a handful of brown grit against my face, a brick of which took out my left eye. Ah, the desert.

Inside, it was just north of an Antarctic winter. "Jesus Christ," said Birdy, "you see a box of mittens? Oops, sorry, Jesus."

You had to wonder what it was costing to keep the place this cold. "I think even He would have asked them to back off the A/C. I've got a jacket in the car."

"I'll just pretend I'm in Chicago."

With the heavily tinted front windows and only a few tiny ceiling lights, the place was in twilight. We were in a spacious, carpeted outer lobby, which, if my catechism memory could be trusted, was called the narthex. I didn't know if that term applied to a place that began life selling Big Mac jeans, but probably.

Running along the left wall was a long, glass trophy case filled with softball, basketball and bowling statuettes next to a number of community service plaques. Above the case were five rows of nicely framed candid photographs showing parishioners doing various church work. At least a third were Asian—I was betting Chinese—and some of those, plus a few others, wore the uniforms of various police departments, mostly LAPD. The officers ranged in rank from patrolman to commander and included two female captains, both Caucasian. I looked for Chuck and Lucille or Wes Crowe, but didn't find them. Maxine Crowe, however, beamed out at me, wearing an apron and showing off a plate of brownies.

One row of pictures was entirely Asian children wearing Santa hats, smiling at the camera like kids always do. I put most of them between four and twelve. An interesting grouping, obviously special for some reason.

Just beyond the trophy case was a narrow offering table under a much larger and expensively framed black-and-white photograph. It had been taken decades ago, and it portrayed a tall, chiseled-jawed man holding the reins of a white horse while a group of ragged Asian children huddled around him and smiled into the lens. Three more children sat on the horse's broad back, and a fourth stood under its neck, her small hand caressing the animal's cheek. An engraved brass plate beneath the picture read

> During the evening of December 6, 1941,
> Riverside CHP officer "Big Jim" Rackmann—
> a man who had not set foot inside a house
> of worship in twenty years—had a vision:
> It told him to go to China.
> The next day, Pearl Harbor was attacked.
> But Big Jim never wavered.
> Because of his faith and commitment, our church exists.
> Please help continue his mission.

The offering basket was labeled THE RACKMANN PROJECT and was flanked by a stack of pledge envelopes and box of new Bibles. I put twenty dollars in the basket.

"Guilty conscience?" asked Birdy.

"I wish it were limited to my conscience."

I steered her in the direction of a wall of red fire doors and pushed one open. It wasn't much lighter inside but enough to see that what had once been an acre of lingerie and lawn mowers was now an ocean of expensive, powder blue theatre seats. And to give the acoustics an obligatory reverential hush, the walls were draped in museum-sized blue and gold-bordered tapestries depicting scenes from the Gospels. I wasn't an expert on fabric and embroidery, but these had cost thousands, so unless, Penney's had left a full safe behind, this was not a cut-rate congregation.

"Snazzy," said Birdy. "The church I grew up in didn't have a single hymnal with all its pages. When we lifted our voices in song, the angels really had their hands full. How about you?"

"The angels had their hands full for other reasons."

Suddenly, there was movement far to the front. A woman had apparently been kneeling, and now she stood. In the half-light and at that distance, I couldn't see her features clearly, but she was slender with streaked hair. She glanced once in our direction, then walked quickly toward an exit sign and disappeared into the dark.

"I think we interrupted someone," said Birdy.

On the far side of the chancel was a lighted hallway. I guided Birdy toward it, but before we got there, a heavyset man appeared, opened his arms and smiled broadly, "Welcome."

For twenty years, Victor Buono gave us some of the best villains ever put on film. Every veteran writer in Hollywood misses him, because if you were too hung over to write the day's scene, all you had to do was type BUONO ENTERS, and crawl back to the couch.

The Reverend Cabot Northcutt could have been Victor's larger twin, and considering that Victor's poundage probably began with a four, that made Northcutt a very large man indeed. He also had Victor's wistful smile, giving him an air of accessibility that probably served him well in his profession. We introduced ourselves, and the reverend led us down the hallway to a nicely furnished office, where a bank of security monitors answered the question of how he had known we were there. He took a seat at his desk and beckoned us to chairs opposite.

"Normally, the doors would be locked, but this is marriage-counseling day."

"We'll be respectful of your time."

He raised his hand. "No rush. The couple I was expecting went to court this morning instead. Probably best for all concerned."

"Boy, there's a switch," said Birdy. "Where were you guys when my mom was getting smacked around?"

"Our founder believed that if you spent your life angry, you weren't doing God or anybody else any favors."

"That would be Big Jim Rackmann?"

He pointed to an oil painting on the wall. In it, Rackmann stood next to a lovely Eurasian lady, well dressed but decades younger. "It would. A beautiful human being. Salty, but beautiful."

"Sounds wise too," I said.

"Sounds like a goddamn saint," blurted Birdy. "Oops, did it again. Sorry."

"I think the walls will remain standing." He smiled.

I nodded at the painting again. "Is that Mrs. Rackmann?"

"It is. The second. Big Jim and his first wife divorced in 1939. When he became a missionary." A smile creased his cheeks as he added, "He met Oona in Hong Kong. After the war. It was a real love match."

"Judging from that, she would have been quite young."

"Twenty-three, but she'd seen more than most of us see in a lifetime. Her mother was Irish, and you may have read how mixed children were treated."

I had. There are no parallels for living through war, and you can double the suffering if you were a citizen of an occupied country. You can double it again if the Japanese were the occupiers. "Is she still living?" I asked.

He shook his head. "Breast cancer. Several years before Big Jim. He kept smiling, but he was ready to go the day she did."

I let my eyes wander over the accumulated keepsakes of Cabot Northcutt. You can learn more about a man from his office than his home. It's always the first place a professional manhunter wants to see. Women are different. Their offices are usually devoid of sentimental possessions. You want to see their purses and closets.

Floor-to-ceiling bookcases took up two walls, their shelves straining to contain mounds of magazines alongside well-worn volumes of history, philosophy and a row of motion picture bios. Squeezed into what space remained were personal photographs and some eclectic pieces of decorative statuary—no tigers.

A man's most prized possessions will usually be the ones physically closest to him, so I was amused to see a collection of martini shakers on the credenza immediately behind his desk. When he noticed me eyeing them, he grinned. "Not quite what you'd expect from a preacher-man." He swiveled, reached out a meaty hand and grabbed a well-polished cylinder engraved with a vaguely familiar, stylized S. When he handed it to me, I could tell from its weight that it was Sterling.

Northcutt leaned forward conspiratorially, eyes alive. "Friday, November 19, 1954. Dawn. Caddie convertible, flying low out of Vegas. Sammy Davis, Jr. heading to a recording session in LA No freeway in those days, just two lanes of blacktop with a bend every now and then. Sammy's tired, but he's made this run before. Problem is, the sun's coming up, and out here, that's like having a flare stuck on your dash.

"Just south of where we're sitting, seventy-two-year-old Helen Boss from Akron, Ohio, misses her turn and does what you always do on a seventy-mile-per-hour highway, stops . . . and backs up. If Sammy saw her at all, it wasn't soon enough, and wham."

Like the professional speaker he was, Northcutt had gradually lowered his voice, and when he got to *wham,* he clapped his hands. Birdy jumped halfway out of her seat, and I could imagine what the reverend was capable of with God over his shoulder and an auditorium full of sinners.

He smiled and went on. "So they rush Sammy to San Berdoo. They get him stabilized, but his left eye isn't going to make it. This would be a big story anywhere, but in the middle of cactus nowhere, it's like *Close Encounters.* Pretty soon, there are gawkers coming from all directions.

"As Sammy's working his way to a full recovery, over the hill comes a line of limos. It's the Copa Girls from Vegas coming to cheer him up."

That's where I'd seen the S before. The Sands Hotel. "With refreshments, of course," I said.

"Four trunkloads. Liquid and cold."

"A few years later, I'm born. Same hospital. Premature and the tiniest kid anybody ever saw." He leaned back and patted his ample girth. "Hard to believe, huh? Spent half my life in the emergency room. My momma had to hold down two jobs to keep us going, so one of the nurses took it on herself to watch for me. Barbara Jacamino. Sammy's nurse. She brought me toys, sang to me, held me when I cried. I think she's the reason I never married. Couldn't find another Barbara.

"Sammy had given her that shaker, and until the day she died, she made herself a martini every night. When I got to high school, I'd go up to her place and have one with her. Child abuse today, probably."

"Death penalty, maybe. And Barbara left it to you."

"It was her most cherished possession. Mine too."

Birdy was mesmerized. "What an amazing story."

She was right. And like Manarca's Balboa saga, it didn't matter if it was true. It *could* be true. When the truth gets in the way of the legend, print the legend. I handed the shaker back, and Northcutt returned it to the credenza.

"How did you and Big Jim meet?"

"Jobs are scarce for new seminary grads, so I was keeping the wolf from the door as a prison chaplain. Terminal Island, mostly. That's where I met Big Jim. I worked the state system too, but it took forever to get your lousy forty bucks a visit. The Feds' checks were on time, so they got more religion."

"Even in the slammer, you get what you pay for. Why two chaplains at TI?"

"Oh, Big Jim wasn't working. He was visiting somebody. Next thing I knew, he was ministering to me too. He had that kind of magnetism. Changed my life, just like he did lot of people's. That's how I ended up here."

"Any chance you remember who he was visiting?"

"Absolutely. Markus Kingdom, a young Pan Am exec doing a year and a day on some kind of white-collar beef. After he got out, he moved to Victorville, settled down, and became one of our most loyal congregants. I'm proud to say I baptized all five of his daughters."

Markus Kingdom? He had my full attention. "He still around."

"Around? My goodness, yes. Markus runs a highly successful business. Kingdom Starr. Do you know it?"

I knew it very well, but I was curious what the local line was. "Something to do with ships, isn't it?"

"A little more than that." Northcutt was on familiar ground—educating the slow afoot. "You can't move much in this world that doesn't touch a Kingdom Starr ship, plane or terminal. They've also got cruise ships, hotels and food service. Markus even has a division called KS High-Value that specializes in transporting racehorses, museum exhibits . . . things like that."

"Now I know who to call when it's time to move my Shamu collection. I presume he's security conscious as well."

Northcutt grinned like a man showing off his firstborn. "You better believe it. Any problem in the empire, and their police force, KSD—Kingdom Starr Defense—steps in. Not people you want to trifle with."

He leaned forward again, like he was about to reveal a state secret. "Recently, Markus has been on a tear buying railroads from the Japanese occupation of the Far East. Remember *The Bridge on the River Kwai*? Believe it or not, that line's still out there. Lots of others too. Sort of the final frontier of freight."

What the reverend didn't know, and I didn't tell him, was that Kingdom Starr had been good friends to Delta, the SEALs—all of special ops. Like the Hughes Corporation some decades earlier, more than one narrow escape out of a hot zone had rendezvoused with a Kingdom asset that "just happened" to be in the vicinity. The CIA also used Markus to ferry gunboats, aircraft and weapons to insurgents and to occasionally make clandestine personnel drops.

My London company, Black Group, competes with Kingdom Starr in some commercial ventures, but despite my past associations, I don't encourage my executives to get into black ops. That has to be a commitment from the people on the corporate firing line, and I only oversee the place from eight thousand miles away. Markus Kingdom and I had never met, but we knew many of the same people.

"I thought Kingdom Starr was based in Singapore."

"For everything but air services. Markus has built his own city at the old George Air Force Base. At any given time, he's got twenty jumbos loading or unloading out there. Hard to beat 360 days of sunshine and a pool of employees that would march into hell for the man."

Not to mention the pool of available cops. KSD has always recruited out of the best commando units and SWAT teams. It wasn't difficult to convince a special operator to trade in his salute for a six-figure income. And Kingdom Starr outpaid everyone.

Northcutt leaned back in his chair, his fingers pressed into a church. "Yes, sir, Mr. Black, Markus Kingdom's been very good to Victorville."

"And the church." It wasn't a question.

"Yes, but StarrLynn has a lot to do with that. She's also where the other half of the company name comes from."

"I assume that's Mrs. Kingdom."

The reverend nodded. "The former StarrLynn Crowe. Sister of our chief of detectives. Never know it to look at the two of them, though. Wes's daddy married himself a cute redhead and got that pretty little girl in the deal."

Bingo. Like small towns everywhere. Walk a block, meet a relative. Walk ten, have a reunion. "I understand there's another brother. Sells ice cream."

"Soft serve, not ice cream. I'm a Häagen-Dazs man myself. That's Melvin, but he goes by Cheater. Great big guy with a chopper as long as my Lincoln. Ink everywhere. The usual, skulls, swastikas, that kind of nonsense. Makes sure everybody sees them. Never wears a shirt, just a black leather vest. No helmet when he rides either, and he's got a real short fuse. Cops gave up ticketing him."

From the description, they wouldn't have to worry about Melvin's fuse anymore. Cheater Crowe was fertilizing

Chuck Brando's woods. "Melvin come in the package with StarrLynn?"

"No, Cheater's Chinese. Just showed up one day last year, and Wes started introducing him around town as his brother. Nobody knows where he's from. Worked as a loader out at Kingdom Starr for a while, but I heard he got fired for busting somebody up. That's when he took out the lease on the Desert Freeze stand. Pretty much all I know. He's not much of a churchgoer."

"Markus and StarrLynn live here too?"

"Real fancy place up in the mountains. Near Wes."

Northcutt's tone suddenly changed. "I sure like talking to you fine folks, but you're not here for town gossip or because I had a hole in my counseling schedule."

I waited a moment, then watched him closely as I said, "I'd like to ask about Chuck and Lucille Brando."

His eyelids fluttered only once, but it was enough. He knew they were dead. Wes Crowe had obviously been working the phones. "Great people," he said as noncommittally as he could manage, but he didn't quite bring it off.

The reverend was also one of those people who, no matter what script he'd been given, was going to ham it up as long as the footlights were on. Wes had to know that too, so maybe he'd just decided he'd handle damage control later. Cops make their living on the type, so they know how to handle them.

"I'm in charge of the estate," I said.

I don't care what deity you kneel to, a guy with a checkbook goes to the head of the line. Cabot Northcutt was no different. He skipped right past feigned surprise and forced condolences and went straight to: "The Brandos told me many times they wanted to remember the church." He tried hard to keep the excitement out of his voice, but as good a storyteller as he was, he was on the other end of the acting scale. Birdy had no idea what was going on, but you didn't have to be overly savvy to notice the change in the room. We'd become royalty.

"Can I offer you something to drink?" Northcutt asked with new oiliness to his voice. "We've got some delicious bottled lemonade made by one of our members. He markets it to gourmet shops all the way to New York."

"No thanks," I said, and Birdy shook her head.

"How long has Big Jim been dead?" I asked.

Once again, his eyelids fluttered, only this time like butterfly wings. He recovered quickly. "Little over two years now. Made it to 103. Came every Sunday and gave me notes on the sermon. Good ones, too."

"Somehow an offering basket and a box of Bibles don't seem like much of a tribute to the man who created all this."

Cabot Northcutt was a polished speaker and probably a good marriage counselor. The essence of both is to never hesitate. This time, his mouth opened, and no words came out. He closed it and tried again, but all he found was, "Well, there's a plaque on the pulpit too. Real nice. Eighteen-karat gold."

"Let's cut the crap, Reverend. Did Wes Crowe happen to mention that the FBI has their panties in a bunch because they can't figure out what's going on in your fair city? If I'm here, they're not far behind. You dance them, and your next visitor is going to be an IRS task force. There was a woman in that house when the Brandos were killed. She was lucky, she got out. I want to know her name, and where she is now."

He looked like I'd thrown his Sammy shaker under the 6:10 to Poughkeepsie. "I don't know what you're talking about," he squeaked. "Honest to God, I don't. Wes said Chuck and Lucille were a murder-suicide, and until they had it sorted out, they needed to keep it quiet."

Murder-suicide! This had LAPD written all over it. What was it Dion had said? *If Maywood's involved, somebody's gonna get it in the ass.* Well, whose ass was more convenient than the dead guy's.

"So what happened? Lucille overcooked the pancakes, and Chuck said, 'The cunt's gotta go'?"

It was crude, but the reverend knew he'd fucked up, and I

wanted to keep the panic on high. I saw sweat stains come through his big and tall suit coat. He stammered a couple of times, then managed, "He sort of intimated it might have had something to do with Lucille's being . . . how can I say this . . . ?"

"What? A tramp?"

"Oh, God, no. Oh, please don't tell anyone I said *that*. I just meant she might have had a boyfriend."

"And Wes intimated it was him."

He nodded.

The best lie is the one people already believe. I had to admit it was a smart way to handle a delicate problem, but I didn't have to pretend it was okay. Somebody, starting with that cocksucker Maywood, was going to answer to me for this.

I changed direction. "What exactly is the Rackmann Project?"

On familiar ground, though his voice was up an octave. "We provide Bibles to developing countries. Make the Lord's Word available to starving souls. We've placed over a million now. A couple of presidents have recognized us."

"Define *provide*."

Some of the beam went out of his baby blues. "I don't know what you mean."

"I'll make it easier. Name some 'developing countries.'"

He hesitated for a few seconds, then, "Korea . . ."

"North or South?"

"Both."

"Both? Really? How about Mexico?"

"We don't consider Mexico a developing country."

"And that would be because of what? Their space program?"

Despite the subzero temperature and the frequent wiping, beads of perspiration continued to form on his brow.

"Let's try another. Saudi Arabia."

"We might have sent some there."

"Sent how? Big crates for the heavy demand at the airport bookstore? Maybe a giveaway at a mall?"

His hands were trying to figure out something to do with themselves.

"One more. China."

"Are you an atheist?" he stammered, the warm façade completely gone.

"No, I'm as much in favor of the Bible as you are. If you want to parachute a few thousand into Darfur or hire the Hells Angels to pass them out in biker bars, I'll write you a check. And if you really want to change the world, how about handing one to every first-year law student?

"What I'm not in favor of are naïve, well-intentioned Americans smuggling banned books into dangerous places with no understanding of the risks. Missionaries make informed choices. A man who sends out a housewife with God in her heart and a false bottom in her suitcase is a reckless zealot—and a coward. And if something happens to her—like maybe a few days of riding a cattle prod or having her hand cut off—then he's also a criminal with no more respect for women than a Taliban mullah." I paused. "And Chuck and Lucille Brando thought so too, didn't they? They also thought you were putting the bigger enterprise in jeopardy."

The last part was a wild stab, but even if I was wrong, I had him running, and that's usually when you learn the most. He burst out of his chair so quickly it banged into the credenza and knocked over the row of martini shakers. I heard Birdy gasp in surprise. Cabot Northcutt was in a rage, and as he came around the desk, I thought at first he was charging me. Instead, he blew by and went to a small closet. He came back with an overflowing banker's box that he upended on the desk. Letters cascaded out, some falling to the floor.

Northcutt grabbed one at random, opened it and began to read, "You have changed my life." He threw it down and grabbed another, "May God bless you and your church." He was onto his third when I stood, reached out my arm and brushed the mountain of paper away, taking with it everything on the desk.

He stared at me with his mouth open. Sometimes being

as big as I am makes a point better than words, and I moved almost against him so he had to look up at me. I kept my voice very soft. "Fuck your letters, Reverend. Fuck the Rackmann Project. Fuck your church. And fuck you. People are dead. Friends of mine. And just maybe you had a hand in it."

Cabot Northcutt then did what I least expected. He started to sob, then fell back into this chair. "It's not because of the Bibles. It's because of the BABIES! Oh, God, I warned them. I WARNED them!"

18

Auctions and Clippers

Carroll Rackmann returned to the U.S. in 1956. He might, in fact, have been the last American missionary left in China. The rise of Mao had forced most to flee years earlier, while those who stayed faced torture—and worse—from roving bands of fanatical young Communists—many of whom had been students of their victims. Rackmann, who survived for a while under the protection of a local mayor, eventually escaped himself, just minutes ahead of an execution squad, by swimming a river, then walking six hundred miles to Vietnam.

But though he left Asia, he did not abandon it. Once home in California, he worked with charities to ease the plight of the hapless souls who were now caught in the grip of a madman intent on propelling the largest homogeneous population on earth back to the Stone Age. Eventually, though, as the Cold War became entrenched, and the memory of what China once had been faded, the romance faded as well, and money raced it to the door.

So Rackmann had gone to the desert. Victorville. A tiny hamlet selling gas and sandwiches to the impatient on their way to gamble and to the beaten on their way back. In those days, a commercial lot on the east side of Route 66 cost twice as much as the same-sized patch of dirt across the road on the theory that those heading to Las Vegas had more in their pockets than those returning.

The reverend began holding services in the common room of a fire station, where his personal Bible remained on display during the week to be touched by firemen on their way to a call. Those were the heady days of innocence before the ACLU enlightened Americans about how devastating casual exposure to the Ten Commandments can be.

His first parishioners were a handful of locals, and because the station was located east of the highway, they were sometimes joined by motorists hoping to ensure their luck at the tables. When the church's finances allowed, Rackmann bought as many used Bibles as he could and shipped them to a student who had fled to Taiwan. The student then smuggled them onto the mainland, where they anchored clandestine worship groups.

Rackmann rescued his first child in 1967, and what the event lacked in sophistication, it made up for in drama. Unremarked upon by the rest of the world, Mao's overt genocide against his enemies was in full, murderous swing. More sinister was the passive slaughter of millions from disease and malnutrition. And as always, children died first and most often—frequently killed by desperate parents trying to stave off starvation themselves.

Late one night, a Victorville ham operator, an ethnic Chinese named Walt Crowe, phoned Rackmann and implored him to come to his home. The reverend knew Crowe only slightly, but the urgency in the man's voice was palpable. When he arrived, he found Crowe talking on his radio with a fellow operator in Perth, Australia. Days earlier, a Chinese trawler filled with fleeing refugees had capsized in high seas. The survivors had been picked up by Javanese fishermen and taken to Surabaya. One was a young boy whose parents had perished and, according to the radio chatter, was being auctioned off by the now-shipless Chinese captain through the Surabaya dockmaster.

Though Crowe's parents had been émigrés from Shanghai, they had Americanized themselves completely, including their name. As a result, Walt didn't speak a word of the language. However, he remembered someone mentioning that Rackmann did. So with patchwork shortwave connection and volunteer translators stepping the conversation through several languages, Rackmann entered the bidding and bought the boy for two hundred dollars—twice what anyone else was offering.

The next day, he cabled half to the dockmaster and headed to the South Pacific. Meanwhile, Walt drove to the Los Angeles passport office and, lying through his teeth, convinced a clerk that his long-lost brother, Wes, had turned up in Java and needed an emergency visa to be reunited with the family. It was a preposterous story, but Walt, a bachelor, was afraid to say the boy was his son because he wouldn't be able to produce a wife or a birth certificate. Fortunately, the clerk never asked how old the brother was or requested any documentation, and a day behind the reverend, Walt was on a plane too.

And that is how Wes Crowe was saved from slavery and came to Victorville to be raised by his "brother." It is also how the Rackmann Project began.

Over the years, the Cathedral of the Testaments spirited more orphans out of misery and placed them with loving Chinese families as far away as New York, some of whom were childless, others who just wanted to play a small role in fighting an incomprehensible tragedy. It was remarkably easy. Immigration laws were not designed to snare small children, and as long as a U.S. citizen represented to authorities that the child was a member of his family, no one intruded.

But shortly after Cabot Northcutt had arrived at the cathedral and had not yet learned about the child-smuggling network, something had gone terribly wrong. A young family in San Francisco, who had recently taken in twins, was shot execution style in their car. And in a grisly bit of theatre, pledge envelopes for the Rackmann Project had been inserted into the children's mouths, a crisp hundred-dollar bill in each.

San Francisco investigators descended on Victorville, interviewing every member of the church and grilling Northcutt and Rackmann. But no one cooperated, and in a few weeks, the cops were gone. No charges were ever filed, but the incident shook Northcutt, and the questions he had been asked during his interrogation lifted the veil. He confronted Rackmann and demanded to know the full story.

But except for talking about Walt and Wes Crowe, Rackmann stonewalled him. There things lay until the old man died, and Northcutt assumed the pulpit. His first order of business was to call in the elders and tell them that the church was officially out of the baby business. And if that was a problem, he was going to call the SFPD and offer them every file, every canceled check, every scrap of paper that the church possessed and let the chips fall where they may. Then he walked out of the room.

A few days later, he found an unsigned note on his desk. All it said was, "It's done." The reverend wasn't naïve enough to think an operation that had been functioning that long had suddenly disappeared. But all he wanted was the cathedral out of it, and he believed he had accomplished that. Until Chuck and Lucille.

We left Northcutt weeping at this desk. Birdy made a final attempt to comfort him, but it was hopeless. Sometimes, the best thing is to let a person get it out of his system. Good intentions had become a dime dance to bad music, and even though it wasn't Northcutt's fault, I didn't care how he felt.

Before we left, I did manage to get out of him the name of the murdered family: Philip Chang, his wife, Wendy, and their two daughters. I now had a few answers but even more questions. Northcutt and I agreed on one thing, though: Chuck and Lucille hadn't died because of Bibles. But I didn't think they'd died because of babies either. Babies were the road marker, but the original Rackmann Project had begun before Chuck knew how to tie his shoes. How many children had been brought in over the years? Dozens? Hundreds? And if there had been an ongoing slaughter of innocents, it would have been evident long before the Chang murders. So why now?

I had a feeling that this was like everything else: find the money, find the prom. And it wasn't going to be in little envelopes in a church hallway. Chuck might have been a contributor, but he'd gone from cop to author, not to oilman.

Wes Crowe knew, of course, but he wasn't going to tell me. At least not voluntarily. He might or might not know what was in Lucille's monthly package to Perth, but I was willing to bet that somebody at Parkinson-Lowe Imports was into ham radio and knew Wes's call sign.

If the Brandos were running a way station for arriving Chinese infants, then based on the FedEx driver's unexpected encounters, the couriers were very attractive Caucasian women, one of whom had been there the night of the mayhem. Chuck had probably fought like a wild man to give her time to escape. I tried to construct a sequence of events, but I didn't have enough information.

Then there was the *Resurrection Bay II*. Three football fields of Bahamian-registered steel. Last known port, Tonga. A place where a few dollars in the right place could buy anything.

I was looking at the very bottom of the pyramid. It was wide, and it was impressive, and it didn't have a damn thing to do with churches, ministers and saving souls—maybe not even children. And somewhere, up where I couldn't see him yet, was the guy in charge. I was willing to bet it wasn't God.

We were back in the Ram before Birdy spoke. "That was the Brandos' house we were in, wasn't it?"

"Yes."

"I knew they were dead. The house felt like it. But I don't want to know how it happened."

"I'm sorry, I should have told you. Given you the option of staying or going."

"I'm only afraid of real things, not ghosts or superstitions. Besides, you weren't going to let anything happen to me."

I felt my jaw involuntarily tighten. I hadn't done so well with a couple of other women in my past.

"You're not with the police, so who are you?"

"A friend."

That seemed to be enough, so while she looked for a radio station she liked, I dialed Fat Cat Saleapaga.

"Hey, I was getting ready to call you." He sounded upbeat. "How's Dion?"

"Goin' home tomorrow, and he better. There's a couple of nurses here who want to strangle the little fucker."

"Tell them to be as rough as they can. It'll remind him to be more careful crossing streets."

Fat Cat laughed. "I managed a few calls on Maywood. Word is he's just punchin' the clock till he turns in his shield. In late, home early, bangin' the steakhouses for a final round of freebies. You want me to dig a little deeper?"

"Let it go for now. You know anybody in the Bay Area?"

"Got a cousin in the mayor's office. In charge of handin' out towing contracts. Would you believe a guy can knock down six figures in a bullshit job like that?"

"He have any pull with the cops?"

"In San Francorrupto? In the towin' business? Please."

"I'm interested in a dead Chinese family. Fifteen years back, give or take. Name of Chang. Two adults and a couple of babies."

"Gang shit?"

"Probably not. I want to talk to somebody who worked it. Find out what they didn't write down."

"I'll have him make the connection, then run up there myself."

"That's not necessary."

"It is if I'm gonna get laid by that sweet little singer in the Mark Hopkins lounge."

As I pulled out of the lot, I noticed that the yellow Mercedes with the wheelchair rack was gone.

The ride out to Kingdom Starr was a straight shot on a mostly deserted two-lane road. Eventually, the landscape was broken by the Victorville aircraft boneyard, where scores of discarded Lockheeds and Boeings sat at silent attention, their engines removed and their windows covered with foil.

Birdy was glued to her window. "That's really spooky."

"Some of them will end up back in service . . . in developing countries."

"That's even spookier."

Having once sat in a lawn chair nailed to a sheet of plywood aboard Air Vietnam, I couldn't have agreed more. Smart people, myself included, who'd walk twenty flights to avoid a noisy elevator, routinely march out to jets piloted by guys who barely speak English and maintained by crews who don't know a wrench from a can of tuna. When it comes to flying, we are a compliant herd.

Back in the good old days of the Cold War, an occasional wiseass F-16 jock would descend over the Mojave to telephone-pole height, then drop the hammer. As he streaked across the desert floor, his wake would cyclone behind him, slinging rocks at bullet speed and uprooting cactus. The purpose of this unauthorized exercise was to cross the I-15, afterburners flaming, and give earth-tethered civilians a close-up of their tax dollars at work . . . not to mention a scare that would last a lifetime. Pilots who were truly pure of heart—meaning the craziest motherfuckers—liked to do it at night.

It's called flathatting, and if you got caught, your career was over. At least that was what was supposed to happen. Usually, though, you got a profanity-laced, eye-bulging lecture from your commander—no paper trial—and you didn't do it again. At least until your next posting. The air force didn't invest several million dollars in your talented ass to cashier it for a wild hair.

I saw the plume of dust and the silver dot just above the desert floor ten miles before it got to us. Only it wasn't an F-16. This was something the size of a DC-10, delta-winged and dead quiet. When it passed in front of my windshield, I could see lettering on its belly, but it was gone before I could make it out. Then the buffeting almost rolled us over.

Birdy sat and stared with her mouth open. "What in the world was that?"

"I have no idea, but it's nice to know the politicians haven't won yet."

The desert is still where our most secret military hardware is born and nurtured, but increasingly, it's also where a growing nation is doing business. Just outside Victorville, governments, banks and businesses have joined to invest billions in the Southern California Logistics Airport. When finished, it will be an air and rail cargo colossus more modern than any in the world. It's a brilliant idea, and how it got done in this state can only be explained by the high desert's lacking enough votes to attract our dim bulbs in Washington. That, and it's difficult to make a good impression on CNN with grit blowing in your face and your five-hundred-dollar haircut standing straight up.

The Kingdom Starr complex was several miles past the main hub of the old airbase and connected to its northern reaches by a maze of newly laid taxiway. Everything was enclosed by a fifteen-foot chain-link fence topped with razor wire, which seemed more appropriate for hardened cons than rogue prairie dogs. Kingdom Starr was its own city, which I guesstimated was something on the order of ten square miles.

A mile from the gatehouse, the road rose slightly, allowing me enough of an overview to count seventeen one-story buildings, the smallest the size of a supermarket. Another dozen taller structures with slightly rounded roofs stood to the rear, probably hangars. It reminded me of a motion picture studio except that it was too far from Nobu.

Northcutt had underreported the 747s in residence. Fifteen were in line on the taxiway heading out to take off, and roughly twice that number sat on designated aprons being loaded by conveyors and refueled by service crews. The aircraft were immaculate, shiny aluminum set off by snow-white tails emblazoned with a large, five-point, cerulean blue star. Inside the star and slightly off center right, was a delicate white script

Kingdom Starr

Allowing for planes in the hangars undergoing maintenance and others airborne or on the ground around the world, Markus Kingdom's business had grown considerably since my days in the army. I remembered hearing that a good operator never has more than 10 percent of his fleet out of the earning stream, so they were running at least hundred aircraft. And if Markus was as sharp as I expected, probably double that.

"I like his logo," Birdy said, "but what's Trippe?" She pronounced it Trippy.

I looked where she was pointing. The lead 747 was just making the turn onto the runway. Under the pilot's window was stenciled

Kingdom of Trippe

"It's a person, and the 'e' is silent. Markus is apparently honoring his old boss, Juan Trippe, the visionary behind Pan American. The best airline that ever flew. We can also thank Juan for the 747. He challenged Boeing to design it, then ordered twenty-five without even telling his board."

"Ballsy."

"It's what we're losing in this country. My father called it the Three C's. Conceit, commitment and courage. The conceit to believe your vision is the right one; the commitment to drive everyone toward it; and the courage run over anybody who gets in your way. We've gone from men like that to having our best and brightest hunched over a computer stealing music."

"Then the best of those become lawyers."

"I sense a scar."

"When it gets to be a scar, I'll give you a call. Right now, I'm just trying to keep the scab on. You're not a big fan of teamwork, I see."

"For execution of a plan, yes. But breakthroughs don't happen that way. Force a dreamer into a partnership, and you kill the dream. What if you had to win a vote every time you worked out a horse?"

"It would confuse the horse and eventually ruin him."

"Exactly what happens with ideas. Show me a teacher who forces her brilliant students to work with lesser lights, and I'll show you a socialist. The gray people will do anything to tamp down excellence because it might take a direction they can't control."

"I never thought about it before, but you're exactly right." She began reading the names of some of the other planes in line. "Kingdom of Paris, Kingdom of Madagascar. So what's that all about?"

"More Pan Am. Mr. Trippe designated his flagship aircraft as Clippers. Clipper Midnight Sun . . . Clipper Pacific Trader. When you boarded one, you became royalty."

"Oh, my God, I just remembered the nose of that plane at Lockerbie. Clipper Maid of the Seas. How dreadfully sad."

"No, sad is for accidents. That was terrorism. Fuck The Hague and European justice. Two hundred and seventy innocent people *and* a company died that night."

Birdy looked at me. "You're one of the most thoughtful people I've ever met—not to mention opinionated."

"There were lots of books in the library at home. But I didn't get to all of them. Eventually, I'll disappoint you."

"And I'll be sure to point it out when you do." She smiled. "I wonder why Mr. Kingdom went to prison."

I did too.

* * *

The wide, spacious entrance to Kingdom Starr was configured around a horseshoe-shaped park, complete with wooden benches and picnic tables shaded by wide palms. Surrounded by so much brown, its lush green was jarring, but it looked more like a movie set than something in regular use.

Fifty yards in, two art deco guard booths flanked a black steel rolling gate. Next to one booth were several white-lined parking spaces, empty except for a lone black Denali with smoked glass. I slowed and turned into the drive. As I passed the Denali, I noticed its plate. KS-771. Interesting car, interesting prefix.

The booth windows were mirrored, most likely to mitigate the hot afternoon sun. It also left you to guess whether you were approaching a retired crossing guard or a squad of Rangers. As it turned out, it was neither. I should have anticipated Northcutt would have called ahead.

A narrow-faced man in his fifties sporting a pencil-thin moustache and a knockoff Armani slid open the guardhouse door and smiled an ex-cop smile. "Good afternoon, Mr. Black. What can I do for you?" His suit jacket was unbuttoned, and he put his hands on his hips so I wouldn't miss the shoulder holster.

I tried to look past him to see if he was alone, but his wide stance blocked my view. "I'm sorry, I didn't catch your name, Sergeant," I said.

He gave me the dead eyes and half smirk that all too often come prepackaged with years of badge-lugging. "It was lieutenant, but we won't be spending enough time together that we need to get acquainted. As I was saying, what can I do for you?"

Sometimes it pays to be composed, and sometimes it's interesting to ruffle a feather or two. I jerked my head in Birdy's direction. "This is Captain Nash, LAPD Internal Affairs. She's here to search your car."

Spit flew out of his mouth. "What the fuck for?"

So much for Jack Webb cool. "It was seen fleeing the

scene of an assault on a police officer. When the reverend remembered you folks have a KS on your plates."

"Goddamn that fat fuck! He didn't say anything about . . ." I watched him as he finally arrived at the party. His eyes went from dead to red. "Lotta assholes who thought they were funny don't laugh at nothing no more."

"Impressive command of the language. I'm betting Markie doesn't invite you to the club."

He'd laced himself back up, "Fuck you, Black. And it's Mr. Kingdom to you. You drove all the way out here for squat. Your dago friend was only supposed to get stuck a little and told to mind his own business. The cutter got a little carried away and got his knuckles rapped. Dion's in the loop now. He'll probably find a little something extra in his Christmas stocking."

"If I were you, I'd still sleep with an eye open for a while," I said.

"What for? Fat Cat? Don't make me laugh. That fuckin' kabong's still trying to figure out toilet paper. We're through here, asshole. Mr. Kingdom's out of the country, so you and whoever the cunt is can turn around and head back to Beverly Hills."

Birdy didn't much like the sound of that and let loose with a, "Motherfucker."

Now that we all had names, I said, "Know where I can find Melvin Crowe."

It took him a second. "If you mean Cheater, word is he split for the coast. Probably a good idea. Sooner or later, somebody was gonna put a full clip in that Chink."

"Hard to believe. A guy like that and a detective for a brother."

"What makes you so sure they're all that different?"

It looked like this guy and Wes didn't spend quality time. "You the one Cheater roughed up out here?"

He scoffed. "I can only fuckin' wish he comes at me."

"When Kingdom gets back, tell him there were a couple

of extra bodies at the Brando place." I paused. "And they're still there."

I saw him run through a mental checklist before he answered. "I got no idea what you're talking about, but so fuckin' what?"

When there's a corpse involved, you don't ask questions, you get as far from it as possible. Unless, of course, you're wondering if it can be connected to you—or, in this case, somebody you work for. "Because I'm pretty sure one is going to have his brother-in-law's DNA on it?"

"Cheater's?"

"Maybe, but I'm betting Wes."

"You said two bodies."

"I did. And the second is even better. I won't spoil the surprise."

As Lieutenant Armani started to say something, I hit my window button and cut him off. I put the Ram in reverse and backed up.

The lieutenant stepped out of the booth and followed me, shouting something that sounded like, "Come back here, cocksucker."

19

Japanese Mountains and a Tiny Dancer

The Resurrection Bay *was a small speck in a big ocean. For the last twenty minutes, Fabian had been checking his watch with increasing unease. They were half an hour outside their window, and he knew he had no right to expect to see the carrier. But suddenly, there she was. Now, no one aboard the PT would know that he would have taken them back to Hong Kong. It wasn't a decision he would have made for himself, but he didn't have the right to condemn everyone else to a watery grave.*

They had left the flare gun with Big Jim, but Fabian had stood watch on that bridge countless times. Somebody could see them; they just needed to be looking.

They were.

It took less than twenty minutes to winch the weakened pilots onto the third deck of the Bay. *The baby had gone up in the first sling, cradled by Luli. The ship's medical staff was waiting, but the pilots wouldn't talk to them until they were satisfied that the kid was taken care of. Fabian sent Pags up, then caught the sling two seamen threw to him.*

As he climbed into it and gave a thumbs-up, he glanced back at the PT and, for the first time, realized there were ten inches of water covering its floorboards. He looked at his feet. His uniform had mostly dried, but he was soaking wet below the knees and couldn't feel his toes. Whatever debriefing was coming, it was going to have to wait for the longest, hottest shower anybody'd ever taken.

The first low rumble reached him just as he came even with the deck. Nobody else seemed to notice, so he dismissed it as fatigue. And then it got louder. He looked up, but there was too much steel between him and the sky to see anything. What he did notice, however, were that the rescued pilots, medical staff and several sailors were now shielding their eyes and squinting directly into the sun. With all that blue up there, what were the odds that an innocent aircraft was somehow coincidentally above them? As he slipped out of the sling and landed on the deck, he answered his own question. Zero.

Like all military men, Fabian had studied the silhouettes of enemy planes and memorized sound recordings of their engines. Because he was a carrier officer, he concentrated on the light, fast, maneuverable fighters and dive bombers that the Bay was most likely to encounter—planes whose engines made high-pitched whines that he could identify in less than a second. What he heard now was more like approaching thunder from a large, deadly storm.

In a throwback to the time of shoguns, when massing armies used to parade in front of one another before battle, some Japanese naval air commanders maintained a habit of overflying their target once before commencing an attack. Whatever impact this may have had on the sword-wielding samurai of the Middle Ages, the only effect it had on twentieth-century Americans was to give them extra time to lock in on their targets.

But this morning, more than a few sailors stopped what

they were doing when they saw what was coming. Approaching at staggered altitudes were least sixty heavy bombers, escorted by wave upon wave of fighters. And then came something no training film had ever covered. Two, dark green, six-engine behemoths that were so large and flying so slowly that their staying airborne seemed to defy logic.

The most advanced aircraft in the Imperial arsenal, Mt. Fuji bombers, had been designed to lay waste to the U.S. mainland. But having never gained a land foothold far enough east to launch them, the only two in existence had lain in mothballs—until now. Carrying fifty thousand pounds of bombs and fitted with four 20mm cannons that fired two thousand rounds a minute, sending them against a single ship said more about the current state of the Japanese war machine than all of the Allied intelligence gatherers combined.

Certainly, no one in American Naval Operations had ever war-gamed this kind of firepower directed at one ship—especially not a carrier with none of its planes in the air. Strategically, it was even embarrassing for the Japanese, but that was small consolation to the men aboard the Resurrection Bay as they watched the twin, 350,000-pound purveyors of death lumber relentlessly toward them.

The first wave of bombs fell so thickly that they actually flashed shadows across the big ship's deck, reminding Fabian less of battle than of a late-afternoon California sun strobing through a eucalyptus windbreak. As loud as the first explosions were, he didn't hear them as much as absorb them. The roiling, unstable water followed by a deep, agonizing, TNT moan that made him sick to his stomach.

The Bay did a three-axis bend, yaw and lurch as concussions hit her from all sides, then plunged into a canyon suddenly created by a mountain of seawater being thrown skyward. Ships twice the length of a football field aren't supposed to be able to make quick turns, but Captain Hackin had apparently read a different manual. As Fabian sprinted along the flight deck toward the bridge, he heard the engines come to full power, and felt the Bay jerk once to port, then almost immediately rotate back. As it did, it fell again, nose down, into another hole, and as steady as Fabian's sea legs were, he lost his balance and didn't stop rolling until the ship reached the depression's trough.

In decades to come, he would remember it as the fall that saved his life, but at the time, all he knew was that his right leg was broken, and his shoes were gone. Then, just as suddenly as the attack had begun, it stopped. From where he lay, he could see the heavy bombers receding in the distance and beginning a long, slow turn that would return them to the killing ground.

The silence was quickly replaced by the earth-shaking reverberations of the approaching Mt. Fujis. They were so low, he could actually see their cannons spit and their bellies slowly open. Fabian watched, mesmerized, as row upon row of bombs walked a path up the carrier's wake until they began tearing through the fantail and mangling the planes tethered there.

As they advanced, a large chunk of the starboard side simply disappeared. Then there was a horrible, grinding scream as one of the Bay's two drive shafts seized, and the remaining screw, still at full power, torqued the ship into a hard right turn. Finally, a five-hundred-pound bomb penetrated the deck, found the aviation fuel storage tank, and the entire bridge superstructure catapulted into the air before slamming back and tumbling across the deck.

Suddenly, the entire world was engulfed in flame.

Fabian staggered to his feet and headed back the way he had come. He passed the charred remains of scores of men who would never again have a beer in Honolulu and saw three gunners, all on fire, pitch themselves over the side. Grimacing with each step, he descended back to the third deck, where the winch and sling sat just as he had left them. Here, there were more bodies, their faces contorted and blood streaming from their mouths and ears, victims of concussion. Most of the rescued pilots, including Tully, were among them, as was the medical team.

Fabian looked over the rail. He expected to see large numbers of sailors in the water, but there were only a few, and they were facedown. Despite the chaos of the last few minutes, the PT still bumped alongside, its thin line having remained attached to the Bay. Seeing how far the starboard hull had already risen, Fabian knew they were taking on water, and the list would only increase. Coupled with the severe right turn, the carrier was, in effect, circling a giant drain.

The line to the PT was already taut. Very soon, it would snap. If Fabian was going to go, it had to be now, and with no one to operate the winch, he was going to have to jump far enough ahead of the smaller craft that he had a chance to catch it as it went by. He only hoped that if he made it, he'd be able to climb aboard with a leg that had gone completely numb.

The Bay suddenly made a terrible sound, as if she knew she was about to die, and rolled even further. Then her remaining drive shaft tore itself loose. The power was now off, but the momentum of a city block of steel pushed her along as if nothing had happened. And the heavy bombers returned.

The last thing Fabian expected was a baby's cry, which was probably why he heard it. Had it been just another random noise, it would never have penetrated his adrenaline-flooded brain. He followed the sound and found Luli's lifeless body lying on top of the infant. She had given her last breath to protect a child she'd known only a few hours. He wished he could have been as honorable, but the first word that came out of his mouth was, "Shit."

The fire found Fabian again and was pouring out of every doorway and racing along the deck. He had no time to consider options. He tucked the baby as tightly against his chest as possible, leveraged himself over the rail with his remaining hand, and leaped as far from impending death as he could. He remembered thinking that this was the second time today he'd left a ship this way and being none to happy about it. Then he hit the water, and the pain in his leg shot through every nerve in his body.

When he came up, he was covered in thick, black goo. The Bay's oil tanks had ruptured, and an inky blob was roiling from her in a great underwater cloud. The bombs were raining down again, and the ship had become nothing more than a smoking target. Fabian saw the PT. It had broken loose and was bobbing on the surface not more than fifty yards away. He'd have to swim for it with one arm, but maybe there was a chance.

And then came an explosion, a white flash, and the sea caught fire.

It was well past sundown, and there were still isolated patches of oil burning. The Bay had been gone for hours, sliding into the deep with a series of protesting bellows followed by an eerie silence. Fabian clung to the waterlogged seat cushion of a Hellcat fighter and remembered once asking a pilot how long they floated. The guy had laughed. "Fuckin' thing don't even pad my ass. How much time you figure the low bidder spent worryin' about sailin' it?"

The baby hadn't cried since they'd jumped. She was on her back on the cushion, shivering as she lay in water that licked at her ears, but she was absolutely quiet. He didn't want her to die, but he had to fight being angry that he had to worry about her. Truth was, though, if she hadn't been there, he might have already surrendered. He'd left exhaustion in his rearview mirror hours ago. The only reason he knew he wasn't dead was because he was hungry, which, all things considered, seemed ludicrous.

In the aftermath of the inferno, he had looked for a lifeboat or at least something larger to climb onto, but there was little debris left. What the carrier hadn't taken with her, the flames had consumed. He'd called out for survivors until he realized he was wasting energy looking for something he wasn't going to find.

The backs of his hands were burned, but his cotton shirt had protected his arms. He couldn't see his face, but when he'd tried to wipe water out of his eyes, a piece of his forehead had come off. Since then, he'd kept his hands away. The baby had been burned too, but there was so much oil on her, he couldn't tell how badly, and after his experience with his forehead, he didn't want to find out.

Earlier, a six-foot hammerhead had bumped him a couple of times but taken off when he jabbed it with his knife. The shark had seemed more curious than aggressive, and he suspected the still-foul water was interfering with its senses. Just in case, he'd left the knife on the cushion and tried not to think about what else might be lurking in the ebony depths.

He dozed off once, coming out of it only when his face dropped in the water. He was aware that the time was fast approaching when that wouldn't be enough, so he decided to try singing. He chose "One for My Baby," mostly because Tokyo Rose had been playing the hell out of the Fred Astaire hit recently, and he knew the words.

Infants weren't supposed to be able to turn their heads, but as he sang, he suddenly noticed the little girl was looking into his eyes. When he finished, he said to her, "You know, little lady, no one should be running around without a name. Since you seemed to like his song, how about for the moment we call you Astaire. I think that's got some real pizzazz, and it beats the heck out of Fred. Besides, you look like you might be a dancer."

He touched the baby's cheek, and for a moment, he thought she looked very scared. Fabian didn't really have the energy to sing another song, but he remembered an incident back on the force when a Louis Armstrong song had made the difference in a man's life. And if anyone needed a difference made right now, it was the two of them. So he cleared what was left of his throat and gave "When the Saints Go Marching In" all he had. Astaire seemed to like it too, and for a moment, he lost himself in the music.

Fabian was lolling half-in, half-out of consciousness. The baby was nearly off the cushion, and as hard as he tried, he could no longer make his fingers work to pull her back. Then *he saw the fin. No, that was wrong. There were several. All of them thicker than the hammerhead's. He reached for his knife, but it was gone, having slipped away when he wasn't looking. He wouldn't have been able to hold it anyway.*

Something hard sideswiped his leg, and the turbulence it created nearly pulled him under. The next one was right behind, and it banged into him harder. He kicked at it, but he had long since lost all feeling in his legs, and the only thing he succeeding in doing was to lose his grip on the cushion and have to use what strength he had left to fight his way back to it. Two more hits came simultaneously, and he knew the end was here. He was actually grateful.

Suddenly, there was a massive displacement of water, and the ocean seemed to rise beneath him. Fabian knew that dying people sometimes imagine things that help them through to the other side, and he wondered why, after all of this, he couldn't have at least conjured up something warm and comforting. Maybe that hot shower.

Then an earsplitting roar of air followed by a burst of salt spray hit him with the force of a shotgun blast, and a dark shape began to emerge from the depths. It was too big to be a shark. Too big even for a whale, but he was in no condition to really know.

His eyes began to close for the final time, and he didn't even try to keep them open. He took Astaire's hand in his and rushed into the darkness . . . just as the USS Parrotfish's *conning tower broke the surface.*

Mad Greeks and Old Friends

Few cities are as intertwined as Los Angeles and Las Vegas. Or as steeped in each other's myths and legends. LA is why there is a Vegas. A Beverly-Hills-obsessed mobster, Bugsy Siegel, invented it; a Central Valley boxer turned pilot, Kirk Kerkorian, started an airline to service it; the wealthiest Californian of his time, Howard Hughes, turned it corporate; and Hollywood provided the entertainment and high rollers to pay for everything. It's a six-decade-long love affair that grows new tentacles every year.

Four hundred times a day, a commercial flight leaves SoCal for McCarran. Another twelve hundred private planes join the procession, and 24/7/365, the I-15 is an endless ribbon of seventy-mile-per-hour steel. And in an aside to my fellow Californians up the coast, nobody screams like a scalded hamster if you call it Vegas.

Birdy and I were both hungry, so before descending the long grade into Nevada, we hit the Mad Greek's place in Baker, the last outpost in the Golden State. We sat on the patio next to a tableful of long-distance truckers who ate, talked, smoked, flexed their biceps and admired Birdy—all at the same time. It was nice to see that not every male in America has gone emo.

While Birdy had tried on clothes at Sears, I'd wandered around the Victorville Mall until I found a nail salon. Like most in SoCal, it was Vietnamese-owned. In this case by Nhu Pham, a twentysomething, very tightly dressed young lady in heels so high every passing XY chromosome over the age of twelve made it a point to check out the polish display in the window.

All the seats were occupied, and I got the twice-over by manicurists and customers alike. They needn't have worried. I had no intention of staying any longer than necessary. To make sure, Nhu walked me out into the concourse, her strong accent anything but friendly. "No men," she said tightly. "You gay, you go to Riki's downtown."

"I just want to ask you a question."

"I no date you. Boyfriend have big gun."

This was going bad before it even got started. "Cathedral of the Testaments," I finally got out.

If I thought that would slow her down, I was mistaken. "I Catholic," she hissed.

"I'm not recruiting. I just want to know if any Vietnamese go there?"

"You fuckin' crazy? That place full of fuckin' Chinese."

"How about other Asians? Koreans, maybe?"

"Where the fuck you go to school?" Then she turned on a very precarious heel and strode back into her shop, while the crowd that had gathered smiled and shook their heads at the dummy she left behind.

I told the story to Birdy as we shoved gyros into our faces. She thought it was hysterical, of course. Why is it when a man gets humiliated, there's dancing in the streets . . . but when it's a woman, men have to bite their tongues and buy her something expensive, or it gets logged into the Big Book of Forever?

While I pondered the imponderable, Birdy went to the

ladies' room, and I wandered out to the truck to make a few calls. Part of me wanted to call Wes Crowe and gauge his reaction when I told him where he could find Cheater. Problem was he would already suspect his "brother" was dead and be ready for the question. He was also a cop, and having me connected to the body in any way would allow him to cloud the issue enough to confuse any prosecutor. Besides, neither Cheater nor Donnie was going anywhere, so I could come back to them later.

Instead, my first call was to Mallory. "You can send the cavalry home," I said.

"Not just yet. Some of the guys are bringing their families over for a swim."

The Beverly Hills PD and I have a very good relationship, but this had all the earmarks of a Mallory-extravaganza with a bill to match. "How many is 'some'?"

"Well, you can't very well offer something like that to just the few who were up here. What kind of neighbor are you? Besides, it's a big pool."

So he'd opened it up to the whole department. My guess, the fire guys too. "And naturally, there'll be food."

"Naturally."

I didn't want to hear any more. It was going to happen no matter what I said, and any suggestions I had for keeping costs down would not only be ignored but countered. "I don't know when I'll be home, but I'll give you a heads-up."

"Don't hurry. I'm just getting into that rack of Travis McGee in the library. By the way, you had two calls. A Ms. Huston and a Ms. Marisol Rivera-Marquez. From the sound of both, your unparalleled charm is still very much in evidence."

No man is a hero to his valet. "Did Ms. Huston happen to mention she was with the FBI?"

"Only six or seven times. Along with a head count of our current guests. Seems she's anxious enough to get her hands on you that she felt the need to threaten my immigration status. I told her to put a rush on it. The beatings are intolerable."

Apparently, Francesca wasn't getting much Beverly Hills love anywhere, but I wasn't surprised she had someone watching the house. "Did Marisol leave a message?"

"Oh, that she did. My Spanish isn't what it used to be, but it went something like, 'Tell Mr. Black I am now without pain, but I shall never again be without disgrace.' If you'll forgive me for saying so, sir, you have outdone even my low expectations."

Well, she hadn't cut me off forever, but I had a lot of work to do to fix a relationship that wasn't even a relationship, which right after neurosurgery is my weakest suit. But Ms. Rivera-Marquez would be getting a few more bullfights under her belt before I had time to try to make things right. And, as damaged as she was, I had my own issues. "Enjoy your pool party," I said to Mallory.

"The officers really like your cigars."

I didn't think he needed a good-bye. My next call was to Jake. "How well do you know Markus Kingdom?"

"He's a Grade-A schmuck."

"Unpaid bill or stolen girlfriend?"

"Fuck you."

Jake didn't get that emotional about money. "Hold the thought. Maybe you can get even. Way back when, he was a guest of the G. Terminal Island. Think you can come up with why?"

"Markus Kingdom had his asshole widened? There is a God." Glee over the tribulations of others is one of Jake's many flaws. As he was hanging up, I heard him yell, "Stella, get in here."

My last call was to Freddie to check on Roxy's new job. Uncharacteristically, he skipped past the usual Freddie bullshit and got to the point. "Your girl's already been to the Pentagon to fill out the paperwork. I got her assigned to carrier group intel, which will bump her a pay grade. She'll meet so many flyboys, she'll have ice down her snatch."

I ignored his last remark, which is the only rebuke Freddie can't argue with. "When does she start?"

"Tomorrow, and I'm supposed to tell you she doesn't want a going-away party."

I couldn't fault her for that. "Thanks, I appreciate the hustle."

"We'll discuss a bonus later."

"Only if I can borrow your car again." Freddie's a material guy, but his love affair with that Bentley borders on the unbalanced. My comment, even in jest, threw him off.

"Where were we?"

"Department 11."

"Murders."

"Murders? That's it?"

"Did I say that was it?"

"If I'm paying a quarter of a mil for a slow dance, skip it, and I'll call somebody else."

"Francesca Huston heads what they call the Extrinsic Homicide Unit. That name is classified, so the geniuses gave it Department 11."

"Extrinsic. If I remember my Sunday crossword, that means extraneous."

"Tangential is closer. Ninety-eight percent of murders, everybody knows who did it and why. It might take a while to nail the perp, but there's no mystery. Another 1 percent are serial killers, and most of the rest are 'who cares.' Mob hits, heroin cut with rat poison, a prostitute in a Dumpster, that kind of shit. But there are a few that don't fit. Wildcases, they call them, which is pretty creative for the FBI."

"What's a few?"

"A hundred a year . . . less. Two categories. First is Joe the Plumber. Never been out of Newark. Wife, kid, current with his bills. No record. Biggest vice is he cheats at bowling. One day, he disappears. A month later, he washes up in Galveston Bay. Didn't have a boat, didn't know anybody in Texas, and the last time he traveled was never."

I thought about the Vegas taxi driver. "What's the other category?"

"Topeka. Sunday afternoon open house. Nice neighborhood. Owners are retired schoolteachers living in Sun City. The Realtor shows up early to put out cookies, and there's a guy with a bullet hole in his forehead sitting in the family room Barcalounger—naked. Clothes are nowhere to be found, but he's wearing an expensive watch and a wedding band. No prints in the system and no missing person report that matches. Oh, and did I mention that his lower torso is all torn up, and his pecker is gone. The cops run his face on TV, and nobody calls.

"In the old days, Joe gets sent home with condolences, and Mr. Barcalounger gets buried in potter's field. Both M.E. reports hit the archives. Over and out, Captain Kirk."

"When were the old days?"

"Before 1995. April 19, to be exact."

I thought for a moment. "McVeigh. Oklahoma City."

"Six years from explosion to execution. It took longer to indict Gotti. But while the Feds were high-fiving each other, some out-of-the-box thinker pissed in the champagne. 'Hey, guys, maybe you haven't noticed, but it's Oswald all over again.'"

He'd lost me, and I said so.

I heard Freddie sigh, but I knew he was enjoying being the smartest guy in the room. "Think about it, Rail. Disaffected ex-military. Weapons expertise. America the Oppressor writings. Unexplained travels. Appearances at extremist events. Shadowy acquaintances. And for the truly paranoid, both men confronted an hour after their event by a lone cop, who apparently doesn't make the connection to the big picture. The difference: Even though he's already killed a shit-ton of people, supposedly for reasons extending all the way back to Thomas Jefferson, and he's got the drop on this Oklahoma Smokey, unlike Oswald, McVeigh doesn't shoot."

I felt my face flush at the same time my blood ran cold. I'd never thought about it before, but now, it stuck out like a neon sign. My JFK-consumed friend, Benny Joe Willis, would have immediately changed neon sign to blueprint. "And the career jockeys got instant nosebleeds."

"You're a pretty quick study for a rich guy. They probably wanted to ignore it, but nobody was going to chance the analyst's report ending up in the *New York Times,* so to pad the file, the task force pulled every unsolved homicide in the preceding two years. Bank jobs too, something no one had looked at after Dallas."

"Bad idea. Never review the tape after the call has gone your way."

"They didn't get the memo. And lo and behold, there were oddball dead people and robberies in places and at times McVeigh was in the vicinity. And since there was nothing to indicate he was a one-on-one killer—even when he was about to be arrested with mass murder on his hands—that could only mean one thing: help, serious help. Want my two cents' worth? The G couldn't get a needle in the guy fast enough."

"And Department 11 is born. Track unrelated, out-of-place murders—wildcases—looking for patterns. If unrelated suddenly becomes extrinsic, you might find a McVeigh before he becomes McVeigh."

"Precisely.'"

"Anybody happen to say how they missed 9/11?"

The silence was deafening. "Same question I had. You're getting the same answer."

I could only imagine. Actually, I probably couldn't. "What about Joe and Mr. Barcalounger."

"Barca's lower body wounds turned out to be from some rodent that only lives in the Society Islands. Nobody'd ever heard of one within three thousand miles of the U.S. Other than that, dead end. Joe, somebody ran a Geiger counter over him, and he glowed in the dark. Plutonium."

"Lot of plumbing in nuclear devices. Delicate, but the same principles."

"Turned out his hobby was building miniature steam engines. Best guess is there's a ship riding around out there with a boom in its belly. I wish I didn't know."

I wished I didn't either. "You earned your keep, Freddie."

"Always do. Just don't charge enough for it."

I hung up and watched trucks come and go from the freeway. I had a feeling I could add a family of four in San Francisco and two dead Chinese accountants and a wife in Los Angeles to the picture. It would have been productive to swap lists with SAC Huston, but that probably wasn't in the cards.

As we rolled into the Vegas city limits, the early-evening traffic swallowed us. I got off the 15 at Windmill Lane and turned northbound on the Strip. Technically, it's simply Las Vegas Boulevard until you hit Russell Road, then it unofficially becomes the Strip. But like Sixth Avenue in New York, there's official, then there's reality.

The Iguazu Country Club is south of the Luxor and one of the city's best-kept secrets. Fifty feet in, you could be in a South American rain forest, complete with howler monkey sound effects and real macaws and toucans. The club's hallmark is that there are falling-water features everywhere. I don't know what golfers with weak bladders do, but I can guess. And with a membership fee in six figures, they probably feel entitled.

We navigated past the guard booth with a dog-eared pass I fished out of my wallet that was only a week from expiring. "Please check in with reception," the uniformed von Stroheim look-alike said as he gave my Ram the same unexuberant once-over he'd given my pass. He closed with a chilly, "Have a nice day," and there we left it.

A wedding reception was in full bloom and a flock of well-dressed guests were standing out front next to one of the tamer waterfalls, knocking back drinks, catching a smoke and watching the sun slowly set. Birdy looked at me questioningly.

"Bring your dancing shoes?" I asked.

The valet took the Ram, and as we parted the sea of revelers, I couldn't help but overhear a loud, slurred female voice. "Tell you what, asshole, I don't care what our tax situation is, you try to take me out of my house in Bel Air and move me to this desert hellhole, you better like sleepin' in that big, fuckin' Mercedes of yours, 'cause that's all my lawyers are gonna leave you with." I didn't hear an answer, so even if the guy was financially right, he needed higher-grade ammo. Maybe asthma.

Inside the row of glass and brass doors, a security knuckle-dragger met us with a well-dressed lady attractive enough to be Miss USA. She was wearing a nice smile. He wasn't. "Is Hassie around?" I asked.

"May I give him your name?" she asked.

"Tell him it's the only guy in Beverly Hills who doesn't lie about his handicap."

She never blinked. "Right away, sir," and disappeared down a hallway, leaving us under the watchful eye of Lurch.

"Is that true?" asked Birdy.

"Yep, but only because I don't play."

I probably used to know Hassie's real name, but I don't remember it. Hassie was all anybody called him at the Army and Navy Academy where we went to high school. I ended up crawling on my belly in Delta Force, and he went to MIT. I'll leave it to the imagination who had better rations. Somewhere along the line, however, he got tired of wearing a pocket protector and became a golf bum—if you can call owning a piece of the nicest course in town bumming. When he comes to LA, he stays at my place, which ruins Mallory for a month because the guy not only plays scratch golf, he cooks like a Michelin chef.

I saw Miss USA returning alongside a familiar curly blonde guy in khaki slacks and a red and green Tommy Bahama Tabasco shirt. No handshake here. He grabbed me and hugged me like a long-lost rich uncle. "Just don't call me honey," I said, "or the lady might look for a cab."

He disengaged, then grabbed me again. "If she's smart, she'll do it anyway. You snore." He finally released me and grabbed Birdy. She didn't offer any resistance, and he took that as an invitation to nuzzle her hair. "You smell wonderful. Got a sister?"

"No, but if you can find me something to drink, I'll swap this guy out. He forced gyros down my throat, and I got a week's worth of sodium."

"Ah, the Mad Greek. What's a trip across the desert without prepping for a bypass?"

The security guard melted away, looking disappointed he wasn't going to be asked to shoot anybody. We moseyed past the partiers in the lobby, and Hassie used a key to open a room on the other side of an antique reception desk. I knew from previous visits that this was his office, but it was set up more like a living room. No desk, only comfortable chairs, LeRoy Neimans and a large, gas fireplace, which was always on. He opened a cabinet next to a liquor shelf that turned out to be a full-size refrigerator. "What's your pleasure?"

"Coke," Birdy said. "High-octane, none of that diet crap."

"Woman after my heart. How about if I pep it up?" I saw him reach for the rum.

"Not unless you want to find me here in the morning."

"Let's hold that thought. How about you, partner?"

"Same. Excuse me minute."

While the two of them chatted, I took my drink, walked to the far side of the room and keyed my phone. After a couple of rings, a familiar voice answered. "Catch you at a bad time?" I asked.

Nick Martz's voice was as smooth as a Marsalis solo. Vegas is a town that doesn't like names. Guys like Nick don't need them. "Are you kidding? What can I do for you?"

"I'm at Hassie's place. Like to stick around a few days. Under the radar."

"No problem. When will you be ready?"

"I just started a Coke. How about as soon as it's gone?"

"Have Hassie take you out through the kitchen. There's a path just beyond the pro shop. Somebody will meet you."

"My truck's with the valet. I need what's inside."

"Done. Looking forward to seeing you. You want a game tonight?"

"I'm dead on my feet, but maybe after a nap."

"I'll make sure we stay open. Got some action you might like. I was going to call you about it. Seems there's a whale convention in town."

Contrary to myth, gaming is not a volume business. The most coveted resource in Vegas are high rollers. They're why skyscraper hotels, million-dollar-a-week entertainers and celebrity chefs flourish alongside the tumbleweed. The roll of nickels and all-you-can-eat buffet crowd gets you what it got Trump in Atlantic City—broke.

But there's a category above high roller. Whale. Men who can and will bet from a hundred grand to ten times that on a single hand—usually baccarat, sometimes poker. And this species is even rarer than the oceangoing kind. There are fewer than three hundred in the world, the majority Asian and Middle Eastern.

"Maybe. Which breed?" I asked.

"Pacific. Island and Mainland at the same time. You get this shit on New Year's, but everybody's in town then, so it's diluted. Never seen it happen this time of year. There aren't enough tables in this burg to keep them apart. And barely enough white paint. My, but they do hate dark walls."

"Which island?"

"Every goddamn one. Had to send to Phoenix for more blondes. All the joints are out of penthouses and villas. Some execs are even giving up their homes."

"But nobody from Sandland?"

"Not a hookah in sight."

"I thought you guys controlled which way the sun comes up."

"Me too. We warned everybody the others were coming, but nobody seemed to care. Fuckin' strange, huh?"

Not strange, unimaginable. For all their money, Asian whales don't like facing each other. High rollers, fine, but whale on whale is usually avoided. Primarily it's ego. These guys do business with one another, and nobody wants to give up a perceived edge—or bragging rights. They love the sheiks, the Europeans and the Latin Americans, whom they consider their inferiors. North Americans, it depends.

Asians are system players who devise elaborate schemes based on superstition, order and precision. You could watch one for a month and not completely understand how he bets, because a waiter dropping a fork on Tuesday afternoon can change everything. By contrast, most Americans, especially Texans, don't care if they're sitting in shit up to their knees, just deal the fucking cards. We're brash, unpredictable and intimidating, which fucks up the Fu or the Feng or whatever. We're also heavy on sarcasm, a concept their cultures don't have, so they miss things, and it unnerves them.

I'm Brazilian-British who became an American. As far as I know I'm my own category, so I'm not automatically on the DO NOT PLAY list.

"Off the subject: you familiar with Donnie Two Knives?"

"Got *Dirty Harry* on in the background, and every time he gets ready to blow some motherfucker away, here comes Donnie trying to sell me a Sony. Act's getting tired. Needs some new material. Why?"

"I'll fill you in when I see you."

"If he owes you a favor, I could use a new flatscreen for my workout room."

"Go wrangle your whales."

When I returned to my companions, Hassie had Birdy on her feet and was standing behind her, showing her how to swing an imaginary club. In some states, he could have been arrested. "Isn't it about time you got some new moves?" I asked.

He grinned. "Lady's got some powerful wrists. Like to get her on the range."

I rolled my eyes, but Birdy flushed. "I play a little but not as well as I'd like to."

Hassie put his chin on her shoulder as he moved her through her stroke. "You're a natural. I'll fit you in for a lesson."

I took a sip of Coke. "Bring your four iron and a stun gun. A name tag's not a bad idea either."

21

Estancias and Macallan

The guy in the golf cart took up most of the front seat, so I put Birdy beside him and got in back. I shook hands with Hassie. "Thanks for the drink. You sure the Ram's not going to be in your way?"

"An hour from now, it's going to have a cover over it and be tucked in our warehouse in Henderson. I decide to rob a bank, I'll get it out. Otherwise, it'll be there when you want it." He looked at Birdy. "I was serious about that lesson."

It was dark now, but even though the path wasn't lit, our driver knew exactly where he was going. "Looks like you've done this drill before," I said.

"Used to caddy at this joint." His tone made it clear he was there to drive not talk, so I shut up and rode.

The car parked just inside the maintenance gate was a black Range Rover, and from the way the door sounded when he closed it behind us, it was armored. That was confirmed when I noticed the light distortion through the heavy glass. When you think of wealth, limousines usually come to mind, and they are the overwhelming ride of choice. Mostly, because of show. People who have money like others to know it—even the ones who play the "regular guy" card.

However, those more concerned with security than stares prefer big SUVs with very experienced drivers. I go back and forth on it, but most of the time, nobody's trying to blow my head off or kidnap my child.

I knew where we were going, and I knew the town, but somehow our driver got my internal GPS turned around, so that when we finally eased into the unmarked drive and past the armed security team, it took me a few seconds to regain my bearings. I had to assume he'd come the circuitous route to be sure we weren't being followed. When you consider that the heavy moneymaking patch of Vegas is only slightly larger than the Mall of America, the way he'd done it took a serious pro.

Birdy's stock kept rising. Since the look she'd given me when I drove into the Iguazu, not one question. Our driver pulled between a ten-foot row of hedges, which I knew from once having tried to walk through them camouflaged a thick, wrought-iron fence. A two-car garage was off to the right, and as we entered a small circular drive, a Spanish hacienda rose in front of us. While our driver helped us out, a smartly uniformed man and woman came out the front door.

"Mr. B., how wonderful to have you back with us," the man said in accented English. "Your things have been put away in the master suite."

I wasn't surprised. Our taking the long way would have given whomever had collected them from the Ram time to beat us there. The woman beside him stepped forward. Her voice was pleasant, but her smile reserved. "Good evening, Mr. B.," she said in the same accent. "The kitchen and wine cellar are stocked, and I've chosen some nice flowers and music I think you'll like. Very new and very cool. But just in case, there's plenty of Frank and Wynton to see you through."

They had both nodded politely at Birdy but not spoken.

That was the town. Until you're sure where people fit, especially friends of important guests, you wait. I took Birdy by the hand. "I'd like you to meet Miss Nash. She'll be staying with me. Miss Nash, this is Bronis and Judita Cermak."

"*Dobrý den,*" Birdy said, extending her hand. She looked at me, "Some of the best horse bloodlines in the world come from Prague."

From the reaction of the Cermaks, love was in the air.

"Will there be anything else, Mr. B?" our driver asked.

"We're good. I assume there's a car in the garage."

"Something a little different. Mr. Martz would like your opinion. But don't hesitate to ask for something else."

Nick Martz is a host at the Inca Resort and Casino. It's a position that doesn't appear on casino organizational charts. They usually have some nebulous marketing title that makes them sound like nobodies. Hardly.

Hosts wield more power than anybody outside the gaming commission. They maintain the personal relationships that enable them to caress high rollers and whales to specific casinos. It's not just a matter of picking up tabs. Whales, in particular, often make exotic demands or have complicated personal needs that the host has to know and accommodate. That's why it's difficult to put two of them at the same table. If their idiosyncrasies conflict—and they can change in the middle of a game—the host and the casino could lose both.

Nick once had a whale in Rome who was convinced his wife was gambling poison, so Nick arranged for her to "find" a boyfriend in the Eternal City. It wasn't long before she was encouraging her husband to do more traveling—alone. For a whale from Chicago, he got the guy's tennis-playing daughter a full ride to UNLV. After all, what doting daddy doesn't like to visit his little girl at college.

Hosts are paid a percentage of the action their clients give the house, but they also have to collect on their markers—a delicate and sometimes dangerous job. As a result, they earn in the high seven figures. On the plus side, no one questions their expenses or watches them too closely, so they live very, very well.

You can't major in host at Stanford or drop off an application at human resources. But if you have a nose for money and the correct people skills, somebody will find you. Nick, who didn't finish eighth grade and now lives on the same street as Steve Wynn, once told me that if he does his job right, a guy who just dropped ten mil will apologize for having to leave town early.

Every client also wants to think he's the only one, or at least Nick's favorite. So when several take a bad beat at the same time, it can mean a lot of sleepless nights holding people's hands until they pay. Nick keeps awake staring at his bank balance.

But smart as he is, he sometimes skates on the edge. Like with Raphael Weathers. Raphael, was a seventeen-year-old street kid Nick took in after he caught him breaking into his car. He bought him a steak dinner and told him he could come to work for him or leave—no questions asked. But if he caught him near the Inca again, he was guaranteed a broken arm.

Raphael became one of Nick's runners, picking up tickets for shows, meeting people at the airport and sometimes taking a high roller's lady friend shopping. Nick didn't pay him much, but the tips were big, and by the time he was old enough to buy a legal drink, Raphael owned a sports car, a closetful of Zenga and was living in a half-million-dollar condo.

But Raphael couldn't quite break himself of his old habits—some of which included violence. His weapon of choice was a pushbutton stiletto with a blade he kept sharpened to Gillette tolerances. And he gave the gift of cruelty often and without consequences, so he came to believe he possessed a kind of reckless invincibility. Those who knew him stayed clear, especially when he was using drugs—

which eventually, was most of the time. He also enjoyed inflicting pain on women, and in a dangerous town, he had no trouble finding dangerous playmates.

Nick knew all of this, of course. Knowing things was his business. But Raphael was good at his job, so he ignored the oncoming train.

The inevitable happened when Raphael got mixed up with a New Jersey Mafiosi's Moroccan girlfriend, a tall, stunning black woman named Daxxene. Nick warned him to stay away from her, but one night, while the boyfriend was in an all-night craps game, Raphael took Daxxene to see Wayne Newton.

Somewhere in the middle of Wayne's second set, they got into an argument, and Daxxene raked her razor-sharp nails across Raphael's face. Raphael lost his mind, and while Wayne was launching into "Daddy, Don't You Walk So Fast," Raphael smashed her in the mouth with bottle of Cristal, then dragged her out of the banquette and began opening her up with his knife. It took four security men to pull him off.

Nick sent Daxxene to Rio for reconstructive surgery, then gave her fifty grand and a ticket to Paris, where she always wanted live. Raphael kicked around town for a few months, then one day, he just wasn't there anymore. Everybody knew what happened and wasn't surprised. Corporations, CPAs and Big Board listings notwithstanding, it's still a jungle town, and the lions bite.

I met Nick when I was a regular at Caesars, and he was an assistant host there. I had never considered leaving. It was like a second home. Then it changed hands, and though the trappings were the same, it felt different. And if you gamble seriously, feel is everything.

I never said a word to anyone, but like the shark he is, Nick smelled it, and next trip I was at the Inca, and so was Nick. I'm told the host at Caesars got shown the door, and Nick got a sizeable finder's fee from the Inca. Neither surprises me. And frankly, the Inca fits me better than Caesars ever did. More importantly, SAC Huston could show up waving a warrant signed by all nine members of the Supreme Court, and nobody would have ever heard of me.

Private villas in Vegas have a tendency to come in two flavors: Babylonian whorehouse or Fredo Corleone's bedroom. There's a perception that sin revels in jeweled ceilings or thirty shades of black, which is mostly true. A lot of whales who are very conservative in the rest of their lives can't wait to slip into a peach sport coat to hit the tables. I prefer things nice but subdued. After a long night, I don't want to come home to a houseful of purple furniture that I don't know how to sit in.

When we entered the villa, I listened for the music and was more than pleased with Judita's selection. It was Brazilian, like my late mother. How Nick found out she was a Carioca wasn't nearly as impressive as his having tracked down a poster from one of her long-forgotten Broadway appearances. As always, it was hanging above the stone fireplace, and as always, I stopped in front of it and tried to remember better times. Unfortunately, the years were making her a stranger.

I'd stayed in this place enough times that it seemed like mine. On the coffee table alongside the obligatory Noah's ark of exotic fruit was a large format, expensively bound book with a picture of the villa on the cover. The title was *Estancia Beverly Hills.* Birdy sat and flipped it open. It was a pictorial of the home, and on page one in bold lettering it read:

WELCOME BACK MR. B.

"I'm blown away," she said. "They did this just for you?"

"Don't be too impressed. If the next guy's from Schenectady, the printer's already working."

"I'm still wowed. Why does everybody call you Mr. B.?"

"It goes back to the beginning of Vegas. No names. The shy avoided the spotlight, and the winners, the IRS. Some of that still holds, but now, it's for security. Doesn't matter if you're the most recognizable face in the world, here you're Mr. D. or Mr. R."

"What about the women?"

"Wives and girlfriends, yes. You'll be Miss N. But it's not a N.O.W. town. If a lady shows up who gives them serious action, they adjust. Gender disappears when it comes to money. So does position. Gates could roll in with Buffett on his arm, and if they aren't players, they'll sit in the cheap seats and get served last."

"I want to meet Mr. Martz. Will he come by?"

"No. That might make me feel like a guest instead of at home. Illusion. Part of the process. Notice there are ashtrays?"

"Yes."

"Smell anything?"

She sniffed the air. "Just flowers."

"As soon as we leave, a team of specialists will come in and eliminate all traces of us. Especially scent. You're in the most subliminally sophisticated city ever imagined. Nothing is left to chance."

"And all this is because you gamble."

"I do. Sometimes worse than others. It's those they count on."

She moved into my arms. "How big is this joint?"

"No clue, but I haven't seen all the bedrooms."

"You won't see more than one tonight either."

I assumed it was my cologne.

I awakened with Birdy draped around me, her soft breath on my neck. I thought about trying to go back to sleep, but the growling in my stomach won. I might have also heard a poker table calling.

An hour later, showered and dressed in one of my own tailor's pin-striped suits taken from a closetful kept on hand, I stepped out of an Inca limo at the casino entrance. As I turned to help Birdy, I was again struck by what Elinor Glyn described as "It"—the combination of intangibles that draws all eyes. Star quality.

It's what built Hollywood, and it's why we still turn our heads when we hear Lauren Bacall's voice. And why a well-past-middle-aged actor seated on a cheap folding chair draws more attention than the basketball team he's watching.

Part of Birdy's It was what God and her parents had thrown together, and part was that she wore her clothes, makeup and hair with a style and confidence all her own. But I've known women who could spend thousands on Fifth Avenue and not come close to what this girl had done in a small-town mall armed with nothing more than radiance and an understanding of herself.

"Rail? Rail?"

I checked back into the present. "Sorry, I was just thinking about the steak in my future."

"Pity, I was hoping it was me." She said it without an ounce of rancor or double meaning.

"You didn't let me finish. We were naked, and you were cutting up little bites and hiding them in strategic places."

"Nice save."

The limo driver thought so too. He winked at me and got back in the car. But before he did, he took another look at the wisp of black dress Birdy was wearing and ran his eyes down her long, long legs.

"Welcome, Mr. B." I turned to see several well-dressed young men coming down the marble stairs toward us. Nick's greet team. The speaker, who could have been a BriteSmile model, nodded deferentially. "I'm Renaldo, sir. Welcome to the Inca." He didn't extend his hand, which was by design. Casino help is trained to never attempt familiarity with a whale. Some might be offended; others, especially Asians, might consider it a bad omen.

Having watched my father shake hands with everyone from the titled to pressmen dripping with newspaper ink, good manners are never out of place. I extended my hand, and Renaldo took it, beaming. I then introduced him to Birdy, whom he openly admired.

If you want to see an entrance handled with style, you can skip the Academy Awards, where dignity has long been out of vogue. Las Vegas hosts can get you through a crowd quickly yet let everyone know someone important has arrived. That may seem contradictory, but it's what presidents do all the time, and it's a real art to be able to do both simultaneously. By the time we crossed the lobby, the entire place knew we were there. They didn't know who we were, but they sensed we were important, and that ratchets up the atmosphere. Always good for the tables.

"My God," Birdy whispered to me as we were led to a private elevator to the penthouse dining room. "This is almost like sex. All these people looking at us."

"Careful, it's addicting."

"Oh, I hope so."

Nick joined us in the Machu Picchu Room after dinner. Birdy and I were seated in a circular booth overlooking the city while we nursed espressos and discussed how we'd let ourselves be talked into the now-gone molten chocolate perversion. His arrival was heralded by a retinue of white-coated waiters bearing four single-malt setups and a bottle of The Macallan 55. I'd always thought the gold-winged Lalique container was borderline gauche and firmly out of character for the Scots, but it was a Vegas natural. At fifteen grand a throw, you need a bigger base than an occasional Masters win or presidential inauguration. I nodded in the direction of Edinburgh for their marketing astuteness.

Alongside Nick was a smartly tailored young lady in her thirties who looked more like a banker than a casino employee. However, in this town, she might have been both. Nick ignored me and bowed graciously to my date. She offered her hand, and he kissed it like a baron.

"Nobody's ever done that before," she said.

Nick let loose of one of his xenon smiles and nodded in my direction. "I'll have to take this guy down to our dungeon for a session with the house inquisitor."

Birdy laughed. "Oh, please let me watch."

"If you don't mind my asking, wherever did you get that hair?"

"Gift from Mom. About the only thing I didn't resent."

"You ever want a change of scenery, I'll put you on the high roller concierge desk. Six figures from me, which you'll triple in tips. And all you have to do is smile and say no."

Birdy really laughed this time. "It's not doing that second part that keeps getting me in trouble."

First Hassie, now Nick. And nobody even subtle. "If I can interrupt the job interview, it's nice to see you, Nick."

"Oh, are you still here," he said, grinning. "I'd like you to meet Yvonne Whitney. Mind if we join you for a drink?" He reached into his inside pocket and came out with an eight-inch gold cigar case. "I brought smokes."

I stood and shook hands with Yvonne. Her grip was firm and warm, her smile genuine, not professional. "By all means."

Birdy passed on The Macallan, so while the waiters poured two fingers for the rest of us, Nick and I fired up a pair of my favorite Arturo Fuente 858 Maduros. If I didn't gamble, I'd still come to Vegas. When the do-gooders in the rest of the country took away our right to have a smoke after a fine meal, they zapped a little bit of America's soul. As my way of saying fuck you, I inhaled.

Nick looked at Yvonne. "The floor is yours, milady."

Yvonne thanked him and turned to Birdy. "My employer was wondering if you might be willing to come out to his ranch and give him some counsel."

Birdy was as puzzled as I was. "Tonight?"

"He's most anxious to get a second opinion on a horse he just bought."

"My opinion? On a horse purchase? I'm not sure I'm the person you . . ."

Yvonne cut her off. "We checked, and the reviews were glowing. You're really well-thought-of, Miss Nash. Anyway, we believe we have a promising two-year-old, but we're concerned we haven't gotten the best advice about getting him ready for next year's Derby."

I had to hand it to Nick. This was beyond anything I could have conceived he'd do. Or even could do. But that's why he's the best.

I watched Birdy go into professional mode and saw the intelligence behind her eyes. "Nevada's not usually considered a hub of Thoroughbreds," she said gently.

Yvonne was right with her. "You're absolutely correct. Much too hot. MrSaturdayDance is just passing through on his way to Santa Anita. That's still your base of operations, isn't it?"

I thought Birdy was going to faint. "Your employer bought MrSaturdayDance?"

Yvonne nodded. "He's also part-owner of the Inca, so when Nick told him you were in town, he asked me to drop by and speak with you. The decision is yours, of course, but he remembers what you did with Song's Harpoon."

Birdy looked at me like she'd just awakened Christmas morning and found Santa had left his entire bag. But there was apprehension in her eyes as well. "Rail, please tell me this isn't some kind of joke, because if it is, I need to go to the ladies' room and cry."

I put my hand on hers. "I'm as surprised as you are, and Nick never jokes this way."

Yvonne handed Birdy a business card. She took it and read aloud, "Yvonne Sykes Whitney, President of Vilcambaba Stables. Oh my God. Now, I think I have to go to the ladies' room and cry anyway." She started to say something to Nick but faltered.

Yvonne stepped in. "Then the only thing left to decide is a fee for your services."

"It would be my pleasure," Birdy said. "Just for the opportunity."

"Nonsense," said Yvonne. "You're a professional, and you should be paid. My employer wouldn't have it any other way."

Birdy looked at me for help, but this was her turf. Finally, she brightened and looked at Nick. "Do you think I could come back here someday and stay in Estancia Beverly Hills?"

Nick smiled. "Tell you what, you've got a birthday coming up in a couple of months. Why don't you get a few girl-friends together and come over for the weekend. I'll have something organized that'll give them a time to remember. Providing, of course, it's okay with Rail."

"I think it's a fine idea," I said.

Birdy looked at Nick and stammered. "I'm not going to ask how you know so much about me, but thank you very, very much."

"You're quite welcome."

Then she added, "Do you think I could get a glass of The Macallan now?"

22

Lake Geneva and the Story of 0

The Inca's private gambling rooms aren't actually inside the Inca. It's an old Vegas deception. Movies like visuals, so big games are portrayed in penthouses with hot and cold running pretty girls and panoramic views of the skyline. The reality is that in a city with no clocks, the last thing the house wants a whale to see is the rising or setting sun, a mood-altering thunderstorm—or, more importantly, a gang of armed thieves coming through the door.

I took my second golf cart ride of the evening, only this four-wheeler had never carried a bag of clubs and was as elegantly appointed as my Rolls. Nick drove us along an underground concrete passageway to a villa on the other side of the complex from mine.

Here, the structures were also walled off by hedges, only much thicker and higher, and just inside the greenery, an array of ceramic geometric screens muffled any ambient sound and kept light at a consistent level. The screens were also used to project images replicating a 360-degree view of any city in the world or scene in nature. This provided the gamblers inside with a sense of space as well as something more interesting than walls to gaze at between hands. Tonight, someone, perhaps homesick for his bank, had requested Geneva, Switzerland, and the lake looked real enough for a swim. Absent a massive power failure or the Apocalypse, years could pass without one's knowing conditions only a few feet from where he sat.

The first floor of the villa was laid out like a vaulted Incan amphitheatre to give players the feeling of a large stage. Men risking millions like to think they're in the Super Bowl, not the Elks Club. By fiat, the open upstairs balconies were locked off and always empty. The Super Bowl it might be, but no one appreciates eyes over their shoulders. The various players' entourages were relegated to a circular pit of deep, burgundy leather sofas, set well away from the action.

In the center of the room sat an oval, green felt table surrounded on three sides by eight padded chairs and presided over by a thin-faced dealer in white, French cuffs. I recognized him. Sydney, the Inca's best. Slightly behind Sydney to his right sat an identically dressed man next to a tall, inlaid cabinet containing neatly racked chips and plaques. I knew him too: Prince, the game's banker, a former Jamaican weightlifter with biceps bigger than most men's legs.

Sydney gave me a professional, "Nice to see you, Mr. B."

"You too, Sydney." I nodded to the banker. "Prince."

Prince gave me his best grin, "Welcome back, Mr. B.," and began counting out my usual buy-in. As he did, a very leggy redhead in pink hot pants appeared and asked if I wanted a drink. I thanked her and passed.

I didn't know the three Asian men already in the game, but Nick had briefed me on our way over. He made the introductions. Takumi Saito from Tokyo, and next to him, a Yale-educated Malaysian named Jerry Merican. Saito's money came from automobile dealerships, and Merican, the son of a sultan, was making a career out of spending as much of his father's fortune as he could get his hands on. They were the high rollers.

The whale was Shi Quan, owner of a construction empire, which no matter where you live operates in the same edgy soup of business, politics and organized crime. In this case, Shanghai. He looked dangerous and probably was. Nick had also mentioned that though Quan was thoroughly Anglicized in speech, there were some missing synapses in the thinking department. I was hoping that applied to cards.

I watched them take in my size. Seldom is being big a disadvantage. It takes people's minds off things they should be concentrating on. Only Jerry Merican stood and offered his hand. So much for the rest of Far Eastern hospitality.

Seeking to establish his primary position in the testicle pecking order, Quan very deliberately eased a Dunhill Fine Cut from a box lying next to him, lit it with a platinum Colibri, and said, "I trust you don't mind if I smoke."

"As long as you don't mind when I take your money."

Saito remained impassive, but Jerry Merican let loose a cackle that showed three gold front teeth. Quan had left his sense of humor in his other pagoda. Someday, a president with a short fuse and a fast tongue will Rodney Dangerfield the wrong guy in Beijing, and it will be ICBMs at forty paces. Fortunately, this guy wasn't in charge of the nuclear football. He simply turned and spit on the floor.

Nick ignored it, but there would be a penalty somewhere. As accommodating as the casinos are to their important guests, they have to keep those in line who have no rules anywhere else. "What's your seating pleasure?" Nick asked.

"As far from him as possible," I said, indicating the spitter. "In case he decides to take a piss."

Quan's eyes went cold. He stood, as did his two linebacker-sized bodyguards across the room. It probably didn't help that Jerry was laughing again. I also caught a flicker of a smile cross Prince's face. There was the possibility Shi Quan might take his bad manners and billions and leave, but I didn't think so. He wasn't a prissy European or gossamer-skinned Arab. He wanted a piece of me, financial or otherwise.

I decided to help him along. I turned to Jerry and indicated Quan's thugs. "Think your guys can handle them? I don't want to be interrupted if things get interesting."

Jerry Merican's crew, four pug-faced men in skintight, black shirts and wearing some kind of royal medallion around their necks, didn't have the height Quan's men did, but they had numbers. They also looked eager to be let loose. "Just say the word, man." Jerry grinned.

Saito's lone bodyguard, a pasty-faced guy no bigger than his boss, didn't move. But as slightly built as he was, he looked like he could handle himself, and I didn't think it would be to help the Chinese.

Ordinarily, Nick would have intervened by now. Out of sight, but only steps away, would be an army of Inca security, and a simple nod would trigger a signal from Sydney or Prince and bring them in. That nothing had happened meant our host was giving the Shanghainese construction boss that overdue lesson in decorum. Quan knew it too. And though he might have been able to snap his fingers and summon up anything else, he couldn't replicate a high-stakes Hold 'Em game with an adversary he wanted to make bleed. He lit another Fine Cut, puffed slowly for a few seconds and sat back down.

"Deal the fuckin' cards," he said.

I took my seat and saw Nick wink at Sydney as he left. It looked like it was going to be a bumpy night. I wouldn't have wanted it any other way.

An hour in, we were joined by a pair of Koreans. Brothers, Iseul and Yong Pak—nonwhales—who were more interested in advancing their rum buzz than paying attention to the cards. They brought with them a collection of loud hangers-on that included several good-looking but very drunk Filipino women, mostly *not* wearing their dresses. The couch area was beginning to look like a map of Asia, complete with ethnic tensions. If anybody else showed up, we might have to have to call in some UN peacekeepers.

The arrival of the Pak brothers and their distractions irritated Saito but allowed Quan and me to carve them up with impunity until Prince advised the Koreans that he had to get Nick's okay to extend more credit. While he placed the call, they wandered over to sofas, where one promptly fell asleep. Shortly afterward, the other brother made a boisterous exit with the groupies, leaving his sibling alone and snoring.

Two and a half hours later by Bert's Rolex, a new dealer and banker arrived to relieve Sydney and Prince. The dealer, Floyd, looked like a small Woody Allen, and the banker, an expressionless blonde named Dagmar, was built like she could handle anybody in the room.

I estimated Saito as even. He played as tight as a widow on Social Security, which made him easy to manipulate but difficult to get into. Very Japanese, and one of the reasons there are no casinos in that country. It's tough for the house to make its nut when you can knit a sweater between bets.

By contrast, Jerry had flashes of brilliance but was reckless, which meant that if you were willing to absorb some bruising, over time, you could eat him alive. As it was, he was down $800,000, which we knew because he made regular announcements.

I estimated the Paks had dropped a million, and since I was up about that, Jerry's money was in front of Quan. The Chinese was a solid player, and his system wasn't as rigid as most. He had a couple of "tells," the most significant of which was that he bet kings harder than aces. This probably meant he had a history of luck with cowboys. It happens. My father almost never won with queens, and neither do I. It's just the way certain cards chase certain players—or don't. The difference is I stagger the way I bet my nemesis. I didn't think Quan was advertising, but we hadn't gotten into it yet.

That was about to change.

Sydney was dealing the last hand before the changeover, and the flop was K-A-7. Quan immediately bet the maximum, $10,000. Saito dithered, then dropped. I hadn't looked at my cards yet, but I called.

Quan smiled at me. "How about we up the stakes?"

"What do you have in mind?"

"No limit . . . unless you don't have the stomach to match your mouth."

"What was it Mao said? 'When life deals you barbed wire, make lemonade.'"

"Fuck you."

I still wasn't making any points.

Saito stood. "I go to bed now."

"I hope you're more exciting between the sheets than you were here," Quan said. "I've had better action from a corpse."

Saito ignored him, and Quan turned to the Malaysian. "How about you, laughing boy? You fuck up bad enough, maybe your old man can adopt me."

This wasn't a game for the Malaysian, and he knew it. Even so, he took a long time before he pushed back from the table. "Too many assholes in the family already." He grinned. To me, he said, "You want me to leave a couple of my guys?"

I thanked him but passed, and Prince began cashing both men out.

I smiled at Quan. "Since it's just us Chinese, you want to rethink your bet?"

Like the spider to the fly, "Glad you asked." He pulled back his ten grand, counted out a million dollars in chips and pushed them forward.

I looked at Prince. "What am I good for?"

"Anything you like, Mr. B."

"Raise ten," I said.

Quan's head snapped up. "What the fuck?"

"You're right," I said. "What the fuck. Make it twenty."

Like it always does when big action begins, the room went quiet, replaced by an electricity that shortened everyone's breathing to only what was necessary. The bodyguards stood and moved closer to the table.

Quan watched Prince carefully fan twenty-one black and gold, mother-of-pearl plaques onto the green felt. A little smaller than a pack of Marlboros, the rectangular tiles were individually hand-engraved with the Inca logo, a unique, seven-digit serial number and the numeric designation, $1,000,000. Before Prince withdrew his hand, he looked at me for final confirmation, a courtesy extended to whales for an extraordinary wager. I nodded, and Prince pulled away.

Quan exploded. "How the fuck can you bet? You haven't even looked at your cards."

"Really? I'll remember to do that next time. You in or out?"

He was stuck. This was beyond cards—or money. I'd embarrassed him earlier. Now I had his nut sack nailed to a board and was sharpening a knife. He grunted, "Call."

As soon as the pot was right, Sydney turned the fourth card. Another king.

"Twenty million," Quan said with a mixture of relief and swagger. He might as well have hired a skywriter. Trip cowboys.

"Raise fifty."

I thought he was going to levitate out of his seat. Now, he knew I had to have a pair of bullets down, so filling his kings did no good because I would fill too—or catch the fourth ace. There was only one card that could do him any good: the case king.

While Quan wrestled with that ugly thought, I reached across the table, took one of his Fine Cuts and lit it. It distracted him and irritated him in equal measure, so I added to it by blowing smoke at him. "I figure these are about to be mine anyway. So tell me something. Why is half of Asia in town? Other than to hope you show up in one of their games?"

There was a long pause while he worked his mouth around his teeth. When he didn't answer, I asked the question again.

"I don't know what you're talking about," he said.

Jerry snorted. "Bullshit. Ever hear of a seventeen-year locust? What we have here is the seventy-year variety. The difference is what these pricks lay waste to never comes back." He stared hard at Quan. "Isn't that right, you motherfucking rapist?"

Without warning, Saito backhanded Jerry across the face. The Malaysian grabbed his mouth, and blood ran between his fingers. Saito spit something in rapid Japanese and raised his hand again. Dagmar moved toward them, but Saito relaxed, and the moment passed.

I'd struck a nerve, but with Jerry swallowing blood, I wasn't going to get anything else, so I turned my attention back to Quan. "In case you lost your place, I raised. Your move is call or reraise You could also drop, but you won't. You set this trap, and you wouldn't sleep for a month if you walked away." I took a beat, then added. "But from where I sit, there's not much sleep in your future either way."

I had him, and he knew it. So did everybody in the room. He couldn't win, he couldn't save face, and he couldn't kill me. At least, I didn't think so.

He gave it all he had. "You must have checked your cards when I wasn't looking."

"I really don't remember."

He then did something I had never seen in Vegas. He tore his cards in half and threw them violently at Sydney. The pieces hit the dealer in the face and landed on the table face-up, confirming the three kings. Sydney, pro that he was, didn't react.

I didn't have to maintain the Inca's honor, so to commemorate the occasion, I threw my hole cards over. Pair of queens. Jerry whooped so loud, they might have heard him in Kuala Lumpur. Quan sat silent, his face ashen.

"You were right," I said. "I didn't look." I pulled in the plaques. I handed a one-million-dollar tile to Sydney and one to Prince, then gave Floyd and Dagmar $50,000 each. Even the unflappable Sydney's hand shook as he took the plaque. That's what I love most about having money. Giving it away.

I saw Quan's right arm disappear, and I shifted my weight slightly. When he launched himself across the table, swinging and snarling and swearing in multiple languages, I let myself slide off the right side of my chair. I saw something flash past my nose, but it missed, and I hit Mr. Shanghai in the back of the head as he went by.

At first, I thought he was just wearing brass knuckles, but it also looked like a blade. As it turned out, it was both. An Ophidian Shuriken is a razor-sharp, four-pointed, steel star about the diameter of a hockey puck. It can be thrown, but it usually isn't. There are three finger holes in its center, and the bottom point swivels out of the way so it can be gripped in a man's palm with the remaining three points protruding outward. The ordinary gangbanger usually cuts himself before he gets to the main event, but in the right hands, an OS slices wide, deep and frequent, and unleashes so much blood the opponent usually flees in terror. I've also seen eyes punctured and one driven through a carotid. It's an ugly weapon with ugly results.

I hit the floor rolling, but before I could get my feet under me, one of Quan's bodyguards threw himself on my back and knocked my wind to Poughkeepsie. While I was deciding if I was going to die, the other clown kicked me in the side of the head.

I used my larger frame to leverage the guy on my back over, and suddenly, Dagmar loomed up and brought a sap down on his forehead. Sheathed or not, lead on bone is not something you want to be on the receiving end of, and the guy immediately let go of me and grabbed what was almost certainly a fractured skull.

My eyesight was blurred and red from lack of oxygen, but I kicked a foot out and caught the second bodyguard on the ankle. I felt it give, and he went down, screaming. I kept moving because Quan had to be close. As I got to my feet, he came from my blind side, and the star cut through my suit coat down to my biceps. I swiveled and banged him twice in the face, hard. He wasn't used to being hit and went out on his feet.

But before he could fall, an Inca security team, along with Jerry's bodyguards, gathered him and his cronies in three scrums and ran them out the door and into what was about to be a sunrise. I saw a couple of the Malaysians get in some licks along the way.

While I settled up with Prince, the villa emptied into a slew of waiting SUVs. On my way out, I looked back and saw the sleeping Pak brother right where he'd been from the outset. He'd be hungover and broke, and he wouldn't have even seen the floor show.

Outside, Jerry had disappeared. Saito was probably responsible for that. Nobody liked the Chinese, but at the end of the day, I wasn't Asian. It was just as well. Right now, all I wanted was a hot shower and a bed. However, as I climbed into one of the Inca's black Escalades to be driven back to my place, I made an appointment with myself to review my distrust of queens.

I fished my phone out of my suit coat and clicked it on to check messages. It rang almost immediately, and Jake's number flashed up. I answered it and heard a woman giggling in the background. "You're up early, Counselor."

"Fuck early, I'm half in the bag and on my way to bed. Judge Cavalcante just called. He chased down Kingdom's conviction. Hold on to your shorts. Elephant trafficking."

"You mean ivory?"

"I mean elephants. Ivory was part of it, but that didn't become illegal until '89. Markus-baby was moving whole fucking heads, feet, bones, even dicks. The penalty for that shit back then was like five grand and have-a-nice-day, but Markus ran into an ambitious prosecutor without enough to do. The guy indicted him for falsifying an international cargo manifest, which takes up about fifty pages of the U.S. Code. Hello fun showers."

"That was pretty rarefied air in those days. How'd he get caught?"

"That's almost the best part. His partner turned him in because he'd been cheated out of a million dollars. And if that wasn't enough, Markus fucked the guy's wife and left a kid for him to raise. This is so fucking great, I might start going to temple."

"I thought you were Catholic."

"I pick and choose."

"Call me if you need directions."

"Good night, asshole."

"Where are you on the Tongan citizenship matter?"

"Did you forget my position on clients asking for progress reports?"

"I didn't, and I don't care. I need an answer. But before you go, I owe you an apology for previous remarks."

"Hold on to it. I want to be sober enough to remember."

Bronis set up a late lunch on the bedroom terrace, then phoned us when it was ready. I'd already worked out, but Birdy was still dead to the world. She managed to wrap herself in a voluminous aqua and orange terry robe and pull her hair into a ponytail before joining me. I thought she looked terrific.

Scrambled eggs and ham on a clear desert afternoon made everything seem new again, and the exhilaration in Birdy's voice as she described her evening evaluating one of the top three-year-olds in the country should have made me happier. Unfortunately, out in the real world, Chuck and Lucille Brando were still dead, and I hadn't felt completely right since that night. I wanted to get moving.

"So how was *your* evening, Grumpy?" she asked.

"Sorry, preoccupied. It was fine. Please continue with your equine adventure."

She shook her head in amazement. "MrSaturdayDance is like no horse I've ever seen. He's as big as Secretariat, and if he's brought along correctly, this time next year, the whole world will know who he is."

"Can I assume you'll be the one bringing him along?"

"They want me to stay for a week and get his diet adjusted so he can travel. Then we'll truck him to Santa Anita. I already know which barn."

"Can I assume you'll go with him?"

She smiled. "What kind of trainer would I be if I didn't?

We've got to get to know each other." She paused. "I must be pretty good at it. Look what happened with you."

I lifted my orange juice. "Bob Baffert, watch out."

She looked uncomfortable. "There a problem?" I asked.

She shook her head. "I gave them a preliminary yes, but I said I had to check with you before I could finalize."

"Check with me?"

Her lower lip trembled. "No one's ever treated me like this before. I'm so overwhelmed I . . ."

I reached across and put my hands over hers. They were trembling too. "I haven't done anything. Nick did. Birdy, don't be tentative when you see a string of green lights. Jump on the accelerator. But I want good seats at Churchill."

She came around the table and kissed me with passion. Too much passion. I gently pushed her away.

She looked at me like maybe she'd done something wrong. "Don't you want to?"

"If you need proof, I'll stand up. But I want that sexual tension in you when we get where we're going."

"Don't worry, I'll be tense. I'm right on the edge. Do I need a briefing?"

"Dress provocatively and pretend you're a little dumb. Not stupid, but eager to please."

"Hey, I'm the chick who went riding with a meth head. I'm a natural."

"Clever, but not funny. Relax, smart people make bad decisions. And no real names. What do you want me to call you?"

"It'll come to me when I need it. You're going to tell me what this is all about one of these days, aren't you?"

"I am, but I'm still figuring it out myself."

"Maybe I could help?"

"You can. Show lots of leg."

When we came out of the villa, Bronis had a silver Genesis sitting in front. You won't find Hyundai on the Christmas lists of many Beverly Hills residents, but maybe it should be—especially the tall ones.

In both my Rolls and Ram, I've had the driver's side seat track lengthened. Even though I can drive most regular-sized vehicles, the extra few inches makes the difference between serviceability and comfort. I own a couple of dozen other cars that I couldn't resist, some of which I can only open the door and visually admire the workmanship. I think of them as expensive paperweights.

But the Genesis seemed like it had been designed with me in mind. It wasn't cavernous but nicely proportioned, and the steering wheel was positioned better than any Mercedes. The proof is always how tight a car sounds when you close the door, and this one was as solid as a bank vault.

As Bronis helped Birdy in, I noticed a folded note on the dash.

> *Don't you just love this damn thing?*
> *Half the price of a BMW and twice as quiet.*
> *And how about that grille? Sensual, huh?*
> *Guy in Seoul sent me a dozen.*
> *He'll guarantee ten rollers a year if I use them as courtesy cars.*
> *What do you think?*

> *—N*

In a tight, midthigh salmon dress cut almost to her navel and matching fuck-me heels delicately strapped above her ankles, Birdy was a knockout. Exactly what I wanted. She'd also accented her deep neckline with a tight, gold collar that was vaguely reminiscent of *Bondage Monthly.* I saw Bronis trying to eye her inconspicuously and not doing particularly well.

When he closed her door, she looked around the interior. "Korean, right?"

"Right."

"Nice, but the seat's cold."

"Ah, as we used to say in school, *le butt du tout nu.*"

"If that means what I think, you wanted provocative, and I'm from the method school."

"Then remember *The Story of O* and no complaining."

"Who's O?"

"Jesus, another thoroughly wasted education. We've got to get you to a library." I made a mental note to check out the Genesis's grille, but in the meantime I had one far more sensual to admire. To the man who insists he prefers conservatively dressed women, I offer: So you'd rather arrive at your reunion in a minivan instead of an Aston Martin? Sure you would.

23

Richer Seas

SIX WEEKS AGO
SOUTHERN CHINA

Cheyenne Rollins was sick to her stomach again. Already, the driver had had to stop the truck twice for her to throw up in the bushes, leaving her soaked and shivering from the cold, unrelenting rain. Between the diarrhea and the vomiting, it had been almost two weeks since she'd been able to keep anything in her system long enough to nourish her, and she was thinner than she'd been in her adult life. Her prized, fur-trimmed Burberry hung so loose, it felt like it belonged to another person.

By contrast, the baby was fine and eagerly gummed the putrid rice balls the orphanage nurse had provided for the trip. Cheyenne supposed that was some consolation, but as she stumbled from the truck and dropped to her knees in the mud, it quickly faded.

The sour taste in the back of her throat wouldn't go away, fueling the nausea further. She grabbed a handful of wet grass, stuffed it in her mouth and forced herself to chew, releasing the chlorophyll. Regardless of what the doctor at the orphanage said, this wasn't a reaction to RU-486, the so-called Morning-After Pill. Both she and Sherry had taken that before, and it didn't make you sick like this. They'd been poisoned, but they didn't know with what.

It's what they had been talking about when Sherry had put her hand on Cheyenne's cheek and told her she was sorry for getting her into this and made her promise to find her sister. "She's going to think I blame her for this, but you need to make her believe I don't. Tell her she's been the best big sis anybody could ever want."

Then Sherry had taken a final breath and died. For a long time afterward, Cheyenne had held the lifeless body and fingered the blackening ligature marks cut deep into her dead friend's neck. They were on her arms and legs too, and the one across her back had sliced through the flesh on her hips. Sherry wouldn't talk about them, and part of Cheyenne was relieved she'd never know. That was only a week ago, but it seemed much longer, and Cheyenne knew that unless she could find a way to eat, she'd be joining Sherry soon.

The plan had been to be at the orphanage only a couple of hours, collect their two children, and depart for the cruise ship waiting in Hong Kong harbor. But both she and Sherry had begun vomiting on the way there, then gone into convulsions. Cheyenne remembered her grandmother telling her that whatever you taste when you're sick is what got you there. If that was true, then the poison tasted like licorice.

So the two hours had turned into twelve days, and their ship had long since sailed, along with their documents. The orphanage director had done everything he could to make them feel unwelcome, and after Sherry died, he told Cheyenne that she had to leave or he would turn her in to the police. She'd stretched it another day to try to gain a little strength, then allowed herself to be put in an old stake-bed truck the director sent for. Two thousand dollars was the last of her money, but she was in no condition to argue price.

She felt guilty about not bringing Sherry's child too. They'd certainly tried hard enough to give the three-year-

old boy to her. But an infected snake bite had forced the amputation of his leg below the knee, and Cheyenne knew she couldn't handle him and her infant too. She promised herself that when she got home, she'd go to confession and ask the priest to say a prayer for Sherry and all the children who were still stuck in that godforsaken place. She'd have to be careful with the confession, though. Not many priests were up to what she could dump in their lap.

Her driver, a scrawny guy with permanently brown teeth and a perpetual leer, periodically glanced at her in a way she knew all too well. At nearly six feet with blonde hair and a pair of breasts that were ordinary in Las Vegas but unheard of in this part of the world, even the puke on her blouse wasn't enough to turn him off. He also smoked incessantly, which, in the enclosed space, wasn't helping her fluttering insides.

Neither spoke the other's language, and her pantomime for him to put out his cigarette drew only a laugh and more staring at her chest. Cheyenne didn't know his name and didn't care to. She called him Shit Teeth, which he didn't get, and if she hadn't been so weak, she'd have kicked his ass out and gone on alone.

When her stomach quieted a little, she spit out the grass and forced herself back to her feet. As she did, she thought she caught a whiff of sea air. She took another breath, and underneath the sulfur, smoke and rot lurked the unmistakable smell of big water. Thank God, she thought. She climbed unsteadily back into the prehistoric rig, grateful for the running board. Shit Teeth didn't wait for the door to close before he lurched forward.

There were no docks on this section of the Pearl River. Thousands of junks and houseboats were simply tied together offshore, forming a city of creaking hulls and rubbing wood. People climbed from one vessel to another to conduct commerce and socialize while swarms of Chinese children scrambled across decks and up and down ropes in a game of tag, oblivious to the rain.

Shit Teeth pulled to the water's edge and stopped. When Cheyenne didn't move, he barked something and pointed to the door, but she had no intention of being left alone in this alien world. She shook her head, and he became enraged, screaming in rapid Chinese, saliva flying. She sat impassive until he finished then calmly said, "You were paid to do a job. Do it." He may not have understood the words, but he got the message.

He banged out of the truck, pulled down his wide-brimmed hat, turned up his stained collar and leaned into the downpour. Cheyenne watched him make his way along the shoreline until he came to a sorry-looking skiff pulled partway onto the sand. A pair of fishermen were working on deck, and Shit Teeth yelled something to them. They ignored him, but after more yelling and gesticulating, one of the men interrupted what he was doing long enough to point farther up the beach. Shit Teeth returned to the truck, muttering angrily to himself.

The deep ruts and hidden rocks made the ride along the beach bone-jarringly unpleasant, but Shit Teeth took no notice of Cheyenne's comfort. Feeling her nausea rising again, she reached over and slapped him. He bellowed and raised his fist to strike her, then changed his mind and slowed a little.

A low, wide pier extended a hundred feet into the Pearl, and waves generated by the open sea a few miles to the south washed against it, occasionally spilling across its planks. At the pier's end sat a medium-sized cargo vessel of ancient vintage showing as much rust as paint. Cheyenne guessed it had once been dark red, but in the gloom, she could have been off by a spectrum. On the bow, peeling white Chinese characters rose above the English lettering:

RICHER SEAS

She wondered if that was a tribute to the ship's past or a prayer for its future. Either way, it didn't apply to the *here and now. It was a dreadful-looking tub on a dreadful-smelling river, and desperation hung over it like a shroud.*

The truck stopped again, and this time Cheyenne got out. She carefully covered the infant with an extra blanket, then took her Tumi valise from behind the seat. The Tumi had been a gift from her boyfriend, Kevin, who'd probably stolen it. Kevin had run off to Dallas with a gay high roller a casino host had pimped him out to—a major violation of the rules—and now, he'd have to take a beating if he wanted to work again. They wouldn't hurt his face, but he'd be laid up for a few weeks, and he couldn't afford it.

That's what had gotten Cheyenne into this mess. Trying to make some money to take care of both of them while she nursed Kevin back to health. Everybody told her she was crazy to be hung up on the guy—even Sherry—but they didn't understand. Cheyenne didn't crave him sexually. He was a selfish lover and mostly interested in men. She longed for his warmth. You can live all your life with everything—or nothing—but awakening in the dark and feeling willing arms around you can't be bought or begged. And Kevin's were the first arms that hadn't abused her, or worse. What she wouldn't have given for them now.

How had a few lousy electronics store commercials turned into this? She wanted to be pissed at Donnie, but it wasn't his fault. She'd volunteered. Hell, she'd badgered him. Miss Quick, her fifth-grade teacher back in Youngstown, used to say that if you don't make your own destiny, you'll end up part of someone else's. Problem was, Miss Quick didn't tell you how to do that when your mom was dead, and your old man was drunk before you left for the school bus.

Cheyenne started for the pier, but Shit Teeth grabbed her by the wrist and led her toward a long, unmarked one-story building set just off the beach. Inside, a few naked, overhead bulbs provided enough light for her to see armed soldiers watching over several hundred ragged, shivering Chinese of all ages. Some huddled in groups, others sat against the walls on crude wooden benches, but despite their numbers, *there was very little noise, only the scraping of feet and an occasional tubercular cough. Fearful eyes turned toward her, making her feel even more conspicuous. Shit Teeth pointed to an empty space on one of the benches, and she gratefully sat, clutching the baby and her valise to her chest.*

An angry, bemedaled army officer approached her escort, and the two began a heated exchange. Occasionally, the officer turned and appraised Cheyenne with undisguised hostility, and she could only imagine what Shit Teeth was telling him. Finally, the driver pressed a wad of bills into the officer's hand, which he pocketed without glancing at them.

Cheyenne had undone the buttons on her coat, and this time when the officer looked at her, his gaze lingered on her chest. She'd been told she'd be traveling with refugees, but with the army involved, this was clearly something more. At a minimum, deportees; at a maximum . . . who knew? There was nothing to do but ride it out, and if that meant she had to spread her legs or lips for this creep, well, she'd done that before.

Suddenly, there was shouting outside and the sound of approaching vehicles. The officer's head jerked up, Cheyenne forgotten. Moving as one, the mass of Chinese humanity crowded toward a long row of windows. Curious as well, Cheyenne clutched the baby to her and did the same.

The rain had stopped, and a dozen troop carriers roared passed the building and onto the sand, split six to each side, then slammed to a stop at the pier's edge. Immediately, a stream of tall, spit-and-polish soldiers dismounted from the vehicles and formed two columns, their bayoneted assault rifles at port arms. An officer blew a whistle, and the columns quick-timed onto the planks, a soldier from each row peeling off at five-pace intervals, then turning and facing his counterpart across the divide. When the last two reached the Richer Seas, *the man with the whistle barked a command, and the soldiers came to parade rest, banging their rifle butts on the pier in a single* thunk.

As if on cue, a massive, black sedan appeared, and the

officer who had been eyeing Cheyenne came out of the building to meet it. Out of the corner of her eye, she saw Shit Teeth exit behind him and begin slinking toward his truck. Soldiers who had not previously been in evidence now ran from all directions and took positions beside the officer, who looked extremely nervous. For some reason, that pleased Cheyenne.

When the sedan stopped, Cheyenne noticed the pair of four-star flags on its fenders and knew that meant some kind of general. The soldier at the wheel bolted out and opened the rear door. A thickset, pock-faced Chinese, wearing enough gold braid and battle ribbons to outfit a roomful of drum majors, stepped onto the concrete. His welcoming committee, already at attention, snapped off a stiff salute.

At the same time, the door on the other side of the car opened, and a civilian got out. Also Chinese, he was in his thirties and wearing designer sunglasses, fashionable jeans and an untucked white silk shirt. His skin was deeply tanned, which set off his expensive gold watch and neck chain. Cheyenne felt her knees go weak. She shuddered and slunk back into the recesses of the building.

She didn't know either man's name, but they were the ones who had taken Sherry away during the party. The general wasn't wearing a uniform then, but there was no question, these were the same men.

She remembered asking somebody where they had gone, and much later, trying to determine how much time had passed, but there were no clocks in the house, and each time Cheyenne's head began to clear, that terrible woman had plunged another needle into her arm, and a new man had mounted her.

And then two men with tattoos on their faces had forced the pills that had made them sick down their throats. "No babies," one said, as they swallowed. Cheyenne had spit at them and gotten kicked in the stomach for it. She'd go to her grave remembering the cold indifference in the men's eyes and those horrible tattoos.

Now, the ground began to shake, and a massive truck came into view. It was so large that from where Cheyenne stood, she could see only its wheels. Fighting down her fear, she pressed forward again.

The eighteen-wheel missile carrier had been converted to cargo duty and painted in fresh camo. Atop it, a ten-foot-square container covered with a tarpaulin was lashed down with white canvas straps. With military precision, a team of soldiers climbed aboard the truck and unfastened them. A forklift appeared, gently lifted the container and brought it to carrying position. The operator waited while the white-shirted Chinese man tugged at the snaps holding the edges of the tarp together. When they came loose, the general lifted one.

The ragged crowd let out a collective gasp, and Cheyenne jostled a man beside her to get a better look. Pacing nervously inside a polished, stainless steel cage was a four-hundred-pound Bengal tiger.

It was after dark when they loaded Cheyenne and the others onto the Richer Seas. During the long wait, the officer had put Cheyenne in his office, where he had spoken to her in impeccable English. "Stay in here no matter what happens. And if anyone speaks to you, do not answer them."

Cheyenne was too sick to do anything but nod. The officer summoned an old Chinese woman from the throng, who gave her what looked like a piece of dried sweet potato. Willing to try anything, Cheyenne took a bite and immediately felt her mouth go numb. A few minutes later, she was no longer nauseous. Cheyenne was out of money, but seeing the old woman staring at the fur collar of her coat, she unzipped it and handed it to her. The woman pressed it to her face and retreated like she had just seen heaven.

Cheyenne thanked the officer but was afraid his kindness might only be a prelude to having to fuck him. Trying to take that off the table, she said "I'm having my period."

The officer looked bemused. "If I were such a man, that

would be of no concern. I'm Major Soong. And you are . . . ?"

"Cheyenne Rollins. Your English is excellent."

"It comes and goes. This is not a good time in my army to be too fluent."

"You didn't learn to talk like that here."

"I've never been out of China. My parents studied engineering at Berkeley. Do you know the place?"

Cheyenne raised an eyebrow. "I'm from Vegas. People from Berkeley consider us barely human."

The major hesitated. "I'm sorry, I am not so good with . . . what is the word?"

"Sarcasm. My apologies, one of my failings. Where are we?"

"On the mainland. Thirty-seven miles north of Hong Kong."

"I don't remember crossing any water, but I was so sick I could have missed Paris. What did that old woman give me? I feel like I've been gargling Novocain."

The major smiled. "Every family has its own remedy, and they keep it to themselves. If you'll excuse me, I have things to attend to. I'll be back when it's time to put you on the ship."

Now, while the Chinese passengers stood in long lines and handed over bricks of cash to be able to board the Richer Seas, *Major Soong escorted Cheyenne to a small cabin, which he said she would not have to share. She thanked him profusely. "May I ask you one more question?"*

"As long as it is not about what you saw today."

"Not what . . . who. The general and the man in the white shirt. I want to know their names."

The major regarded her for a moment. "Why?"

"It's personal."

The officer walked across the cabin and stared out the small porthole. "The general I will not tell you. The other man is the leader of the Hu-Meng. The Tiger People. They live in the mountains not far from here."

"That's not what I asked."

"He goes by Zhang, but that's not his name. The original Zhang warlords are long gone, but the honorific remains."

"What is an honorific?"

"An expression of respect . . . and power. Like Caesar."

When Soong had gone, Cheyenne bolted the door and, for the first time since her arrival in China, felt somewhat safe. The room was dank and damp, but it was paradise compared to the open deck where the rest of the passengers were scavenging anything they could find to erect shelters.

She tended to the baby who, despite her untreated cleft palate, gnawed at another rice ball, drank some apple juice, then promptly fell asleep, propped against a pair of pillows. She watched her for a long while, marveling at the tiny hands and face and trying to imagine what she would look like once a good surgeon repaired her mouth. Beautiful, she thought. She felt herself bonding with the little girl, and she fought it back. This was someone else's child, not hers, and the last thing she needed was to become emotionally involved.

Using the cold, brown water from the single faucet, Cheyenne tried to wash as best she could, but she was still a mess. She comforted herself with the thought that as soon as she got home, she intended to break the Guinness Record for the longest, hottest bath in the history of indulgence. The $50,000 that would be in her bank account for delivering the child was consoling too.

She suddenly realized that she was desperately hungry. There were cabins on either side of hers, and she could hear people moving about in them. She contemplated knocking on a door and trying to beg some food, but decided not to risk it until they were well out to sea. She lay down and fell fitfully asleep.

Cheyenne was awakened by the absence of sound. The steady drumbeat of the engines had stopped, and without forward motion, the ship was rocking gently from side to side. The northern coast of Australia was days away, and *there were not supposed to be any stops. Her first thought was pirates, but she could see nothing through the porthole. The baby was still asleep, so she stepped into the unlighted passageway, let her eyes adjust and made her way back toward the deck.*

She stopped at the wooden door and heard people running on the other side. Cracking it slightly, she peered out. Illuminated by red emergency lights, sailors moved about quickly, directed by hand commands from one of the ship's officers. She pushed the door a little further. Only thirty feet of deck separated her from the port railing, but it took several moments to realize that just beyond, looming in the dark, was the hull of an enormous ship. Thick steel cables connected the two vessels, and sailors were hanging rubber bumpers over the side of the Richer Seas.

From Cheyenne's angle, she could only make out part of the new ship's name, Kingdom of Sam . . . *She thought about moving farther along the deck so she could read it all, when part of the larger ship's hull suddenly began sliding away. A cavern-sized opening appeared, and several Asian men, surrounded by Caucasians in blue jumpsuits and carrying automatic rifles, came into view. Somewhere, motors sprang to life, the cables tightened and the two ships began being drawn together. Simultaneously, sailors started dismantling a section of the* Richer Seas *railing.*

Then, without warning, the Chinese man in the white shirt rounded a corner only feet from where Cheyenne stood. Even in the dark, he was still wearing his sunglasses, which made him seem even more ominous. She receded a step, but he took no notice of her. He was followed by the forklift, carrying the covered cage. As the lift passed her, a sudden, bloodcurdling roar echoed through the night, and the sailors stopped working, fear in their eyes.

The ships were only twenty feet apart, and a long ramp was extended from the larger one. Zhang shouted angrily at the ship's officer, who frantically yelled for his men to get back to work.

Cheyenne saw another man step into the gaping opening of the second ship, almost close enough to touch. Like the guards, he was Caucasian but taller and broader, gray-haired and wearing a black sport coat, black turtleneck and black trousers. He lit a cigarette and drew deeply on it.

Suddenly, a tall, slender woman emerged next to him. She was dressed entirely in tight, red leather, and her stiletto-heeled boots looked awkward on the steel decking. A gust of wind caught her shoulder-length black hair, and as she turned to sweep it back, she looked directly toward Cheyenne.

For a long second, the two women locked eyes across the water, then Cheyenne shuddered and retreated into the dark passageway. She couldn't be sure the woman had seen her, but she knew she had just stared into the face of evil. It was the woman from the butterfly house. Cheyenne turned and ran back to her cabin.

24

Chipmunks and Helicopters

Las Vegas doesn't have a Chinatown in the conventional sense. Not like LA or San Francisco. Because of the relative newness of the city, theirs is a collection of strip centers wrapped by pan-Asian residential neighborhoods. That the Chinatown designation dominates is more a function of economics than embracement. Tourists understand Chinatown—not so much Koreatown or Little Saigon.

Donnie Two Knives' place took up forty feet of frontage at the end of one of the lesser centers. I hadn't seen his commercials but was surprised at the place's shabbiness. It was jarring when compared to the sleek electronics and billion-dollar logos in his windows. But then I remembered that, in that business, price is everything. If a customer goes home thinking he got a great deal, he doesn't care if he was standing in six inches of dirty water when he got it. In fact, it makes a better story if he was.

Before we got out, I said to Birdy, "There's no way to tell how this is going to go, so be ready to zig or zag."

"Hey, stop worrying. In this outfit, if the guy has a pulse, he won't be paying attention to my acting."

The interior of Donnie's wasn't much of an upgrade from

outside. Boxes of appliances and electronic gear were stacked in every conceivable space, leaving customers to pick their own path though the maze. Half the overhead lights were burned out, and the A/C had either failed or been turned off. Fans moved languid air from one place to another, but it all smelled like stale sweat. There were a few shoppers, Asian men, wandering among the clutter, stopping occasionally to point at something, then exchange rapid comments in a language I didn't understand.

One of them glanced at us and saw Birdy trying to step over a Sony flatscreen, showing pretty much everything she owned. Suddenly, they were all looking and smiling and chattering. I heard broken English that sounded like, "Donnie bee TB gol," which I translated into Donnie's big TV girl, but I could have been wrong.

"Can I help you?"

The voice reached me before I saw its owner. And I'd heard it before. On the cell in the Brandos' woods. An Asian man appeared from behind a wall of boxes, but if he was smiling, it was on the inside. I pegged him at slightly over six-two, and he had his long-sleeved white shirt rolled up to his elbows, revealing a pair of forearms that hadn't gotten that size shelving microwaves. He moved well too. On the balls of his feet and with short steps, which is always a dead giveaway that a guy's been trained.

"I'm here to see Donnie."

If he recognized my phone whisper, he gave no indication. He looked me up and down, then made an appraisal of Birdy like a predator sizing up something that had wandered into his cave. He seemed to be trying to decide whether to eat it or fuck it.

"Donnie's not here." Just like before, no trace of accent at all.

"When do you expect him back?"

"He's on a buying trip to Singapore."

The lie was natural, no trace of having to think about it. Donnie'd been gone a few weeks, but even though this guy probably didn't know exactly what had happened to him, he knew he wasn't coming back.

"Just my fuckin' luck," I said. "We made a deal for a couple of girls next time I came through. Was supposed to be here a fuckin' month ago, but got hung up. Then only one of the bitches wanted to come."

The guy turned and stared at the customers who had assembled in a group a few feet away. As the silence got longer, the men began to look uncomfortable, and finally, they skittered out the front door. The guy turned back to me. "Who are you?"

I decided to give the Garden State some love. "Johnny," I said. "From Jersey."

"That it? Just Johnny from Jersey?"

"That's it. Who are you?"

It took him a moment. It didn't smell right, but he was curious. "Major."

I decided to test the waters. "As in next promotion you're a colonel, or what?"

Birdy laughed out loud. I don't know if she thought I was funny, or she was just into her part. Either way, it was perfect. The guy's jaw tightened.

Then Birdy reached down and slowly inched up the hem of her dress until Major got the full chipmunk. She held it and smiled at him, licking her lips carnally. If the guy hadn't suddenly snorted like a bull, I might have forgotten what we were there for.

"Just Major," he said, never taking his eyes off Birdy. "So Johnny from Jersey, what was your deal with Donnie?"

Donnie and Major's office wasn't any plusher than the showroom, but at least it wasn't full of merchandise. I sat in a plastic chair two sizes too small, and Birdy sank into a deep sofa to my right that had her crossed knees as high as her shoulders. That's why I took the chair. Delta trains you to never sit in overstuffed furniture. The extra half second it takes to pull yourself out could mean that's where you'll wait for the body bag.

Major ignored the desk and sat directly across a low coffee table from me in a leather banker's chair.

"Here's the drill," I said. "Donnie wanted some girls—"

Major interrupted, "I heard you the first time. Who the fuck you kidding? This is Vegas, man. A thousand new broads show up every week." He looked at Birdy, and I saw his eyes go to her lap, but the curtain was down. "No offense, of course."

"Of course," she said.

I stood up. "Sounds like Donnie thought you were a moron, Maj. You don't know shit. I'll wait till the man gets back."

A dark cloud descended over Major's face. I'd gotten under his skin. "Sit down, motherfucker."

I stayed standing and turned to Birdy. "Come on, doll. I never argue with waiters. All they can do is spit in your food."

Now Major stood. "I said, sit down." His voice was throaty, rage just below the surface.

"No, you said, 'Sit down, *motherfucker*.' We're gone. Donnie's got my number."

Birdy started to get up.

Major looked at her. "You got a name besides 'doll'?"

She looked at me and waited like a pro. I took a full beat then nodded.

"Marlene," she said.

Major smiled. "I like that. Major and Marlene. It has possibilities."

Sometimes you have to guess if you've leveled the playing field. I sat, and so did Major.

"Donnie's going to be gone a little longer than expected." He let that sink in, then added, "And just so we understand each other, he worked for me."

I wasn't surprised, and I didn't indicate I was. "So how do you want to handle this?"

"What exactly did Donnie tell you?"

"That the girls had to be smart and able to take orders."

"And?"

"No record. A misdemeanor or two, okay. Nothing heavy."

He seemed to be waiting for something else. I hesitated, made a decision. "They had to be willing to please . . . anybody . . . or anything."

He smiled slowly, then looked at Birdy. "That you, Marlene?"

She never took her eyes off his while she uncrossed her legs and parted her knees just enough. When he had taken in another eyeful, she smiled back. "I like a challenge."

The office was hot. The temperature was now up another few degrees, and all of us were wearing a little sweat. Major forced himself back to business. "Donnie was maybe smarter than I thought, but this gig requires a pair."

"I told you, this is it. Take it or leave it."

"She got a passport?"

"Yes," I answered.

"Saturday. She'll take the eight o'clock to Hong Kong. Be here four hours before with one bag. Carry-on only. I'll have her ticket and a visa. Any questions?"

It was Birdy's turn to show the flag. "I want to know what I'll be carrying"

Major shifted his gaze to me. He was weighing his answer when I took it out of his hands. "Nothing on the way over. A baby coming back. Isn't that right, Maj?"

"Donnie tell you that?"

"I wasn't going to reach out to this kind of talent for a mystery tour," I said. "But if it matters, he didn't volunteer. I had to help him."

He relaxed slightly. "Figure two weeks, maybe a few days longer. You'll do a little entertaining while the people on the other end get the documents together. Then you'll go on a nice cruise and bring back an orphan for a wonderful family. Very simple. Think of it as God's work."

"What else will God's mule be carrying?" I asked.

He flashed angry . . . started to say something . . . stopped. I waited. Finally, he said, "All she's gotta do is present some paperwork on this end."

"The wrong paperwork gets her the same sentence as a key of China White strapped to her ass."

"That's not the way this works. The paperwork's for the baby, and it will be completely legit. That's all you need to know."

"Is there a dress code?" Birdy asked.

"Just like you are now, and let people know you got a pair of tits. Don't be bashful about flashing man's best friend either. Understand?"

Birdy smiled. "I like clothes. A carry-on isn't going to cut it, especially if I'm . . . entertaining."

"Everything you need will be provided . . . but this kind of entertaining, you're not going to be going out much." He let that sink in. "For the return, pack comfortable. A coat's a good idea too. It can get cold out on the water."

"You missed something," I said.

"You'll get paid when she gets back."

"We need to go through the stand up, sit down routine again, or can we just cut to the chase?"

He didn't like my attitude, but he bit his tongue. "How much did Donnie promise you?"

I shook my head. "I got to tell you, Major, where I come from you'd have been dead before first grade."

He hesitated, then stood and walked to the desk. He bent, and I heard a heavy drawer slide open. When he came back, he was carrying several bundles of banded cash. "Half, now. You want to count it?"

When I didn't answer, he grabbed a yellow plastic Donnie's Electronics bag, shoved it inside and handed it to me. "We all set?"

"No."

"What the fuck do you mean, no?"

"How do I know you're not selling her? That I won't be meeting ships a couple of weeks from now with my Johnson in my hand?"

He should have told me to get the fuck out, but he didn't. That meant he was behind schedule. The look in his eyes also told me he was on the hook to somebody a lot more dangerous than he was.

"What do you want?"

"Let me see your wallet."

He looked unsure, but he got it out and handed it over. I fanned through his cards and let him see me memorize his address. I also now had a last name to go with Major—Martin. I took out a picture of a couple of kids. Boy and a girl, maybe three and five. "Yours?"

He nodded.

"Marlene's going to call me twice a day. Noon and midnight. She's five minutes late even once, you'll be down to one. She misses twice, you can't run far enough. And if you're thinking of sending the family away, remember what city you're in and where I'm from. You ain't going back to China, so sooner or later, I'll settle up."

He tried to hide it, but he was shaken.

"We on the same page . . . motherfucker?" I said.

He recovered, but not all the way. "See you in a few days."

Major walked us to the front door. "Where you staying, Marlene?" he asked.

I stopped and looked at him. "You're kidding, right?"

"Can't blame a guy for trying. There a last name to go with Marlene?" When she didn't answer, he turned to me. "I need it for the visa and to get things started in Hong Kong."

I nodded an okay to Birdy.

"Monroe," she said.

He forced a smile and tried to get some of his strut back. "This is getting better all the time." But he'd lost his rhythm.

We were half a mile away when Birdy pointed to a deserted construction site. It looked like a new mall had hit hard times. "Pull in," she said, her voice suddenly husky.

I followed her directions to a ramp leading to what would eventually be underground parking. As we wound down to the second level, the sun disappeared. "Stop," she said, her voice trembling. "I can't wait any longer."

I did, and she reached over and turned off the car. Seconds later, she was naked except for her shoes and collar as she tore at my jeans. When my engorged cock sprang free, she inhaled it, masturbating herself at the same time. We both only lasted seconds, coming in spasms and shudders.

We climbed into the back, and I sat while she faced forward and pounded herself down on me. I held her hips and thrust into her as deeply and as violently as I had anyone in my life while she hugged the driver's seat and bit into the headrest. None of the noises we made were human.

Finally consumed, we held each other. She tried to say something, but all that came out was a small whimper. I felt tears on my chest. She tried again, and managed, "My God, Rail, I can't find myself. I've never wanted a man more. Not any man. You."

"It's called a danger fuck. Wars are full of them. Careful, they're addictive."

"God, I hope so."

I put my finger to her lips to indicate she didn't need to talk. She took it in her mouth and began sucking it. Then she returned to my lap.

When I awakened, I didn't immediately know where I was. Then I felt the cramps in my legs and remembered. My cock was against her sleeping lips, and as she breathed, it started to respond. I moved her onto the seat, got out and dressed. Then I found a blanket in the trunk and covered her.

Before I did, I admired her nakedness. I didn't know where Birdsong Nash left off and Marlene Monroe took over, but I liked them both.

Judita met me at the door of the villa, and I motioned toward the car. A few moments later, she led a still-naked and out-on-her-feet Birdy up the stairs. I stripped and got into the downstairs shower, where I stood for a long time letting the 360 degrees of hot needles work their magic. While they did, I thought up a couple of songs for Hyundai I didn't think they'd use. I reserved judgment on the one entitled "Danger Fuck Zone," but they might want to install mouthguards on the headrests first.

After toweling off and putting on a robe, I found a cold Tecate, sat on the couch and counted the money in the Donnie's bag. Twenty-five grand. Lot of cash for a plane ride. I went to the hall closet. As usual, the combination to the safe inside the phony electrical panel had been set to my father's birthday.

I returned to the couch and turned on my phone. The mailbox was full. Fat Cat.

The Inca heliport was well away from the hotel, adjacent to their golf course. Arriving by chopper for your tee time has an up-your-ass resonance not easily duplicated at most country clubs. Personally, I hate helicopters just a little more than I hate golf. At least with golf, there's a bar at the end. With helicopters, all you can do is wait for it to go down, something I managed to live through in the army—twice. One also saved my life by pulling me out of an off-the-books combat zone, but I was barely conscious at the time, so I don't count it.

Nick drove me directly onto the pad and offered to ride to San Francisco to keep me company. I almost said yes but decided against it. "Depending what happens up there, I might be gone a few days. That going to be a problem?"

"What, with the villa? Forget about it. Besides, I want you to feel beholden. What do you want me to do with your lady friend?"

"She's going to be busy horse bonding during the day. Maybe, you could see that she doesn't get too lonely after work."

"Consider it done. I've got a couple of escorts who'll show her the time of her life and know how to keep their hands to themselves."

"Hands aren't the problem."

"You get a look at the arms on Bronis? They'll behave."

He pressed a small envelope into my palm. "Valium," he said. "One should be enough."

I took two. After all, flight time to McCarran, where the hotel jet was waiting, was ten minutes. Before I got out, I handed Nick the phone from the backpack I found at the Brandos. "There's a number on this."

"You want to know who it belongs to?"

I shook my head. "Only if it's not a guy named Major Martin. I'm interested in who might have been in the background telling him what to say. It would be somebody who speaks Chinese."

Nick tossed the phone on the dash. "I can tell you right now. Major is Donnie Two Knives' brother, and if they were taking orders from anybody, it was their old man, Lew. He runs the police union over here. The boys used to be cops too, but they couldn't stop stealing."

"What's the threshold to lose a badge?"

"Lower than you might think, but these two would have exceeded unlimited. Their big brainstorm was to catch a cab driver pimping or dealing and put him to work."

"Doing what?"

"The cabbie'd lay a hundred on a casino valet to bring him to the front of the line when a well-dressed single came out a little too drunk. Before we had cameras all the way down the drive, Donnie and Major would be waiting down at the end. They'd get in, hit the guy hard enough to make him groggy, then drop him buck naked a couple of miles out of town. Sweet deal. They were picking up five, ten grand a week."

"And nobody reporting it."

"Not something you want to discuss with the little woman back in Omaha."

"I think I can guess how it came apart."

Nick nodded. "This is a town where you better stick to pistol-whipping 7-Eleven clerks. We were all running decoys, but it was the Polynesian that got them. Anybody else would be playing shower tag upstate or anchoring a subdivision in the desert. But Lew made some problems go away for the right people, and the boys got a pass."

"After that, they'd put their dicks in a meat grinder if Lew told them to."

"Lew Martin. Doesn't sound Chinese."

"Used to be Martino. Changed it when they ran the mob out of the big hotels. Went from an asset to a liability overnight. The boys are adopted. There's another brother and a sister too. Older, but I never met them. Separate transactions. Like maybe twenty years apart. Same deal, though, Chinese."

"Then I assume the mother is?"

"Was. She's been dead a while. They met when Lew was a Marine in Taipei doing embassy duty. He came home speaking Mandarin and married to a Miss World. I remember her when I was a kid. One sweet-looking lady."

"You and Lew acquainted?"

"After a fashion. He's using his language skills to make inroads with the restaurant workers. Much bigger deal than fuckin' around with cops. Right to the head of the payoff line. But I gotta warn you, Rail, he's one nasty asshole, so don't be nosing around with half a plan."

"I'll check with you for the part I'm missing. Thanks for the lift."

"Get the fuck out of my car." But he was smiling. "Oh, one more thing."

"Yeah?"

"Thanks to you, my best dealer turned in his retirement notice."

"What about Prince?"

"Shit, he's already made me promise to let him work your next game."

"Bring back Quan."

"That's not gonna happen. I had to comp him a floor so he could fly in some friends and party. God knows what that's going to cost me. But you better brace yourself. Word's going to get around, and some other schmucks are going to show up asking for you. Gonna want to take down the man who took down Quan."

"Make it soon, will you."

"That's what I was hoping to hear."

"By the way, forget your Hyundai deal."

"Really?"

"You use those courtesy cars, nobody'll take time to gamble."

"I don't get it."

I winked and got out. "Check with Birdy."

At McCarran, I stepped off the big Bell, walked five yards and got on the G5. We were into our takeoff roll before I was belted in. Now I could spend an hour thinking about dropping into some Bay Area fog in a second chopper.

The dead hack driver in Victorville now made sense. He'd almost certainly been one of the drunk-rolling team and was probably shaking down the Martin family or talking to a reporter or any of a thousand things that might screw up Lew's new union plans. He had to go.

But whacking a cabbie is one thing. A famous cop and his wife are something else. Smart guys like Lew Martin don't kill unless there's no other choice, so going to Chuck and Lucille's afterward had been Donnie's play. And since the car he'd arrived in was already in a storage shed with a body in it, he needed a ride to the next event.

Calling a local cab or renting a car was out, so who was the other person? It had to have been somebody who could drop him away from the ranch, then be cool enough to sit in the dark and wait. Somebody who wouldn't seem out of place if another car happened along. And it wouldn't have been Major because he wouldn't have bolted on his brother.

I dialed Eddie Buffalo, my excellent but mostly lawless pilot who couldn't hold a left seat until I hired him. His phone rang seven times and went to voice mail. I told him to get back to me in a hurry. Ninety seconds later, he did.

"Where are you?" I asked.

"Thirty-one thousand feet over Arizona. Fuckin' driver's

crawling along just fast enough to keep this goddamn thing from being a road hazard. About ready to go up front and show him where the throttles are."

"Isn't your cell supposed to be off?"

"It's cool, I'm in the john."

In the background, I heard pounding, then a woman's voice. "Hey, are you on a phone in there?"

I heard him call out, "Scared of flying. Talking to my imam." Then he was back with me. "That should send them to the PC handbook. What do you need, boss?"

"Assuming you're not in federal lockup, I'll meet you at the Huntington tonight. So before they wrestle you out of your booth, call up there and tell whoever's on duty I want that big suite on the second floor, and I don't care who they have to move." Normally, it doesn't matter where I sleep, but every time I'm in San Francisco, they seem to have an earthquake, and Nob Hill is high enough without adding extra stories.

"You care which airport?"

"Use Oakland. Less hassle if we need to leave in a hurry."

Helicopters and earthquakes, all in the same night. I didn't have enough Valium. Then I got really lucky. As we went into our descent, a thunderstorm was waiting.

Lonny, my pilot for the third and last leg, was good but way too chatty for sideways rain and Tilt-A-Whirl winds. I also could have lived without the endless loop of Mick Jagger's "Brown Sugar" dialed up to head-pound.

Over the music, Lonny ranted about other galaxies listening to our radio signals and rap music fucking up their perception. He had some interesting observations about earth's being hit with a death beam to keep us from infecting the rest of the universe and that a mandatory Stones Hour on every station would let the aliens know we had our shit together. I might have written down his Web site, but I was busy helping drive since he felt he had to look at me while he talked.

Fat Cat had gotten clearance for us to land at the Hall of Justice, which on a clear day was probably spectacular. Tonight, I would have settled for a controlled crash. Somehow, Lonny got us down on all fours, and as I dashed through the rain with my overnight bag slung on my shoulder, I made my umpteenth promise to never, ever fly in a helicopter again. Somehow, I didn't think it would hold any better than previous ones.

25

Missed Miracles

Page Bacon Hospice was a 1907 Victorian in Haight-Ashbury that had once been a hotel. Even though they deal with the terminally ill, hospices are usually more inviting than hospitals, where noise and indifference compete with healing. There's no such pretense in a hospice. Men and women who choose to spend their time providing comfort and dignity to the dying don't watch clocks or consult their pocket copies of union rules when they're having a bad day. They're also low-paid or no-paid, so it's a calling.

And for those who live in big cities and can't abide homosexuals, I suggest you don't die, because there's a better than even chance that the guy who empties your bedpan when you can no longer drag your own ass to the toilet will be gay. I don't know if that's because gays are more compassionate or just willing to take unpleasant jobs, but it doesn't matter.

Retired Detective Stojan Kujovic's room was on the top floor. As Fat Cat and I trudged up the three long flights of worn carpeting and rickety handrails, we cut through a dense cloud of cannabis. Every six-year-old who squirms twice gets Ritalin jammed down his throat, but we won't let a guy with his brain rotting away smoke a completely legal joint. My compliments to the bureaucrats who never met a cross they couldn't be offended by but can't work up the same passion for the terminally ill.

"This was above and beyond," I said to Fat Cat.

"You're telling me. My singer's working a cruise in Vancouver. Sorry to drag you up here on a night like this, but the guy's a Serb, and he wants to die over there. Noon tomorrow, he's outta here. That's why I blew up your in-box. Seems like a long fuckin' trip to give it up in front of strangers when you was born in Daly City, but then, it ain't happening to me."

"He was on the Chang case?"

"He ran it. They tell me he used to be one handsome dude, but that was a hundred less pounds ago. Some kinda gut cancer. Now he's the color of vitamin piss and looks like a blowfish. Don't mind seeing guys busted up or bleeding like Dion. This shit's not for me."

"How much did he tell you?"

"Enough to know you need to hear it from the horse. That, and he got a hard-on that he has to meet the man with the plan. You got a plan?"

"Not that I know of, but I'll see if I can dance to it."

Wes Crowe again. Jake calls it badge disease. They all think they're geniuses at reading people, so they want to give you the I'm-a-cop-motherfucker-stare. Jake believes half the cops protecting their assholes in prison would still be on the job if they hadn't insisted on a face-to-face. They know it's a pain in the ass to get a wiretap approved, and that most come up worthless, but they still insist on locking eyes. IA's biggest job is making sure there's film in the camera and enough cuffs to go around.

Detective Kujovic's room was small and close. Twin beds, a thrift shop chair, a couple of lamps and a poster of Dirty Harry brandishing his .44. He was sharing it with an emaciated young man, not more than twenty-five, who probably didn't top seventy pounds. From the sores on his face, I guessed AIDS. He was sleeping, but his breathing was dangerously shallow.

Fat Cat hadn't exaggerated. Kujovic was severely bloated, which meant his kidneys were failing. He'd also been charitable about his color. The ex-cop's skin looked like an overripe banana, dirty yellow splotched with brown and trying to squeeze shut a pair of yellow-orange eyes. He wasn't going to be the most popular guy on that transatlantic flight.

With two more large bodies in the room, there wasn't any space left, so we stood shoulder to shoulder while he sat on his bed in a loose, batik caftan and a pair of paper slippers. "Nice fuckin' outfit, huh? Back in the day, we took somebody down wearin' one of these, we busted him up good." He stared at me. "So what the fuck you want, since you ain't no cop?"

He didn't seem to want to talk about the 49ers' draft picks, so I plowed in. "I've got dead friends, and the Chang murders might fit in. Anything you didn't share?"

"Share? Like in if I write this down, motherfucker, you gonna keep me off the promotion list?"

"Somebody didn't want them solved?"

"Let's just say there was an incentive to leave it for the archaeologists."

"Care to elaborate?"

"Didn't have nothin' to do with what went down. Just the usual pussy shit upstairs."

"So a guy adopts a couple of kids and gets killed for his trouble. Money issue?"

"Fucker was drivin' a BMW 750. What's that tell you?"

All it told me was maybe he had a big car payment. "They were shot, right?"

"One each. Forehead. Mr. and Mrs. belted in, the kids in car seats. A 9mm. Not neat, but something left to identify. Jesus Christ, ask the right fuckin' questions, will ya?"

It's a wonder more lawyers don't shoot cops right on the stand. "It's supposed to be a conversation asshole, why not save us both some time?"

Suddenly, he grunted in pain and hit himself in the chest. I guessed he was wearing a morphine injector. A few seconds later, he took a deep breath, and some of the hostility disappeared. "They were left in front of the guy's parents' house. Big joint. Private street."

"So it was a message. We can get you anytime, anywhere."

"Yeah, but not for the parents. The old man didn't know his own name. Alzheimer's. Totally gaga. Mom was all twisted up in a wheelchair."

"The Chinese community isn't known for its swagger. Raise your family, earn a living, keep your head down and your mouth shut. Want to be John Wayne, go live with the white people."

"Keep going," he said.

"You can do business with outsiders but don't get mixed up with them."

"And those two things, my friend, is why we're discussing the *late* Mr. Chang. A bold motherfucker can make everybody a lot of money, but bold is like stupid, it never takes a day off."

"He needed to be reminded with a bullet?"

"My guess is he got told half a dozen times, but his wife couldn't conceive, and not many Chinese kids come on the market in this country. He sure as shit wasn't gonna get a white one, so eventually he convinced himself that he was too valuable to fuck with. Grew up here. Never grasped the concept that some people don't give a shit about money. There's no question his brother, Randy, pulled the trigger. Prints were in the car, and he put one in his own ear a year later. Same weapon."

"But you didn't close the case."

"My way of fuckin' with the system."

"That won't fly, even with an archaeologist."

We listened to him breathe for a while. No wonder he was angry. Worked his ass off for a career, and for his trouble, he was going to die eight thousand miles away, screaming.

"If I'm right, somebody had a gun on the brother while he did it."

So there it was. The same crap you see from the Middle East to Middle Earth. And as far as the authorities are concerned, once the bodies are in the ground, if nobody's marching outside, let it collect some dust, then send it to archives. Whatever you do, don't scratch around and find out something you don't want to know . . . get mixed up in cultural or political shit none of us understand.

But two Chinese kids shouldn't have meant four people had to die—no matter how they got here. I didn't really want to hear the answer to my next question, but it had to be asked. "I'm still missing who sent the message."

He waited so long, I thought he hadn't heard me. "Some of the street thugs up here don't work for the godfathers."

It was what I was afraid of. "Beijing," I said.

"On the surface, what they do looks like ordinary bullshit. Extortion, arson, kidnappin'. But it's actually intimidation. Keep the expats in line. Break the faces of the natural-borns who might have ideas. Problem is Wang the Tailor can buy from the right suppliers, kick back to the right tong and vote the way he's told, but one day, somebody sees him having lunch with Ling the Silk Merchant, who Wang thinks is just another businessman. Only Ling's a mover in Free Tibet, or his nephew's a general in Taipei. If Wang's lucky, all that happens is they cut off his wife's tit.

"The day those Communist motherfuckers take over that shitty little island next door, there's gonna be a bloodbath in a hundred Chinatowns. Lots of names on lots of lists. State department oughta open an embassy on Grant Avenue. They'd make more progress.

He was right. The American melting pot cracked when we decided not to mandate English as our official language. That was in 1795. It's not about commerce or thought control or waging war on other cultures. It's about unifying a population under the same set of laws. Multilingual is fine. Unilingual isn't, unless it's the one we adjudicate in. Otherwise, there will always be communities whose only connection to the rest of us is the weather. And because the politicians just care about votes, the people who need the law most can't even call a cop.

Carroll Rackmann had stuck a thumb in the eye of the Chinese government and kept twisting. They didn't care about babies, but they did care about control—and about being embarrassed. And what could be more embarrassing than watching little kids they were going to kill or let die be raised in freedom and with means.

Each time a new one arrived, it was like putting up a billboard in a thousand villages. And the bosses in Beijing didn't count it as one lost out of multitudes but as a bullet fired on their sovereignty—and their dignity. Most Westerners can't comprehend the concept of face, but Rackmann did, and as much as he wanted to save children, he was just as interested in waging war. As it turned out, he was better at it than all the uniforms and all the spooks in Washington. It was hard not to be impressed, but I wished I'd never had to know. And I dreaded what I didn't.

"If killing the Changs was to make a point to the locals, why schlep all the way to Victorville?"

"Easy answer. A few days away from the desk. Nice per diem and some new ass to chase. We laughed all the way down."

For the first time, I smiled. "Victorville? Ass?"

"You'd be surprised. Couple of guys had been there before."

I stopped smiling. "Before? What for?"

"There's a famous cop who lives down that way. LAPD. Got some big-time friends up and down the coast. People who like to get together on his birthday."

"Chuck Brando."

"Never heard of him."

"Who are *you* talking about?"

"Fabian Cañada."

"Who the fuck is that?"

"Never met the guy, just heard that if a cop's in a jam, he's the man to see. Unless you need a miracle. Then you go to Serbia."

So Kujovic wasn't going home to die. He was taking one last chance. The Sacred Water of the Caves. How he intended to get to one of the most remote places in Europe in his condition was anybody's guess. "Black River Monastery," I said.

He looked at me like I'd slapped him. I'd intruded. This was between him and God. "None of my business," I said, and quickly changed the subject. "When you were banging around in Victorville, did you happen to run into somebody named Crowe? If he was a cop then, he would have been a greenhorn."

"Never heard of him, but it wasn't my town."

"Who told you about this Fabian Cañada?"

"Vic Innunzio. He knew every cop and every piece of ass from Seattle to Tucson. But Vic's waitin' for the Rapture out at Our Lady of the Worms, so you ain't gonna get much out of him. For all I know, Cañada's dead too. He was supposed to be old back then." He held my eyes for a long time like he was waiting for something. "You want to tell me why you haven't asked about the others?"

I didn't know what he was talking about. Fat Cat stepped in. "First thing I did after you called was have my cousin hump over to the *Chronicle* and pull the Chang obit. Wasn't there, at least not where you said."

"I'm not following."

"Somebody gave you bogus info, my man. The Changs were killed several years earlier. During the Chinatown Massacres."

"Never heard of them."

"Neither had the *Chronicle*. Or the *New York Times*, the *London Daily Mail*, the *Sydney Morning Herald* or anybody else. Just this guy."

I looked at Kujovic. "What constitutes a massacre?"

"If you take the sixteen we had here in those two weeks and multiply by the number of major cities with Chinatowns, five hundred give or take. Factor in a few others, adjust for collateral damage, could be twice that. No way to know for sure."

"Two weeks?"

"Sixteen days, to be exact. Same as the murders. To the Chinese, eight's a lucky number, so they like to work with multiples. Tiananmen Square minus sixteen."

It hit me like a falling safe. How had I missed it? Tiananmen Square was the Kennedy and King Assassinations, the Oklahoma City Bombing and 9/11 all rolled into one. The single, unifying event in the national consciousness of more than a billion Chinese. Every person from the tiniest hamlet to Shanghai could tell you exactly what he was doing at the precise moment he heard about it. Right down to the fear he felt.

"You said minus sixteen. If it was retribution, you mean plus."

"I might look like Jabba the Fuckin' Hut, but I ain't out to lunch. I said minus, because I meant minus. Sixteen murders in the sixteen days *before* Tiananmen."

I was rocked again. This was Department 11 territory, only there hadn't been a Department 11 then. "So Beijing knew it was coming and tried to prevent it."

"Maybe. More likely, they knew they couldn't, so they were making sure it didn't have legs. And have you seen any? How about them fuckin' Olympics, huh?"

"Kill the activists. Watch the sheep run back to their pens. And for good luck, round up to a multiple of eight."

"Things got a little dicey a couple of places, but there wasn't any Shah of Iran or South Africa shit. Whole world eatin' their ass to make a change. I ain't no Nostradamus, but seven months later, the Berlin Wall came down. Ask me, it was part of a package. First Asia, then Europe. Bye-bye Big Commies."

"Instead, they ended up a superpower."

"God loves a good laugh."

"Earlier, you talked about a future bloodbath. So that would be the second."

"That we know of. Lotta years since those fuckers took over."

An old state department hand once told me how they used to manipulate the press into chasing bullshit so they could hide what was really going on. But this was too big, cut across too many lines. "How is it this goes unreported, but you know?"

"That's two questions. First, when it comes to Chinatown—any Chinatown—unless something goes down where an outsider sees it—like four dead Changs in a nice neighborhood—if the community holds its water, it didn't happen."

"And the second part?"

He looked past us for a moment, remembering something. "My partner was from over there. Sam Martin—name's a long story. His sister, Glenda, was a leader in the Defiance— that's what it was called. Sam and I were the ones who found her—what was left of her anyway."

Martin? "Any relation to Major Martin?"

There wasn't much elasticity left in those puffy eyes, but what there was opened all the way. "Who the fuck are you?"

He wasn't going to buy that it was just a shot in the dark, so I went the other way. "He's probably going to be joining both of them. Another brother too. I'm pretty sure there's a connection to what you just told me, but I don't know what it is yet."

"But it's on the wrong side."

I nodded.

"So how soon's this Major thing gonna happen?"

"Maybe ahead of you."

He seemed to like that. "Families. Glad I missed the boat."

"Somebody once told me that we hate the ones we love because they deserve it."

He didn't answer, but I didn't need him to. It was obvious the detective and Glenda had been more than friends, and he wasn't over it. "So what about Sam?"

"He went after them. Wouldn't tell me who it was. Just that he was the only one who could get close. Coroner said he fell under a cable car on its way back to the yard. No witnesses. That his hands and eyes were missin' didn't seem to bother anybody."

I shook my head. "So people get buried, loved ones mourn, and everybody goes back to work."

"More importantly, meetin' halls go empty. They still are."

Except for a big church in the desert, I thought.

"Word in Chinatown was Tiananmen was a D.C. operation, but that sounds like smoke to me. The only people who know for sure don't talk to each other, so what are the odds of the rest of us findin' out? Also, right after, you couldn't order an egg roll around here without gettin' your picture taken and your balls busted. I think they were trying to figure it out too."

"CIA?"

"Every letter in the alphabet. I wouldn't have said anything to them, but it wasn't because they didn't try. Sat outside my apartment for almost a month. Fucked with my neighbors—and my bosses."

"That's why you left the Chang case open. That and Sam. Maybe there'd come a day."

"Hero shit. I blame Woodward and Bernstein. Think I can sue? Lotta fuckin' good it did. Twenty years, and I'm about to join them."

"If it matters, there's something in the works. Besides Major."

That seemed to brighten him a little. "Put me down for a pound."

"One more question. Were the Changs the only children among the sixteen?"

He nodded. "Only family. Others were one at a time. All leaders, no soldiers."

"Then how do you know they fit? That they weren't involved in some other beef, and the real Defiance count was twelve."

Kujovic looked at Fat Cat as if to say, where did you get this clown? It was the same look Wes Crowe had given Del

Brockman. I thought he wasn't going to answer, but he finally did. "First, twelve ain't a multiple of eight. But I don't know. Maybe it was because somebody burned out their offices the same night."

"What kind of business?"

"Happy Asia Tours. In that part of the world, the biggest then, the biggest now. You want to take a few hundred of your closest friends to Disney World or grab a week of Broadway and booze, you're with Happy Asia. Sister took over. Suzanne. Wouldn't spit in our direction. What do you think?"

I was still thinking about Wes Crowe. *We all know Asians do Vegas like it's around the corner. Charter 747s. Bring the whole village.*

"She still around?"

"Channel 5 did a special on San Francisco's Most Eligible. She was Number Two, right after some guy who had his hair dry cleaned. Said she was worth half a billion. Who the fuck has that kind of money? Looks pretty good too for a broad in her forties. Probably iffy on fat Serbs, though."

"I should say thanks, but it doesn't seem like enough."

"Don't bother. My ears stopped listenin' for that word years ago."

I shook his hand, and it was like shaking a wet loaf of bread. He was a tough guy, but he wasn't going to get to that monastery. I think he knew it too, but trying was better than sitting around in paper slippers.

As we turned to leave, I noticed the kid in the other bed was still asleep. I stopped and put my hand on his wrist. He opened his eyes, and I patted him. He tried to smile but couldn't quite get there. "Safe journey," I whispered, and he nodded.

Fat Cat was waiting on the landing, "Where I grew up, it was better to kill a man's brother than humiliate the man. Death is an eye for an eye. Humiliation buys you a thousand-year vendetta."

I thought about that. Big Jim Rackmann started humiliating in 1967. On Fat Cat's clock, that time line wasn't even out of diapers. Now people were dying again. Was it a new kill-off or a continuation of the old? Or was it something coming the other direction? But most of all, where did Chuck and Lucille fit?

In Fat Cat's rental car, I dialed Yale Maywood. He sounded groggy. "Rub the sleep out of your eyes. I've got two words for you. Fabian Cañada."

"You didn't hear that from me."

"No, why would you help?"

"You sound a little out of sorts."

"That would be one way of putting it. You and I will handle this face-to-face someday, you pompous fuck."

I hung up. As soon as I did, the message light came on. I called my voice mail. Jake's voice stopped, then started a couple of times. It sounded like he was in a wind tunnel. Finally, he got it out. "Sorry, got the top down. On my way to San Diego for a depo. About that Tongan thing. What'd you call it? Protected Person. Only one of them took out papers. The wife. Did it just before they closed the program. Probably had a plan she wasn't ready to implement and wanted to preserve her options. My guess is the husband didn't know shit because her application said 'Single.'

"Something else. Same week she leased the ship, she applied for and received Tongan import-export status. She was acting as an agent for some Aussie outfit called Parkinson-Lowe. Seemed odd, so I checked the laws. If you're a citizen and licensed like she was, as long as you don't off-load anything, your ships aren't subject to a customs search. Any kind of search. You could sit there for years with a hold full of Peruvian Flake or hot Corvettes, and nobody's even going to ask. How about that?"

Yes, how about that. Board anywhere in the world with Bahamian paperwork, then sail into Tonga under a law that forbade a search. And I'd be willing to bet that if you sat there long enough, the attention paid to you dropped to zero, and you could just walk off. Or on.

26

Lofty Hotels and Air France

No one in San Francisco thinks Los Angeles is worth a pitcher of warm piss. On the LA side, no one thinks much about San Francisco at all—except to occasionally twist some NorCal tit by calling it Frisco . . . or NorCal. A century ago, California was so sparsely populated that the state ran ads to lure the adventurous to cheap land, unlimited opportunity and no more winters. Many of us would like to have a chat with the guy who came up with that idea.

Today, our ever-expanding economic sunrise has been exchanged for an empty promise attached to a mountain of debt. On the plus side, we can take our driver's license exam in thirty-two languages, which, since the courts haven't yet mandated the same for highway signs, provides entertainment for the commuters who are not busy exchanging insurance information. Then there is the added bonus of additional cars on our leisurely roads.

San Francisco, like its two larger sisters down the coast, survives in spite of its leadership. It has been whipsawed by elected morons for so long that, other than breadlines and thumbscrews, most Soviet Russians would feel right at home. Spit-flying speeches, political purges and rampant corruption, followed by retirement to lush dachas somehow purchased on public service pay.

That said, this ever-increasingly generic world contains just five cities of such breathtaking beauty that even the heavens smile. And San Francisco is one of them. I rank it first. In hotels, it's 1-A with London. And for quiet, personal service, the Huntington is second to none. It's also on the highest ground in the city, so you can sip champagne in a lofty suite and commune with a view unmatched anywhere. Unless you happen to be traveling with me, who never seems to miss an earthquake. Then, the Golden Gate keeps changing windows.

Eddie, Fat Cat and I sat at my regular table in the far left corner of the Big Four dining room. We'd spent the first half hour after checking in at the bar, listening to tales of local scandals told by a most engaging white-aproned bartender named Wylie. In between, I'd given Eddie my standard lecture about not flying the BBJ alone. He'd then bullshitted me for a while about how contrite he was, then added that since the FAA hadn't caught him, it was almost like it hadn't happened. You can't argue with that kind of logic.

Now we were well into dinner and a bottle of very good Barolo, while another breathed nearby. Eddie had ignored his fish but polished off a plate of fries smothered in Heinz, then taken his wine and headed outside for a smoke. Meanwhile, Fat Cat had downed three appetizers and was tearing into a double order of truffle/lobster mac and cheese—a new one on me. I doubted Fat Cat had seen it before either, but from the sounds he was making, it was agreeing with him.

"You know an ex-lieutenant who does security for Kingdom Starr?"

"The freight outfit?"

I nodded. "Probably LAPD. Walt Disney moustache and keeps himself in pretty good shape. Doesn't have a very high opinion of you."

"That would take you into triple digits, but the guy you're

talking about is probably Perry Duke. Killed his partner. She somehow got between him and a carjack suspect . . . about a week after she told him she was pregnant with his kid."

"A tragic accident, of course."

"Not the term Mrs. Duke used. IA either, but the carjacker got Perry's second round between the eyes, so the witness list was a little thin. Sorry to hear he landed on his feet."

"He was there the night Dion got sliced. Probably set it up."

Fat Cat was silent for a moment. "I knew my boy was holding something back. Now I know why."

"I don't think what happened to Dion was connected to what I'm looking into, but he should probably get a new phone. If that means you want to take a hike too, no problem."

"And maybe miss spending some quality time with Perry? Not a chance."

"I can't have anything personal crop up at the wrong time."

"Never happen. But I can't speak for him."

"Fair enough."

"Dion said you weren't much of a partner last time."

"It was a shotgun marriage. Wouldn't happen now. You'll know what I know."

"Doesn't mean shit unless I know *when* you know."

I put out my hand, and he shook it.

A few minutes later, Eddie was back. He topped off his wine, then wordlessly took an empty glass off the next table, filled it and left with both. I wasn't particularly hungry, so I picked at a salad and ran though the Kujovic conversation again with Fat Cat. After Eddie's second trip for two more wines, I indicated he should stay put.

"Fuckin' doorman's gonna wonder what happened."

"He's not supposed to be drinking on the job."

"You know how miserable it is out there? Guy doesn't even have a heater."

"Please remind me of the last time you were concerned about somebody else's comfort."

Eddie leaned close. "His name's Harvey, and he's been

here twelve years. All that time, he's been hitting up rich guests for stock tips."

"Did you notice he's still a doorman?"

"That's what I said too, then I got to thinking about how many times you hear about some working stiff leaving a wad to his fuckin' Chihuahua. Listen to this. There's a company right here in San Fran sucking gold out of seawater."

"The operative word being *sucking*. You got extra dough, give it to your wife."

He shook his head. "No upside. Ten bucks or ten grand, I still only get laid twice a week."

They'd just met, but Fat Cat thought everything Eddie said was hilarious, even while he was shoveling food in his mouth. "Dion ever meet this fuckin' guy?"

Eddie looked at me. "Jesus, boss, you know DiMooch? I'm fuckin' nuts about doo-wop."

Fat Cat had no idea what Eddie was talking about, but he laughed anyway. I shook my head. "Different Dion, Eddie." To Fat Cat, I said, "Manarca'd get about halfway into his Balboa spiel, and Eddie'd ask about Stallone."

"You're gonna make fun, I'm gonna hang with Harvey."

For Eddie's benefit, I went over the events since Yale Maywood had shown up at the *Sanrevelle*. Some of it was a repeat for Fat Cat, but like a good cop, he listened as if he were hearing it for the first time.

When I finished, Eddie said, "Jesus Christ, boss, what the fuck's going on?"

I didn't have an answer.

"You thinking what I'm thinking?" Eddie asked.

I nodded. "We need to talk to Coggan."

Eddie was born Edward Lafayette Bufreaux. One of the original Cajun clans from the Acadiana swamps, the Bufreauxs migrated to the Big Easy in the twenties and through hard work and harder fists, rose from fishermen to power brokers on the docks. Now, very little moved through the New Orleans waterfront that didn't pick up several sets of the family's fingerprints.

Like many of their relatives, as soon as they were old enough, Eddie and his two younger brothers, Jimmy and Coggan, changed their last name to Buffalo. It was easier to spell, and nobody forgot it. After a couple of lackluster years in junior college, Eddie left home to pursue flying. Few tears were shed. He'd been a difficult kid, and he was a more difficult adult. Jimmy, the middle brother, spent much of his life in one jam after another before getting things turned around. He'd died tragically the previous year on my boat. I miss him.

Coggan, the youngest Buffalo, was the biggest and most academically gifted. Powerfully built and with no concept of pain, he was a four-year defensive end at Ole Miss and an Academic All-American. But despite being on the Cowboys' draft chart, he passed on the NFL and headed to graduate school, emerging with two doctorates: one in Asian studies, the second in space sciences.

An hour after graduation, Air Force Intelligence offered him an undercover job that sent him to the Far East for three years. He spent two more running around the U.S. fine-tuning surveillance satellites aimed at the world's newest superpower, until returning to Mississippi as chairman of a think tank that dreams up new ways to conduct espionage.

When Coggan's not devising electronic leashes for our future enemies, he moonlights as a bar owner. His place on the Oxford square is called Nasty's, and I once spent an evening with him, having my eardrums numbed by Afroman, while a mountainous bouncer named Wal-Mart conducted a headlock clinic on drunk football players, Ultimate Fighter wannabes, and Sigma Chi bad boys.

Coggan had no use for Eddie, and even brief encounters often ended in violence. While he was alive, Jimmy refereed, but with him gone, Mama Bufreaux had to put Eddie and Coggan on home visit rotation. Eddie never said what the underlying problem is, just that it's Coggan's fault. I know them both, and I'm betting the other way. As my father used to say: *Why hate strangers when you don't have to leave the house.*

"You know, you're gonna have to be the one to call him," Eddie said.

"First, you're going to promise to put a screw through that tongue of yours. There are lives at stake here."

"I'll give it a shot, boss, but that motherfucker starts in on me, and . . ."

Fat Cat was tearing into something chocolate, runny and large. Without looking up, he jammed three fingers of his free hand into Eddie's armpit and twisted. Eddie jolted upright and went white with pain. Fat Cat pulled his hand back then shot it upward again. I thought Eddie was going to pass out.

"There'll be no trouble," he managed to croak out.

Fat Cat withdrew his hand and continued eating with pure exhilaration. "As soon as I order another one of these fuckers, I'll get on the horn and check out this Fabian Cañada."

Looking at the now very docile Eddie, I made a mental note to revisit my book on nerve bundles.

I hadn't pulled the drapes and was awakened by a blast of San Francisco's famous white dawn. After the previous night's rain, the city glistened like a jewel. I had a pounding headache, and since I'd cut myself off the wine early, I diagnosed it as not having eaten enough. Fat Cat was staying with his cousin and would meet us at Happy Asia at ten. I had time for a workout.

I dressed in jogging clothes and walked seven blocks down Taylor, turned and ran back—hard. Running's not my forte—I'm a swimmer—but I wanted to get the blood flowing, and Taylor is one of those streets where you expect to have to jump out of the way of a green Shelby. Straight up and straight down. When I hit California Street on the return, I resisted the urge to call for a paramedic and hung a right to the Mark Hopkins, lapped Huntington Park twice, and arrived back at the hotel with my tongue hanging out.

I could tell from the doorman's avoidance of eye contact that he thought I was nuts. He was probably right. I showered and called Eddie. While he was getting ready, I rang Birdy. Bronis put her on the phone, and I was surprised to hear how peppy she sounded. "I figured you'd still be asleep."

"Hassie's waiting out front," she said with far too much enthusiasm.

"Let me guess—his regular foursome canceled."

"How did you know?"

"He's an A+ in golf, but a D- in clever."

"When are you coming back?"

"Don't know yet. You need anything, ask Nick."

"He set me up with the most fun guy last night, except that he handled me like he needed asbestos gloves. Is everybody that afraid of you?"

I could only imagine what Nick had said to him. "Keep the oven stoked, I'll be back as soon as I can."

"Hurry, I miss you. I need some more of that danger stuff. Hey, if I'm going to Hong Kong, I need a passport. Can Nick handle that?"

"Probably, but you're not going anywhere, Miss Monroe. You did great on opening night, but the show closed."

"But, Rail, there's a baby involved."

"There are babies everywhere."

"Yes, but we know about this one. And we took his money."

"No, and that's final. We'll give the cash to a home for wayward Thoroughbreds. Now, blow me a kiss and get ready to fend off the world's most attentive country club owner. There won't be a shot all day he won't have to help you with."

Stuffed full of French toast and peppered bacon, Eddie and I hoofed it down to Chinatown, then killed half an hour looking in shop windows and watching some little kids set off firecrackers. The older I get, the more I enjoy the sound of children laughing. The purity of the innocent living each moment without care ends sooner with each generation. It's hard to believe we got along so many years without kindergarteners knowing how to waterproof a banana.

Fat Cat was waiting in front of the glass-fronted tour office that was sandwiched between a Chinese grocery and a dim sum palace. He was decked out in white shoes, white slacks, red and blue silk shirt and a white straw hat. I presumed somewhere under all that fabric was a gun and a badge.

Eddie looked him up and down. "Jesus Christ, who the fuck dressed you? Air France?" Right on cue, Fat Cat burst out laughing. Except for its deepness, it sounded a lot like the kids with the firecrackers.

"How'd you do with Cañada?" I asked.

"Lives in Nevada. Someplace called Suicide. How do you like that shit? It ain't on the maps, but I called an old homicide guy in Vegas, and not only did he know Cañada, he said the only way to get to him is through his doctor."

"He sick?"

"No clue, and the cop clammed up. But I got the doc's name."

"Okay, let's go see about a tour."

27

Lavender Bathrobes and Flaming Snapple

The Happy Asia office was spartan, just a large open area of gray metal desks with a waiting area of mismatched furniture. The light blue linoleum was buckled and cracked, and the only decorations were travel posters slugged haphazardly with the company name. Three ceiling fans moved air slowly, a fourth was out of commission. The owner might be worth in the hundreds of millions, but she wasn't putting any of it into interior design. Probably better for business. Who wants to think they're keeping their tour operator in Maseratis.

A half dozen attractive, young Asian women, all wearing skintight, green silk sheath dresses were standing and chatting in Chinese over Starbucks and Virginia Slims. California is still trying to decide if the penalty for smoking should be caning or mutilation, so until they get it straight, I've stopped making citizen's arrests. I gave the women a few seconds, but when it became obvious they weren't going to fight each other for the chance to talk to us, I walked over. "I'd like to see Suzanne Chang."

A model-pretty lady in her twenties took in my height, then did a slow evaluation of my associates. "No in," she said.

It's standard procedure in ESL communities to go language stupid when you're not sure who you're dealing with. I took out my card and handed it to her. "Richy-richy man. Berry important." It was crude, but I knew she spoke English as well as I did.

"Is that supposed to be funny, cocksucker?" I was wrong. Better.

"Put me down for a hate crime, but I need to see your boss."

She tossed her head and turned on her heel. I watched the green silk move in all the right places as she strode to the back and pushed the button for an elevator.

When word came back that Suzanne Chang would see me alone, Eddie and Fat Cat went looking for the Starbucks, while I was escorted to the second floor.

In stark contrast to the downstairs bullpen, the owner's office was elegantly appointed. Delicate, hand-painted, coral wallpaper perfectly showcased the oversize black and coral antique Chinese art deco rug, and a wall of eight-foot multipaned windows looked out over a flat red roof down to the bay.

Behind the very feminine white, gold-trimmed desk stood a young woman with her back to me wearing nothing but a high-hipped turquoise thong. Her sleek, black hair hung to her waist but didn't hide her exceptional figure. She was doing something with her hands, and I realized she was brushing somebody's hair.

When she finished, she stepped aside, and though she was as beautiful as I expected, her breasts tight and the aureoles large and dark, her face was as expressionless as a mannequin's. She gave no indication of being aware of my presence.

The desk chair then swiveled, and a handsome, not gorgeous, fortysomething Chinese lady with her hair pulled back by an ivory comb and wearing a little too much bloodred lipstick and heavy eye shadow rose to greet me. Her deep-cut lavender silk robe was high-end designer and showcased some excellent plastic surgery. But there was something wrong with the fit, and when she came around the desk, I saw what it was. She had a malformed right hip, which caused her to walk with a rolling limp, and over the years, the unnatural movement had twisted her spine off center.

She extended her hand smiling. "The older I get, the more I enjoy being made love to in the morning. How about you, Mr. Black?"

"Only if she doesn't snore in my ear."

Her laugh was warm, genuine. She took in my size. "I doubt that's ever a problem. I've read about you. I'm pleased we're able to meet, or have we done this before?"

The scent of jasmine filled my nostrils. It fit the lady. "We haven't. And thank you for seeing me without an appointment."

Suzanne Chang took a seat in a white, upholstered chair and indicated its mate to me. While I got settled, the woman in the thong knelt and helped Suzanne work her bad hip into the right position to cross her legs. Though difficult, it wasn't clumsy or self-conscious, and the younger woman was expert at the manipulation. When she was comfortable, Suzanne said, "This is Meong. She will stay."

Meong made no attempt at a greeting or even eye contact and moved to a sofa on the other side of the room. The same green silk dress worn by the women downstairs lay there, but she made no move to put it on. Instead, she sat, lit a cigarette and began paging through a magazine. I didn't need a scorecard, but it was an interesting dynamic.

"Do you have a wife, Mr. Black?"

"No, I don't. Please call me Rail."

She nodded. "And I'm Suzanne. Well, Rail, if you ever get one, and her doctor tells her it's no problem to deliver breech, remember me and slap the son of a bitch until his ears bleed. My mother just lay there while they pulled on my leg. Thank heaven, there was a pretty good brain on the other end, because it's been slim pickings in the dating department. If you know anything about Chinese men, you understand."

"It's not limited to the Chinese," I said.

"Probably not, but they're the ones I have a PhD in." She looked at Meong, who seemed to be engrossed in her magazine. "But if life deals you lemons . . ." She didn't sound bitter. On the contrary, her voice was matter-of-fact. "Okay, lesson's out of the way. What can I do for you?"

"I'd like to ask you some questions about your family."

She nodded gravely. "I didn't think you were here to book a tour."

"I apologize for delving into things that might upset you, but some friends of mine died recently. Very unpleasantly. I'm trying to find out if there's a connection."

"From over twenty years ago?"

"It's complicated, but possible."

"Then you must be the kind of friend most people never have. I'm sorry about your loss. Were they Chinese?"

"One was. Her husband, no. Chuck and Lucille Brando."

"I don't know what I can tell you. I'm not familiar with either of them." I couldn't tell if that was the truth or not.

"Forgive me if I don't seem organized. Did Randy leave a family?"

She looked at me with a mixture of dismay and sadness, and I thought for a moment she might ask me to leave. "No, Randy never married. Philip and Wendy had the children, Allison and Abigail."

I saw no advantage in asking her to revisit what we both knew Randy had done. "Were the brothers close?"

"No, Philip was six years older—a lifetime when you're a kid. I was a year younger than Randy. Both boys were highly intelligent, but in different ways. Randy was quieter, more introspective. Philip was always challenging. He had a gift for big ideas."

I thought about Kujovic. Bold, he'd said. "What kind of ideas?"

She waved her arm at the room. "My father built this business from our kitchen table into the largest Chinese tour operator in the country. But as successful as he was, he stayed within the community, mostly sending wealthy Asians from the States to Hong Kong. When Philip joined him, he immediately saw that Japanese companies were far more profitable because they concentrated on tours from the home islands to Europe and the United States rather than the other way around.

"At that time, people in China were just beginning to accumulate money, but they never considered traveling outside the country because it was impossible to get a passport. Philip convinced the right people in Beijing that allowing Chinese to go abroad and shop for things they couldn't get at home would increase demand for consumer goods. Goods they could then begin manufacturing or knocking off. As Philip used to say, 'You've got to know what it is to want it.' "

"Very smart."

"That wasn't the half of it. Then there were the travel taxes, the import duties and the fees for currency conversion. It was like pointing to an ocean of money, and all the government had to do was to issue some passports. It also didn't hurt that Philip took care of the right officials. My brother didn't invent the economic revolution, but he gave it a vitamin."

"And in the process, Happy Asia got an exclusive contract."

"Ten years."

"The markup on tours didn't make you as wealthy as I hear you are."

"Those goddamn lists. I think what really pisses me off is that they're accurate. Who finds out that all that stuff?"

I smiled. "I feel your pain. If I were more motivated, I'd buy *Forbes* just to delete myself."

She smiled, and it was warm. "But you'd leave everybody else on."

"Of course. I always read them."

"Me too." She laughed. "But you're right. The real money

began to flow after Philip came up with the brilliant idea of inviting malls to partner with us. It also made the exclusivity irrelevant. Once we had the shopping centers, Beijing was locked in. You have no idea how many Chinese have never laid eyes on LA or New York but know Houston and Minneapolis like the back of their hand."

"And Vegas, of course."

"They owe us a couple of hotels, minimum. But it didn't happen until Caesars built the Forum Shops. Unlike Americans, Chinese men like to gamble *and* shop. And they outspend their wives."

"So I have the Changs to thank for jamming the aisles at Neiman Marcus when I need a tie."

She laughed. "Guilty as charged. And for dressing my help to attract the decision-makers."

"That wasn't lost on me."

"In that case, may I make a suggestion? Linda, the young lady who brought you up here, knows the city quite well. I'm certain she'd be pleased to show it to you."

I wasn't so sure that was how Linda would have viewed it. "Thanks, but I'm flying out tonight." Somewhere, Linda breathed a sigh of relief. "Do you do business with Markus Kingdom?"

She seemed surprised at the question. "Why do you ask?" It was as good as a yes, and when I didn't answer, she added. "He's a little high on the totem pole. We work mostly with his managers."

"How about personally? Are you two friendly?"

"No." Her tone had an edge that seemed unnecessary, but I didn't want to lose her, so I shifted gears.

"Was Randy jealous of Philip?"

She seemed glad to get away from Mr. Kingdom. "No, not at all. Philip made the deals, Randy ran the company. Everyone loved him. Philip was impetuous, temperamental. Randy never got angry, so he was an ideal inside man. Unfortunately, I am like neither, but I'm good at hiring, so I get by."

I suspected she did a lot better than get by. "How did you get along with Philip?"

"I barely knew him. We grew up in the same house, but that was it. Philip was always off doing something to call attention to himself. He was a ranked tennis player and dated glamorous girls, not necessarily Chinese. Compared to Philip, Randy and I were wallpaper. Very dull wallpaper. Our parents used to get this beatific look on their faces whenever Philip walked into a room. I don't think they had any idea, but Randy and I sure did. The oldest boy . . . well, you know the drill."

I smiled. "So it was Randy and you against the golden child?"

"Kids. Seems silly now. Philip earned everything he got, and nobody was starved for love. But to answer your question, yes, like me, Randy was very sensitive, so I mothered him, and he did his best to protect me from the jerks who thought my walk was the funniest thing they ever saw."

I nodded. "More than once I've grabbed some kid by the scruff of his neck. Once, one screamed he was going to have me arrested, and I handed him my phone. He ran. I'd rather have grabbed his dad, but there aren't many of those around. Interesting world we've created."

"The person on the receiving end never forgets. Even this many years later, if I want to have a good cry—and what girl doesn't sometimes—I can conjure up an incident or two. My father used to just shrug it off and say it would toughen me up." She looked at the ceiling. "Hey, if you're listening up there, I don't feel so tough."

The window behind Suzanne's desk was open, and a typical bay breeze was blowing. To keep the floor-length draperies from billowing, someone had tucked their hems into the bookshelves on either side of the window, obscuring much of the shelves' contents. Suddenly, a strong gust of wind blew one drape loose, and as it fell away, a large, jade statuette of a tiger came into view.

The now-free drape began flapping loudly, and Meong got up. "I'll get it," I said, and crossed behind the desk.

I wedged the drapery into a space on a different shelf, stepped back and admired the tiger. It lay on its stomach, eyes closed, and though different in pose from the other two I'd seen, it had been created by the same hand. Or at least under the original artist's guidance. "Definitely not Pier 1," I said.

"It belonged to Randy. I don't know who carved it, but it's supposed to be quite old. Randy said it was from a collection, but I've never seen any of the others. This one is Sleeping Tiger, and he said there's an Attacking Tiger and a Waiting Tiger. Others too, but I don't remember anymore. It was very important to him, so I kept it after . . ."

Her voice trailed off, and I returned to my seat. "Did you ever hear of a Fabian Cañada?" I asked. "He might have been a cop. LAPD."

She looked past me. Not a good sign. When a person's eyes wander after a direct question, it generally means they're evaluating which shade of deception you're most likely to buy. "It's an unusual name. One I should remember. It doesn't ring a bell, but a lot of years have gone by."

Way too much information for what should have been a simple yes or no. "How about Big Jim Rackmann?"

It was like I'd cracked her with a bullwhip. She went rigid, her mouth twisting into a grotesque sneer. "That piece of shit! That lousy piece of sanctimonious, Bible-spewing shit! May the motherfucker die of cock cancer and the maggots eat him twice!"

Meong was suddenly beside her, caressing her face, trying to comfort her. I waited for Suzanne to get herself under control, but she let loose with another screaming stream of profanity stronger than the first. When she ran out of new words, she repeated the others until she had to stop to catch her breath.

While her chest heaved, and the pulse in her neck

throbbed, I got up and opened cabinets until I found a set of sambuca glasses and a half-empty bottle of B&B. Not exactly a breakfast drink, but I poured three fingers and handed it to her. Suzanne took a slug, snorted and took another. When she calmed sufficiently, Meong gave her a lace handkerchief and went back to her sofa but not before mentally shoving a dagger through my Adam's apple. I noticed that when she sat down, she began texting on a cell phone.

"I'm so sorry. I knew that name was coming, but I hadn't heard it for so long . . ."

"You're not doing yourself any good holding on to that kind of anger."

She took another sip of B&B, and I noticed a tremor in her hand. "I know," she said. "What's the saying? 'Hate is like taking a little poison every day and hoping the other person dies.'"

"It's true."

"Then why are you here? I felt your hand when we shook. That kind of hardness doesn't come with a man who turns the other cheek."

I didn't have an answer for that, so I plowed ahead. "How did you know Rackmann?"

"My father was one of his students. Before the war."

I did a quick calculation. "Then he was relatively young when he became ill."

"Sixty-two. Early-onset Alzheimer's. The body's not broken, so it's death by millimeters. Seven years of hell. My mother had so many strokes, she became less coherent than he was. Never happen to me. I keep a loaded gun next to the bed and a backup in the basement."

"The wife of a good friend says the day her guy stumbles over something that's not there, she's buying him the big Harley."

That seemed to lighten her a little, but I also thought she was looking for an excuse to come back. "I haven't asked your father's name."

"Ellery. I don't know what it was originally. I don't even know if he was born with the name Chang. Until the missionaries found him, he lived in the streets. The kids called him Rat because he was good at finding food. Rackmann didn't like that, so started calling him Ellery."

"After the detective."

She nodded. "My father would have done anything for that motherfucker, and look what it got us."

I hated what I had to do, but it was time to puncture the balloon. "The jade tiger was Ellery's, wasn't it?"

She opened her mouth to protest, then closed it and nodded. "He was using the tour company to get babies out. He said he owed Rackmann his life, and if he could save even one child from what he'd gone through, he was damn well going to do it. Whatever the consequences. Well, he sure as fuck got plenty of those."

While she dabbed at her eyes, I helped her along. "So when Ellery became ill, Randy stepped in. To honor him but also to have his own sense of purpose. Something separate from his brother. Maybe to see that look in your father's eyes that was reserved only for Philip."

The wind seemed to go out of her, and I went on. "So all this fury really isn't about Rackmann. Philip was the chosen one, then Randy got his moment. But you were still the shy little girl with the limp whose father never saw that you were smarter and more capable than both of them."

"Goddamn you," she said, but there wasn't much conviction behind it.

I was going to hate myself in the morning, but as long as I was breaking eggs, I needed to go all the way. If she knew something that could help me, she had to focus on what was real not some personal myth.

"But no hate comes close to yours for Philip. A guy, who for all his brilliance, was so arrogant that he ignored all the warnings and brought the twins here anyway. And who never grasped that the people who made him rich cared less about balance sheets than raw power. What makes it even more difficult is that for all its brutality, you completely understand what happened and why."

I watched her fight it through and her eyes turn to stone. "Philip signed his own death warrant, and his selfish, controlling bitch of a wife deserved it right along with him. I felt sorry for the kids, but I barely knew them."

I prodded. "Ellery got a pass because he was sick and harmless, but when you're dealing with families, you can't take a chance that the quiet brother won't suddenly find his stones."

She dropped her glass, and what was left of the B&B, spilled onto the Chinese rug. She buried her face in her hands, and her shoulders heaved with sobs. "Oh, my dear sweet Randy. What did they do to you, my little baby?"

I heard Meong get up behind me. I stood and glared at her. She faltered and returned to the sofa. I went over to Suzanne and put my hand on her shoulder. "If there's something you haven't told me, I need to know it."

She looked up. "Everything you said is true. Everything. After Randy died, some people came here. They said they were from a church. I remember looking it up. It was out in the desert."

"Victorville."

"Yes. They wanted me to continue, but I was confused . . . angry." She hesitated. "I hate myself for saying it, but I was afraid too. How could anybody think I would help them after what happened?"

"Because they knew how much it had meant to your father," I said. "And you were in a position to save lives. The most innocent ones."

"That's almost word for word. I called them terrible names and threw them out."

So the Chang appendage had been severed. Sleeping Tiger was dead. Or was it? "They didn't let it drop that easily, did they?"

She shook her head. "No, somebody came every year.

Like clockwork. Always a different person, always very polite. I offered them money, but they wouldn't take it."

"That would have let your conscience off the hook. They needed your ships."

"Well, apparently, they got tired of hearing no, because last year, they tried something different. They sent one of us."

"One of us?"

"A man on the lists. Closer to your spot than mine."

"Who?"

He voice turned into a snarl. "The man you asked about. Markus Kingdom. His pitch was that we had obligations we couldn't walk away from because they were inconvenient. That it was our duty to hold civilization to a higher standard. I told him he could go fuck himself and every obligation he could find. As for civilization, it was pretty busy fucking itself."

"What did he say?"

"Nothing at first. He just hit me."

Her answer caught me off guard. "Hit you, how?"

"With his fucking fist, that's how. Right here in this office. He had a goon with him he called Duke, but Markus did the hitting himself. Knocked me clear over the desk. He would have kept at it if one of my girls hadn't heard the commotion and come in. I've never seen a man so angry.

"Then he started yelling that he wasn't even Chinese, and he was tired of carrying the whole load himself. That he had important business with powerful people, and the kids were in the way."

"So why not just quit?"

"That's what I asked. And he got even angrier. Started yelling it wasn't that simple. That two trains can't run on the same track at the same time—especially if there's only one locomotive."

I didn't say it to Suzanne, but a man in Markus Kingdom's position doesn't lose his temper. At least not where outsiders can see it. At his level, everything is a chess move, and anger gives the edge to your opponent. The only time it happens is for effect or if the man is backed into a corner. The punch settled which this was.

Before I could ask another question, I heard running footsteps on the roof. Not heavy, but fast. I turned and saw two young Asian men barely out of their teens. Each had a MAC-11 or the latest knockoff in one hand and an amber-colored Snapple bottle with sparks shooting out of its top in the other. Probably firecracker fuses inserted into det cord. When it ignited, it would amplify the Molotov cocktail ten-fold.

A volley of gunshots slammed into the panes, sending glass shards in all directions. I jerked Suzanne to the floor, so the desk was between us and the windows. Meong didn't drop. She ran to the open one and began shouting angrily in Chinese and pointing in our direction. The first Snapple bottle came through where the glass had originally been.

Pros like to score bottles with a glass cutter so they'll break if they contact anything stiffer than cotton candy. Fortunately, these two hadn't read the manual, and the heavy carpet absorbed its fall. I rolled, swept it up with my right hand and threw it back. I heard it break and the familiar *whoosh* of unleashed flame, but it wasn't going to do much damage to an asphalt roof.

The second cocktail hit the window frame, shattered, and splashed its contents onto Meong. A split second later, she burst into flame. She got off only a partial scream before another flurry of bullets cut her dead. The pungent odor of gasoline and burning flesh reached me at the same time as the heat.

As the men fled, I bolted up, tore off one of the drapes and smothered the flames on Meong. It saved the office, but it didn't matter to her. There were shouts in the hall-way, and I knew Suzanne would be looked after. Getting her head around Meong's betrayal would take longer. I climbed through the open window and onto the roof.

28

A Flag and a Fish

The shooters had split up. The decision of which to go after was made for me. Only one was visible. He had leaped onto an adjoining rooftop and fallen. As he struggled to his feet, his clothes were torn, and his hands and face were sliced open from belly flopping on the rough gravel surface. Unfortunately, he still had his gun.

I hit the edge of the Happy Asia roof at full speed and tried not to look down. As I clawed for altitude, I half expected to feel a shower of lead plow into me, but my quarry had disappeared into a service stairwell. Being as tall as I am, I leap pretty well, and I needed every inch. Normally, I would have hit and rolled to lessen the chance of breaking an ankle, but having seen what happened to the kid, I bent my knees and took the shock on the soles of my feet. I felt it all the way up my spine.

At the stairwell door, I stopped and waved my arm past the opening. Immediately, several shots rang out, kicking loose pieces of the steel frame. When I heard footsteps descending, I went down too.

When I reached the sidewalk, I saw the shooter turning the corner a block away. He was heading back the way we'd come. The kid was fast, and by the time I reached Grant Avenue again, he was gone. People avoiding pursuit tend not to cross streets unless they have to, so I turned right and walked briskly along the storefronts looking in. I had gone about twenty feet when I heard chickens squawking and a man yelling. I ducked into a Chinese grocery.

The place was so jammed with merchandise, I couldn't see much of anything. Then suddenly, a flock of chickens came cackling past me and ran out the front door. I heard tires screech as they made it to the street, then shouts and people running after a free chicken dinner.

I threaded my way past barrels, boxes and several older women talking excitedly and pointing toward the rear. I pushed through a beaded curtain into a narrow hallway.

The back door was twenty feet ahead, and it had a burglar bar across it. Another doorway opened to my left, and I took a breath and ran past it. MAC-11 bullets tore plaster off the opposite wall. As soon as the firing stopped, I dove through the doorway and rolled behind the cash register counter.

I was in a small restaurant not accessible from the street. It was decorated with mismatched Salvation Army furniture and old martial arts posters, and whatever was cooking was mouthwatering. About half the tables were occupied, their occupants shifting their gaze from me to the back, where I presumed the kitchen was. In a corner to my right, six older men wearing black suits sat playing cards at a large, round table. One looked up long enough to nod, then went back to his cards. I guessed I was in a tong restaurant and had just been given an okay to handle the problem. Unfortunately, nobody slid me a Magnum.

I worked my way to the other end of the counter and used a mirror on the wall to look in the kitchen. The shooter was slamming another clip into his weapon, while the cookstaff stood next to the stove watching him. One of them caught my eye in the mirror and pantomimed opening a drawer.

I reached up, pulled on the knob under the register and felt inside the drawer. The gun was a Raven .25, not much bigger than a pack of Camels. The cops call it a Saturday night special. I call it an amputation-in-waiting. Maybe I could ram it down his throat.

The shooter saw me watching him and blew the mirror to pieces. That sent a few, but not all, of the patrons running into the grocery. The old men dealt another hand. While I was considering my next move, the shooter stuck his gun around the corner and fired wildly. He didn't hit anything significant except a long fish tank filled with black water. It exploded, setting free a swarm of four-foot eels. They slithered past me faster than most people can run, and what the bullets had failed to do, the eels accomplished. Women screamed, and men knocked their wives out of the way running for the door.

I used the distraction to grab a straggler by the tail, and before it could turn on me, I flung it in the general direction of the kitchen. Blind luck wrapped it over the shooter's wrist, and it sank its teeth—serious teeth—into his wrist. He did the eel dance for a second, then regained his composure, changed hands with the gun and shot it. He kept firing as he ran past me and out the door. I heard the burglar bar clank, and by the time I got to the alley, he was gone.

I caught up with him on the next block. City workers were rebuilding a stretch of sidewalk, and four cement trucks were lined up, waiting to disgorge their loads. The shooter had climbed into the lead mixer, which was painted bumper to bumper like a giant grinning shark. He was frantically trying to start it while the driver pulled at the door and yelled obscenities. When the kid pointed the MAC in the driver's face, he opted for discretion and backed off.

Seconds later, the mixer roared to life, and the shooter ground it into gear. I was already running toward the second truck. The guy in the cab didn't look like he was going to surrender his rig easily, but I got lucky. The driver behind him got out to confront me, probably assuming I was some kind of jacker. Unfortunately, he was right, and I brushed him out of the way and got behind the wheel. My ride was painted like an American flag, and as I wound through first and second gears and headed downhill, I liked my look if not my chances.

From the way the shark was swaying, I thought the kid was having a little trouble getting the feel of seventy thousand pounds of steel, chrome and shifting viscosity. But he wasn't tentative. His brake lights came on only intermittently, and while he banged into parked cars, he continued accelerating.

San Francisco's one-way streets seem to have been determined by drawing names out of a hat. If there is a discernible pattern, it's one I don't recognize. At the next block, the kid went left, which put us on a two-way level surface and closing on a traffic jam ahead. In any other city, the next street would have headed uphill, so he would have had to turn against cars coming at him. But it headed down again, and the kid took it.

There was some kind of street festival taking place, and as I swerved to avoid taking out a popcorn wagon, an Asian woman with an infant strapped to her stomach stepped in front of me and froze. I looked at her, and she looked at me, and in that split second, I imagined her disappearing under my bumper. I wrenched the wheel right, but there was no hope. Then, at the last possible instant, a hand came out of nowhere, grabbed her by the back of neck and jerked her out of my path.

I glanced in my mirror and saw the red-and-white-striped coat of the popcorn man clutching her. I hit the horn in appreciation, but I doubt anyone guessed what it was for. Certainly not the motorcycle cop who flew out of an alley and had no choice but to lay down his bike and let it slide under my wheels. He was able to grab on to a tire of a parked car and miss being mashed into his Harley.

The kid in the shark was doing better on the downgrade, missing most of the vehicles. But when I saw that my speedometer was approaching seventy, I knew it was only a matter of time before we both hit something that would kill us and a lot of innocents. Then his cement feeder trough broke loose, swung out and began disgorging wet sludge onto parked cars. The fail-safe chip in the truck's computer immediately jammed the transmission into a lower gear and began grinding the shark to an involuntary stop.

I got the American flag down three gears in less than half a block, hearing steel tear with a shriek like a hundred cats in heat. When the brakes caught, the truck jolted to a stop, slamming my chest into the steering wheel.

The kid was already out and firing his MAC. I dove down in the seat and pushed open the passenger door, preparing for another foot chase. Any other criminal would have taken off, but this was a teenager who'd probably been driving cement mixers on his Xbox since he was in diapers. While he kept me pinned down, he refolded and rehooked the trough and ran back to the cab. If I had moved right away, I might have gotten to him while he was fighting the truck into gear, but I might have also gotten a hollow point between the eyes. I was back on my own accelerator while the blue smoke from the stop was still in the air. My passenger door closed itself against a FedEx van.

The streetcar near Lombard Street was traveling away from us, and the kid hit it with such force that windows rattled in Oakland. The car's rear third came off the tracks, and the mixer slid along its right side, where his extended mirror took out every window. When I passed, the conductor was doing his best to get the trolley stopped, and the passengers were clumped together on the opposite side.

The Golden Gate Bridge isn't that easy to get to. The shark managed to do it without dropping under sixty. I'd been expecting a fleet of squad cars and helicopters since we'd begun, but when I finally heard the first siren, it was by itself. A single black and white was sitting about thirty yards behind me and making no move to come any closer. I couldn't blame him. There's less paperwork for shooting somebody than wrecking a department vehicle. And the outcome for tangling with a couple of concrete behemoths at freeway speed seemed obvious. I figured they'd probably be waiting for us at the toll plaza.

They were—about twenty of them. Plus a couple of cone trucks they'd commandeered from the Bridge Authority. But Shark-Boy didn't come off the gas an inch, and that much tonnage behind the leering grin of a man-eating fish sent the Marin sheriffs into a jailbreak trying to clear what had been a limp-wristed attempt at a roadblock. The kid took out half a tollbooth, and I finished the job. I didn't see anybody inside, but they'd forgotten the cash drawer, and as I looked in my mirror, I saw dozens of motorists bolt from their cars and wade into a cyclone of currency. It was nice to know somebody was having a good day.

I was trying to anticipate where the kid might go when he took the guesswork out of it, got off the highway and headed east—which was also straight up. It made sense in that guys on the run seem to try to stay close to home, but a cement mixer wasn't what that narrow road was designed for.

29

High Ground and Long Magazines

Ninety-nine percent of the visitors to San Francisco have no idea the Marin Headlands are anything other than picturesque hills. Part of the reason is that nobody's turning a buck up there, so the tour books funnel you to the normal fleecing stations. The other part is the city's anathema to calling attention to the military—except to ask if there's any more free land they can have.

The headlands, however, are where America's *Guns of Navarone* were.

Shortly after the turn of the twentieth century, the army began constructing cannon emplacements across the bay to protect the country's most important West Coast port. In the run-up to WWII, antiaircraft batteries were added along with massive sixteen-inch guns that could fire a one-ton shell thirty miles out to sea. To man and secure these weapons, hundreds of soldiers lived and worked in remote installations hidden among the ridges. The locals knew they were there, of course, but details were classified, and to ask questions was to invite a cold cell and several long evenings with the FBI.

During those years, the movement of every vessel that

passed through the Golden Gate—from carrier to mine-sweeper, cargo ship to tug—and every aircraft that ventured overhead was carefully orchestrated by the military. The secrecy of the operation, along with the tightly controlled identities of the personnel and the state-of-the-art equipment were components of the Japanese internment decision.

Though very few outsiders know about the headlands' former use, almost everyone has seen photographs taken from high above the Golden Gate Bridge looking across to San Francisco. Most are not the aerial shots they appear to be. You get them by standing on a narrow spit of dirt on the edge of a thousand-foot cliff with your heart in your throat.

During my high school years at the Army and Navy Academy, we traveled to the headlands for two weeks each summer to bivouac with other military schools and play war games. The food was lousy, it always rained, and trying to stay awake standing watch was impossible. But they could have doubled our discomfort for the one Saturday night each year that we were turned loose in San Francisco.

What had begun as a postcard-perfect day had been gradually darkening since the shark and I hit the bridge. Now, ascending the hill at an angle steeper than any street in the city, fog rolled over the hood of the mixer, and the temperature dropped twenty degrees. Twain never said, "The coldest winter I ever spent was summer in San Francisco," but he should have.

I raised my window to keep out the wet gauze and turned on my wipers against the increasing mist. Ahead, the shark disappeared, and when I gave my truck more gas, I almost missed a bend and barely recovered to avoid plunging over the side. When I could no longer see the road, I hit my lights, then quickly switched them off when they reflected back in my face.

The procession of law enforcement kept falling farther back until it was completely swallowed by the gloom. Even the sirens disappeared. Since we were now on federal land, somebody higher than a patrol officer would be making decisions. Hopefully, that would give me time to figure out how to avoid having them reopen Alcatraz for me.

As I approached the top, my memory said that as soon as the terrain leveled, the ruins of one of the artillery batteries would be thirty yards off to my right. I turned in what I hoped was the correct spot, and in a few seconds, I could make out what looked like a two-story concrete motel with its outer wall removed. Welcome to 1942.

I angled in so that I was parallel to it and almost ran into the shark. The kid's engine was still running, but the door was open and the cab empty. It made sense that he would know the place. He'd probably graffitied it along with countless other drunks, druggies and gangbangers. I drove past the idling truck until I was enveloped in fog again, stopped and got out as quietly as possible, leaving my engine on to cover any extraneous noise.

The gravel had been paved over since the last time I'd been here, and the brown cement was wet from the mist, causing the soles of my deck shoes to squeak slightly. I thought about taking them off, but a sea of broken glass changed my mind. With visibility only inches, I kept to the wall, unable to see the overhang of the second floor above my head. I entered the first doorway I came to, and though it was dark inside, there was much less fog.

It was a square room with rusting artillery shell racks built into the walls. At the rear was a stairway leading up. As I moved toward it, I noticed something under one of the racks. When it didn't move, I got closer. The guy was wearing dark blue sweatpants, matching hooded CAL sweatshirt and Adidas cross-trainers. He'd taken two shots to the face and several more in his chest. He hadn't felt much pain.

Keeping against the wall, I took the stairs one slow step at a time. Halfway up, I found a St. Francis Hospital clip-on ID in the name of Joanne Trufant. From the picture, Joanne was a black girl in her twenties with an engaging smile. Just under the small gold crucifix around her neck was the bold lettering:

**TRAUMA TEAM FOUR
SUPERVISING R.N.**

Two steps beyond, a pink-and-white running shoe lay on its side. There was broken glass here too, and fresh blood on the cement. Suddenly, a volley of shots ricocheted off the concrete above my head. Not a good time to be tall. I retreated down a couple of steps.

"Hey, Jaws, you don't need the girl."

His answer was two more bullets. I knew he couldn't see through the fog, but I also couldn't avoid the glass underfoot, so I might as well have been wearing a cowbell. I needed him thinking about something else.

"You okay, Joanne?" I shouted back.

"I'm fine, but this motherfucker's crazy."

She didn't sound like she was about to fall apart.

"How's Carmine?" she asked.

She'd obviously seen him shot, so I told her the truth. "Dead."

"Shit, he seemed like a nice guy."

The kid spit a stream of angry Chinese, and Joanne let out a muffled yell. "Goddamn it, stop pulling my hair!"

I heard scuffling, and it was just what I needed. I bolted the rest of the way up the stairs into the open air of the roofless second floor. I ran in the direction where I thought the shots had originated and came upon the kid trying to hold on to Joanne with one hand and level his MAC with the other. He didn't get either right.

Joanne sank her teeth into his free wrist, and I got to the MAC just as he pulled the trigger. I jerked it up, and it fired wildly for a few seconds before the clip ran dry. If I had hit him with the left I threw, it would have knocked him cold, maybe worse. As it was, it just grazed his temple and sent the gun flying but didn't put him all the way down. He spun, caught himself with one hand on the floor, regained his balance and headed for the stairs.

Other than a bloody foot and some mussed hair, Joanne looked okay. I left her and went after the kid. I heard the shark's engine rev and the gears engage. I got close enough to see the soup close around its taillights. I listened as it gained speed, but instead of turning onto the road, it went straight. Maybe the kid didn't know his geography after all. I ran after him.

You couldn't miss the noise of the truck going through the fence, but it was a low barrier, and as high as the kid was sitting, he might not have seen it. Then the engine surged and underbrush began breaking. I slowed because I knew the edge was close. Still, I almost misjudged it.

Standing between the tire tracks, I listened to the mixer sliding down the side of the cliff. It continued for a couple of seconds, then hit something hard and stopped. The engine was still roaring, so the kid might have been unconscious with his foot on the gas.

I moved carefully parallel to the abyss, hoping to get an angle that would let me see. Like the eye of a hurricane, a round tunnel of sunlight suddenly opened, extending all the way to the water. Two-thirds of a mile below, a flock of white seagulls skimmed the whitecaps. And then there was the crack of a tree trunk splintering, and the shark suddenly fell out of the clouds into the light. It bounced once against the cliff face, flipped and plunged upside down into the bay. I waited for somebody to bob to the surface, but it didn't happen, and the hole closed.

I was on my way back to the battery when I heard a helicopter. He passed over me then swung around and came back and hovered directly overhead. We couldn't see each other, but he must have been equipped with thermal imaging, because there was no question he knew I was there.

Joanne had both shoes on and was bending over Carmine. She looked up. "Did you get him?"

"He got himself."

"Fucker."

I nodded at the dead guy. "You two weren't together?"

She shook her head. "Just jogging the same route when the weasel almost took us out with that goddamn truck. You a cop?"

I ignored her and went back upstairs. I found the kid's MAC. It was well used and devoid of markings. I ejected the long, nonstandard magazine. Half-inch dashes were etched along its edge at irregular intervals. I recognized the clip's design. It had been manufactured for the Ministry of State Security, and its capacity would be a multiple of eight. Fifty-six for this one, I estimated. There would also be an identifier engraved inside its base that corresponded to an agent.

Being able to link a specific piece of equipment to a specific operator might seem counterintuitive, but the Chinese are almost as long on personal accountability as they are on brutality. In other words, carelessness with state property can get you executed. The kid wouldn't be an officially recognized asset, but considering the brazenness of the attack and immediate response to our arrival at Happy Asia, he was being run by a professional.

I pocketed the magazine, took the MAC and headed back downstairs. Joanne was standing in the doorway looking up at the opaque sky. The helicopter was still there, and the fog was getting thinner.

"Sounds like somebody's going to be here pretty soon," she said.

"I know, and I'm sorry to leave you with this mess."

She looked at the gun in my hand. "How are you going to get past anybody on that little tiny road?"

"A little cadet magic. But it would be helpful if you never saw me."

She nodded. "Way too much fog to have seen anybody."

"You going to be okay?" I asked.

"Where I work, this wouldn't even make the day's top ten. How bad is the heat going to be?"

"I think they're all going to go into a room, and when they come out, none of this will have happened."

"Then one day, you can buy me dinner and fill me in."

I shook her hand and felt its warmth. "It's a date," I said.

I wiped the American Flag mixer free of prints and made a mental note of the owner's name painted on the door. J. G. TARANTELLO. J. G. would get something nice for the trouble I'd caused him. Maybe a new Escalade to ease his commute.

As I jogged west down the ridgeline, I threw the MAC as far as I could, knowing there was water out there somewhere. About a mile farther along, I found the old trail. It was in a lot worse condition than I remembered.

During my military school excursions, we'd discovered a shallow cavern in the hill about two hundred feet down. Since it provided a clear sweep of the bay, rumor had it that it had been a sentry post against a possible Japanese commando landing. To me, that sounded like army-speak for: *Here's another place to bore some dogfaces to death.*

Wanting to honor those who had come before us, our group turned it into a drinking club and cut crude steps down to the tiny beach to get the beer up once it arrived via the tug captain we'd paid. I suppose the steps put us at risk of a frontal assault, but we kept a church key handy just in case. Never underestimate the industriousness of young men with too many rules and too much money.

I wasn't as nimble as I'd once been, but half an hour later, I was hoofing it along the Golden Gate Bridge approach. An empty cab heading back to the city stopped where he wasn't supposed to when he saw the hundred-dollar bill I was waving.

It was still a mess at the toll plaza, but the cops were doing their best to squeeze the four northbound lanes down to two. I made a silent apology to those I'd inconvenienced. Southbound was clear but moving at a curiosity crawl that was somewhat mitigated by the Bridge Authority having suspended toll collection. My cabbie, an aging hippie named

Walt Wingo, caught my eye in the rearview mirror. "I still gotta charge you for the toll, buddy."

"That the law or because you saw the C-note?"

Walt got a little ouchy. "You want, motherfucker, I can stop right here and call one a them pigs over to 'splain it to you."

"Lighten up, Walt, the sixties are over. If the extra few bucks will make a difference in your life, fine. Just don't jerk my chain."

He brooded for a moment. "Two fuckin' airport runs with a carful of Gandhis. Counted out the fare to the fuckin' penny . . . to the fuckin' PENNY. Then I get sent out to Sausalito, where I drive around for a fuckin' hour lookin' for an address that don't exist. I got me a roommate that don't pay his share of the rent and picks up stray cats that eat my fuckin' food. So, you'll fuckin' EXCUSE me if I got a little attitude."

I had Walt drive past Happy Asia. There was crime scene tape blocking the sidewalk, and some cops standing around smoking. An old Asian woman, pulling a grocery cart, broke through the tape and started across the restricted area. One of the cops said something to her, and she spit a stream of brown liquid on his shoe and kept walking. The cop's buddy almost fell down laughing.

Down the block, next to Starbucks, were more tape and more cops. No old ladies. I saw no sign of Eddie or Fat Cat, but I'd been gone two hours. I had Walt stop at the next intersection, where I got out and handed him the entire hundred. He might have grunted, but he didn't smile.

You can only checkmate a Fed for so long, and my time was running out. With my plane now in operation, it wouldn't be difficult for my dear friend, Francesca Huston, to find me. I didn't need more aggravation. It was time to play a customer's game. As I hoofed it back to the Huntington, I bought a throwaway phone from a street vendor.

"You and I need a face-to-face," I said when she answered.

"I couldn't agree more," growled SAC Huston. "Where are you? I'll send a car."

"If that's your sweet voice, you don't date much. A friend of mine has a soft spot in his heart for law enforcement. Benny Joe Willis. You should be able to come up with an address. I'll give you a hint. LA."

"Fuck off, Black. The only reason I haven't put out an arrest-on-sight is . . ."

I interrupted her. "Are we going to have to go through the hang up/call back routine again? You're not going to arrest anybody because you've got a sick feeling that you're way over the horizon from something very big and very ugly. Well, you are, and it's a good bet you're going to get a whole lot sicker before you get better." I gave her a moment. "So, do I have your attention?"

"Benny Joe Wills," she snarled.

"When you run him, the computer's going to say he's crazier than a shithouse rat. He probably is, but before you make a mistake that puts you even further out of the loop, call over to the NRO, and get somebody important on the line."

"The National Reconnaissance Office? What for?"

"Because Mr. Willis is one of theirs, and they're going to tell you all you need to know. When Benny Joe confirms you're at his place—alone—we'll take the next step."

"You can't expect me to go anywhere without backup."

"Why? There's not a felon in sight, and the only one who's shown any violent tendencies is you."

She waited so long to answer I wondered if I'd lost her.

"When?"

"Tomorrow. And don't underestimate this guy. He'll know in ten seconds if you're jerking him off. Or his dogs will."

"I hate dogs, and they hate me."

I thought about Benny Joe's four slobbering Dobermans and their low regard for human life. "Then this is going to be even better than I anticipated. And Francesca, my love, if you even think about trying to screw over my friend, and he doesn't get you, you can bet your cold, dead, D.C. heart I will." I clicked off before she answered. I wanted to hate myself, but the lingering pain in my right kidney talked me out of it.

I dialed Benny Joe. "I'm sending you an FBI agent."

"I'm flattered, but my fuckin' freezer's full." With Benny Joe, that might or might not have been a joke. In addition to being a magician with all things photographic, he's at war with the government, which is interesting, because even though they retired him with extreme prejudice, they can't stop rehiring him. No one teases images out of a frame of film like Benny Joe. Throw in consulting fess from the news networks and patent royalties, and he easily knocks down half a million a year. All it does is make him more paranoid. Did I mention he can't open his mouth without saying *fuck*?

"She won't be there long. Just make sure she's alone. All the way alone."

"A fuckin *she*?"

"Special Agent in Charge Francesca Huston. Very pretty. In a flesh-eating sort of way."

"In other words, like my fuckin' ex-wife. Maybe the freezer's not as full as I thought." As Benny Joe started into a riff about the former Mrs. Willis, I handed the phone to a homeless guy on the corner. When I looked back, he appeared to be telling Benny Joe a story.

30

Takeoffs and Bullies

Eddie, Fat Cat and Coggan Buffalo were waiting in the lobby of the Huntington, but not together. Fat Cat and Coggan were on a sofa, talking. Eddie was across the room, glaring. I thought I saw him rub his armpit.

Eddie jumped up when he saw me. "Jesus Christ, boss. What the hell happened at the tour place? We were across the street, and all of a sudden it sounded like Patton taking Palermo. Then this kid comes running toward us with a gun. Fuckin' clip musta been this long." He held his hands eighteen inches apart.

I took my clip out of my pocket. "Like this?"

"Shit, yeah. Where'd you get that?"

"Did you see where the kid went?"

"See? Hell, yes, I saw. Some guy stepped out of a doorway and shot the motherfucker right in the face. I was this close."

"Asian?"

Eddie nodded emphatically. "Black suit, black hat, the whole rip."

Fat Cat and Coggan joined us. Coggan, even more muscular than I remembered, was wearing an acre of Hugo Boss jogging suit and an untied pair of Nikes. Together, they were an impressive assemblage of sinew and bone that could have hired out as a windbreak. I shook hands with Coggan. "Good to see you again."

"You too." He looked at Fat Cat. "I'd like to hire this guy. Can you imagine him and Wal-Mart moving in on a pack of drunks? Especially in that red, white and blue outfit."

"I was just telling him about the kid who got shot," interjected Eddie, not looking at either man.

"Cops show up, I assume?" I asked Fat Cat.

"They were on the usual ACLU delay, but yeah, eventually. Two black and whites. One for the agency, the other for the kid. Then half a dozen detectives, but no Chinese-speakers, which is par for the course. That, and a lotta yawnin'."

"What happened to the shooter?"

"He just walked back in the building. After that, who knows?"

"I thought all you cops couldn't resist a chase."

"Couple of guys with Glocks closed ranks behind him, and silk looks like shit with holes in it. I jawboned with a pair of homicide guys until the meat wagon got there. A big Irishman and a dude named Ramos. They didn't know shit, and wanted to know less. 'Asian guy in a black suit . . . in Chinatown? What the fuck?' I got the message."

"And, of course, none of the locals saw anything."

"Whole block was suddenly struck blind."

I turned to Eddie. "You find a right-seater?"

"Jody's waiting at the airport."

I motioned to the concierge, and he hurried over. I handed him two C-notes and told him we were leaving.

"Want me to send everything to Mr. Praxis as usual, Mr. Black?"

"Please. And anybody asks, we weren't here. Think you can square that with the rest of the staff and wake up the limo driver to take me to Oakland?" I peeled off another couple of bills.

"No problem, sir."

* * *

I sent Fat Cat and Coggan back to Chinatown. I wanted Coggan to see Sleeping Tiger, and the detective would be able to get them past any cops. Meong hadn't died over a shuffleboard dispute on Lido Deck. If Suzanne was into something, and it wasn't the baby trade, I wanted to know what. Meanwhile, Eddie and I took the hotel's stretch to Oakland.

At the general aviation terminal, I handed the MAC clip to Eddie with instructions to find a mechanic who could cut off its base. Then I showed the lone security guard my ID and walked out to my plane.

Jody had the BBJ gassed and ready, and in the cabin, I found a stack of CPK pizzas and a case of Sam Adams on ice. I made a mental note to give Jody a bonus—a large one. I was starving, but I needed a shower more, and when I saw my torn clothes and dirty face in the mirror, I wasn't surprised Walt the Cabbie hadn't treated me like royalty.

Clean, and with a couple of small cuts bandaged, I grabbed a Sicilian pizza and a beer, plopped myself down in a soft leather seat and ate like a condemned man. Eddie had apparently been there while I was changing and left the two pieces of clip next to my chair. I assumed he was up front running through the preflight checks with Jody.

Between bites, I picked up the clip's butt end, which was about the size of my fingertip, held it so I could catch a ray of light from the window and squinted inside. As expected, there was a tiny, gold Chinese character at the bottom. I didn't feel any satisfaction at having been right. At some point, I fell asleep and only awakened when Fat Cat and Coggan came aboard.

I looked at my watch. It had been over two hours. "Trouble?" I asked.

"On the contrary," answered Coggan.

Fat Cat was already ramming pizza in his mouth, but he talked around it. "A couple of the agency girls were still there. One of them was that chick who took you upstairs."

"Linda," I said.

"Right, and her friend, JinJing. My man, Coggan here, is hell with the ladies."

"You own a bar, you learn to talk to everybody," Coggan said.

"Bullshit. I can talk with the best. These chicks wanted to bookend you."

I was surprised civilians had been allowed back inside. "I figured they would have sent everybody home."

"They tried," said Fat Cat, "but the girls said they had cruises at sea and had to be able to monitor them. If the cops wanted them out, they were goin' to have to use cuffs."

"And that worked?"

"You've been forced to take a hundred fuckin' hours of sensitivity training, and the only thing you know about Chinatown is you like the food. What do you think?"

"What did they say about Meong?"

"Called her a cunt. Not because she was boffin' the boss but because she wouldn't make sales calls and could barely operate a computer. The other girls had to cover for her. Hey, is *boffin'* the right word when it's broads?"

"So she was put there by somebody to watch Suzanne."

"That's how I'd write it," said Fat Cat.

"Any idea who?"

"It's like Kujovic said. The cops don't know shit from Shinola about Chinatown. Long as what they do doesn't spill onto the regular folks, have at it, motherfuckers. But just to stay current, they use business types like Suzanne Chang. The Triads know it and use the same channels in reverse. Maybe call in a little blue retribution for an upstart or help the cops fix a small problem before it gets out of hand. Small stuff. Neither side wants too much information in play."

"Very clubby."

"This ain't like no other city in America. Miss Chang seem like a pain in the ass to you?"

"Hot, cold and emotional."

"Which means weak and probably slated for a dirt nap sometime soon. So when her minder reported in that she was talkin' to us, they just sped up what they were goin' to do anyway."

"Now that there's a spotlight on her, she'll get slapped around a little and assigned a new handler. Probably one that doesn't eat pussy. She's smart, she'll move to Hawaii."

"Let's get this crate in the air, and we can compare notes."

I pressed a hidden button, and almost immediately, I heard the auxiliary power unit disengage. As we rolled into takeoff position, I noticed Coggan was sweating heavily and gripping the armrests so hard he was leaving dents. Sort of like me in a chopper. I gave him credit for getting through it.

The fog had dissipated, and the late-afternoon sun was bright and beautiful over the bay. Eddie pulled the nose of the 737 into a steeper climb than usual, and I noticed the engine RPMs were up—way up. The moment the landing gear retracted, he cut power completely, and the world went silent. After we'd dropped a couple of hundred feet, he restarted everything, jammed the throttles forward and jerked us skyward again. It was like bottoming out on a roller coaster. My insides, like those of my guests, went weightless for twenty seconds, which seems a lot longer when its happening.

Fat Cat was oblivious, but Coggan was straining against his lap belt and doing all he could to choke back a scream. I didn't say anything, and a few minutes later, we were at sixteen thousand feet and making a wide, slow turn to the south. The seat-belt sign went off, and Fat Cat immediately got up and went for another Sam Adams. He offered one to Coggan, who first shook his head no, then changed his mind. The hand he took it with wasn't very steady.

When I had my BBJ's cabin blueprinted, I told Preston Gage he could do what he liked everywhere else, but I wanted my office right behind the cockpit. Preston, owner of F&G Yacht Design in San Diego, is another Delta guy. He lost a leg in Sierra Leone and got hooked on design from killing endless hours in doctor's offices reading *Architectural Digest*. He'd never tried a plane, but he'd done such a magnificent job keeping the Kelly Wearstler interior of my boat current that he was the only guy I called.

He tried talking me into positioning the office in the rear, ahead of the bedroom, to dampen any cabin noise while I slept. But I'd been aboard Air Force One and believed the prez had it right. You want to be as close as possible to the people who have your life in their hands. Besides, when someone was going to be sharing my bed, I left the crowd at home.

I went up to the office now and called Eddie on the phone. A minute later, he joined me. "What's up, boss?"

"You're fired."

His jaw dropped so far I couldn't see his shirt collar. Until he met me, Eddie was chronically on suspension, on probation or on food stamps. The FAA had tried to cashier him, the pilots' union had blacklisted him and most employers fell somewhere between contempt and wanting him dead. He was as good a pilot as there was, but he couldn't take an order or stay out of things that weren't his business. He also wasn't above going deaf when an air traffic controller gave him instructions counter to what he wanted to hear, which for me, sometimes comes in handy.

But Eddie and I had an understanding. He didn't fuck around with my plane or my passengers, or he was out. No warnings, no questions.

"But . . ."

I didn't let him go any further. "You know how much I hate bullies, Eddie, and that takeoff was your way of fucking with your brother, who, not incidentally, is my guest. It was also dangerous, and in case you've forgotten, our asses are currently being held aloft by *my* $60 million worth of Boeing."

He started to say something, then dropped his head. "I'm really sorry, boss."

"Fuck you, Eddie."

I walked past him and into the cockpit. Jody Miller has been my on-again, off-again first officer for a while. He's considerably younger than Eddie, and a terrific stunt pilot with his own Stearman. But when he's at my controls, he's as smooth and steady as a Buckingham Palace chauffeur—and as reliable.

Like every other flight school grad, Jody wanted to work for the airlines. Unfortunately, the only jobs available would have forced him to move east, and he likes to spend time with his blackjack-addicted mother in Lake Tahoe. My schedule's loose enough and my salary high enough to afford him a good living and plenty of time in his Stearman. I also like him, which is getting harder to do as young people become less educated and more imbued with entitlement.

"You up to running this thing full-time, Jody?"

He turned and looked at me, then at Eddie behind me. "You serious, Mr. Black."

"Dead serious."

"What about Eddie?"

"He's unemployed. But it's your cockpit now, so you make the call who rides shotgun."

There was a long moment's hesitation before he said to Eddie, "It won't be a problem for me if it isn't for you. One thing, though. No more smoking up here."

Eddie stood there long enough for the shock to wear off, then said to Jody, "You want to move over to the left seat?"

"We'll make the switch next run."

I left as Eddie was buckling himself in. You can tell in the sandbox which boys are going to be the bullies. Just ask them to tap each other as softly as possible. As sure as night turns into day, one is going to say, "Fuck this," and hit some kid hard enough to make his eyes cross. He'll do it all his life.

31

Satellites and Market-Makers

When I got back to the main cabin, Fat Cat said, "You gotta listen to this guy. He's wired different."

"The floor is yours."

"Let's put the jade tiger aside for a moment. I know where it came from, but it's just a symbol. Right now, I need your mind in an expansive state."

He leaned forward. "Pretend you're a spy satellite in geosynchronous orbit. Your job is to monitor your little piece of the planet 24/7/365. Let's say, Beijing. If there's a festival, you enjoy the fireworks. It rains, you can see through it. Need a close-up, no problem. But if a president gets assassinated in Dallas, you don't care. Unless . . ."

"Unless something that shouldn't be on my screen suddenly is," Fat Cat said.

"Correct," said Coggan. "Or something that *should* be *isn't*."

"I think I'm with you."

"Look at it this way. Books and movies have taught us to find the clues, decipher them, and the mystery's solved. But that's not the way strategic intelligence works. If you go looking for individual items, you miss the big picture. Your value as a satellite is overview. And absence is often as telling as presence. No response to a major fire until everything is burned. A school playground empty at recess."

"Shit like that's important?" asked Fat Cat.

"Everything's important when you're looking for broken patterns and nonevident relationships. So you watch your target, and computers model and analyze the data. In the old days, you could run maybe a million permutations a month, but with billions of possibilities, statistically, you were still wandering in the dark. Faster systems and software based on chaos theory now let you sift through nearly everything."

As a ground-pounder at Delta, I'd learned that even if the Washington brain trust does know something, it doesn't do much trusting down the line. You're lucky if they tell you anything. Ask Pat Tillman. "What you're saying is to take a step back."

"Correct; if we make what we know now our alpha position, we'll burn a lot of shoe leather and end up with exactly nothing. So if we go back to the satellite, what's missing?"

"The girl with the baby," said Fat Cat.

"Yes, but the cops said Lucille was done first. And the killers used ATVs from the house to get out there. That means the girl had already escaped, and Chuck was out of commission. So why not chase the quarry rather than hang around torturing people to find out where she *might* have gone? No, what they wanted, Lucille had, and it was only when they couldn't get it out of her that they returned and tried Chuck."

"Which is why they were even more violent with him. Pure fury."

"And you said the Pullman wasn't trashed, so it was something Lucille knew."

I thought about it for a long moment. The FedEx driver had a standing order. For Perth, Australia. And he'd seen an artist's easel and heard a man's voice. I took out my cell phone and held it so my associates could listen.

The Reverend Northcutt didn't seem as happy to hear a

sinner's voice as a man of God should have been. "This will only take a minute, then you can go back to handing out Bibles. In that collection of cops you minister to, is there an artist?"

"An artist? I'm sure we have lots of people who can draw."

"If you want to be coy, I can stop by and discuss it in person."

"Milt O'Keefe."

"And Milt was a friend of Chuck and Lucille's. A good friend." They were not questions.

"Yes."

"And a cop?"

"Not a cop, but he worked for the LAPD. But only to put food on the table. Milt was classically trained. In Rome. He did a lot of really fine work on Lucille's train car. Painted a mural in their dining room too."

"And if I wanted to talk to Mr. O'Keefe?"

Northcutt's pause was confirmation, but I waited until he said it. "He's dead."

"As of when?"

"Just before Chuck and Lucille. Couple of weeks, I think. He was target shooting in the desert and didn't come home. Coroner ruled it a suicide."

A couple of weeks. The same time Lucille had gone to see Maywood. When the dominos had begun to fall. I hung up.

"Looks like Milt was drawin' girls," said Fat Cat. "Probably so somebody could recognize them."

"Why?" I asked. "When you could take a picture and shoot it around the world in a few seconds. Besides, when the FedEx guy saw them, there were babies there, so they were already back from their trips."

Coggan nodded. "Milt was a police artist. He was drawing something being described to him. And he'd been doing it for some time, meaning whatever Lucille was doing, it wasn't spur-of-the-moment."

"Sounding more and more like Department 11 all the time," I said.

"What's Department 11?" asked Coggan.

After I ran it down, he seemed genuinely impressed. "I didn't think the FBI had that kind of thinking in them. Sounds like they didn't stretch for a person to run it, but it's nice to know they're finally in the game. That makes this guy Wes Crowe and his radio gear even more interesting."

"Why?"

"In most places, an Internet connection and a Dell will get you all the connectivity you need. But in China, they've got something called the Golden Shield, less glowingly referred to as the Great Firewall. It's their own blocking technology that State Security uses to track citizens who might pose a threat."

"In other words, anybody with an idea not invented by the Central Committee."

"The term is *harmonization,* as in all content must be harmonized with policy. You'd think that would be impossible in today's world, but the big dotcom players pitch right in. Helping Beijing crush radical concepts like human rights is the price of admission to their market. We estimate there are hundreds in prison for doing nothing more subversive than checking the weather in Taipei. And some have gotten a ride in an execution van for not much more. Motherfuckers."

"American companies? Are you shittin' me?" asked Fat Cat."

"They make a lot of noise when their complicity leaks out, but as soon as the heat's off, they go right back to business as usual. That kind of control goes all the way through the system. Try to sneak a PDA into the country, and you'll be lucky if all they do is confiscate it and beat you senseless."

I knew some *Falun Gong* refugees, so I understood how paranoid Beijing was about free expression. I made a mental note to check with my executives to find out if Black Group was playing that game. If we were, there were going to be some changes.

Coggan finished his thought. "Radio is low tech, reliable, impossible to shut down and everywhere. So Crowe might be helping get a few kids to freedom, but he didn't build the kind of capacity you describe as a hobby. To anyone wanting to bypass Beijing, what he's got is worth its weight in gold."

"Or jade," I prodded.

"Okay, the tiger. It's the work of the Hu-Meng, the mountain people of South China. The statuettes were used to identify their safe houses on the Tiger Road. There are eight basic shapes—sleeping, drinking, sitting, stretching, running, leaping, stalking and attacking. They're all roughly the same size, but depending on the artist and the year carved, there are wide variances in detail."

The number eight again. "The Tiger Road anything like the Silk Road?"

"Same concept, but it's not linear. More like a web with its epicenter in the high country north of Hong Kong. The tentacles reach into the major tiger habitats, India, Indochina, Sumatra, Bali, Afghanistan—at its peak, a dozen and a half countries. Including, the biggest prize, Siberia. If you were one of the lucky few deemed loyal enough to be granted a jade tiger, you automatically became the wealthiest person in your region—and the most feared. God help anybody crazy enough to fuck with you."

"How many is a 'lucky few'?"

"The Tiger People—that's what Hu-Meng means—could travel thirty miles a day with a hundred animals. Lodging was the exception, not the rule. They tried to steer clear of population centers. I'd guess no more than a few dozen statuettes—give or take.

"And the cargo, are we talking pelts or live tigers?"

"The only reason you'd have a pelt was if the animal died during capture or transit. It would be the value difference between a Vespa and a Ferrari. But there was also a downside to being tied to the Hu. If they suspected you were working with anyone else, they stripped your flesh, painted you with snake venom to keep the blood flowing, broke off the jade tiger's head, and stuffed it in your mouth. Then they tied a rope around your neck and led you behind the caravan. When you couldn't go any further, they tossed you to the tigers and took bets on how long you'd last."

"Can I assume this tiger trade is in the past?"

"You can assume it, but it wouldn't be true. It almost died during the dark days of Mao, but it reappeared about two decades ago. There aren't as many tigers now, but the money per animal is staggering."

I was afraid that was going to be the answer. "So if the Hu-Meng are in the capture and transport business, Markus Kingdom must be the market-maker. Sort of the DeBeers of endangered species."

"You gotta help me here," said Fat Cat. "Guy's got planes, more ships than the navy, all kinds of shit and a *billion fuckin' dollars*. What's he doing hustlin' tigers?"

"Because he was always a criminal. He just got rich legitimately too," answered Coggan. "But I work for institutional bucks, so I might not be the one to ask."

They both looked at me. "There isn't any way to say this without sounding like a jerk, but when you have a vast amount of money, your thinking is different. I have to fight every day to maintain a semblance of reality, and I still don't do a very good job. Often, the only thing some people think about is how to one-up their peers. It's not accidental that the business press covers mobsters, drug lords and dictators right along with oil barons and Internet tycoons. We're all part of the same ego game.

"One gives billions to science, so a second gives more to save rain forests. Then there are the spenders. Biggest yacht, best sports team, most trophy properties. It's an I'll-see-your-foundation-and-raise-you-a-Jackson-Pollack-No. 5 kind of world. And ordinary folks slugging it out for a paycheck like to know what the newest billionaire causes and toys are too. *Forbes* would be out of business if the rich suddenly turned shy. Essentially, every one of them wants to be Jack Nicholson. But if they go to a Lakers game, nobody notices. So they buy their own cameras and point them at themselves."

"I don't think of you like that," said Coggan.

"Then you would be wrong. I don't have a publicist, but I smile just as broadly as the next guy when people find out something I wanted them to know but didn't want to get caught pushing. Like I said, I fight against it, but I don't always win."

"Son of a bitch."

"Tigers allow Markus Kingdom to occupy a place in the world no one else does. That none of the others would even consider doing it makes it all the better. It marks him as dangerous and a renegade too."

Fat Cat sat back. "I think I'll stick to donuts and choke holds."

I picked up the butt of the MAC clip and handed it to Coggan. "You'll have to get the right angle, but does the character in the bottom mean anything to you? It will be the code name."

Coggan positioned the base so he could see into it. "It's in an archaic style. Xin Dynasty, maybe as far back as the Western Han. Only somebody very important would have this attached to him today."

"My dynasty knowledge is rusty, what's that in years?"

"Two thousand, give or take a couple of hundred."

"And how long have the Hu been in the tiger business?"

"The first mention of them is in 220 B.C. During the Salt Wars. Hong Kong was founded on the vast salt beds of the Pearl Delta, and after the emperor's army seized them for his own exploitation, the indigenous tribes were forced to find other employment. The Hu ran the caravans, so they had established trade routes, and since they were already dealing in the occasional tiger to supplement their income, it was a natural transition."

Coggan handed the MAC-11 clip back to me. "This character denotes a color. A very specific one. Crimson. Known then as Blood of the Tiger."

Fat Cat let out a whistle. "More tigers. What the fuck."

It was time to tell them about Jerry Merican's seventy-year locust remark.

Coggan thought for a moment, then seemed to be weighed down. "My God."

I didn't like the sound of that. As it turned out, I didn't like the answer any better.

"It's been exactly seventy years since the last great tiger hunt. It lasted two years and is said to have resulted in the capture of more than seven hundred animals. The Hu smelled WWII coming, and they were preparing for it."

"Bad news for the tigers."

"Bad news for everybody. From that point on, extinction in China was irreversible. Then, when Mao consolidated power, he tried to finish the job. The great Commie murderer had read his history and knew the Hu weren't picky about what they'd transport on those trading routes. Without tigers to support them, they wouldn't be around to move weapons either."

"Jesus."

"It gets worse. Care to guess which animal corresponds to this year in the Chinese and Japanese zodiacs?" He let it sink in. "If you possess a tiger before the year ends, your soul becomes immortal. But it has to be a live one."

I sat back. That's why the Asians were in Vegas. They were waiting for the auction. But why Vegas? It could only mean they were going as a group. With someone they trusted. Someone who also knew how to move live animals. Markus Kingdom.

Coggan looked at us. "Babies and tigers. The two trains on the same track. The dead taxi driver is important too—for what didn't happen. This Department 11 should have either logged it and moved on or taken over the investigation. Instead, they're just hanging around. They don't seem to know about Donnie in the corral or Cheater in the ravine either. And they're not running around town violating people's civil rights, which is definitely not like them. Rail, you're not going to like hearing this, but you need to talk to that Huston chick again."

"My stomach's turning, but I'm way ahead of you. Which brings us to the *Resurrection Bay II* and Parkinson-Lowe Imports. It could be something as simple as Lucille's taking Kingdom out of the loop with a ship of her own. But that would require a network inside China, and if she had that, she could have dumped him years ago."

Coggan looked at me. "It might be a dead end, but we also have to find the girl with the baby. She's the last person who saw Chuck and Lucille alive."

I also wanted to talk to this Fabian Cañada. But no matter how you sliced it, sooner or later, we were going to have to go to Tonga. Fat Cat and Coggan could handle themselves, and Eddie could shoot and drive anything. Jody had to fly the plane, so he was operationally out. I had a plan forming, but it would require at least one more.

I looked at Coggan. "Think Wal-Mart would be up for a long flight?"

"You couldn't pick a better man."

"He's a Mississippi boy, so I figure he can handle a gun."

"Just don't get between him and a buffet table."

32

Flying Foxes and Clean Sheets

FOUR WEEKS AGO
SOMEWHERE IN THE INDIAN OCEAN

Cheyenne heard the gunfire over the storm. Rain and waves had been pounding the Richer Seas *for three nights, and she had just dozed off after another long session trying to calm the screaming infant. The next shots hit the ship so hard, the concussion rocked her cabin. Outside, she heard crashing glass and people screaming. She bundled up the baby, cracked her door and looked out. The corridor was empty, so she ran, being tossed from wall to wall as the deep swells pitched the ship in all directions.*

On deck, chaos reigned. Waves crashed over the railings, and through the flashes of lightning, she could see a warship no more than fifty yards away firing its deck gun. This new fusillade tore away chunks of wood as big as Cheyenne's fist. She squinted against the rain, trying to read the boat's name. HMAS Flying Fox. *Where had she seen HMAS before? And then it came to her. On a modeling trip to Sydney. So why were Australians shooting at them?*

Looking around, she had her answer. The Richer Seas

was firing too. Near the bow, a man fed ammunition into a .50-caliber machine gun while his partner raked the superstructure of the cruiser, tracer rounds visible through the rain. On the cargo ship's bridge, other men fired rifles into the dark.

Suddenly, night became day as an intense floodlight bathed the Richer Seas. *Immediately above where Cheyenne stood, a Chinese retaliated with a shoulder-fired RPG that took out the spot and splashed the attacking vessel with flames.*

Then all hell broke loose.

Wave after wave of bullets hit the boat and ricocheted across the deck. The terrified cries of the innocents rose above the din as people tried to find cover. But there was nowhere to hide. Many died where they sat. One woman ran toward the bridge screaming and waving her arms. A volley cut her in half. Cheyenne screamed and pulled the baby close, feeling the child's little hands clench into fists. Then their engines stopped.

Cheyenne and the baby went into the water shortly before dawn. The attack had mortally wounded the refugee boat, and it had been left to drift. But the shooting had also torn loose a long rubber bumper, which was sliding around the deck. Cheyenne managed to pin it against the rail with her shoulder and lash herself to it, clutching the infant against her. A few minutes later, the Richer Seas *slipped quietly beneath the waves, and she and the child were adrift in the blackness. If there were other survivors, she didn't see them.*

She had a cut on her forehead that was bleeding into her eyes, and the baby was crying again, but at least that meant she was alive. By the time the sun was up, the storm had ended, and Cheyenne was alone on the water. She drifted, kept afloat by the bumper, but unable to maneuver. Around midday, she heard engines and saw another military vessel cruising nearby. She tried to call out, but her words were lost to the sea.

Then, suddenly, the ship turned toward her.

* * *

Cheyenne awakened in the ship's infirmary. A female naval officer was taking her pulse. A nurse sat at the foot of the bed, feeding the baby from a bottle capped with a latex finger cut from a glove. The child was happily sucking away.

"Nice to have you back with us." The officer smiled.

Cheyenne shivered and looked anxiously at the IV in her arm.

"Nothing to worry about. Just glucose. What's your name?"

"Cheyenne Rollins. I never been so cold."

"An American. I'm Commander Gibson, Royal Australian Navy. Aside from some minor hypothermia, both you and the child seem fine. How in the world did you end up in the water?"

Cheyenne had seen a lot of bad things happen because people couldn't keep their mouths shut. This didn't seem like a time to start blurting things about tigers and soldiers and gunfire at sea. "I don't know. I was asleep, and the next thing I knew we were in the water. I guess I was lucky to find that bumper."

The officer looked at her skeptically. "What was the name of your boat?"

Cheyenne took her time, seemingly trying to recall. "I don't remember. It was a yacht. A big one. I just met the owners, Terry and Marcy Something-or-Other, and they invited me to bring my baby and go for a cruise."

Even Cheyenne didn't think that was much of a story, but it was the best she could come up with in her present condition.

The officer smiled. "If I don't ask any more questions, I won't have to listen to any more raw prawn answers."

"Raw prawn?"

"It rhymes with bullshit."

Cheyenne's eyes apologized, but she held her tongue.

"We picked you up in a military restricted zone where deadly force is authorized. You're very lucky to be alive."

She let that hang there for a moment, then continued, "Normally, we'd off-load you onto a refugee transport headed for Christmas Island—a most unpleasant place. But since you're an American, I'll speak to the captain about getting you to Perth." She started out, then turned. "You've got no papers, and I'm pretty sure you don't want anybody checking for your mystery yacht, so here's some advice. Pick a name for the baby, a birth date, and a good explanation for a father. Then stick to your story. Nobody can twist what you don't tell them."

Cheyenne smiled. "No raw prawns. I'm pretty good about sticking to things."

"I'll bet you are."

After China, Perth was like dying and going to heaven. Clean sheets, good food, smiling people and English. They put her in a suite in the Richardson, with a view of the botanical gardens and around-the-clock nanny service. The American consulate was closed for some local holiday, so she would have a full three days to herself. She intended to spend them with sleep, hot baths and plenty of room service.

On Saturday, the phone rang, and a man, introducing himself as Mr. Smithson, asked if she could come down to the bar for a beer. "Thanks, so much, but I don't think so," she answered.

Before she could hang up, he said, "I represent the Brandos' interests in Perth."

Foster Smithson was a tall, lean gentleman in his early sixties who moved like a man half his age. His suit said London, and his platinum Patek Philippe said $200,000. His accent was all Aussie.

When they were seated at a booth well away from anyone else, and their beers were in front of them, Smithson clicked his glass against Cheyenne's and sipped. Cheyenne waited. "I want to thank you for seeing me, Miss Rollins. My associates and I have arranged your passage home. You'll be on Qantas 667 this evening."

"But the consulate . . . I don't have a passport or paper-work for my baby."

Smithson withdrew a thick envelope from his inside pocket and pushed it across the table. "Here's everything you need," he said.

Cheyenne opened it and found three first-class tickets on top. "It's a long flight," Smithson said. "You'll want the child to have its own space. One of our people will be accompanying you—in the event there are any problems with the authorities. She's an American with excellent connections. She's also a trained nurse, so you'll have help if you need it."

Cheyenne also found five thousand dollars in hundreds and a passport with the faces of herself and the child facing the camera. "Is this passport real?"

"It is."

"But how?"

The man ignored her question. "We will, of course, take care of your hotel bill. A car will call for you at seven."

"But . . ."

"You must not be here tomorrow. Some men from the Australian government are flying in to see you. And we cannot let that happen."

"I don't know anything."

"Then you will be put in detention until your memory improves. And you will never see the child again. So what's your pleasure, Ms. Rollins? A first-class seat home or a long stay in a dirty cell?"

Cheyenne got the message. "I'll be ready."

Smithson nodded. "I appreciate your cooperation. I just need one question answered before I leave you to your packing. Was Zhang killed?"

She stalled. "Was who what?"

"You know exactly who he was. Was he killed in the battle?

Cheyenne shook her head. "We met another ship shortly after we left China."

"The ship that took the tiger."

"Yes, the man you're asking about, Zhang, was very possessive of the animal. I think he went with it."

Smithson smiled. "That's good to hear. Very good to hear."

33

Fresh Starts and Last Stops

The faint taste of metal hung in the back of my throat as the afternoon sun beat down on the roof of the Ram. A-bomb thirst. That's what the old-timers called it. The residue of hundreds of nuclear tests moving randomly with the perpetual dust of the high desert. It still gave local milk a Geiger counter reading decades after the last blast.

I wished now I'd stopped at the Circle K fifteen miles back. A Coke and a pack of Twinkies would have cut the grit I'd been swallowing and made at least a small dent in my empty insides. But my sleeping passenger, Daniel Jenkins, M.D.—or Dr. Dan as he preferred—said that the turnaround time between Las Vegas General and the patch of Nevada sand known as Suicide was seven hours no matter how you sliced it, so the Coke and Twinkies would have to wait.

I always marvel at this broad expanse of nothingness and unforgiving heat. Of the sun-hardened souls who scrape out an existence in temperatures nobody in my native London could imagine. Where pasts are no longer than the storyteller wants them to be, and a man can slip in and out of existence without a mailbox or even a last name.

To some, the desert is the last place in America where

fresh starts are still possible—a ripcord for the day the final backup fails, and there's nothing between you and the ground but a scream. It's not what I'm looking for, but it's nice to know that the day they show up to put a chip in our crotches to tax hard-ons, there's an option.

Before he dozed off, Dr. Dan told me he'd come west from Boston because he'd killed a man. Helped him die as I saw it. Watched his fists unclench for the first time in months and listened to his breathing slow and his heartbeat disappear into the stethoscope. Saw the man's eyes flutter one last time and the corners of his mouth turn up in a small smile of silent thanks. He'd touched his forehead gently, imagining the cancer realizing that now it too was dying, then he'd thanked the man one last time for the summers of baseball, catching fireflies, fishing trips, midnight talks, his deep infectious laugh . . . and the safety of his arms.

Afterward, Dr. Dan said he'd taken a walk along the river where he and his father had walked together so many times and tried to remember the story about how the river wasn't really a river but a magic place where the best dreams lived. But as he walked, the details seemed to drift further out of reach, and pretty soon, he couldn't remember the parts he liked. And when he looked at the water, he knew that it was just a river now, and that's all it would ever be.

Dr. Dan said he hadn't minded starting over. Being last in seniority behind young doctors who hadn't seen half of what he had. And he didn't mind what was called Mars Patrol, the trips into the arid, barren wasteland to check on patients who'd been released and couldn't or wouldn't come back for follow-up. It was a chance to be the kind of doctor he'd always hoped he'd be, and during the long, empty miles of driving, it was also a chance to think—or not.

What disturbed me most about what I'd uncovered so far about Chuck's and Lucille's murders was the sickness that hung over everything. I've seen many things I wouldn't wish on anyone, but this was different. I regretted I was looking for more.

My traveling companions were back in Vegas at the MGM. Jody would hit the deli, then turn in early. Fat Cat would work his phone, and Coggan would wander the Strip cataloging every detail in his computer brain. Eddie, I didn't want to think about, but in the past, a bail bondsman had been needed.

Since landing, I'd called Birdy a couple of times and come up empty. I tried Nick, but his secretary said he was "not reachable" until midnight. That probably meant a whale was losing the price of a McCartney divorce and needed to have his ego stroked—or he was winning and wanted somebody to celebrate with. I'd been in both positions and preferred to be alone either way. Someday I'd have to check with an analyst about what that means.

While I was on the phone with Nick's secretary, I got the Cermaks' private number but didn't call. If this was what I suspected—Hassie and the erection that wouldn't die—putting the Inca help in the middle was bad form. Hassie was a great friend who'd give you the golf shirt off his back, but he was compulsive about bedding other people's women. Wives, girlfriends, fiancées, hell, if he met a lesbian couple, he'd make a pass at one. He was the embodiment of the phrase, "Mine's better than yours, but I better fuck yours just to be sure."

I didn't have a claim on Birdy. She was a free agent. But like most men, I expect a modicum of manners from my friends. Barring that, discretion. This was blatant enough to replace the WELCOME TO LAS VEGAS sign.

I called Mallory and gave him the Cermaks' number. One of the many lessons I learned from my father is that when you want information, bishops should talk to bishops. It didn't take Mallory long to get back to me. "According to Bronis, your bird has been with someone named Hassie since you left town. Isn't that your friend with the golf course?"

He knew it was, he just wanted to get in the "your friend" part. "That's what I thought. Thanks, Oprah, you can go back to your couch."

"Not today, there's a houseful of electricians here to . . ."

"I'd prefer not to know."

A crossroads with a rusty arrow pointing left jolted me back to matters at hand.

SUICIDE—12 MILES

Underneath, somebody had stapled a torn piece of cardboard with a third-grade scrawl.

KEEP GOIN
YOU DONT GOT NOTHIN WE WANT

I turned off the two lanes of blacktop, hit the unpaved road and got on the accelerator again. Double cyclones of dust billowed out behind my fishtailing pickup, and the jostling woke Dr. Dan. He got his bearings and told me there was a washout ahead, so I backed off to a more stately speed.

"LA's a little short of docs with this kind of commitment," I said. "You decide you want to smell salt air again, I know some people who'd be happy to meet you."

"Thought about it a couple of times, but always ended up agreeing with my old man. Legs are about promise; tits are about the obvious. California mostly sits around playing with its nipples."

"Living in Vegas, I can see how that might offend you."

"The difference is the change girl at Caesars isn't dreaming about anything except finishing her shift and getting off her feet."

Point made. I negotiated the Ram though the washout.

Dr. Dan had exaggerated. Suicide was barely even a spot, let alone a wide one. A tattered Getty filling station broke the monotony of the brown desert, though just barely. A faded sign dangled by one corner from the listing portico and announced the place as Sal's. However, the sand had drifted high enough to touch the single pump's handle, so

Sal was obviously long gone. It looked like I was going to have to keep dreaming about that Coke.

Spread out behind the station was a randomly distributed cluster of three dozen, weather-beaten double-wides, and off to the left, an ancient Greyhound sat on cinder blocks, its wheels stacked against a barbed-wire fence around a ragged garden. The bus's paisley curtains were pulled tight, and a pair of chickens out front pecked lethargically at what looked like nothing.

Dr. Dan directed me past the trailers until we came to a steel prefab in Cape Cod style, complete with white picket fence and a rooster weather vane on a faux-brick chimney. Out of place was an understatement. A yellow Mercedes with a wheelchair rack sat under a carport. It might not have been the one from the cathedral, but I wouldn't have bet on it. Unlike the rest of the lots, this yard was neatly raked and dotted with bricked cactus beds and an awning-covered sitting area. "Somebody put some hours in," I said.

"Neighbors," the doctor said. "Funny thing about desert folk. They'll work harder on somebody else's place than their own."

"Probably says something about the guy who lives here too," I said as I turned off the Ram and started to get out.

Dr. Dan stopped me. "Wait here. Sometimes he needs to get himself organized." He grabbed a plastic Walgreens bag off the floor. "I replace his medicine when I come out, but the seals won't be broken on the last batch. Man won't even take an aspirin, but at least I feel like I'm doing something." He opened his door.

I hadn't seen the two guys come up behind us, but there was no mistaking the sound of a shell being racked into a shotgun. "Step out nice and slow so we can see all of you . . . and that includes your hands." The voice was flat, devoid of emotion. It belonged to someone who wasn't going to make a stupid miscalculation, which was comforting. I just hoped we agreed on what was stupid.

I glanced in my door mirror and saw a red-bearded man

a few feet off the Ram's taillight steadying a "Just in Case" in the vicinity of the back of my head. "Just in Case" is what Mossberg calls their no-stock, pistol-grip 12-gauge. The ATF prefers the term *illegal*. Fortunately, the Founding Fathers anticipated the need for an occasional dose of buckshot to somebody's vitals and footnoted them into the Second Amendment.

The only thing I could see of the second guy was his right hand. It was holding a Ruger .357 long-barrel, and there wasn't a piece of steel between us that would even slow the slug down. I got out as easily as my large frame would allow. When I turned, I took a good look at both men. They were either twins or had been living together too long. Regardless, it had been a while between baths. I saw them appraise my size, but there wasn't an ounce of shake in either weapon.

"You miss the sign at the turnoff?" asked the one with the Ruger, staring at me.

"Goddamn it, Shorty!" Dr. Dan yelled. "How many times we gotta go through this drill?"

"Easy does it, Doc," answered the guy with the shotgun. "We don't know your friend here."

Dr. Dan was having none of it. "And it's no fuckin' business of yours who he is. He's with me, and that's all you need to know."

Shorty looked at his partner. "Whadya think, Buzz? Need some target practice?"

"Only if I can shoot the doc too. I get goddamn tired a his smartass sometimes."

Dr. Dan gave them a wave of dismissal and got a better grip on the Walgreens bag. "You clowns ever get tired of rubbing your brains together looking for a spark, call me. I know some researchers who'd crawl out here on their hands a knees for a swab of your DNA."

He turned his back on Buzz and Shorty and headed for the trailer. I watched him negotiate the sideways V of the white-railed wheelchair ramp, then knock and go inside the house before anyone answered.

The twins and I stared at each other for a while, then they ambled up the road toward the wheelless Greyhound. "It really is a very nice sign," I said. Buzz looked over his shoulder, started to say something, then didn't.

Ten minutes later, Dr. Dan appeared in the doorway and gestured me inside. As I went by, he said, "Sorry about the welcoming committee. Half of it's neighborly concern, the other half's whatever they're doing in that bus."

Welcome to the desert.

34

Chesterfields and Rockwells

Except for a few slivers of sunlight around the tightly closed Levolors, the living room of the Cape Cod was dark, the faint hum of an air conditioner the only sound. As my eyes adjusted, I could make out a slightly built figure half-sitting, half-lying in the corner of an oversized sofa. He was wearing dark sunglasses, and a blanket covered him from the lap down. However frail he might have otherwise appeared, a pair of thickly roped forearms protruded from the rolled-up sleeves of his flannel shirt.

My late friend, Bert Rixon, the Michelangelo of prosthetics, had a term for arms like that—wheelchair arms. After Bert sold his original company, he founded Rixon Radicals to develop cutting-edge devices for disabled men and women seeking high performance, and those were the kind of arms he sought out.

As it turned out, the number of applicants was so large he had to start a second company to devise special testing methods so he could identify those at the very top of the pyramid. What he discovered was that not only were these individuals exceptionally strong, many had measurably better sensory skills and reaction times than elite athletes. And because of their unique physiology, a few showed a considerably higher tolerance for altitude, cold and g-forces.

Always a pain in the ass to bureaucrats and small thinkers, Bert badgered the Pentagon to let him outfit an F-16 for a paraplegic—at his cost. He wanted to train his pilots his way, then let the military run anybody they wanted against them in a dogfight. They'd put the whole thing on television as a recruiting tool, and as an added incentive, Bert would ante up $10 million to begin funding training of disabled Top Guns. Needless to say, it didn't happen. Now Bert's gone, and it never will. Pity, I think he was onto something—not to mention the ratings.

One tiny beam of light hit an end table where two black-and-white photographs sat in matching frames. The first was of a handsome young man in an LAPD patrolman's uniform. Fabian Cañada in younger days, I presumed. The other was of a pretty young Asian girl, about ten, dressed in a schoolgirl outfit only Catholics could have designed. She was standing in profile next to a sharp '53 Merc convertible with wide whitewalls and fender skirts, and her smile was as big as her tiny face could manage.

I'd asked Dr. Dan to keep my identity sketchy. The doc hadn't much liked the idea, but he agreed to try. As it turned out, the former cop hadn't pressed, so what I said in the next few seconds would elicit as pure a reaction as I was likely to get. I stepped past Dr. Dan and approached the man on the sofa. As I reached the coffee table separating us, there was a sudden flash as Fabian lit a cigarette, fumbling several seconds to get the flame to the tip.

The turtlelike appearance of a person with catastrophic facial burns is something you never get used to, and I was glad when he extinguished the lighter. But it had been on long enough to see that his hair, ears and lips were gone, and all that remained of his nose was a nub of white cartilage, necessitating his sunglasses be held in place by a neoprene strap. Crudely grafted skin had been drawn tightly across his cheekbones, and it was spiderwebbed with thick keloids brushed a splotchy red by random clusters of capillaries. This was as bad as any I'd seen, and I'd seen my share.

"Fuckin' scary, ain't it?" He pitched the pack of cigarettes onto the coffee table. Chesterfields.

"Didn't know you could still get those," I said.

"Same fuckers that killed Bogart. Finally found something the Internet's good for. Help yourself."

"Thanks, but not right now."

"Don't blame you. Me, I've been trying to get the Big C for sixty years and can't even work up a good cough. Pretty funny considering, don't you think?"

I didn't think he was looking for an answer, so I started to introduce myself. "Mr. Cañada, I'm . . ."

He cut me off. "I know. Rail Black. Haven't heard my name pronounced correctly for quite a while. Fuckin' Boston here thinks taco rhymes with Waco. How'd you find me? It wasn't that preacher in Victorville. He's so wound up, he's pissing himself. Had to be Maywood."

So much for pure reactions, but I'd half expected it. We'd overlapped at the church, and Cal Northcutt was an anxiety infection agent. Dr. Dan sat in one of two straight-backed chairs, and I took the other. "Actually, it was somebody who never met you. Another cop. San Fran."

"Surprised they still got a force up there. They're not allowed to arrest anybody."

I skipped the editorial. "Long drive to church," I said. "Make it often?"

"You here to check up on my soul?" His laugh was more guttural than his speech, so I guessed his lungs and throat had been burned, and he'd taught himself to talk without using his diaphragm.

He took a deep drag and a third of the Chesterfield glowed. "Me and God made us a deal. He doesn't assign me to any more flattops, and I don't give him shit about why he's not killing the assholes I tell him to. Course, if I had it to do over, I'd ask for the cancer."

The guy was in his nineties and sharp. When you want

people to open up, you listen to what they want to talk about first. "Any assholes in particular?"

"Take your pick, but how about starting with the cocksuckers who think slitting a stewardess's throat gets them a ticket on the eternal starship. Tell you what, I'm a chick and somebody says I gotta spend *my* afterlife being sweated over by one of those douche bags, I'm going to have me a serious talk with the Man."

He was just getting started. "The fuckin' ganoushes didn't invent anything. Mosques, churches, beer halls. What's the difference? They're just places where deals get made. The genius is in keeping your followers stupid and the young ones dying. Formula's worked for everybody who's used it."

"Only when helped along by cowards on the other side," said Dr. Dan.

"Shit," sneered Fabian. "This country's always had plenty of pussies who'd hand over the keys to the first asshole who pissed in our direction. But we also had ourselves a tussle of men who'd take a good spit and say, 'Let's go kill us some motherfuckers.'"

"Tussle. I like that."

"My granddaddy's word. Lived to be 102, the cocksucker. You taken a hard look at the males we're breeding lately? Ones who ain't holding hands are being raised by single moms who'll put Little Joey on phenol if he says the word *gun*. Hell, even the criminals can't shoot. Ten of them, firing at each other, and all they hit is some five-year-old playing on her porch. Hey, assholes, holding the goddamn weapon sideways takes several hundred years of balancing and sighting out of the equation."

I smiled. "I got a friend. Benny Joe Willis. You two need to meet." I gave him a moment to light another cigarette, which is usually an indication a person is settling in. "Can I ask why you left Victorville?"

"Didn't. We split our time. Little more elbow room out here."

That rang about as true as one of Northcutt's smiles. "I thought maybe it was the pounding surf."

He didn't think I was funny. I waited, and he finally got there. "Truth was, once Big Jim was dead, things weren't the same. Lotta influences rose up past their worth."

"Markus Kingdom."

"That'd be one."

He flicked his ash and changed the subject. "Dr. Dan says you're okay. He's a shitty doc but a good judge of character, so that's enough for me."

Just then, there was commotion at the back of the house, and a door slammed. A moment later, a pair of Rhodesian Ridgebacks came flying in, ignored me and the doc and jammed their panting muzzles into Fabian Cañada's lap. He must have had some kind of treat under the blanket, and as soon as he handed it out, the beggars moseyed to the other side of the room, lay down and began munching.

A woman came around the corner, her voice light. "First Athena scares up a jackrabbit, and we all run for a mile, then Spice decides she wants to visit every bush in the desert." She saw me and the doc. "I'm sorry, I didn't know we had company." She shook her head. "Fabian, darling, how many times do I have to tell you we're not moles." I could now see enough of her to tell that she was Asian, but she had no trace of an accent.

She crossed the room and dialed open the Levolors. Sun flooded in, and suddenly, a gallery of museum-quality art appeared on the walls. An extraordinary Rockwell oil hung over the sofa, while others by Federico del Campo, Montague Dawson and the staggering *Presenciando una Corrida de Toros* by Rodríguez Clement, occupied every available space. I'm not up on my auction pricing, but just what was visible had an insurance value of more than $15 million, making the prefab in Suicide, Nevada, one of those places *Antiques Roadshow* dreams about when they're planning Begging for Dollars Week. Only these people weren't eccentrics eating cat food and hoarding. They were escapees from a society that had gotten too complex and too unpredictable.

The woman was in her sixties, naturally thin and moved like a dancer. Her gray-streaked hair was cropped medium short, and she wore tailored cargo pants and a dark blue blouse that showed off a very fit figure. She reminded me of a Chinese Audrey Hepburn. Combined with the yellow Mercedes, it was the same woman whose prayers I had interrupted at the cathedral. She recognized me too.

Dr. Dan and I stood, and she embraced him. "What is it about men?" she said. "Leave them alone for an hour, and they take off their underwear and sit in the dark."

"Sun's bad for the art," Fabian grumbled. "And my Jockeys are tight but on."

"Then we're making progress," she said. "The paintings will have to fend for themselves. If you didn't want me to look at them, you should have put them in storage or sold them with the rest of your family's things."

As she turned to shake my hand, I saw that the right side of her face and her right arm were scarred. Not nearly as badly as Fabian's, but still noticeable under her makeup. She was also wearing a wedding ring. "I'm Astaire Cañada," she said, and her smile made the already sunny room brighter.

"Rail Black."

She took me in with a pair of onyx eyes that seemed to hold the wisdom of a hundred generations. "You're the man Lucille said would come, aren't you?"

I shouldn't have been caught off guard, but lately, it had been happening more than I liked. The inscrutability of the Orient is real and, to the rest of us, as ungraspable as a fistful of water. "I am," I answered.

"She didn't tell us your name. We were there that night. But if you're as smart as Lucille said, you probably knew that."

It hadn't even crossed my mind. Sorry again, Lucille. I keep letting you down. And then I had to take time off from feeling sorry for myself because I was too busy catching Astaire as she collapsed.

Dr. Dan raced out and got his bag from the truck, but by the time he returned, she had come to. She told me where I could find a bottle of Hennessey, and when the doctor objected, she gave him a stare that ended the conversation.

After she had a drink in her hand, I suggested we leave and come back, but Astaire was adamant. "Why, so I'll feel better? I don't think that's going to happen anytime soon, do you?"

I didn't.

"If my daughter trusted you, then we do too." She looked at Fabian, and when he didn't jump in with his vote fast enough, she added, "Don't we?"

"I know about the children," I said to get past the moment. "And I've spoken with Suzanne Chang and a few others. Northcutt obviously. Some of it I think I understand, but I'm missing the framework."

Fabian wasn't finished. "I'd like to know why my daughter picked you?"

"A fair question. A logical one too, but unfortunately, Lucille didn't let me in on it either. I have a reputation for helping friends, but it would have made more sense to tell me *before* something happened. I've been designated to handle the estate too, but I'll be happy to have my attorney put that in your hands. You would know better than I what she and Chuck wanted."

"No," said Astaire, "Lucille always knew exactly what she was doing. If she selected you, we have no reason to second-guess her." She looked at her husband. "Fabian, why don't you start at the beginning." Turning to the doc, she added, "How about that drink now? And I'm going to need another too."

With a beer in hand, Fabian began. "Our home in Victorville is on the other side of town from Chuck and Lucille's. When we were there, we got together on holidays and Super Bowl Sunday, but most of the time, the girls just talked by phone. You know how it is. Families are nice, but they're nicer when they're somewhere else."

I did. I never loved my mother so much as when she wasn't talking to me, but she was a drunk, so that might have factored in.

"We were supposed to have dinner that evening. At their place. I didn't want to go, but Lucille was insistent. She said she had a big announcement, and we were supposed to bring champagne. Well, when she pushed, Daddy always got with the program, except I told her to stick the champagne, it was going to be brewskis or nothing."

"Any idea what the announcement was?"

"None, but both Chuck and Lucille were like that. Close-mouthed and full of surprises. Like that crazy railroad car. We hit their exit just as the sun was going down, and we pulled off to watch it set. Out here, people do that. They think it's a desert thing, but we did it in the navy too. All you need is a horizon line to bring out the Nat Geo in even old fucks like me. If we just hadn't stopped . . . maybe . . ."

I didn't want to lose him. "You and Astaire would be dead too."

He knew it, but hearing it from me gave him something to hang on to. "It was pretty dark by the time we got to the ranch, but I could see two cars up by the house, and some of the ATVs were out of place. I wasn't happy. That's wrong, I was pissed. Lucille knew I hated most of her asshole friends. I wanted to turn around and go home, but Astaire does the driving, so I was stuck. Just as we got next to the barn, three people come running out of the house and pile into the cars—one of them half-naked with a towel wrapped around her arm."

"Three women?"

"Two women, and a guy. All Chinese."

"It was dark. You're sure they were Chinese?"

"Well, Chinese or pygmy. I get them confused."

When was I going to learn? I shut up.

"Anyway, they come flying past us, almost out of control.

We get to the house, and I'm so anxious to get inside, I forget I can't fuckin' walk, and Astaire has to waste time getting me off the ground and into the chair."

He looked off into the distance. "It was a mess. I saw a lot of things in the war I don't ever want to see again, but this wasn't like that. It was a man I knew and loved, hung up like a prize hog on butchering day. My baby's husband and one helluva cop. I know it doesn't fuckin' matter, but I can't seem to forget they even killed the goddamn puppy we gave Lucille for her birthday."

At that point, Cheater would have already been dead. "Can you describe the man?"

"Young guy. Handsome. Wearing sunglasses at night, which is something that frosts my ass. I got to, and I fuckin' hate it when jerks do it because they think it's cool."

"What's young?"

"Under seventy." He was getting some of his attitude back. "But this guy was about Lucille's age."

"Why don't you just tell him who it was?" Astaire snapped.

"Because we can't be sure."

Astaire looked at me. "It was our nephew—my nephew. Bolin. Bolin Ran."

35

Returns and Relatives

"Mommy, there's a monster on the plane!" The girl was no older than five, but her scream was worthy of Hitchcock, and her panicked sprint down the long aisle of the 747 had brought crewmembers running. It had already been a gruelingly long flight for Fabian, who had tried for several hours to ignore the furtive stares of his fellow first-class passengers. After the incident with the little girl, Astaire and the copilot had helped him up the winding stairs to the lounge, where he retreated to a quiet corner and chain-smoked the rest of the way across the Pacific.

Now, after a day's rest in their Peninsula suite, Astaire pushed Fabian's wheelchair past a line of bellboys, resplendent in starched white uniforms and matching pillbox hats, and let the Hong Kong sunshine wash over them. It had been thirty-two years since Fabian had last smelled the airborne brew of fish, vinegar, ginger, charcoal and flowers, but it was exactly the same. And the years had added something new—prosperity. Everywhere he looked, skyscrapers loomed, and from curbside carts to boulevard shops, commerce was being conducted at a frenzied pace.

"Hey, Ensign. Get a move on, you're holding up progress." *Big Jim Rackmann unbent his large frame from the tiny Toyota and strode across the sidewalk, grinning like a vacuum cleaner salesman. He clasped Fabian by the shoulders, causing him to juggle the crutches lying across his lap, then Big Jim turned and swept Astaire into his arms, kissing her on both cheeks.* "How do you like your old stomping ground?"

"My feet were a little small to have done much stomping, but I'm overwhelmed." *Astaire grinned.* "It's a long way from Victorville."

"Long goddamn way from anywhere," *grumbled Fabian.*

Astaire smiled. "Cheer up, Grumpy. This was your idea, remember?"

A traffic policeman on a motor scooter pulled up behind the Toyota and beeped an unimpressive little horn. Rackmann turned, and the cop shouted something unintelligible, but a translation was unnecessary. Move it, jerk.

"Our chariot awaits," *Big Jim said, and helped both into the car.*

Crossing to the mainland by ferry, they endured the usual incompetence and practiced delays of Communist border agents, exacerbated by their visas having been stamped with the wrong color ink in LA.

"You want to tell me how we're supposed to know that?" *Big Jim thundered, and a nervous soldier went scampering off to fetch a more senior official.*

While they waited, a guard got interested in Fabian's scars and pinched his face roughly as if he might be wearing a mask. Fabian slapped his arm away, and a tense moment ensued when the guard jammed his AK-47 into Fabian's belly. Finally, the boss arrived and approved their paperwork. After having their picture taken twice, once individually, and a second time grouped beside the car, they were waved on. Fabian raised his arm to extend the interna-

tional thank-you, but Astaire anticipated him and wrestled it down.

A couple of hours later, standing on the beach where he had landed three decades earlier, Fabian remembered the dead sailors floating in the surf as if it were yesterday. He maneuvered his crutches through the soft sand until he was at the water's edge. The Pearl was busy, as it always is, sampans and junks running their cargo up and down the river. Somewhere to the north, Pags and he had fired their flares, and in the other direction, they had ridden their horses into the hills. As the memories washed over him, he felt the tears starting to come, and he let them.

The ride into the hills was more civilized this time—and more noisy. Though crude, a strip of blacktop had been laid through the jungle, and all manner of livestock and conveyances jockeyed for space along its length. Big Jim honked and yelled and swerved around the buses, bicycles, pigs and recalcitrant pedestrians until Astaire could no longer watch.

The pavement ended in a small village, but they continued on. It was the dry season, so though the Toyota threw up a tremendous cloud of dust, Big Jim was able to hold it at a steady 30 mph. Fabian didn't recognize the place where the dogs had met them. The area had been cleared of trees and replaced by a ramshackle army garrison. Big Jim handed a scraggly, underfed commander a hundred-dollar bill and a bottle of Haig & Haig he had under the seat that the first checkpoint had miraculously missed, and nobody said anything about ink color.

The cut in the mountain had been widened, but the previous order and color of Hu-Wei had devolved into mush. The few people they passed were ragged and malnourished, their faces drawn and gray. The plaza was still circular, but that was all. The coral and jade inlays on the buildings' façades had all been pried out, and even the carved roof beams were sawed off.

When they got out of the car, Astaire seemed to be having

trouble walking. "You might have a touch of altitude sickness," Fabian said with concern.

"It's not the altitude. I can't process what I'm seeing. I feel so ashamed for letting a few scars affect my life when people are living like this. My people."

Rackmann put his arm around her. "You can't think like that. It's paralyzing. You have to live your life to its fullest and help where you can."

"Is that in the Bible?"

"It would have been if God had thought of it. Now let's go meet your mother. I think you'll like her."

Fabian felt like he'd entered a time capsule. Everything was precisely as he remembered it down to the stale air and matched pair of jade tigers flanking the carpeted aisle. Big Jim was pushing the wheelchair, and Fabian looked over his shoulder as he gestured at the candles. "Is it my memory, or is this just . . ."

"Just like we left it? Yes, I couldn't believe it either."

Ai was not in bed this time. She was seated in a wooden chair with red silk cushions on the seat and back, a silk shawl around her shoulders and blanket across her lap. She smiled kindly, but it was one of anticipation, not recognition. Her eyes were as opaque as glass on a frosty morning. She was blind.

Astaire knelt at her feet and spoke softly. "Mama, I'm here."

The old woman leaned forward and put her hands out. She touched Astaire's hair, then ran her fingers along her face, pausing over the scars on her cheek. She spoke softly, and Big Jim translated. "I told her about the burns earlier. She wants to know if you had much pain."

Astaire took her mother's wrists and held her hands in place, framing her face. Then she shook her head no. With the reverend translating, the two women reached into each other's hearts the way only a mother and lost child could. Years, cultures, languages and regrets disappeared, and they became two people inseverably connected.

And then, it was Fabian's turn, and the old woman finally

wept when she felt the steel chair then touched his face. "You were such a beautiful young man. You gave so much to save my children."

"I received much more."

Later, when Ai's attendants insisted that she rest, the three Americans gathered outside. Fabian smoked, and Astaire held his hand, her other clasped in Big Jim's. "I've thanked you both before," she said, "but it wasn't enough."

Rackmann put his finger against her lips to quiet her. "Enough. We'll stay until she wakes up, then we'll try to see your brother."

"Do you really know where he is?"

"Yes, but it is not easy to get in."

"But you saw him and told him who he was?"

"I did, but I don't think he believed me. He has now had time to confirm the story. The question is, does he want to pretend it didn't happen."

"Who wouldn't want to know his family?"

"Only someone with very much to lose."

At first glance, the sprawling military installation looked like any other. It was only when they reached the guardhouse that it became clear it was not. These gatekeepers were not the civilian bumblers of the ferry crossing or the scruffy conscripts at Hu-Wei but a whip-hard, jackbooted Praetorian Guard with stony expressions and staccato efficiency. As two approached the Toyota, two others goose-stepped back and forth behind the iron gate that blocked the road.

Big Jim conversed with the man on his side, while the other stood at a safe distance, his AK-47 pointed a few degrees lower than the passenger-side windows. It was clear they were expected, but instead of opening the gate and giving them directions, the soldier ordered the reverend to park next to the guardhouse, where they were transferred to the backseat of a military sedan. Fabian's wheelchair went into one of the identical cars that bookended them.

As the procession got deeper into the camp, the Americans could see rows of long, wooden buildings set among the tall trees on either side. From a distance, they might have been mistaken for barracks, but their heavily barred windows and doors quickly corrected the impression. And if that weren't enough, the commandos with dogs patrolling them did. One could feel the horror that lay within.

"Welcome to Disneyland," said Fabian gravely.

A soldier in the front seat turned. "No talking," he said harshly.

The administration building was a two-story brick affair and military plain. Here, the guards were less theatrical but equally on alert. Big Jim, Fabian and Astaire followed their escorts up the walk, Big Jim pushing the wheelchair.

Though only a fraternal twin, the gray-uniformed man who rose from his desk to greet them was identical to Astaire in almost every respect. He was thicker, like his father, but there was no question they were brother and sister—or that they were the son and daughter of Zhang. However, unlike the warm greeting one might have expected, he shook his sibling's hand perfunctorily, bowed slightly then did the same to the men. "I am Colonel Ran," he said. "There is no need to introduce yourselves."

He gestured to chairs across from his desk, and Fabian rolled himself between his companions. Colonel Ran lit a cigarette and offered the pack to his guests. The red label read KRONG THIP.

"Thai," he said. "Very strong."

Fabian took one and used his Zippo. The colonel stared at the burned former sailor, but not with curiosity. "I am indebted to you for saving my life, Ensign Cañada. I assure you, I have made use of it."

"Just Fabian, please. Seeing this place, I probably wouldn't do it again."

Colonel Ran nodded without expression. "Accepted. But the prisoners here are not ordinary criminals. Each has committed himself to destroying the revolutionary goals of the Chairman. It is important that we debrief them completely to prevent future occurrences. But you have not come so far and gone to so much expense to debate the internal politics of China. I assume it was on behalf of my sister."

Astaire vibrated with anger. "Then you would assume wrong, my callous brother. I was interested in meeting you, of course. Out of curiosity, if nothing else. But having lived with scars my entire life, and now seeing that you are part of a machine that inflicts them, I wish I had skipped the jet lag."

The colonel was unmoved. "We were discussing why you have come."

Astaire put her hand over Fabian's, and he could feel it trembling. "Very well, my beloved husband believes that every man should know his history. And since he and the Reverend Rackmann were the only ones who could put you on the track to yours, they spent years trying to find you."

The room was silent for a moment, and Ran lit another cigarette. As Fabian watched him, he thought, This is not a man I would want to face for interrogation. Cold, emotionless, deliberate. Unquestionably, highly skilled. The barred buildings on the road might be filled with misery, but they would be a welcome refuge after a session here.

When the colonel spoke, it was still measured, but he had allowed a faint human quality to enter. "I'm sorry. I am not given to displays. I am quite pleased to see you. The reverend has urged that I visit your mother, and I have taken his suggestion under advisement."

Astaire wasn't having any of it. "You're kidding, right? Under advisement? She's not your mother too?"

"The Hu-Meng are nonpersons. The tribe has been disunified from the rest of Chinese society. Many of the recalcitrant reside here."

"What an interesting word. Disunified. Will you now disunify yourself?"

Fabian saw a flicker in the colonel's eyes, but it didn't stay long. "Modern men are what we believe, not what runs through our veins. Nevertheless, perhaps a trip up the mountain would be a worthwhile journey."

He was struggling with this, and Astaire read it. She took her wallet out of her shoulder bag and handed a picture to him, her voice softer. "This is our daughter, Lucille. Your niece. She'll be four in November."

Colonel Ran accepted the picture and stared at it for some time. "I have a son. Bolin. He is one. Unfortunately, my wife died delivering him."

"I'm sorry."

"I am too. She was quite beautiful and quite anxious to be a mother. May I keep this?"

"You may. Do you have one of Bolin?"

Fabian knew at that moment that the colonel would not only go to Hu-Wei. He would go soon.

36

Ifs and Handkerchiefs

Everybody plays the "IF" game. Next to feeling sorry for ourselves, it's mankind's most popular pursuit. If JFK had let the Secret Service put the roof on the limo in Dallas, your father wouldn't have disappeared into the gulags of Vietnam. Or if you hadn't had the Dodgers game on in your hotel and looked up from your PowerPoint at just the right moment, you wouldn't have seen your wife sitting in the stands with your neighbor, and your son wouldn't now be living in Colorado.

I have my own version, and I play it every day of my life. Only my son isn't in Colorado. He's at the bottom of the Caribbean, still inside my wife. Astaire didn't say anything, but I knew what she thought each morning when she awakened and each night before she fell asleep—and a thousand times in between: If we hadn't gone looking for my brother, our daughter would still be alive.

"What happened after you met Colonel Ran?" I asked.

"At first, nothing but good things," said Astaire. "He used his position to end the government-mandated starvation of the Hu, and he gained releases for many in the prison system. He declined to become the new Zhang, but he encouraged the younger men to reestablish the old trading routes and pursue the exchange of goods with other provinces. Many of the children we brought out during that time were Hu-Meng whose parents had died during the long years of deprivation.

"Then the Changs were murdered, Tiananmen Square exploded onto the front pages and the pipeline ruptured. When Suzanne Chang refused to continue her father and brothers' work, Big Jim introduced us to Markus Kingdom. We had no idea of his prison record then, but I should have realized after our first meeting that he was too eager. I should have also reminded myself that Big Jim was a great man but gave everyone the benefit of the doubt. What none of us knew until it was too late was that, almost from the start, Markus began whispering into young Bolin's ear that his family were the rightful leaders of the Hu-Meng, and if his father wasn't going to accept that responsibility, it was both his birthright and his obligation to do so."

"Let me guess. Bolin listened, and pretty soon things went bad for the colonel."

She nodded. "He was arrested, tried and executed. We never determined the charges. And Bolin was no longer Bolin. He was Zhang. And Markus Kingdom was a trading power in China."

I was worried Fabian might be fading, but he opened a new pack of Chesterfields and took a deep drag. "So after you found Chuck, you went out to the Pullman."

He shook his head violently. "No, I was hoping Lucille was away. Or maybe just late getting home. I knew better. Her car was parked next to the corral, but it was so tough. We called Maywood and waited."

So much for some concerned cop just checking up on the Brandos. I tried to imagine Yale's conversation with himself on his way out to my boat.

It was past dark, and Astaire suddenly stood up. "I don't ever want to have to do this again, so let's get some food in us." With nothing but several cups of coffee in my system, I was with her.

Fabian reached behind the sofa and pulled a previously unseen wheelchair around. He threw the cover off his stumps and, with remarkable dexterity, leveraged himself up and in. The doc started to help, but I'd grabbed his arm. Fabian noticed and nodded. If I had learned anything from Bert, it's that the disabled despise being treated like invalids. If they want something, they'll ask.

There was a raised, fenced-in, cement deck out back that ran the length of the house and was fitted out with a gas grill, a round, teak table and some very comfortable chairs. Astaire tossed a salad, and I grilled steaks and portobellos while Dr. Dan stood behind me pulling on a Ruby Mountain Amber Ale and making suggestions, most of which were what you'd expect from a guy who ate most of his meals out.

While I cooked, Fabian cut up two more steaks—raw—and fed the ridgebacks. They noisily wolfed them down, then curled up next to his chair and went to sleep. "Keep one eye open for Gilas," he warned. "There's thirty feet of liquid fence around the house, and snakes won't cross it. Lizards, though, don't give a shit and like to screw with the dogs' heads."

When we were all stuffed, we sat back with fresh beers, and I joined Fabian in a cigarette. I don't smoke often, but when I do, I like to taste them. My preference is an English Oval, so American strong doesn't bother me.

Dr. Dan brought us back. "Neither of you should be alive," he said. "It's a real testament to your strength."

"Bullshit," Fabian answered. "I was ready to go. That sub shows up ten minutes later, I'm spared a lot of aggravation. I was in Bethesda three months before I had any concept of having been rescued, and two more before they brought me a mirror. At first, I laughed. Then I decided to throw myself out a window, but they'd been through the drill, and there were bars on everything.

"There was this nurse, Linda Lucille Lane. Not very attractive. No, that's a lie. She was as homely a woman as I ever saw. Beautiful voice, gentle hands, but just nothing to work with in the looks department. Another thing me and God haven't gotten right with—why that mattered.

"Gradually, I came to the realization she was always there. Every day. Every meal. Every rehab session. Later, I found out that most nights, she slept on a sofa in the lounge. I got angry. I didn't deserve that kind of care. There were men who would get well and lead productive lives. I asked her why, but she'd just smile and encourage me to cut my roast beef or work harder at walking on those goddamn wooden legs.

"After about a year, they were getting ready to move me to an apartment to ease me back into the world, and I was happy as shit because the first thing I was going to do was buy myself a gun and eat it. Then one day, Linda sat down next to me and put her hand on my forehead. 'It was because of the light,' she said.

"What are you talking about? Light? What light?

" 'You wanted to know why I stayed with you. It was because of the light in your eyes. There's so much goodness inside that I couldn't allow it to die. And so I didn't.' "

Fabian Cañada lifted his sunglasses and showed me his eyes. "You see any goddamn light? Far as I'm concerned, they're as dead as the rest of me. And you'll notice there's not even a picture of her in here. That's the kind of asshole I am. She cared for me unconditionally, touched me when no one else would, but I'm still not able to get past what she looked like. Sort of like the bearded lady not wanting to be seen with the three-legged man."

There are times you don't want to get inside somebody's life because the demons are too familiar. I didn't like what Fabian Cañada was saying because I'd acted the same way and hurt good people. My father didn't care if you were a king or a beggar, handsome or on the other side of the universe from it. His smile was always genuine and his embrace warm. The older I get, the more I understand that said more about him than all the money he made and the empires he built. But it's a legacy I have to work very hard to live up to. It never feels natural.

"You named your daughter after Miss Lane. That's a stronger statement than any picture."

"Might have been if she'd still been alive when it happened."

I turned to Astaire. "Would you mind if I asked how you ended up here?"

She seemed to welcome the opportunity. I understood. I never lost a child I had raised, but after my parents' deaths, I talked more about them than I ever had when they were alive. And, of course, I thought of all the things I should have said and the questions I'd never have answers to.

"At first, I went to an orphanage," said Astaire. "Several, actually. They kept bouncing me around because nobody was interested in a burned Chinese kid. And every time I was transferred, they gave me a new name. I didn't remember Astaire, of course, so sometimes I was Jane or Barbara, sometimes Ling or Xue. I was really jealous of the kids who had the same one year after year. I don't know why, but I thought Kathy was the most beautiful name in the world, so I picked it as my secret name, and that's what I called myself. I'm still Astaire Kathy.

"Linda Lane found me. She'd stayed in touch with Fabian's family, and when she found out he was looking for me, she began using her vacations to search up and down the East Coast. She'd just about run out of places to look when somebody told her the Catholics sent a lot of kids with disabilities to Chicago. She figured that might mean burns too, so she went to work. You're not supposed to be able access records, but they'd never come across anybody like Linda. She'd wear you out."

"An understatement," said Fabian.

"I was in the Polish Children's Home. Think a scarred Chinese kid stuck out? But they were wonderful to me, and I'll still drive miles for *golumpki*. In those days, a single woman had no chance of adopting—not even the irrepressible Linda. But Fabian's family could. So good-bye cold winters and five girls to a double bed, hello mansion in Pasadena. Not long afterward, Fabian came home, and we were a family."

I didn't want to ask the question. Astaire saved me. "Pretty creepy, huh? Guy marries his sister. Or his kid, depending on who's doing the counting. Then there's that pesky age thing. Well, don't blame my husband, blame me.

"Growing up, I had four dates, and three of them were because somebody put out a rumor I was an easy lay. Which was pretty funny because I was so self-conscious about my scars, I took baths in the dark."

"You're a beautiful woman," I said. "And I'm not being patronizing."

"Thank you. I think so too—now." She smiled. "But I was thirty before I heard it the first time." She stood and crossed the room to her husband. "And this is the man who said it." She bent and kissed his head. "Linda Lane was right. There is a light in his eyes—and in his heart. A magnificent light. He won't say it, but he's the one who made it possible to save so many children. Big Jim had the bluster and the bullshit, but Fabian had the tenacity and wrote the checks. You see what's happened, don't you?"

I did. Fabian Cañada had become Linda Lane. I didn't think he needed to hear me say it, though.

"When Fabian's parents died, we stayed on in the house, but after a while, it got to be too much of an expense."

"If you're going to tell it, tell it right," said Fabian. "The good people of Pasadena drove us out."

Astaire looked at the floor. "They painted horrible things on the walls along the street. 'Sister Fucker' and 'Gookenstein' were some of the nicer ones. On Halloween we'd leave town because they threw so many rocks at our windows. One year, on the Fourth of July, somebody fired a rocket onto the garage and burned three generations of photographs. It got worse after Lucille was born. People sent cards to the hospital that said, 'I hope your baby dies,' and set dolls on fire and tossed them over our gate. The worst part, it wasn't all kids. I'd see some of them at the supermarket."

"So you moved to Victorville."

"It was like being reborn. Wonderful people, wonderful friends. Lucille grew up strong and smart and loved by everyone. I'll never leave the desert."

I gave them a moment, then looked at Fabian. "I realize your family was wealthy, but what you're talking about with the kids is too much money over too long a period of time for an individual. Besides, you knew you couldn't live forever."

Astaire looked at her husband. "You want to tell him, or should I?"

"Voodoo tax," Fabian said.

The bulb finally went on. "That's why there were so many cops involved." It also explained what Yale Maywood meant about Chuck's "handling something sensitive."

Dr. Dan wasn't on board. "Could somebody enlighten me."

I turned to him. "A voodoo tax is the price a senior cop extorts from a crooked underling to look the other way. It's the title of one of Chuck's pictures."

"I like it. Dirty money doing some good."

"I figured why fuck around," said Fabian. "All those cops in Victorville who knew the score and kids dying in China. Rackmann knew, but he didn't, if you follow."

"Nobody knows a dirty cop better than another cop, but you need cooperation upstairs. Somebody who can pull IA off a case . . . or put them on."

"Over the years, we had a whole line of them in several departments. Maywood was the fourth at LAPD. I never wanted Lucille near any of it, but . . ."

"It was the family business," I said. "Then she married a cop."

He nodded. "Got herself a good one too. As soon as he got some seniority, he began doing the collecting. Fuckers paid fast too. Especially after that picture."

He sounded proud, and I understood.

"Eventually, Chuck and Lucille took over," said Astaire. "More Lucille than Chuck. She was totally committed, and he loved her so much if she had wanted to raise ragweed, he would have started plowing. Lucille got lots of young people involved. And some of the kids we'd rescued years before had grown up and wanted to adopt others. Fabian and I were burned out. The doctors said we had to find a less stressful life. That's when we moved out here."

"But Chuck and Lucille couldn't escape Kingdom."

She wrung her hands. "At first, the tigers were just a rumor. Then an open secret. Lucille tried everything to find other ways to get children out, but each time she set up a new network, it would be shut down and the participants executed."

"No mystery there. Your nephew enjoyed living high and wielding influence. And that was the Hu way, wasn't it?"

"So now she had those people's blood on her hands too. Finally, she told Kingdom they were pulling the plug. Know what he said? Fine, the kids are a pain in the ass anyway."

Of course, I thought. Walking away wasn't going to stop the tiger trade. "Then Kingdom began demanding women—and more money."

"We didn't know about that until the day Lucille told us a man might come, and we were to do whatever he said. I wanted to ask her what she meant, but she wouldn't have told me. I was just happy to see her smiling again. And Chuck had stopped being gone for days at a time.

"I have to believe that wherever they are now, the children they saved outweigh anything else." She bent her head, and I saw her whisper a quiet prayer.

I'd always liked Chuck, now I liked him more. It was also clear why Maywood had drawn my name out of the hat. It wasn't my propensity for helping friends or my civic-mindedness. It was that I was cynical enough not to get wide-eyed, and I wouldn't rat anybody out. But the biggest reason was that he knew I'd clean up any messes the cops had left behind. Make sure two friends didn't get their reputations sullied.

The chief was out of the operational loop, but he knew. It was also why the department put the lid on Chuck and

Lucille's murders. There wouldn't have been enough seats in the grand jury room for the suspects. Somewhere, lots of cops were doing lots of sanitizing, and others were doing lots of sweating. And if the first group did its job right, the second group would be holding a banquet.

After a little bit, Fabian wheeled himself into the house. He was gone a few minutes, then came rolling back with a Nordstom's garment bag on his lap. He stopped in front of me and pushed it my direction.

I unzipped it. Inside was a WWII naval officer's shirt, or what was left of it. The years hadn't been kind, and the burned sleeves and shoulders didn't need any explaining. Neither did the outline of an ensign's bar on the one remaining collar point.

"Open the pocket," Fabian said. "The left one."

I started to undo the flap, and the button crumbled in my fingers. Gently, I slid out a handkerchief with an FC monogrammed in script. The combination of seawater and age had turned the linen as brown as the shirt, but it was as neatly folded as if it had been ironed yesterday. I glanced at Fabian, who was watching my hands with such intensity that I felt like an intruder.

As I carefully unfolded the square, the cloth became white again. In its center, I found what looked like an eight-inch piece of tapered gray-white string. I touched it and felt its stiffness and glossy finish.

I knew what it was, but this was Fabian's ghost, so I waited.

"It's from a white Siberian," he said. "It was supposed to be buried with me, but I want you to take it." His voice drifted away.

I accepted it without speaking.

37

A Brave Lady and a Connection

It was close to three o'clock in the morning when the doc and I left the Cañadas. We'd been invited to spend the night, but I'd begged off—stupidly, as it turned out. As they saw us to the door, I asked if they were aware their daughter had leased a ship.

"I doubt it," said Fabian. "Chuck didn't even like to put on hip waders to fish."

"It's a container vessel. Parked in Tonga. She named it the *Resurrection Bay II.*"

Astaire looked at her husband, but with his sunglasses on, I couldn't read his eyes.

"Maybe that was the announcement," he said with a catch in his throat.

Neither of us believed that, but I let it drop.

We were halfway to Vegas, and Dr. Dan was snoring, which wasn't surprising considering he'd matched Fabian beer for beer. Off to my left, I could see the eastern sky just barely beginning to lighten.

For the past hour, I'd regretted not grabbing some shut-eye in Suicide. I was almost as sleepy as I had been coming out of Chuck and Lucille's back in what seemed like another lifetime. I found a truck stop and pulled into a slot between a couple of dark big rigs. I was out before my head hit the back of the seat.

I awakened to my cell going off. I noticed Dr. Dan was gone. Probably inside grabbing some breakfast. That he had gotten out without my hearing him said all that was necessary about how tired I'd been.

Julius Watson was on the line. "Wake you?"

"I'm good."

"Meant to call last night, but I went down to the station house to watch the Cowboys and Dolphins play Super Bowl VI and ended up shooting the shit. How'd we live without the NFL Network?"

"Good game," I said, making an effort to connect with him on any level.

"Fuck Dallas," he answered.

Well, maybe another time. "Have any luck with the girl?"

"She's staying in the South Bay."

"That narrows it down to about a million and a half possibilities."

"All you're going to get. She's one scared lady."

"How's the baby?"

The question caught him off guard. Apparently, he hadn't asked, and she hadn't volunteered. "You can cover that when you talk. She'll call you sometime today."

"Not good enough, Julius."

"It'll have to be. Like I said, she's scared."

Something didn't sound right in his voice. I didn't want to think he was making up his own game, but he'd lost a daughter, and that changes a man. Maybe he was trying to protect someone else's. "Look, Julius, whatever you think of me, fine. Fucking up somebody else's life in the process isn't."

He let me sit long enough to consider hanging up before finally saying, "Gladstone's. I'll bring her. When can you be there?"

"Gladstone's isn't anywhere near the South Bay, Julius, and nobody as scared as you say she is would get on the road for a minimum of forty minutes. So cut the bullshit. And no, you won't bring her. You've got an axe to grind, and this isn't the time." I looked at my watch. "I'll see her there at eight thirty this evening. Should be a thin enough crowd that we can sit for a while. Tell her if she gets there ahead of me to take a table inside. All the way in the back."

I heard him snort, but he didn't argue. "She was going to ask this when you talked, so I'll give you the heads-up. She wants to meet somebody."

"Who?"

"An FBI agent named Huston. Francesca Huston. You know her?"

"Tonight. Eight thirty."

I dialed Benny Joe. The phone rang a long time. I was about to hang up when he answered, out of breath. "Jogging?"

"Fuck you, Rail. This broad you sent me is like fuckin' cancer. Just when you figure you got it all, it breaks out someplace else."

"So she didn't come alone."

"Like the fuckin' president. The whole hill's full of un-markeds. No choppers, though. Checked with a friend at the federal hangar at LAX who said she threw a fuckin' hissy fit tryin' to requisition one, but couldn't make a case."

"Where is she now?"

"Out in the yard with the dogs."

"I thought she didn't like dogs."

"Who gives a fuck what she likes? Lulabelle's trained to sense anything emitting a signal, so once she passes inspection, I'll bring her in. She's probably gonna need a shower though."

Lulabelle? That was the first time I'd ever heard a name for one of those nasty mutts. Of course, I hadn't asked either. I got a mental picture of Lady Huston rolling around in front of a pack of snarling Dobermans. I hoped Lulabelle'd take her time.

"Where you want her?"

"Gladstone's. Nine thirty, no earlier. Later is even better."

"Gladstone's? Jesus Christ, that's all the fuckin' way across town?"

"Benny Joe, you live in LA. Everything's across town. Don't tell her where you're going, and if you see anything out of the ordinary, keep driving. Otherwise, drop her at the valet stand and make sure she walks straight in. How do you intend to handle the distractions on the hill?"

"I'm gonna call the TV stations and every fuckin' paparazzi assignment desk in town and tell them my neighbor's havin' another pool party."

I remembered that one of the recent crop of showbiz bad girls had bought the house next to Benny Joe's, and she liked to get high and naked with a few dozen of her celebrity friends. The narrow, twisty streets under the Hollywood sign weren't designed for more than an occasional car, so fifty trying to beat each other to a front page were really going to fuck up the landscape. Not to mention the floodlights on the choppers.

"Another little gift to the homeowner's association."

"Fuck them. Where were they when my ex was shootin' up my 'Vette?"

"That old Norton of yours up to off-roading?"

"With your little G-girl pressin' her hard titties into my back, I can hardly fuckin' wait."

"My best to Lulabelle."

I locked up and went looking for Dr. Dan.

When we hit the Vegas city limits, I toyed with stopping to see Birdy, but she'd probably be on her way out to the ranch. Besides, she hadn't returned my last two calls, so she apparently didn't need any cheering up. Instead, I dropped the doc at the hospital and swung by the MGM.

Fat Cat, Coggan and Wal-Mart met me in the coffee shop. I let Eddie and Jody sleep. I had a feeling they were going to need all they could get.

Wal-Mart looked even bigger than I remembered. He was going to make a nice impression where I was sending him.

"Coggan, I want you and Man Mountain here to pay a visit to one Wesley Crowe. You'll know the best questions to ask."

"If he's a cop, I think I'd have a better shot," Fat Cat said.

"That's exactly why I'm not sending you. This isn't about his being a cop. It's about his being Chinese. And a very rich man's brother-in-law."

"Should be fun," said Coggan. "People like to talk to me."

"What about me?" asked Fat Cat. "I thought we had a deal. No fuckin' secrets."

"You're going with me. I may need you to handle a fireman."

"Jesus, I hate those self-important assholes." He lapsed into singsong. "Hey, look at us. We're everybody's heroes, and we don't even carry guns."

"You'll be perfect."

My record time Vegas to Beverly Hills is three and a half hours. Maybe with a badge in the car, I could run fast enough to get a couple of hours in my own bed before meeting Cheyenne Rollins.

I awakened at seven feeling fresh. There's something about your own bed. There's also something about your own shower. Despite the cataclysmic predictions the water department spews out with the same regularity that the *Today Show* announces the end of the human race from the flu or a shortage of Priuses, I stand under *my* hot water—which *I* pay for—until I decide to get out. Here's a thought. We live on a fuckin' ocean. Figure it out.

Fat Cat had taken the Ram and run home for his own nap and a change of clothes, and he was waiting in the living room with Mallory. They were munching cashews and comparing notes on the correct way to roast a pig, which suddenly made me very hungry. I grabbed the bowl of nuts, and Fat Cat followed me downstairs to the garage. In the background, I heard Mallory say something like, "Bring back the bowl. It's part of a collection." I never really had a mother, so he does his best.

Fat Cat looked at my car collection with interest but not drool. "Dion said you had some fancy wheels. Looks like you got a thing for black and red too."

"I'm working on that. I'm negotiating for a DeLorean, and they only come in stainless. You ever drive a Rolls?"

"Only the ones in the department."

I tossed him the keys, and he eased us into the Beverly Hills evening. "I could get used to this," he said as he headed toward Sunset.

The late, lamented Beverly Hills Gun Club used to be hard by the railroad tracks in a seedy part of West LA, five miles from the nearest border of its namesake. It was one of my favorite hangouts. Cordite and attitude. Not to mention gangbangers taking target practice alongside the cops they'd be exchanging Uzi fire with later.

In the same tradition, Gladstone's 4 Fish is actually in the Palisades. That doesn't, however, keep them from claiming Malibu—and Santa Monica from claiming them. People from Pacific Palisades don't claim anything, except being rich, and that most tourists haven't figured out a lot of famous faces live there.

Sandwiched on fifty yards of sand between the PCH and the surf, Gladstone's is people watching, big food and bird attacks at their finest. And like the gun club, I have a romance with the place. There are beach joints up, down and across this nation's coasts, but nowhere else is it possible to run into Spielberg or Schwarzenegger working on a plate of garlic fries while he dodges flying seagull shit and a homeless guy sleeps on the sand ten feet away. It doesn't make the food any better, but it says everything about my adopted home of LA. I couldn't live anywhere else.

Fat Cat self-parked the Rolls at the far end of the lot, and we wandered slowly toward the restaurant until I saw the red Wrangler. It had a fresh scrape on the driver's side fender, and there were scattered papers and a map on the passenger seat, indicating no one had ridden here with her.

Cheyenne Rollins had her back to me and was tucked into a wide wooden booth at the end of the far dining room. The nearest occupied table was a section away. She was a handsome lady, in clothes a little too tight for Sunday mass but ideal for a margarita and nachos, which is what she was working on. As I got to the table, I saw a baby wrapped in a pink blanket lying on the seat next to her. The cleft palate on the happy, gurgling child was severe, but I'd seen worse.

"I promised myself that if we ever met, the first thing I'd do is tell you how brave you are."

She looked at the two large men standing over her and didn't miss a beat. "If you'd see me crying sometimes, you'd retract that in a hurry." Cheyenne Rollins was one of those people who was completely self-possessed. It's rare, so it's always impressive.

"I've seen men cry in combat and keep firing their weapons. You're a keeper, young lady." I pointed to the baby. "Someday, you'll have to tell her how she got here."

"And if she's like every other kid, she'll roll her eyes and groan."

We introduced ourselves, and I saw something else. She and Fat Cat had connected. Not the thunderbolt of *The God-father* fame, but a quiet emotional connection when a strong but damaged soul stares into a light she didn't know existed.

"What's your real name?" she asked Fat Cat.

"Hugo."

"I like that. So that's what I'm going to call you. Hugo." It wasn't a question, and you knew it wasn't open for debate.

She slid the child farther into the wide both, and Hugo sat beside her. I sat across. The pert, short-shorts server had apparently been waiting for us and pounced before our rears got settled. "I'll have a glass of Stella," I said.

"Same," said Fat Cat.

"How about one of our great starters?" she asked.

"I'm good."

Cheyenne pushed her nachos toward us. "Please," she said. "All I seem to do is eat and worry."

"Running for your life is hard work," I said.

"Do you think maybe you could do something about that?"

"That's why we're here," said Fat Cat, and I heard a huskiness in his voice that hadn't been there in the car.

"Did that fireman mention I was really anxious to talk to Francesca Huston?"

I nodded. "She'll be along shortly. But I thought we might cover a couple of things first. Ms. Huston isn't much with small talk."

"Shoot."

"Can you take us through everything step by step?"

"Everything? Okay, but a lot of the China stuff's a blur. When we weren't sick, we were high."

"Okay, while you're still fresh, start with the most difficult part."

She nodded. "A Chinese guy who barely spoke English met us at the airport in Hong Kong and took us to a dive where they pushed drinks on us. That's where we got slammed with the drugs. It was dark when we left, and Sherry and I were leaning on each other just to walk. The guy put us in his backseat, then drove a long time. At some point, I realized we must be going up because my ears started to pop."

"Victoria Peak," I said.

"Can you like see the whole city from there?"

"Yes."

"Then that was it. Jesus, was it high. The next thing I remember was this gate with a butterfly on it—one that broke in the middle when it opened. The driver dropped us at what I'd call the service entrance where this pretty, but very cold Asian woman was waiting for us."

I was betting Crimson. "Name?"

Cheyenne shook her head. "I asked, but she said we were there to entertain not sell Girl Scout cookies, which I thought was hilarious at the time, but it was probably the drugs. The house was really crazy inside. All kinds of big art but with these like curtains everywhere."

"Curtains?"

"Yeah, white ones. Hanging from the ceiling, the walls, everywhere. And the place was dirty. Like the housekeeper was on strike. Plates of food sitting around, cigarette butts in the carpet, unflushed toilets. Disgusting. The woman took us to a bedroom that was a little cleaner and told us to get undressed. Nothing but heels. The highest we had.

"Even fucked up, I didn't like that, but when I started to say something, she hit me like I hadn't been hit since my old man died. 'No clothes,' she screamed. 'If somebody wants you to put something on, you do it and don't argue. Otherwise, nothing but shoes. Now let me see your bush.'

"I was, like what? My bush? It's fuckin waxed, bitch. But she looked anyway and rubbed it for a minute like I was gonna lie down and beg for more. I just looked at her, and she stopped. Then she checked our breath and armpits. Jesus Christ, I said, we weren't there to join the fuckin' army.

"I guess she didn't appreciate that, because she called in some guys who held me down and gave me a shot. After that, all I did was fly. And fuck. Fly and fuck. The sun came up and went down I don't know how many times, and people kept leaving and new ones kept coming, but Sherry and I were still fucking. Sometimes guys, sometimes women, sometimes both. Sometimes each other. They must have let us sleep, but I don't remember much except having things stuck in me."

"And was everybody else Asian?"

"Of some kind, yes. There was this one guy who spoke like an American and came in a few times. But he didn't get involved. He just talked to the woman, then left again."

"Big guy. Gray hair. Sixties, but could pass for younger."

"I never saw him. He was always in a shadow or behind one of the curtains, but if you know his name, don't tell me. I'm working on forgetting."

The waitress came back, and Cheyenne said, "I could go for a burger."

Fat Cat and I ordered the same. "Why don't you tell us about your escape from Chuck and Lucille's," I said.

She looked grim, but soldiered on. "I've got to get it out sometime. I'd just stepped out of the shower when I heard a commotion in the living room. People shouting and furniture breaking. Then Chuck started yelling, 'INSPECTOR SANDS! INSPECTOR SANDS!' "

"Who the hell is Inspector Sands?" asked Fat Cat.

"Not a who," I said. "It's the London transit system's emergency code. It's derived from 'Mr. Sands,' the phrase theatres use for a fire in the house. Chuck cross-trained with the Brits after the subway bombings. Probably where he picked it up."

Cheyenne looked at me. "I didn't know that. Chuck just said if I ever heard it, I was supposed to run and not stop running until I got to the safe house." She suddenly smiled. "It's probably not cool to make jokes, but I wish he would have said something about getting dressed first. That was one long, uncomfortable drive. Thank God the agriculture checkpoint was closed."

38

Working Unrestricted and Investment Banking

As Cheyenne finished her narrative, our server cleared our empty plates and brought us fresh drinks. "Did Lucille tell you where the two children were going?"

A curious look crossed her face. "If you guys were friends, I thought you would already know. They were for them."

"Chuck and Lucille?"

"She told me they wanted to give two kids who would end up on the streets a chance at a real life. And that nobody would interfere if they were visibly disabled."

So that was going to be Lucille's big announcement. Fabian and Astaire were going to be grandparents. "Do you know how much money was involved?"

"I don't, but she told us that the Chinese had begun waiting until girls showed up to collect children, then demanding double what had already been paid. And she couldn't go back to the families, because most of them had mortgaged their houses. So Chuck had done some . . . uncomfortable things to make up the difference."

"She used that word, *uncomfortable*?"

"No, that's me trying to make it better. The word she used was *dreadful,* and that Chuck had put his career on the line."

I didn't see the need to get into voodoo taxes, and that Chuck had probably had to cast his net even wider to cover the extra money. "Wasn't buying children breaking the law to begin with?" I asked.

Cheyenne suddenly got very angry. "Since when is rescuing a baby from a terrible death wrong? You want to fire up the indignation engine, then let's start with, 'I'm feeling a little blue today, should I shop Armani or Africa?' Or how about the Hamptons social climbers trying to improve their multicultural cred."

She put her hand on the baby's forehead. "If you could see the place this little doll came from—hundreds and hundreds of kids with missing limbs, twisted spines, Down Syndrome or just a lousy cleft palate, all piled into rooms the size of closets—you'd kill somebody. And because they're classified as 'abandoned,' their goddamn government won't even let them be citizens, meaning that sooner or later somebody's going to stop feeding them. My God, if I ever got elected president, I'd start a war with those motherfuckers."

She was right. My neck was on fire just listening to it. To quote Detective Kujovic, "How about them fuckin' Olympics?"

"I'm sorry, I didn't mean to snap at you. I just can't get that vision out of my mind no matter how hard I try."

"No explanation necessary. The Brandos had been at this baby business a long time. Do you have any idea why they picked now to adopt kids of their own?"

"Lucille said they couldn't risk it before because somebody might have tried to hurt their kids to get at her and Chuck. That what started out as getting a few government officials laid by hot American chicks so helpless kids could escape destitution had turned into something so sick that she and Chuck couldn't bear it anymore. She said she woke up every night vomiting over what they'd become. So they were closing down the operation."

Closing it down? The words hit me like a shot. You don't lease a ship at twenty grand a month and park it within range of the Chinese coast if you're getting out of the business. "Are you sure that's what she said? Closing down?"

Cheyenne looked at me angrily. "No, I'm making it up. What the fuck is wrong with you? Suddenly, I'm delirious?"

"I'm sorry. It just caught me by surprise. Is that all she said?"

"No, she said there were going to be some very angry people, but they wouldn't stay angry long. I've got no clue what that meant."

I didn't either, but I couldn't get bogged down with it now. "I know this isn't a question you probably want to answer, but I need to know how were you recruited."

"At this point, I'm beyond caring what anyone thinks, so sure. All the girls in the Vegas flesh business knew you could pick up a ton of money if you were willing to do two weeks unrestricted in Hong Kong. And that the connection was this guy Donnie Two Knives on TV. It was like, hey, if I really fuck up, I can always call Donnie."

"Define *unrestricted*."

Her tone got ugly. "You're over twenty-one. Use your imagination." Fat Cat put his hand over hers, and she clutched at it with both of hers. "I'm sorry. That was uncalled for. I'm still trying to readjust. Basically, it means if you can fuck it, or it can fuck you, put a smile on your face. I thought it was for DVDs because there are a lot of rich collectors in Asia. And it was . . . kinda. Sometimes you'd see a guy with a handheld, and he'd asked you to moan louder or talk dirty, but it wasn't the really raw stuff, so it was probably just leverage over the officials. But then Sherry disappeared, and even in the fog I was in, I got so scared I remember this guy slapping the shit out of me because I was screaming."

"You lost me. Why were you suddenly afraid?"

"There was this girl a few years ago who got invited to party in Brunei and didn't come home for like a month. She couldn't remember what had been done to her, but she got a lawyer and got paid off. In my world, everybody knows the story. Well, before we left, Lucille said if we tried that with these guys, they'd cut off our heads and feed us to the tigers."

"Tigers?"

"Not a threat you forget. Frankly, she had me with the head part. It was almost like she was trying to keep us from going. But we both needed the money really bad, so it wouldn't have mattered what she said. It's like a guy who knows a loan shark. He never intends to borrow from him, but it's nice to know it's there, just in case. And, of course, if that's how you think, just in case always happens."

"And what young lady doesn't have a soft spot for babies?"

She smiled. "Not to mention the first-class cruise on the way home so you could get yourself together. I don't recommend mine, though. A little short on casinos and cute cabin boys."

"Let me go back to Australia for a moment. This Smithson who spoke to you in Perth, did he mention a company called Parkinson-Lowe Imports?"

"I don't think so, but I was still pretty shaken up. And when he told me I was in danger of losing the baby, I didn't hear much after that."

Cheyenne needed a break from talking, so I left Fat Cat to regale her with how he got his name and walked out onto the beach with my phone. It was a beautiful night, and the surf was barely lapping at the sand. I looked off in the direction of the Land Down Under and asked the operator for Parkinson-Lowe Imports again.

The same young man answered, so I slipped into my dormant, but still passable, British accent. "Foster Smithson, please. Mr. Black calling from London."

"I'm sorry, Mr. Black, we're just a service."

"Oh, yes, it was mentioned that he uses a buffer. This is a bit of an unusual situation. And quite sensitive. Can I bring you into my confidence?"

I could hear the anticipation half a world away. "You certainly may, sir."

"One of our wealthier clients is interested in purchasing an interest in an Australian import company. One with current licenses and excellent contacts in China. Our man does several hundred million pounds a year there, and he's tired of paying usurious commissions. Mr. Smithson and Parkinson-Lowe were recommended as being quite well-thought-of . . . and very discreet." I let that hang there for a moment, then added, "Would you mind holding a moment? I've got the prince on the other line."

"*The* prince?"

I winked with my voice. "Let's say *a* prince and leave it at that. We manage some royal assets. I'll be right back."

"While you're doing that, sir, let me see if I can reach someone at Parkinson-Lowe."

I flashed onto call waiting and walked for a while. When I reached the lifeguard station about a hundred yards down the beach, I reconnected. "So sorry," I said.

"I completely understand, sir. I have a Mr. Holden on the other line. If you'll hold, I'll patch you through."

There were a few clicks, and a voice that would have been considered rough even in the Outback said, "Who the fuck is this?"

"Mr. Black calling from London. Do you represent the owners?"

"There's no Parkinson, there's no Lowe, and there's no imports, so let's cut the shit, mate."

When in doubt go with the truth. I dropped the accent. "Black's the right name, but I'm in California. Chuck and Lucille Brando are dead."

There was a moment of silence, but not a long one. "You made that point the first time you called. Okay, you've told me in person, that it?"

"You don't seem surprised."

"It's a dangerous world."

"There's not going to be an envelope this month. Is their account in order, or did they leave outstanding obligations?"

That stopped him, but only momentarily. "You don't know shit, do you?"

Fuck this guy. "Look, friend, I don't give a fat rat's ass if you're dealing coke or hot kangaroo pouches. I'm trying to keep some other people alive, and if I have to run ten kinds of law enforcement up your ass to do it, I will."

He didn't seem impressed, but he didn't hang up either. "You another one of the Brandos' cop friends?"

"Cop, no. Friend, yes. And I don't like playing catch-up. But Lucille asked me to get involved, and dead women get my attention. Especially ones who were tortured on the way out."

"The Brandos are even with the board. No outstanding obligations. My condolences to the next of kin." He hung up.

I called the virtual office again, and the same young man answered. "I'm sorry, I didn't get Mr. Holden's first name."

"Rennie. I had no idea he was involved with the company. He's a real legend around here."

"In what way?"

"Mr. Holden's a hunter. Takes people all over the world to shoot big game. Really rich people with expensive guns and private planes. Every kid in Western Australia grows up reading about him. I wonder what he does for Parkinson-Lowe?"

So did I. The difference was I knew how to find out.

Jackie Benveniste used to be the State Department's organized crime guru for the Mediterranean. Now, he's retired on the hills of Dana Point, a few dozen miles down the coast from where I was standing. Since we'd met, I'd had him and his thirty-year-junior significant other, Nancy, out on the boat a few times, and we'd become good friends.

I could hear his boxer barking when he picked up. "Give Annie a cookie, you cheapie."

"Rail, how the fuck are you? Nance, open another bottle of red and let that crazy mutt out on the patio. She sees that mouse up close, she'll pee herself."

"Sounds like a big night, I'll make it quick. Rennie Holden. Aussie. Company called Parkinson-Lowe Imports, but I think it's a dummy."

"That part of the world was out of my sphere, but I can make a couple of calls. How soon you need it?"

"Anybody ever call this late and say, no hurry?"

He laughed. "Nance is teaching me how to text. That be okay?"

"Better than okay. New number, though. Got a pen?"

I went back inside the restaurant and used the head. I was on my way to my table when I saw SAC Huston striding fast toward us. She looked a little the worse for wear, and her face wasn't hiding her displeasure. Her mouth was open, ready to make some kind of threat, when I said, "I'd like you to meet Cheyenne Rollins."

She gave my dinner partner one of those looks professional women reserve for hookers and stay-at-home moms. "Another one of the Rail Black punch crew? I'll pass."

I don't like rudeness in any guise, but Cheyenne handled it with a grace I wouldn't have been able to summon. She extended her hand. "I'm really pleased to meet you, Francesca. You're even more beautiful than I expected."

Francesca looked at the offering like it was covered with boils. "I'm sorry, should I know you?"

"I heard so much about you from Sherry, I almost feel like another sister."

Francesca's entire body went rigid, and her tone turned accusatory. "Have you seen her?"

"I was with her when she died. In China."

The agent sucked in her breath, then staggered. I caught her before she fell and helped her into my side of the booth. The server saw what was happening and hurried over. "Is everything all right?"

"The lady could use a glass of wine."

Francesca shook her head. "Vodka, rocks."

I gave her my untouched water, and she took two large gulps.

"Please," she said to Cheyenne. "Tell me."

An hour and several vodkas later, SAC Houston had left the FBI behind and become almost human. I say almost, because a lingering accusatory tone showed itself every now and then. Cheyenne was too polite to ask the right question, so I did it for her.

"What did Sherry mean you'd think she blamed you?" I asked.

I was expecting the pat FBI comeback, "None of your business, asshole," but she surprised me. "She asked me for a loan, and I turned her down."

"We talking lunch money, or rent?" I asked.

"Thirty-five thousand."

"Not likely working for Uncle Sammy, right?"

Francesca looked at her lap, then at her drink, then out the window. If she'd been interrogating a suspect, she'd have given Special Agent Curtis the signal to hit the guy with another several thousand volts. Finally, she got out, "We owned a piece of property together. My mother's house in Palm Beach."

I don't know much about Florida, but my Rolls guy is always complaining that the Palm Beach dealership puts the glom on extra cars before they even get off the ship. Cheyenne wasn't so challenged about Sunshine State real estate. "That has to be three million, minimum."

"Seven-five," Francesca said. "After Dad died, Mom took their savings and got into the stock market. Turned out she had a gift."

I tried to throw her a lifeline. "But the house wasn't liquid."

She seemed to need to get all of it out. "My ex was a no-good cheat, but he made up for it by being an earner. My lawyers had enough on him that he settled up without a fight. I wouldn't have missed $35,000 or ten times it."

Cheyenne couldn't believe it. "Sherry didn't do drugs. She didn't even drink. So if she needed money, she *really* needed it."

Tears formed in Francesca's eyes, but they didn't fall. "I never asked why."

This was one of the things that makes me want to strangle people. I could have let it go, but sometimes you have an obligation to punish the self-righteous. I'll gladly take my beating on Judgment Day. "Forget what it was for and what you had personally. Why were you in control of the house?"

"It was in both our names, so I would have had to sign off on a loan."

"Would your mother have given her the money?"

She didn't even hesitate. "Yes, of course. Mom died from an aggressive form of Alzheimer's, and that last year was really rough. Sherry moved back to Florida to take care of her. She practically lived at the nursing home." She paused. "I wanted to be more help, but I was . . ."

"Busy busting people's asses?"

Her lip started to tremble. Cheyenne put her hand over Francesca's. "No," I commanded, "she's not finished."

Cheyenne jumped at my harshness, but Francesca was so caught up in her own confession she might not have even heard me. "I told her that if she couldn't find the money anywhere else, I'd see if we could work something out."

"In other words, you investment bankered her."

"I don't understand."

"Sure you do. You gave her hope, then dragged your feet. With Wall Street guys, the perverseness is genetic. With individuals, the party line is usually that they're helping someone become a better person. Sound about right, Francesca?"

She didn't answer, so I jammed it in harder. "So when Sherry couldn't get the money and came back—desperate— you told her no, which was what you always intended to do."

She was about to lose her composure. "How do you . . ."

"Because people who can fuck with others' lives, usually do. And I'll bet she never once complained about changing your mother's diapers. I'll also bet she listened sympathetically to every slight and travail about your tennis-playing prick of a husband."

Francesca looked at Cheyenne. "I suppose Sherry told you what a bitch I am."

Cheyenne shook her head. "She never said anything but the nicest things. About how important you were, and how smart, and how much she admired you."

That was all it took. I've never held an FBI agent while she wept, and I wasn't about to begin with this one. Like all bullies, she disgusted me, and if she'd had a fucking heart attack, I wouldn't have called the paramedics until she was cold. There was a word for her, and as far as I was concerned, she'd wear it the rest of her life.

When she pulled herself together, she seemed to want to say something more to Cheyenne. "Did Sherry . . . ?" Eventually, she got it out. "Do you know why she needed the money?"

I looked at the beautiful young lady across the table. After what she'd been through, she didn't deserve this. Sometimes, though, life just keeps handing out turds to the virtuous. I could tell she knew the answer, but that it would hurt Francesca even more. Cheyenne Rollins was a better person than I.

"No," she said, "she never told me."

That was when I saw a pack of FBI agents led by Jerk Curtis running toward us, guns drawn. I shook my head as some of them herded the staff and remaining patrons outside while the others crouched and leveled their weapons at us.

"Keep your hands where I can see them, motherfuckers!" Curtis shouted. He eyed Fat Cat warily. "Who's this asshole?"

I looked at SAC Huston. "I thought only SACs used that kind of language."

"Shut up," Curtis shouted. "And hit the floor. All three of you. NOW! Francesca, are you all right?"

Francesca? Now I was really amused. "Huston, don't tell me you and Captain Sandpaper are pistol-whipping each other after hours?"

She turned beet purple. "Everything's okay. You can stand down."

"But I thought . . ."

"I made a mistake. I'll explain later. Leave somebody to drive me and go back to the hotel. I'll give you a full debrief when I get there."

"Pardon me, ma'am, but I don't think that's wise. This man . . ."

I'd had enough. I stood and put my hands out, wrists together. "Cuff me." Curtis looked confused. "I mean it," I said. "Get a pair of cuffs on me, then I'm going to beat you through this place until every piece of furniture is broken. And when there's nothing left but splinters and pulp, we're all going down to the Federal Building and explain to the Office of the Inspector General why SAC Huston used a wildcase investigation to pull Department 11 into a personal matter."

You could have heard a pin drop.

39

Oklahoma Drills and Headphones

On my way back to Beverly Hills, I called Coggan.

"We're just finishing up with Detective Crowe," he said. "Give me half an hour."

Fat Cat had volunteered to escort Cheyenne home, and after what she'd been through, she deserved some easygoing company. After watching him watch her for the past couple of hours, he certainly qualified. He could also field the guaranteed call from Julius and reinforce that I hadn't destroyed yet another fine young woman. My assurance wouldn't have been worth the breath it took to offer it.

I cruised by Tacitus, my favorite eatery—if you can use the word *eatery* to describe the finest Tuscan food this side of Florence. The valet was on duty but looked ready to bolt, which meant there were stragglers inside, and he had a hot date. I parked at the curb, handed him a twenty-dollar bill and pocketed my keys. I think he was more grateful I hadn't given him the car than he was for the money. I waved to the lone paparazzo on duty and pushed open the iron gate.

Tacitus Gambelli is an old friend, but I've been treading lightly around him since getting myself shot on his front patio. When you have money, you get a pass on most indiscretions, but in this town, giving the paps an excuse to set up shop on a restaurant owner's sidewalk is worse than sleeping with his girlfriend. No matter how many guys she's banged, he won't find her on his roof taking pictures through the skylight.

I felt doubly bad because Tacitus had gone out of his way to avoid being a flavor-of-the-month restaurant. That can sometimes get you a lot of ink and a slew of Hollywood elite—mostly looking for comps—but when they move on, so does your income. Tacitus had slowly built his clientele from neighborhood regulars and conventional businessmen, with a few "faces" thrown in whose publicists didn't hire a skywriter every time they went out to dinner.

Tacitus saw me coming, put on a big smile and crossed the room hand out. "Rail, *buona sera*, *buona sera*. Where have you been?"

I gestured toward the door where I'd seen the photographer. "I see you're down to only one vulture."

"And not even an important one. The old paps send the pussies here to break them in."

"I'll see if I can do something to get you back on the A-List."

"And I'll see that there's ground glass in your ravioli. Come, sit. I have a recent addition to my wine collection. And cigars."

"I thought they took smoking away in Bev Hills."

"You ever hear of anything so *stupido*? Even the cops roll their eyes. There's one old broad in the condos next door who complains, so I send her a *sfogliatelle* every night, and she straps on a gas mask and goes to bed."

We were on the patio and well into our second bottle of something very dark and very rich, and I was wondering how much it was going to cost to have one of the waiters drive me home when my cell went off. Tacitus usually doesn't allow phones in the restaurant, so I asked permission. "I can step out to the sidewalk."

He threw up both palms. "Please, go ahead. I have to

check with the kitchen about tomorrow's antelope entrée. Can you believe it, I've got a vegan chef, and somebody else has to cut the chops."

Coggan was laughing. "If you can believe it, we're on our way back down the hill with a plate of Maxine Crowe's ham sandwiches. Well, the plate anyway. Fuckin' Wal-Mart doesn't share."

"Sounds like it wasn't as difficult as I expected."

"Little rocky at the outset, but after half an hour of Oklahoma drills, we found common ground. Did you know Wes played a little running back up at Fresno State?"

I wasn't sure I heard him correctly. An Oklahoma drill is basically three-man football: a blocker, a running back and a tackler. The back gets handed the ball by a quarterback or coach, and while the blocker occupies the D, the back tries to run past him. The only rule is that everybody has to stay within narrow boundaries.

On its face, it's a simple exercise. In practice, it's *Gladiator* without the compassion. It's only trotted out when everyone's blood is up—often to punish some miscreant for something serious, like an untied shoe. And the longer it goes on, the more fury is unleashed. Some of the great humanitarians among coaches have special cages built so the runner can't get wide on the tackler, and I've personally heard collisions from several blocks away. I was also present when some of my fellow Delta operators nearly killed three Fayetteville townies by introducing it in a bar after way too many shots of tequila. It wasn't something a cop in his forties would have volunteered for.

"Where did this all this fun take place?"

"Wes's office. Little cluttered, but that made it more interesting. You should have seen Wal-Mart. I don't think he missed a tackle. Course, blocking was never my strong suit."

The mental picture of the three of them crashing around Wes's private retreat made me smile. "So can you give me the CliffsNotes version?"

"I can. Crowe claims he didn't have anything to do with

Chuck's and Lucille's murders, and I believe him. We can get into the details later, but I think he had a thing for Lucille. Maybe they didn't do anything about it, and maybe they did. Cops are gone a lot, and restless wives have been known to find somebody to keep them warm."

I was inclined to agree on the murders. Not because I liked Wes Crowe but because it would have been a cleaner job with a chief dick involved. At the very least, a cop wouldn't have left a chunk of forearm behind. As for an affair, I gave up my illusions about husbands and wives when my mother took her first boyfriend. "What about the late Donnie Two Knives?"

"Enter Cheater Crowe. He and Knife-boy heard that the Brandos were personally paying some kind of added extortion the Chinese were demanding to release kids. And naturally, they got it in their heads there was a pile of cash in the house. Down South, we see this all the time. Couple of dim bulbs who never heard of a wire transfer kill an entire family looking for a stash that isn't there.

"The place was supposed to be empty, and Donnie went in while Cheater waited down the road in Wes's car—which he borrowed without asking. Only Chuck and Lucille were just up at the Pullman and came back while Donnie was crashing around inside. Then, instead of doing the smart thing and beating feet, Donnie grabbed Lucille and held a knife on her while he called Cheater on the phone to come help.

"Cheater said no fuckin' way, and while they were arguing, Chuck took Donnie down. I guess in the process, Lucille got cut a little, and Chuck lost it. Tied the little fucker to a chair and jammed the guy's blades in his ears. Afterward, he set him out on the lawn under a floodlight. Then he hit REDIAL and told Cheater to come take a look. Cheater didn't, but later, Wes did. He got Chuck settled down, and they buried him together."

Surprise. Cops looking out for cops—and cops' brothers. Not to mention Lucille getting cut. No wonder she wanted out.

"There's another body too. Some Chinese CPA in LA. The guy was handling cash for Chuck and got whacked by his partner on some unrelated matter. Chuck had to clean up the mess before it got too far into the system."

"Grand jury gets hold of you, you might as well buy a house out here."

"Not me, partner. Too many clearances. They'd send in the A.G. first."

"Okay, the tigers."

"It's a radio auction, like the one Old Man Crowe bought Wes in. Wes runs it from his place, with Kingdom sitting right beside him. For security purposes, the boss doesn't speak. Neither do the principals. They're all present at their respective locations, but they have stand-ins to do the bidding."

"Makes sense. Somebody wants to run tape, all they got is a bunch of no-names probably talking in code."

"Correct. What's different this time is that because of this zodiac thing, Kingdom's insisted on a live event. He thinks the bidding will be more ferocious if the buyers have to be there in person. The only people excluded are the ones who've had their passports lifted. They'll still be on the radio, but if Kingdom doesn't hear their actual voices, their bid will be ignored."

"Greedy prick, but very, very smart."

"He's been on a tear with tigers too. Normally, every couple of years, he moves one or two. The word is that the Hu-Meng have stockpiled nine for the big event, which in this day and age is probably the monetary equivalent of a railcar of gold bars."

"Are you kidding? Nine animals and two dozen guys with nothing but money. There isn't an equivalent."

"We'll soon find out. Vuku Island, one week from today. I think there's a ship there you're familiar with."

"Which makes even less sense after tonight."

"Not really. Wes tipped Lucille the auction was coming. Pillow talk, would be my guess. Right afterward, she leased the boat. He thinks she was planning to ask you to use it to rescue the tigers. I think he's right."

I didn't. "What you're talking about takes months to plan."

"Then explain the notation in her appointment book for the day *after* she and Chuck were killed. 'Call Rail. Finally! He HAS to do it! There's NOBODY else!'"

"Somebody's bullshitting you."

"Then he's bullshitting my eyes too, because Wes grabbed her book before the LAPD got it—probably because he was worried about what was in there about him. I saw it myself. She jotted down her feelings with every appointment. Even the goddamn hairdresser: 'Tell Sue she has the cutest smile and to get back in circulation. Divorce doesn't end your life.' And it would take a team of experts to fake her handwriting. All kinds of curlicues and loops and hearts dotting the i's. The entry didn't mean anything to Wes until he met you. Then all he did was put two and two together."

"I still think he came up with seven."

"Get a grip, Rail. Your learning curve on something like this would be next to zero. But if she told you too soon, you'd find a way to stop it or talk her out of it. The safe thing to do was wait until the train was pulling out of the station. And frankly, I think she read it just right. She just didn't expect to be dead."

I thought about Jake's wiseass remark. *Looks like they left you a mandate and the means. Now, all you're looking for is a mission.* "There might be a way," I said, "but it isn't what Lucille had in mind. How are you with a camera?"

"Still or movie?"

"Movie. Something light and digital that'll handle one of those super high-res government lenses that they won't let civilians buy."

He laughed. "Stop hanging out on the conspiracy Web sites. But yes, on all counts. What's your thought?"

"I think it's time to make Markus Kingdom a star."

"Why not. Cameras are the new guns. Who needs assassination when you can ruin somebody's life. Count me in on this guy."

"I want two views. Wide and close. How about Wal-Mart?"

"Give me a few hours with him, and he'll be Jim Cameron. Minus the third-grader dialogue."

"What're you going to do about Wes?"

"He's coming to work for my think tank. Once we got on the same page, we liked each other, and his shortwave knowledge is something we don't have. Oxford's also about a tenth as expensive as California. But the deal I made with him is he stays on the job until the auction's over."

"Have him record it. I want a sound track. What about his wife?"

"Maxine feels like a lot of women who grew up with an asshole older brother. There's not a grave deep enough. Plus she's had it up to here with cops. She thinks she might want to go back to school."

"I guess I should say, nice work."

"Thanks, but I struck out one place. Wes was a blank on Parkinson-Lowe."

"I've got a little more on that, but not enough yet. I'll fill in Fat Cat, and you handle the others. Tell Jody to get a flight plan together for anyplace within boat range of Vuku. We'll leave late tomorrow."

"I'll get the lenses."

As I got off, Tacitus was returning. "Good call?" he asked.

I raised my wine. "To *sfogliatelle* and Oklahoma drills."

He didn't get it, but he drank anyway.

Vanda, Tacitus's accountant and chief assistant came around the corner with her usual look of disdain. I used to think it was me, but she's just one of those people who couldn't work the front of the house at a graveyard. I love her eyes, but that's all. "Excuse me, Mr. Gambelli, but a man called looking for Mr. Black."

"I'm right here," I said.

She ignored me. "I told him he was here, and he said not to leave."

Ten minutes later, Nick came through the front gate. "Cedars helipad," he said. "I take care of their docs, and they take care of me." But his voice wasn't cool. It was cold, and in guys like Nick, there's a difference. "It's Birdy."

Not wanting it to be something worse, I took it my own direction. "If you flew all the way here to tell me she's sleeping with Hassie, I already figured that out."

"What the fuck's wrong with you? That girl's head over heels. And it ain't for some golf bum with an eye tuck and a bad line of bullshit. She didn't show up at the ranch yesterday. Or today. When I got around to checking, Bronis and Judita hadn't seen her either. And the Hyundai was missing. I figured she might have gotten homesick, so I called Santa Anita, but no dice there either."

I didn't like the sound of this. "Spare me the journey. What's the destination?"

"I sent two of my guys out to look for the car, and they found it around five this afternoon. It was in a ditch ten miles from any road she needed to be on. With four blown tires. You know how hard it is to blow a tire anymore?"

I did, and I was getting sick to my stomach. Fortunately, or unfortunately, I also knew who to ask.

Despite what some Pentagon popes with a case of Senate Hearing Room Shakes would have you believe, there is no debate. Torture works. One of my instructors at Delta had a saying: Asking a general about the dirty side of war is like asking your ex-wife what she thinks about your girlfriend's tit job. Why bother?

Civilians equate generals with bravery and brilliance. While it's true some were once very brave, and most can recite Napoleon's moves at Austerlitz, to attain flag rank, you have to be more like Ted Kennedy than John.

As with all promotions of commissioned officers, to wear a star, your superiors and the president must nominate you. Then the Senate must confirm you. No one outside the military pays the slightest attention to promotion lists—until it comes to general officers. Then, senators go over each name like crazy girlfriends checking your text messages. Naturally, this sends candidates into a wild frenzy of ass-kissing.

And so flag officers enter their new jobs compromised and beholden. Because what can be bestoweth, can be unbestoweth. And only the Senate determines which generals retire with three or four stars. It's not that much difference in pay, but it matters when you're calling for a tee time.

This civilian wedgie on generals is part of checks and balances, and in theory, it's a fine idea. But downstream, the guys who get dirt under their nails are never comfortable that some squeamish chair-warmer could blow a secret mission because he can't hold his water in front of a microphone. So, whenever possible, nobody tells a general anything.

Colonels—and navy captains—run the military. No one in the outside world knows who they are, and they're usually the best officers in the ranks. To put it another way: You might show off a general at your birthday party, but if you needed somebody to protect your back in a bar fight, you'd call a colonel. So ask one. Torture absolutely works. All kinds.

But you have to know how to apply it.

Waterboarding is excellent for long-term interrogations. It turns even the baddest of the bad into babbling schoolgirls. The downside is that you get so much information it requires months to evaluate and prioritize. Extreme distress changes brain chemistry, and waterboarded intelligence comes in such a rush that it often gets jumbled with aborted plans, misinformation, even dreams. That's what the generals who keep getting quoted in the *New York Times* are trying to say without saying it. What they don't mention is that it's not pain that gets you what you want, it's the absence of it.

Interrogation professionals love the William Goldman masterpiece, *Marathon Man*. In it, Laurence Olivier does masterful work on Dustin Hoffman's molars with a set of dental tools. But he doesn't get down to serious questioning until he applies oil of clove to the exposed nerve. That's because during the pain-creating process, people will say anything to make it stop. The critical step to getting what you want is lowering your subject's adrenaline level so the brain can begin working rationally again. Then, all things are possible.

But beyond technique, the essence of Olivier's interrogation is that he's only interested in the answer to one question. No long exchanges about historical inequities, no justification for past crimes, just a simple yes or no to three words: "Is it safe?"

In the business, this is called a 220-Interrogation, or just a 220. The name is derived from the number of beats per minute at which the human heart fails, and if you're assigned one, it means the situation is so dire the guy needs to be broken in minutes, not hours. Unfortunately, on occasion, the bad guy will hit 220 before he talks, but that's the price of eggs when you're saving lives.

I was always very good at 220s. I was about to find out if I still had what it took.

Major was beginning to come around. While he'd been out, I'd moved him to his office, secured him to the banker's chair with knots that tightened if you fought them and gagged him with a baseball-sized wad of plastic packaging tape. Then I went shopping in the store.

When I returned, he was trying to push the tape out with his tongue while he fought against the restraints and wasn't having much success with either. His eyes focused in on me, and he stopped struggling.

While I set up, he watched intently and tried to communicate with some indecipherable grunts. I ignored him. A few minutes later, I placed a pair of professional headphones over his ears and ran several loops of tape around his head to hold them in place. He tried to make it difficult, so I jabbed him in the throat, and he choked a little, then settled down.

You hear a lot about breaking terrorists with heavy metal music, but since I didn't have to report back to the Justice Department, I decided to skip Black Sabbath. I worked the dial of a top-of-the-line international radio receiver until I found a nicely shrill squeal not unlike amplifier feedback at a rock concert. When I was satisfied I had just the right pitch, I plugged in the headphones and dialed up the volume as far as it would go.

The shriek leaking around the pads made me wince where I was standing. I could only imagine what it sounded like inside Major's head. He bucked like he was strapped into Old Sparky, and I had to put my foot on the chair to keep it from dancing across the room. I gave him thirty seconds, turned it off for thirty and repeated. When I stopped the second time, he seemed to want to say something, but he only *thought* he was ready.

I positioned myself so he could watch me strip the female ends of three electrical cords I'd removed from a row of Sony flatscreens. After plugging the good ends into a power strip switched to the off position, I tore away Major's T-shirt and clamped one frayed lead into each armpit, then ran more tape around his upper torso to secure them. He was sweating like a rutting boar, so I expected a good connection.

When I picked up the third cord and unbuckled his pants, I was surprised at how loud he was able to scream through the tape. I ran the wire down his front but purposely didn't push it all the way to Johnsonville.

I wanted him to appreciate what was coming, so I found a Coke in a small refrigerator, opened it and took a long swallow. Then I sat down at the desk and started writing on a legal pad I found there.

When I finally hit the power-strip button with my foot, I didn't know what to expect. I'd selected the highest rated unit, but electronics are assembled in sweatshops, so I couldn't be sure it wouldn't explode. It didn't. The lights in the office hummed and dimmed, and I heard popping coming from Major, then smoke appeared, and the unmistakable smell of burning flesh permeated the room. His pants also caught fire.

I switched off the strip and doused the flames with what

was left of my Coke. When I took stock, Major was conscious, but foaming through his nose. I gave him another shot of the radio to bring him back to the present and waited.

When he stopped convulsing, I showed him the legal pad. It said:

> *I'm going to take the tape out,*
> *And you're going to tell me where Marlene is.*
> *If you stutter, I plug everything back in and leave.*
> *Understand?*

I gave him a moment to get that processed, and when he nodded, I took the pad and added:

> *And IN THAT CASE, the cord in your pants*
> *will be touching what it's supposed to.*

Five minutes later, I had my answer and was in my car. As for Major . . . maybe he'd get lucky, and the circuit breaker would trip.

Fragrant Harbors and Butterfly Gates

The polished cowlings of the 747's four engines shimmered in the triple-digit afternoon as Singapore Airlines Flight 11 swooped smoothly across the harbor before dropping into final approach in steamy Hong Kong. Framed against the distant mountains, a long row of international flags flapped in a stiff ground wind, which reached the plane, buffeted it and forced the pilot to jog slightly left. Our descent, however, remained gentle and unhurried.

I looked north, to where the vast expanse of the world's most populous nation lay in quiet, green repose. A thousand years ago, China was unknown to the West. Today, it touches the life of everyone on the planet. And it is still unknown.

Even its vaunted wealth is a myth. The Chinese have money, but it is other people's debt, not their own capital. The only way to sustain a long-term-growth economy is by manufacturing goods to which you add value, then exporting more than you import. If every Chinese trademark in existence—financial, industrial, consumer—were to disappear tomorrow, no one would notice. They create nothing and produce no must-have product. They have no significant assets in the ground, grow less than it takes to feed their population and possess limited gold reserves. What they do have is a large, inexpensive labor pool that, instead of adding value, shaves it from each item produced, an unsustainable economic foundation.

Worse for them, that labor pool is rapidly pricing itself off the world stage. That is why the Chinese are tightening their influence over the emerging economies of Southeast Asia and why they permit North Korea to remain starving and ruled by Daffy Duck. Beijing needs all the subsistence workers it can lay its hands on.

They would love to add the multitudes of India to their stable, but the Indians are too smart to let that happen. And the Pakistanis are saddled with Islam, which the Chinese won't let near those extra billion people they have sitting around. They couldn't even abide the Tibetans, and they're pacifists.

Russia scares the shit out of them because Russians are immune to both reason and the bludgeon. The only thing you can do with a Russian is give him what he wants or kill him. Unfortunately, even if you give him what he wants, sooner or later, you're probably going to have to kill him anyway.

But contrary to popular opinion, China has no ambition toward the United States. Our financial markets are the only method they have of monetizing anything. Plus, like everyone else, they're fans of Coke, Levis and Hollywood movies.

What the Chinese want is Africa. Plain and simple. There are more natural resources there than anywhere else on earth, few organized governments and a perpetually hungry populace that can be bought with a barrel of flour. More Chinese businessmen, diplomats and military advisors go to bed each night on the Continent of the Exploited than in the rest of the world combined. Someday, somebody's going to notice. As the wise man once said, "Keep your powder dry, my friends."

In decades past, landing on old Kai Tak Airport's short Runway 13 was something the uninitiated never forgot and produced sweaty palms on even the most hardened flyer. It was nice to see air operations had finally caught up with the century.

Things had changed for the better inside the SIA cabin as well. Gone was the old first class, replaced by private seating pods that, once I figured out the buttons, were more than comfortable for someone my size. The food remained exceptional, and the flight attendants, the most beautiful in the world.

This was my first commercial flight in seven years, but Fat Cat and Coggan needed two days to assemble the team, so I left the BBJ with them and flew on ahead. I was also impatient. I had no idea where Birdy might be, and none of the possibilities were pleasant to contemplate.

As the Boeing touched down, first-time visitors craned their necks for a look at the Orient, but mostly what they saw was the controlled chaos of too many airport vehicles on too little land. Flight 11 turned off the runway and began the two-mile trek to the terminal, but halfway there, we made an unexpected right turn and came to a bouncing stop on a concrete apron between two taxiways.

Moments later, the engines shut down, and the pilot came on the intercom. "Ladies and gentlemen, please remain seated. In a few minutes, airport security will approach the aircraft. There is no danger, and we should be on our way soon. Thank you for your patience."

A murmur ran through the cabin, and I saw people looking over the tops of their pods. Seconds later, a middle-aged businessman with a Brooklyn accent and a severe case of don't-you-know-who-I-am, stood up in the aisle. "This is bullshit," he bellowed.

I couldn't have agreed more, but I decided to let him go it alone. Two well-proportioned Asian men in 1950s' suits approached Mr. Indignant. I'd seen them boarding during our refueling stop in Singapore. "Sit down," one grunted.

But he was a New Yorker. "Hey, fuck you, Commie. My company does a billion bucks' worth of business in this country. When I'm done, you assholes will be lucky to have jobs."

Without warning, the second man clipped a handcuff around the man's wrist, snapped the other ring to his own arm and pushed him back into his pod, disappearing with him. I heard a couple of thumps and a groan, then the remaining suit said in a loud voice, "We are officers of the People's Armed Police, and this man is now under arrest for failing to follow an order. Any further disturbance will require a quarantine of the aircraft."

Welcome to the *new* China.

Fifteen very quiet minutes later, the outside door opened, and sunlight and humidity streamed in. I heard a lift motor, and soon, a smartly dressed Asian woman stepped into the cabin and came down the aisle, obviously looking for someone. When she saw me, she broke into a broad smile. "Mr. Black?"

I purposely hadn't told my Hong Kong office that I was coming. I didn't need anything from them. This was a personal mission. More importantly, I was hoping to avoid anyone's radar. I'm sure my annoyance showed. "And you would be . . . ?"

"Miss Lou. Regina Lou. Black Group's security liaison. Do you have a carry-on?"

I stood and took my beat-up Orvis duffel out of the overhead, conscious of the caustic stares from my fellow passengers. Miss Lou tried to take the bag from me, but I shook my head. "What you can do," I said, nodding in the direction of the Chinese cops, "is go up there and tell Stan and Laurel to cut that guy a break. That a problem?"

She hesitated.

"Otherwise, I'm not getting off."

That, she understood. She huddled with the People's Police, during which a lot of words were spoken and some arms waved, but in the end, they pulled the cuffs off the newly docile American and deplaned with us.

A black Mercedes flanked by two airport SUVs waited on

the tarmac. "Do you have additional luggage?" Miss Lou asked. "If so, I'll send someone for it."

I shook my head, and we got into the backseat. As our driver fell in between the escort vehicles, I gave Miss Lou a less-than-warm stare. "Whose idea was this?"

"Mr. Fleetwood told me to get it done and to not be subtle."

"Put yourself in for the bonus. You succeeded."

Brice Fleetwood was waiting at Black House, the Black Group's residence in the Central District. Sitting just off the water, the three-story colonnaded home with recessed porticos on the second and third floors is one of the last standing nineteenth-century mansions built by the British lords of commerce during the colony's glory years. Hong Kong traffic being what it is, we justify its extraordinary expense by its proximity to our offices in a larger, adjacent mansion plus the ever-escalating value of the real estate. Fortunately, we're a private company and don't have to try that logic on stockholders.

As irritated as I had been, I had calmed considerably on the ride into town and was now actually pleased at the prospect of being comfortable. If I've got a beef with Far East accommodations, it's that the majority of hotels look the same inside—minimalist décor with impossible furniture. When you're my size, you want to sink down in an overstuffed chair every now and then and sleep in a bed that doesn't end at your shins. What's interesting is that the Chinese are as big as Westerners, but they don't build accordingly. Black House is furnished for use, not how it photographs for a Web site.

Miss Lou had said very little, probably in an effort not to ruffle my feathers further. I let her stew so I could ride in silence and remember a place that held so many wonderful memories of my father. A place I hadn't seen since the handover in '97.

As it always had, Hong Kong still felt more like a London borough than a Chinese city, and all indications were that it was still the most civilized place in Asia. I find no coincidence in that where the British colonized, economic, political and legal stability followed. In the reverse of the rest of the great sea powers, my forebears were traders first and acquisitors second. The French, Belgians, Dutch, Germans, Portuguese and Spanish enslaved. The British ruled.

And despite the efforts of the Nobel committee and Hollywood to convince us otherwise, the results are in. The greatest loss to freedom in the world was the fall of the British Empire. Anyone needing further proof can check the GNP of her former territories—and the quality of the justice they left behind.

When the schoolteacher who rails to his captive students about the evils of English-speaking people finds his own liberty—or life—at stake in some distant land, he still runs headlong past every other embassy to the one flying the Union Jack. My American citizenship notwithstanding, I wear my British heart on my sleeve. And given a free vote, Hongkongers would race back into the arms of the Crown.

My silver-haired Hong Kong managing director greeted me with a smile and a handshake that wasn't as firm as I remembered. I also noticed that he swayed slightly as he stood. I suggested we sit while we talked, and he quickly accepted. Pimm's in hand, we made ourselves comfortable in the brocaded study in front of a window looking over the harbor.

"It's been a long time," he said.

"Too long. It seems each time I'm in London, you've either just left or won't be arriving until I'm gone. I was beginning to think it was me."

He chuckled, and his blue eyes had the same twinkle they always had. "If you haven't heard, I'm retiring at the end of the year. Molly insists, or she's sworn to leave me. Fifty-two years is enough for any man, she says, and this time I think she's right.

I touched his glass with mine. "It's been an honor to have worked with you."

"My last act will be to stand with you at your investiture as the new Lord Black. I did the same for your father, and it would be an honor to pay homage to his very worthy successor. That is, of course, if you'll have me."

I hadn't thought about the knighthood since Lord Rittenhouse's surprise visit. "Don't book your flight just yet. As for retirement, I hope you'll stay on as an advisor."

"If you think I can be of service."

"My father would insist."

"My God, how I miss him. Every single day when I walk by that big portrait in the boardroom, I feel a chill."

I was moved. "I miss him too. There will be no more like him—or you. That time has passed."

He turned serious, "Your father is the reason I had Regina meet your plane. One of the last things I promised him was that I would look after you."

"I detect the fine hand of Mallory."

He nodded. "Don't blame him. Your father gave several of us the same charge."

"I gave up trying to manage Mallory years ago, but he can be a bit of an old lady."

"Hazard of the job. Monitoring the reckless young."

"So what do I need protecting from?"

"I have no idea why you're here. That's your business unless you decide to confide in me. But we have been advised by our contacts in the government that your name has surfaced as a kidnapping target, which in Hong Kong simply means you will die somewhere other than on the street."

"Did they tell you who?"

"They claimed not to know, but of course they do. The problem since Beijing took over is that the people investigating the crimes often have offices next to the ones committing them."

"Why should Hong Kong be any different?"

He shook his head. "Time was, it was. Another reason to retire."

"I appreciate it, Brice. I'll take precautions."

"Regina can be helpful. She's young but connected—and motivated. Her parents disappeared into the Chinese gulag, and she knows she'll never see them again."

"I'll keep that in mind. Now, how about you and Molly joining me for dinner?"

"I'll ring her up. She's probably already dressed and sitting by the door."

The next morning was overcast, and the clouds had dropped the temperature to where it was almost comfortable. Heeding Brice's words, I ignored the row of taxis parked along the street in front of the residence, turned the corner and walked two blocks until I saw an empty one sitting in front of a McDonald's. The driver was gnawing on the Hong Kong version of a Big Mac, which is identical to the one in the States except that it costs the same as a car. He tried to wave me off, but I got in before he could lock the doors. The unfailing politeness of Asia isn't quite as universal as Tony Bourdain would have you believe.

Initially, he tried to ignore me, but when he realized I was prepared to wait him out, he mumbled something I didn't catch and made angry eye contact in the mirror.

"The Peak," I said.

"No English," he threw back.

I waited.

"Address?" he finally barked with disgust.

"I'll tell you when we get there."

This didn't make him any happier, so he dropped the hammer and began a hair-raising dash through the heavy traffic. For a few minutes we rode like a couple of clowns. Me, trying to keep from sliding around in the back; him, head snapping from side to side, one wrist casually over the wheel, while he finished his meal. If this were a kidnapping, he was owed an Oscar for deception.

Victoria Peak is Beverly Hills, Greenwich and Coral Gables, rolled into one. The locals brag that it's the most expensive real estate in the world, and at a recent price of $200 million for an unimproved acre, no one's come forward to challenge the claim. The narrow, winding road to the top is also one of the most dangerous, but the views are so breathtaking, many brave the heart-in-your-throat drive for the photo op. What the travel brochures don't tell you is that distracted gawkers sometimes wander into the wrong lane or over the side, and more than one tourist has closed out his vacation watching the sights go by at terminal velocity.

I try not to second-guess drivers in other countries. They know the local traffic rhythms. But as I mentally gauged my reaction time to the blind corners we were flying around and the slower traffic we were dodging, I knew it would be impossible to adjust to anything unexpected. But not wanting Mr. Big Mac to go even faster, I mentally crossed myself and concentrated on searching the turn-ins for Cheyenne's butterfly.

The road bent back and forth in tight hairpins as it terraced its way up the mountain. From time to time, the tram to the summit flashed into view then disappeared again in the trees. Eventually, we left the shops and small neighborhoods behind; and then we left the haze as well and broke into sunlight. The landscape changed too. Here, the vegetation was allowed to grow unchecked, creating an additional layer of security for the residents of hidden estates. Unlike lower down the mountain, no cars were parked along the roadway either, and few passed going in the other direction.

Then, suddenly, that unexpected happened.

An old man stepped out of a blind driveway directly into our path. Swerving right wasn't an option. That was straight down. So my driver jerked the wheel left. A massive bougainvillea offered little resistance, but the thick hedge behind it pushed us sideways so we hit the approaching wall at a glancing angle. After scraping along ivy-covered concrete fifty feet or so, we finally jolted to a stop.

Other than being angry, I was okay. In the front seat, though, my driver was groaning and holding his head. As I got out to see what I could do for him, part of me was rooting for the pain. He probably had a concussion, and he'd lost some teeth against the steering wheel, which he was clumsily feeling for while blood ran down his chin.

Regina had given me a local cell phone, but it might as well have been a ham sandwich. I couldn't even get the satisfaction of static. I heard another car coming up the mountain. It was an old Rolls Phantom IV, like the ones the queen uses on state occasions—only this one was white.

The chauffeur in the right-hand-drive vehicle was wearing a man's uniform with the hat brim pulled down, but there wasn't any question it was a woman. Asian, and without makeup, which is unusual in Hong Kong. She also had on a pair of black driving gloves and a man's watch.

I walked to the car and saw another Asian woman seated behind her in the cavernous backseat. Beautiful wasn't a strong enough word, but it was the kind of beautiful that was almost too perfect. The kind where anything could be hiding beneath. Swathed in red silk and a black, wide-brimmed hat over saucer-sized sunglasses, she'd gone to a lot of trouble to look like a wealthy wife out for lunch. My gut, though, told me she and her pal had been following us. I'd checked several times, but the twisting road could easily have hidden the big Rolls.

I went around to her side, and she lowered her window. "Is anyone hurt?" Her voice was slightly husky with a hint of Chinese and a vague European inflection, perhaps Portuguese. A constructed voice. One you didn't so much hear as have slip around you. And that could lure the unsuspecting to promised pleasures and unpromised fates.

"My driver probably has a concussion, but I don't mind." I held up my phone. "Unfortunately, *no habla*."

She smiled like a woman who had also enjoyed the suffering of others. "We saw you ahead of us. I assumed it would end badly. There's very little cell availability up here. If you wish, you may use the phone at my home."

I walked to the taxi to tell Asshole I'd send someone for him, and the Rolls pulled alongside. I got in back on the left side, and my seatmate's perfume enveloped me as had her voice. I'd never smelled anything like it. Whatever nameless fool decided we needed to replace the descriptive "Oriental" with "Asian" needs to get out more. This fragrance was pure Orient. A coalescence of flowers, spices, history, superstition and intrigue that wouldn't have been the same on Park Avenue or the Champs-Elysées. In the Far East, the first touch of lovemaking is scent. I had to remind myself it wasn't why I was here.

Now that I could see all of her, the woman was Oriental too, a modern version of another era. Chalk white skin, highlighted by deep red lips, upswept hair pinned under her hat with ivory combs and a six-inch-wide gold cuff pushed halfway up her left forearm. She wore a couture copy of an ancient Chinese dress pinched at her narrow waist with a wide red and gold sash. And instead of white stockings and wooden sandals, her red silk Jimmy Choos, also embroidered in gold, had been given an extra inch of heel. Her single nod to the twenty-first century was a thin gold anklet accented by an ivory teardrop charm.

I gave her Beijing masters points for the name. Crimson was perfect.

Our driver, who wasn't introduced, was a very careful lady. Part was the road, part the car. Straight eight, 1950s Rolls-Royces weighing two tons aren't geared for steep grades or hairpin turns. But even accounting for the less-than-responsive behemoth, I could have walked faster. After what seemed an interminable climb, we turned into a steep, tree-lined drive. The deciduous oaks reached far to the sky, shutting out most of the sun and all noise. We could have been in a woods in Pennsylvania instead of on a mountaintop in China.

The gray-green gates were a dense steel weave decorated with an elaborate butterfly, gracefully executed by a sculptor of exceptional skill. The driver pressed a button on the dash, and the butterfly broke in half as the gates swung inward.

As the drive rose, I could see through the trees the partial outline of a spacious home. I was about to comment on the architecture when everything went to shit.

The chauffeur suddenly accelerated and jerked the wheel left, right, then left again. The soft shocks and low center of gravity turned the heavy Phantom into a drunken whale, and I grabbed the hanging strap with my left hand. To my right, I saw a flash of red and gold as Crimson raised her left arm. I lunged for it, but the car wallowed again, and I slid toward her and missed. I grabbed again and got the gold cuff, which slid down to her wrist. The mouth-sized wound on her forearm with sutures still in it wasn't autographed by Chuck Brando, but it should have been.

I didn't feel the hypodermic go into my thigh, but I saw it there, and a split second later, my leg turned white-hot, followed by ice-cold.

"You were lucky once, Mr. Black. We were waiting outside the Red Roof Inn. We'll try to get it right this time."

I elbowed Crimson in the jaw, and she flew against her door. I tried to think, but my head was filled with bees. I grabbed for the door handle with a rubber arm that seemed to be a mile long and getting longer. I wrenched it open and threw myself out. I was lucky. The car was just swinging to the right, so my jump took me away from it. I hit the edge of the cobblestone drive and rolled into the soft ground cover.

I pulled the syringe out of my flesh, staggered to my feet and broke for the closing gates. It was downhill, and I was running as fast as I could, but the entrance seemed to be receding. I shook my head and tried to focus. Just as the two halves came together, I threw myself at them, banged my temple on one, my shoulder on the other and went through.

My vision had begun to tunnel, and my arms and legs were blocks of granite, but I willed myself forward. I looked over my shoulder and saw the gates reopening. The main road was only a dozen yards ahead, but it took me a week to reach it. By then, the Rolls's grille was so close I could feel its heat.

I stumbled across the blacktop, and when I heard gravel

under my feet, I leaped. The harbor looked far, far away, but I remember thinking it was beautiful. Then I was falling . . . and falling . . . For a brief moment, I thought I saw a great grinning shark tumbling above me, but, as I tried to reach into my memory for why it looked familiar, everything began to fade, and I rushed into the welcoming darkness.

High Places and Silk Houses

I awakened to the sound of a jet. A big one, climbing out toward some faraway place. I think it was day, but I dropped back to sleep before I could be sure. The second time, I managed to force my eyes open, but the effort wore me out. I don't know how long it was before I came to again, but it was dark and raining. I was lying on my back and so thirsty I couldn't get past it to think anything else.

I tried opening my mouth, but that didn't work. While I pondered the problem in the heavy web that had replaced my brain, I felt something wet hitting me in the head and running over my ears. I gathered my strength, heaved myself over and pressed my face into it. It tasted like earth, but I didn't care. One of the things you learn in survival school is just how much crap your body will allow you to insult it with. Considering some of the scrounged feasts I'd choked down over the years—clotted camel blood being one you never forget—this particular mud tasted pretty good.

When I pulled myself away, I was still maddeningly cotton-mouthed, but I had taken in enough to keep my kidneys from failing. The residual thirst was the result of whatever had been in the hypodermic. Animal tranquilizer, probably, which meant my liver wasn't going to be very happy. To make up, I promised to send it a few beers as soon as I could.

My head was beginning to clear, and I took stock. I was on a steep grade, 70 percent, at least. The good news was that I was head up, which might have saved my life. More than one mountaineer has died from nothing more than being trapped upside down. My hands and feet worked—though one of my shoes was gone—and other than what felt like a severely skinned back and a knot behind my left ear, I was intact. My legs were jammed solidly into a sweet-smelling bush with ropelike branches, and when I reached up, there was another like it.

When I finally got a look down, my elation disappeared. The bush was growing out of a narrow ledge of rock beyond which was a black abyss. I listened, and through the rain, I heard distant surf—too distant. Victoria Peak is eighteen hundred feet, and I'd been near the top. Whatever portion was below me fell into a category of information I didn't want to know.

My cell phone had apparently joined my shoe, and in another move of divine brilliance, Bert's watch was right where it would do me the most good—on the dresser at Black House. I had obviously been lying there for hours, but how many?

I had two choices. Wait for daylight and try to signal for help, or climb. Inaction hadn't brought the Marines thus far, so hanging around didn't seem smart. I'd also get weaker. I try not to ask God for personal favors. He's never been much of a listener when I asked him to help the Cowboys. I took a shot anyway. Who knew, it might just be an issue with Jerry Jones.

Normally, you don't invite a guy my size to go climbing. Long muscles, wrong center of gravity, and too much weight. But during the first six years of my life, I lived on Clarissima, my family's Caribbean island where there were no other kids, and I had to make my own fun. Mostly that meant tagging along with Magé, our Brazilian foreman.

Magé taught me the rain forest like it had been taught to him by his grandfather, including how to hunt boar with a spear and a knife. You started in a tree, but you had to drop next to the boar to finish the job. If it went bad, you had to be able to get back up—in a hurry. I learned to climb everything, even palms. And later, when I went to England for school, I led my classmates on some of the wildest excursions ever chronicled by the Derbyshire constable—a hapless chap who spent a lot of his time driving under us.

In Delta, you train hard in all disciplines: scuba, desert, jungle, arctic, alpine and a host of others. I try not to talk about my worst, but building an igloo at forty below figures in. Fortunately, one of my best was alpine.

The first ten feet were a breeze. They only took me an hour. Then, a little while later, I stumbled onto a half-pipe concrete drainage ditch where I was able to get a cleaner drink and use it to scale the rest of the way.

I crested the ridgeline just as the sun broke over the horizon. The rain was gone, and it looked like it was going to be a beautiful day. After a thorough assessment, I discovered there was considerable blood seeping through my shirt. Torn, bleeding and wearing one shoe, I wasn't much of a candidate for hitchhiking, so I began walking.

A couple of miles later, I arrived at the spot where my taxi had gone into the wall. It was another thirty yards from where I'd left it and deeply entangled in a creeper vine. Apparently, my genius driver hadn't been any better off-road. I checked for keys, found them in the glove box, and the engine turned over after a couple of tries. I spent the next hour collecting pieces of stone to put under the wheels and tearing away the vine—which in keeping with my current run of luck was thorned.

By the time I had the taxi back on the road, my sock was almost as bloody as my shirt. I took it easy heading back to the city, but I couldn't help thinking about Birdy.

* * *

I had to expect someone would be watching both Black buildings, so I parked up the street where I could observe pedestrian and traffic patterns in my mirror. Half an hour later, all I knew was that if somebody was there, they were either inside a building or so good I was never going to see them. I took a deep breath, got out and headed for the door of the residence, half-expecting to feel a bullet.

I tried to let a long shower do its magic, but several soapings later, there was still blood running down the drain. I wrapped my back in towels, put on a white terry bathrobe and made myself two sandwiches. After inhaling one and washing it down with Evian and a tall Tsingtao, I picked up the private line and dialed Regina's extension.

She answered on the first ring, her voice not hiding her alarm. "Mr. Black. Is everything all right?"

"Everything but your cell phone. I must have left it somewhere."

"I'll bring you another. Are you back at the residence?"

"I am."

"You certainly don't have to check in with me, but someone's been calling for you. Twice yesterday and three times the day before."

Two days. No wonder my head felt like a bag of broken glass. Quite probably, my substantial body mass had saved me. "Did they leave a name or number?"

"No number, just a name. A funny one. Birdy. Could that be right?"

My muscles tensed. "Yes, it's right. How did she sound?"

Regina seemed surprised. "Other than arrogant, I'd say she was fine. From her accent, I think she's from the northwest. Manchuria, would be my guess, but when I asked, she ignored me."

Not Birdy, Crimson. "Did she leave a message?"

"Not until her last call about an hour ago. She said if you showed up to tell you she's sorry she didn't get to entertain you."

Of that I was certain. "That's it?"

"No, she wanted you to know she and her friends have left Hong Kong, and they won't be back for some time. Maybe a year, maybe longer."

I didn't buy it. Nobody needed to run as long as I stayed dead. "If she calls again, you still haven't seen me. And put some alarm in your voice. Think you can do that?"

"Yes, sir."

"Regina, when I came in, there was a battered taxi parked up the street. In view of the kidnapping threat, maybe it's wise to have the authorities check it out."

"Absolutely."

"I'm also going to need a couple of things. Can I count on your discretion?"

"Of course, Mr. Black."

She was fast and surreptitious with the doctor. They came through the Black Group offices and entered the residence via a side door that wasn't visible from the street. He was a young Chinese who'd studied at the University of Texas, and while he dressed my wounds he kept up a running commentary on Lone Star women. He was a fan, as was I. What he didn't do was ask questions, and I skipped mention of the tranquilizer. Regina watched him work without comment.

"You'll be fine after a few days rest," he said. "The scrapes on your back are mostly superficial, but there's one nasty gash that probably could stand a few sutures. I can butterfly it, but if you do anything strenuous, it'll open up again."

I've always been a fast healer, so I skipped the needle. "How about my foot?"

"It looks worse than it is. I'll leave some antibiotics. Just avoid sandals until there's no longer a danger of infection."

When he left, Regina handed me a piece of paper. "This part was difficult. Most of the air tours here are done by helicopter. Since the handover, fixed-wing aircraft are limited to government and approved businesses. Being British, we don't qualify."

"I'll see to it you're rewarded."

She shook her head. "That's not what I meant. I can't vouch for the pilot. At the very least, he'll be an informant."

I wasn't about to tell her I was prepared to risk beheading rather than ride in another helicopter. "I'm sure he'll be ideal."

"The police towed the taxi. It looked like they brought the entire department."

"Then I'm glad we called."

I could tell she wanted to tell me to cut the crap, but she was too polite. If you treat people like children, sooner or later, they'll act like it. I tried to make nice. "Look, Regina, you're a thorough professional, but I don't know what I'm dealing with, and if I stir up a hornets' nest, I'll be gone, and you won't."

"May I speak freely, Mr. Black?"

"Of course."

"China is a Communist country run by a brutal regime. There's no Bill of Rights or presumption of innocence. Not far from here is a building where they use cattle prods and branding irons to interrogate dissidents. Most are young people caught drawing graffiti. You can hear their screams while you're eating lunch in the park. That's by design. Whether you tell me or not, I'm still going to have to clean up your mess. If I know some things ahead of time, I can divert attention. Bureaucrats are lazy. If there's a reasonable explanation, they'll take it."

She looked like she wanted to say something else, so I waited. "Did Mr. Fleetwood tell you about my parents?"

"He did."

"Then you will appreciate I have my own reasons as well."

"I'm going to need a car. Four doors, black and fast. Can you drive? I mean, really drive?"

"Very well."

"Good, dress in dark clothes that you can run in if you have to."

"Anything else?"

"A roll of duct tape. Can you buy that here?"

"Are you kidding? The city would grind to a halt without it."

"Now for the hard part. A gun."

She didn't bat an eye. "What caliber?"

I liked this girl. "Something heavier than a nine, but if that's all you can come up with, I'll make do. And the noisier the better."

"It'll be heavy *and* noisy. How much ammunition?"

"If I need more than a clip, I'm in trouble. Last item. Is there a way to get in and out of this place without being seen? I've got something I have to do this afternoon; then you and I will be going out this evening. Around nine thirty."

She looked me up and down, then stepped forward and put her arms around my waist. She was warm and smelled like jasmine, which reminded of Suzanne Chang. Only this woman wasn't a whiner or a coward. "Shall I put on some music?" I smiled.

She stepped back without acknowledging the remark. "There's a tunnel. From the war. I've heard many rumors about what it was used for, but no one really knows. I think you'll fit, but it's going to be tight."

"Tight I can handle."

Her businesslike demeanor suddenly disappeared. "May I ask you a question?"

"Please."

"This Birdy you have come for. Is she your lover?"

"We have made love."

"There is a difference."

"I don't discuss relationships."

She pondered that for a moment. "Very well, then would you mind very much if I made love to you?"

"I don't know what Brice told you, but that's not necessary."

"I do not share my body because it is necessary. Ever."

She put her head down, and I realized I had shamed her. I reached out and tilted her chit up. "I apologize. No excuses."

She came into my arms in a rush. She was so much smaller than I was, I had to bend to kiss her. It was worth the effort. Her diminutive mouth was warm and willing, and our tongues found each other. She pulled back slightly, "What do you like from your women?"

"Mostly, I just like to know when they come."

A slight smile crossed her lips. "Then you will not be disappointed."

She unclipped a band of gold from a snug chain around her neck, pulled her long hair back and threaded it through into a tight ponytail. Her small face was now completely exposed, and I kissed her again as she began unbuttoning my shirt. I reached out to do the same for her, but she pushed my hands away. "I will do everything."

She kissed each part of my body as she uncovered it, lingering over my nipples and the underside of my penis while she made small murmuring noises in her throat. When we were both undressed, she stood, and I rolled her nipples between my fingers. She put her hands over mine and made me pinch them harder, her head lolling back as she sucked in her breath.

She took my manhood in both hands, her fingertips doing things I couldn't describe. I reached for the tiny strip of hair between her legs, and she moaned. She stopped what she was doing to me and watched my hand work. Then she looked into my eyes, and said, "Do you like my cunt?"

I had my first sexual experience in my teens and quite a few since, and no woman had ever asked that. I didn't think the head of my cock could get any larger, but it did its best. As an answer, I let my thumb part her folds, then gently massaged the throbbing button between them. She shuddered and came without trying.

A few moments later, she took my hand and placed it on the top of her head. She put her own fingers into what was now a very wet vagina until they glistened with her juices, then she drew them across her lips and flicked her tongue to get some on its tip.

She knelt. I closed my eyes and waited to feel the warmth of her mouth engulf me. Instead, she put the tiny tip of her velvety tongue in the hole of my penis, gently swirled, then drew it out. The second time she did it, I exploded onto her lips. It was so unexpected, I felt my knees buckle slightly and realized why she had put my hand where it was. I steadied myself while she took the rest of my pumping orgasm in her mouth.

She never took her lips away, and shortly I went from indecision to even harder than before. After a while, she led me by the hand to the bedroom and turned down the sheets. She got onto the bed, turned and knelt on its edge. I stepped forward, and she clutched my buttocks with both hands and pulled me into her mouth again.

This time, as I was about to go, she turned quickly and impaled herself on me, coming again and again as she groaned and gasped for breath. She reached up and pushed her ponytail into my hand, and I grabbed it, pulling her head back. "Yes!" she grunted. "Pull it! Make me your cunt. Make me your cunt!" I put my other hand on her shoulder and jammed her hard rear against me with such force that she momentarily lost her breath, then I pounded into her so ruthlessly I thought I might break her.

Suddenly, I felt her body tense like it had not before, and my heart reached the same rhythm as my thrusts. "Yes!" she screamed. "YES!" When we came together, she made a bestial sound that was exceeded in wantonness only by my own.

I remember falling into bed, still coupled, and her pressing her back into my chest. I reached down and pulled up the sheet, but I don't remember letting go.

Regina didn't have to worry about the plane. Buddy Leeds was a sixtysomething Brit holdover with a 1941 DC-3. A forty-year expat, the Chinese had let him continue operating his charter service, Buddy Leeds, You Follow, as long as he made himself available to ferry government functionaries back and forth to the provinces.

"They all got a piece of ass somewhere, so mostly, I just fly guys with a hard-on. Not that I got anything against a little toss, mate, but these cheap cocksuckers fight me over every buck and don't even slip me a bottle of gin. Day I feel the big one comin' on, I'm gonna aim my baby here right into Government Hill. Those pricks can't die fast enough for my taste."

Of all the aircraft ever conceived, nothing comes close to the "Three." Thousands were built and won countless wars and opened markets from Abilene to Zanzibar. Most of the last generation took their first flights watching twin Cyclones and six blades bite reliably into the sky. It was a real joy to be up in one again.

Buddy had the cabin decked out in all its antique beauty, but I rode up front with him. When a couple of fighters appeared, he grinned and waved. The jets held position long enough for their cameras to get what they wanted, then waggled their wings and blasted away, giving us a substantial slipstream jolt in the process.

"Assholes. The jerk on the left is fuckin' his general's wife, and the general's fuckin' some nurse upriver. I can't tell you who the prime minister is anymore, but I know who can't get it up without a dildo in his ass."

"Maybe you should put out a newsletter." I laughed.

"Oh, I got it written down, all right."

In his line of work, probably a smart idea. "What do you know about the Peak?"

"If you're lookin' for real estate, you gotta spread some big money around before they'll even let you inside one."

"Right now, I'm just interested in a house with a butterfly on the gate."

He was silent for a moment. "You here to kill somebody?"

That wasn't exactly the response I was expecting. "Why? Does it need doing?"

"People been goin' in there and not comin' out for a long time now. Somebody was bound to come along with a grudge and the skill. You look to me like you got both."

I didn't answer, and he turned into the sun. Ahead was the Peak.

"It's not a butterfly. It's a moth. A silk moth to be exact. They call the place the Silk House because everything inside is supposed to be made of the stuff."

"Whose is it?" I asked.

"American guy. Wired all the way to Zhongnanhai—that's the private city in Beijing where the elected murderers live, in case you didn't know."

I did.

"Owner's name is Kingdom. Markus Kingdom."

According to Buddy, everybody in Hong Kong knew he worked for the government, so he could wander back and forth over the Peak as long as he liked without somebody complaining. On the flip side, the old DC-3 wasn't particularly nimble, and Buddy babied it, so after we made a pass, he'd run out a few miles before making a wide, sweeping turn and coming back.

On our first approach, I got a look at where I'd spent the last two nights and was glad I hadn't been able to see much before I started climbing. Buddy noticed me staring. "They lose about ten cars a year over that. Sometimes they get a body out, but mostly not." It reinforced what I'd thought. Right now, Crimson was getting comfortable with my being dead. She'd stay put.

The Silk House gate wasn't visible from the air, but the white Rolls was parked next to a freestanding, four-car garage. The sprawling one-story house was built of massive redwood beams with the corners curved dramatically skyward like the bow of a Heyerdahl ship. That this uniquely American wood, much romanticized by poets and politicians, had been carted across the Pacific to create a weekend getaway for a billionaire trading partner seemed appropriate. Beijing now controlled the Panama Canal, most of our manufacturing and the majority of our money. Why not our forests?

The house was set thirty feet from the ridge with a hundred-foot-wide wall of glass overlooking the distant city and harbor. Guests would surely be awestruck. The combination of altitude and deep eaves prevented my seeing inside, but it was probably just as well. I was powerless.

On a second pad, well down the mountain, sat an infinity pool and tennis court. I looked for stairs and saw none. On our next pass, I was able to pick out a small recess in the green hill near the pool and guessed there was an elevator between the two levels.

Three sides of the residence were windowless, and a line of narrow fence posts delimited the interior property line. I pointed to a long, narrow structure partially obscured by trees. "Any idea what that is?"

Buddy banked the plane and took a look. "No, it's new. Within the last couple of months."

We came around one more time and ran parallel to the cliff so I could get a look at the neighbors. None were closer than a quarter mile.

I saw a line of black Mercedes coming up the mountain. I pointed. "Somebody's getting some important company."

Buddy craned his neck. "Not company, the owner."

Moments later, the lead car turned into the Silk House drive and disappeared under the trees. The entourage followed.

Rowland Rounds and Red Hands

Regina, dressed in a black leotard, black Nikes and a black baseball cap, led me into the company offices, then down several flights to the basement for the second time that day. Her long, raven ponytail protruded out the back of her cap, and as I watched it bounce, I tried to keep my mind on the stairs. I noticed an athleticism in her gait that hadn't been evident in heels, which told me I wasn't going to have to worry about how she'd react if she broke a nail.

I was wearing black cargo pants, a long-sleeved black T-shirt and a pair of black deck shoes. She'd brought me an artist's charcoal stick I'd use later.

The tunnel was behind a false wall in a fireplace, and when I'd seen it earlier on my way to meet Buddy Leeds, I didn't think there was a ghost of a chance I would fit. "It widens once you get in," she'd said. Then she'd smiled, and added, "But you've probably heard that before."

The Shecky Greene neighborhood of my brain had flashed something drop-dead clever, but I kept it to myself. This time, there was no banter. I took the flashlight she'd brought and went in first. That way, there'd be somebody to tell the coroner whose feet he was looking at.

It seemed even narrower than before, and I scraped both shoulders wedging myself in. The shaft angled down slightly, and the combination of gravity and my willingness to ignore what was happening to the wounds on my back, allowed me to pull myself thorough the sixty or so feet. Eventually, I broke into another basement, turned and helped Regina out.

She led me through the maze of passageways until we came to a rickety stairway flanked by stacks of boxes labeled in Chinese. Earlier, it had been dead quiet down there, and we had continued straight to door that opened onto an alley. This time, I smelled food and heard dishes clattering and people shouting.

Regina stopped. "At night, the security people take their breaks in the alley." She pointed up. "We go this way. Act like an owner."

"What do I own?"

"The Ritz-Carlton," she said.

At the top of the stairs, we walked out into an industrial kitchen in full operation. People stared at us. I picked up a wok, looked at the fish frying in it, frowned and said something in gibberish to the chef. He winced, and everybody else quickly went back to their tasks.

The car was a new, midnight blue, right-hand-drive Maserati, and it was parked against the wall in the valet section of the garage. "Sorry about the color. It was the best I could do."

"It's fine."

A handsome young Chinese man in a Ritz uniform appeared out of the shadows and held the keys just out of Regina's reach until she jabbed him in the solar plexus, and she took them while he was trying to get his breath. He glared at me, then said something in rapid Mandarin to Regina.

She wasn't interested. "Give it a rest, Tommy. Who I'm with is none of your business. You want to fuck around, I'll tell Mr. Fleetwood we need to put our guests somewhere else."

Tommy held out his hands in mock supplication then

spoke English. "Always with the threats. You owe me a movie, remember. I'm not letting you off the hook."

She waved him off dismissively, and we got in the car. "If you listen to those old fuckers in Beijing, there are 20 percent too few women in China. In my age group, it's thirty to one."

"Sounds like a marketing opportunity."

"That would presuppose a semblance of intelligence. No, they'll do it the old-fashioned way. They'll start a war."

Unfortunately, she was probably right, and as she burned the Quattroporte past Tommy without looking at him, I felt sorry for the kid.

I'm not a Maserati fan. The styling's too much like Buick and not enough like Pininfarina. However, I have no complaint about the power plant. Only Ferrari has a better roar, and as Regina shot toward the Peak, I was able to appreciate the car's performance in the hands of someone who knew how to show it off.

Fog and a slight mist had rolled in, keeping the sightseers home and leaving the road empty. We didn't talk as she wheeled the Quattro through the hairpins and hammered it on the straightaways. I didn't tell her where we were going, so she blew past the Silk House driveway doing sixty. It's human nature to slow as you approach a target, and modern surveillance systems pick up variances in speed and send a first alarm.

Half a mile farther up, I saw another drive, this one illuminated by a coach light on a stone pillar. I pointed, and Regina slowed and pulled over. "I'll get out here. Find someplace to get a cup of coffee and come back in an hour and a half. Stop up the hill and stay dark. Flash your lights every sixty seconds, and if I'm not here after fifteen flashes, go home and forget you ever met me."

She opened the glove box and handed me a roll of three-inch duct tape and a heavy, padded envelope. I tore off a small strip of the silver tape and handed it to her. "Before you come back down, put this on your right headlight, vertically."

She understood. "So you'll know it's me. It's pitch-black out there. Do you want the flashlight?"

I shook my head. "There's a footpath that cuts back and forth among the houses."

She nodded. "The nature trail. It used to be private, but several years ago, they opened it to the public. The home-owners are still screaming."

"The proletariat's a bitch. Ask anybody with California beachfront."

"You're going to the Silk House, aren't you?" When I didn't answer, she said, "I thought so."

"What can you tell me about the place?"

"They throw loud parties. Somebody complained once, but they got a visit from the Third Bureau."

"Third Bureau?"

"State Security, Hong Kong Affairs. They keep the dis-sident herd thinned. They're the ones who took my parents."

"I'm sorry."

"It's a big club." She got back to business. "Stay on the trail. Otherwise, you'll trip the lights that are supposed to keep people from wandering over the edge."

I opened the padded envelope. Inside were a new cell phone and a modified Sig Sauer 1911 along with a full clip of ammo. "You said you wanted it noisy," said Regina. "How do you feel about Rowlands? Hollow point."

In stopping power and wince-factor, a Rowland round is just this side of a Magnum. The difference is a less violent recoil. At the very least, I would deafen somebody.

"You ever get tired of the Far East, I know a hundred spe-cial operators who'd walk barefoot over broken glass to hear you say Rowland."

She laughed, and I put the phone back in the envelope. "I'll leave this here. They have a habit of going off at the wrong times."

Just then a set of headlights broke out of the gloom behind us, turning the interior of the Mas into daylight and us into silhouettes. I quickly grabbed Regina and kissed her passionately. She played her part well, and I felt myself reacting. The car went by. A black Mercedes. Then another and another. Six sets of headlights later, I released her, but it was slightly slower than it should have been.

"Looks like Mr. Kingdom is going to the top for dinner. I'll do some recon while I'm there."

"Don't take any chances."

Her face got serious, and she reached between the seats and pulled out a 9mm Brazilian-made Taurus, no larger than the palm of her hand. Tiny, but deadly. "There are many of us," she said. "Young and committed. We may not rid our country of this vermin, but they know we're here, and they worry. It is what an American would do, isn't it?"

I had to learn to stop judging people by their age. It hadn't made any sense when people were doing it to me, and it didn't make any now.

"It's exactly what an American would do."

I reached up, switched off the dome light and got out. I thought about thanking her for our earlier intimacy but didn't know how to say it. She leaned over, grabbed my wrist, held something to her mouth, kissed it and put it in my hand. It was the gold band that had held her ponytail.

"*Yi ri quan li*," she said. "One day, a thousand miles."

The going was rougher than I expected. Trees with thick, twisted limbs grew among dense patches of bamboo and giant thornbushes to create a web of wet vegetation that was nearly impenetrable. Add in the usual nocturnal insects and predatory bats, and I was very happy when I finally reached the trail.

I had hoped the fog would have the same effect here as on the road, but it was more like Central Park. A pair of lovers were strolling hand in hand, followed by a tiny old man who paused every few steps to do a Tai Chi move. Then a bony swarm of joggers panted by. Worse, the path lights were on as far as I could see.

In my dark outfit with a heavy Sig in one pocket and a roll

of tape in another, I felt like a walking billboard for the ITT School of Cat Burglary. Nevertheless, no one paid me the slightest attention.

Just before the Silk House, the trail bent right and doubled back on itself to circumvent the property to the rear. Seeing no one nearby, I left the path and made my way into the brush. I knelt and used the charcoal stick to darken my face, then moved silently toward the house.

The grounds were different here. Tended and thinned. Not good. Then I saw the five thin black strands of barbed wire, which, at first glance, didn't seem strong enough to slow down a determined rabbit. As I got closer, I revised my thinking. The wooden posts that had been visible from the air were dotted with plastic insulators, and the wire had been unprofessionally strung through them. Even from ten feet away, I could feel electricity coming off. I wasn't up on my protons and ions, but I knew that meant the fence wasn't grounded properly, which made it unpredictable—and deadly.

While I pondered my next move, I heard someone coming on the other side of the wire. I melted back and into the trees. Shortly, motion lights on the Silk House property blinked on, and a thick-trunked Asian man came into view. His arms were heavily tattooed, which ran up his neck onto his face, and he was leading an enormous reddish brown dog. At least I thought it was a dog. Considering the mane, it could have been the MGM lion. I remembered not paying much attention to Fabian Cañada's description of the Tibetan Mastiffs of Hu-Wei and made a mental note to be smarter next time my hide was on the line.

When the dog got directly opposite me, it stopped and faced in my direction. My gut said to move deeper into the foliage, but I fought the impulse. The animal already sensed me and almost certainly heard my breathing. As many people as I'd passed on my way here, this wouldn't have been the first time the dog alerted to a person outside the fence. The smell of fear would be something different. Not knowing the animal's ability to see in the dark but expecting it was excellent, I waited.

The dog walked to the fence, and the handler kept the lead short and went with it. The mastiff and I locked eyes, and I could feel him sorting through his instinct bank. The man watched his dog watching me, then squinted in my direction, but he was flying blind. I hoped the dog would decide I wasn't a threat and move on, but its perception equaled its size. I saw its breathing become more rapid. Time to have some fun.

Magé hadn't just taught me how to hunt boar but also how to call them. In Delta, I'd used the sounds to communicate with my team. Now, I pressed my lips and teeth tightly together and grunted from deep in my throat. Not loudly, but audible to the man and like a thunderclap to the dog. The mastiff exploded toward the fence, and only the handler's strength prevented the animal from impaling itself on the barbed wire.

I expected a "Cut" command, but none came. Instead, dog and man wrestled each other for supremacy, the mastiff's eyes never leaving me as he snarled and bit at the air. I grunted again, lower but with more aggression, and the mastiff went wild, throwing himself in all directions.

The fence was down a slight slope from the walkway, and the man's balance was tenuous. He tried to grab the dog by its mane, but it head-butted him, and he stumbled backward toward the fence. The hum increased as his bulk hit the top wire and broke it. The remaining four strands caught him across the back and legs, and sparks flew in all directions. Somehow the guy's right arm got tangled in the broken strand, and as he jerked involuntarily with the juice, large chunks of flesh came off. He screamed an inhuman scream. And then his hair caught fire.

As more men came running, the dog ran along the fence, looking at me and barking wildly. Then, inexplicably, he turned and charged one of the new arrivals. The man didn't hesitate and rammed a Taser against the dog's nose. It squealed and ran off. Someone shouted a command, and the fence's hum stopped. While the victim was being dragged off the wire, I circled deeper into the trees then cut back to the fence and crossed. When I did, I noticed that the driveway was full of cars. Expensive ones.

At the back of the house just beyond the garage, I saw another security type in an open doorway smoking a cigarette. He too had tattoos on his arms and face. I approached him like I belonged there, and by the time he realized I didn't, I had taken him out with a chop to the neck. The snap told me he wouldn't be getting up again. I pulled the body behind a hedge, drew my Sig and went inside.

Some less-than-pleasing, extremely loud techno was being piped through an internal sound system. It sounded like the shit we'd used in interrogation school, which after a couple of hours, would make Sister Mary Catherine confess to killing Kennedy. This was cranked up enough to cover a chain saw.

The kitchen was a mess. Open liquor bottles, dirty dishes and food strewn everywhere. A cat sat on a counter, his face buried in a mountain of caviar I could smell from across the room. To my right was a long, dark hallway that I assumed led to bedrooms. I didn't see any movement, so I pressed my back to the wall and moved on. The smell of drugs cooking burned my nostrils.

The long wall of glass at the back of the house looked out into darkness, but inside, soft pink lighting cast the teak-beamed living room in warm shadows. Low white sofas, faux-stone tables and eccentrically shaped chairs were scattered over a field of Oriental rugs on a dark hardwood floor. I don't know what I was expecting from something called the Silk House, but what I got were dozens of billowing sheets of white fabric draped from the ceiling that could be pulled around individual pieces of furniture—for privacy, I assumed.

The centerpiece of this Christo mélange was a block of white limestone large enough to have come from the Pyramids, atop which sat a life-sized, dark jade tiger fitted with carved ivory teeth and claws. The animal's head was tilted playfully, one forefoot elevated as if pawing at some imaginary object. In my less-than-professional opinion, ivory against jade added a gracelessness more appropriate to Tony Montana than tony collectors.

These guests didn't care either way. Thirty or more men and women were engaged in various sexual encounters or drug use or both. Twosomes, threesomes, whatever, and they seemed perfectly comfortable sharing their experience with anyone who wanted to look. The men were all Asian; the women, a mix, including a milk-skinned blonde doing a sixty-nine with a heavily freckled redhead while two men shared a pipe of something and watched. No Birdy.

One privacy curtain was drawn, and just as I started toward it, a young Asian woman pushed the fabric aside and stepped out. She was wearing heels and nothing else—unless you counted the fourteen inches of ribbed, black dildo belted to her pubis. The Asian man reclining on a chaise was naked, masked and handcuffed, and when he said something to her, she turned, grabbed his genitals and squeezed, hard. He let out a moan, and she smiled.

When she walked past me, I noticed her eyes were glassy, and there was a zombielike quality to her stride. She noticed my gun, seemed to try to process it, then pointed at the dildo. I shook my head, and she shrugged and walked on, eventually turning into the kitchen, strap-on swinging.

I retraced my steps and headed down the hallway I had passed. The techno was not being piped here, and I could hear my footsteps on the Berber runner. Then there was a sudden burst of different music from the far end of the hall, where I could see a vertical sliver of light.

The corridor ended in a T, and the light was coming from between a set of double doors. So was music. I stood and listened. Nick Cave's "Red Right Hand" again. Suddenly, it went off, and there were voices, then a slap followed by a moan. Then metal clanking and more moaning, and the music began again, even louder.

I gently tried the door handle. Locked. I pushed on the wood to gauge its strength and wasn't surprised to find it rock solid. If there were security inside, this is where it would be stationed. I might be able to John Wayne my way through, but if I didn't get in on the first try, I might not get a second chance.

I took a left and walked down the hall alongside the room. Forty feet farther, I came to another smaller door, but as I reached for the handle, I heard a motor and saw lights at the end of the corridor. An elevator. Probably the one to the pool. I moved to a position beside it and pressed myself against the wall.

When it opened, light spilled into the corridor, and two Asian men got off, naked and holding hands. The elevator door closed behind them, and they made their way down the hall and turned right toward the living room.

I went back to the door. It was unlocked, and I crouched and pushed it open. It swung noiselessly inward to no reaction. I could make out a king bed and seating area. Both were unoccupied. I entered and closed the door behind me.

To the right was an open door into a dark bathroom. There was another door on the opposite side with light under it. A connecting bath. Just as I started in, the music stopped again, and the opposite door opened, flooding the bathroom with brightness. I retreated. A mirror allowed me see a heavyset man entering. Over his shoulder he said in English, "Hold for a sec. I gotta take a piss. And Christian, dial down the fuckin' bass before my ears bleed."

The guy closed the door and didn't turn on the bathroom light. I heard him unzip and a stream hit the toilet. The fat roll around his neck made a chop risky, so I stepped behind him and slammed my gun into his skull. I felt bone give, and he collapsed.

I deposited him on the floor, opened the door and went

through. A blast of heat hit me, and I remembered Chuck Brando's bedroom. My view was blocked by an array of generators, lighting equipment and photographic screens. A slender woman heard me coming and started to turn, "Doug, we're getting a shadow across her face."

When she saw it wasn't Doug, she opened her mouth to shout, and I hit her on the chin with the heel of my hand before she could get anything out. The blow audibly slammed her teeth together and lifted her completely off her feet. She was unconscious before she felt the floor. I stepped past her, the Sig leveled.

Two digital movie cameras, a sound boom and three halogen floods were aimed at the center of the room. Birdy was strapped facedown on a rape rack. Dogmen use a canine version to breed fighters, but this one hadn't been built with pit bulls in mind. Three four-foot-long pieces of I-beam had been welded to the points of two triangles made from square steel tubing to create a sawhorse-type device that was bolted to the floor so it couldn't be rocked.

Birdy was bent lengthwise along the top beam, her torso supported by only a few inches of steel, her bare breasts hanging below. Three wide steel bands, one at her neck, one across her back under her arms and a third over her hips dug deeply into her skin as they held her in place. Her arms were banded to the front triangle at the wrists and biceps, and her legs had been drawn far apart, then banded to the rear triangle at the thigh, leaving her feet dangling off the ground. She was wearing one red high heel, the other lay under her.

Behind her, a muscular, burly guy of indeterminate ethnicity stood naked. A life-sized tattoo of a sword began at top of his pubic hair, its tip resting against his Adam's apple. Kneeling in front of him, the chauffeur of the white Rolls had her very large, very stiff penis in her mouth. However, neither seemed emotionally engaged, just ready.

It was my first look at the rest of Crimson's driver, and she wasn't what I expected. Her thin face and slender neck belied a fireplug of a woman with chunky thighs and tiny breasts. Her arms were thick and hard too, like she lifted weights. If she hadn't been sporting a waxed snatch, which looked like original equipment, I'd have bet she'd once been a man.

Crimson, wearing a pair of tall, red high-heel boots, stood at the side of the rack next to Birdy's head. She held two fistfuls her hair as she pulled the prone girl's face into her sculptured bush. But she too, seemed to be just going through the motions of some overrehearsed script.

And then I saw why. Off to one side stood another undressed man, a leather hood covering his head and face. From his drooping breasts, flaccid middle and the wiry gray hair around his half-erect manhood, I guessed he was at least sixty, perhaps a decade older. In his right hand, he held a gleaming, jewel-handled dagger.

All the snuff team had been waiting for was Doug. Apparently, the guy was particular about lighting the face of the woman whose throat he was slitting. It was the same lighting that would catch his ejaculation when Birdy's blood bathed his five inches of humiliation.

I wasn't surprised that most of the dozen or so people in the room, now frozen and staring at me, were, like Doug, Caucasian. I was willing to bet they also had 818 area codes. If you want good production values, the San Pornando Valley is the place to go. I saw one man inching toward the double doors and suggested he not. He quickly returned to his original position and stood there, twitching.

"Step back," I commanded Crimson. She looked into my eyes, then at my gun, and her mouth twisted into an ugly smile. Very slowly, she released Birdy's hair and took a half step away. Birdy looked languidly in my direction. I saw her trying to focus, but she was under the influence of something. A part of me must have registered, however, because tears began streaming down her face.

The chauffeur still had the Big Penetrator in her mouth, but instead of pointing at the guy's chin, it was now checking out his pedicure. I motioned for the driver to get up. "Let's get a look at the guest of honor," I said. "Take off his hood."

She stood and looked at Crimson, confirming that she understood English. Crimson shook her head no, and the chauffeur glared back at me in defiance. I noticed that the man in the hood had begun urinating involuntarily. "Come to think of it," I said, "I'll pass." I raised the Sig and shot him in the face. In the enclosed space, the roar of the Rowland was like a howitzer, and a female camera operator screamed.

At that range, hollow point notwithstanding, had the decapitator-in-waiting not been wearing a hood, his head might have exploded on the technician beside him. As it was, except for some brain tissue that shot out of the eyeholes, the thick leather contained most of the gore. He staggered back slightly, then pitched face forward into his own pool of piss. It doesn't happen often, but every now and then, karma is immediate.

Crimson ran to the man and bent over him. When she turned to me, her face was contorted with rage. "Do you know who this is?" she spit.

"I don't, but if you can wake him up, I'll shoot him again."

"You fool. It's General Maa, First Class General of the Army. We are all dead now."

"Well, he only had a second-class hard-on, so I'll take my chances."

Crimson stood, her fury barely under control. "The general is who kept your friends' precious children flowing. Are you even smart enough to realize that you've ended that?"

I'd had about enough of her, but I couldn't kill her yet. "And somewhere, a tiger just lit up a cigar. Fuck the general, and while we're at it, fuck you."

"Security will have heard the shot and . . ."

I cut her off. "Not over that bullshit music out front." I pointed the gun directly at her. "But if I'm wrong, you won't know it. Now, you and your girlfriend please undo the lady."

It took Crimson and her chauffeur a couple of minutes to get the bands unhooked. While they worked, I made an observation to the naked, red-booted addition to my fan club. "This was supposed to be Sherry Huston, wasn't it? But when she told you her sister was a big deal in the FBI, you backed off. What I don't understand is why you poisoned her. It seems counterintuitive."

Crimson turned, "An unfortunate error in judgment by some overzealous associates. They will not be repeating it."

"But it left you with the worst possible scenario. The FBI agent's sister dead, a living witness and a general with half a hard-on who still wanted a neck to cut. I'll bet Major wasn't happy to see you come through the door and even less happy after you left. That's a tough ad to run. 'Free trip to China. Oh, by the way, no high collars.' General Maa must have been a very demanding client."

"Not a client, a business partner. An important one. He'd never gone all the way before . . . and he wanted to."

"And who better to make that happen. Miss All the Way herself." I grabbed her arm and turned it so her wound showed. "Did you warn him that they sometimes bite?"

"All the motherfucker had to do was talk."

"Sure, so there would be more bodies. You wouldn't have let the baby live either if you'd found it, would you? At least you got your rocks off. You and Stumpy there. Does it bother you when she has a cock in her mouth?"

I thought she was going to charge me, and part of me was disappointed when she didn't. "Fuck you," she sneered.

I smiled. "It's nice to know you feel something." Chuck would have approved. I thought about the women the general had probably maimed and who would bear the scars forever. I turned and put another bullet in his body. Crimson jumped a foot. It was unprofessional, but it felt right. It also kept the room guessing.

Deep bruises were already forming in Birdy's flesh, and as I helped her to her feet, she swooned against me. One of the male crewmembers had that look in his eye that he might be thinking about becoming a hero, so I gave him the opportunity to look down the Sig's barrel. "The picture's been canceled," I said. "You still want to die for it?" He decided he didn't.

"Where are her clothes?" I asked him.

He hesitated and looked at Crimson. Apparently, everything went through her. I was going to kill the chauffeur anyway, this gave me a chance to get something for it. I turned and shot her in the chest. The bullet came out her back, splattering the sword tattoo of her former fellatiate. The guy I was talking to choked back his vomit, and blurted, "In the other room. The one you came from."

I pushed Birdy toward the bathroom. "Get dressed, I'll be along in a minute."

She stumbled away, and I turned to the group. "Everybody have a seat." They complied quickly. As Crimson started down, I said to her, "Not you, sweetie. You and I have a lot of Q&A ahead. Let's start with where's Bolin?"

Her eyes flashed, but she didn't say anything.

"Good, I was hoping you'd make it difficult."

I could see her tensing to kick. Since she'd wielded the syringe in her left hand, I gambled she'd go with the same foot. She was really good and really limber. She got the red boot as high as my head. I leaned back to let it go by then banged her in the face with a fist. She wasn't out, but she was woozy, and I grabbed a handful of black hair and pulled her to me.

While she was trying to get back to today, I fished the roll of duct tape from my pocket and tossed it to one of the seated men. I gave him instructions, and he pulled Crimson's arms behind her and wound several loops around her wrists then several more above her elbows—tight. After he'd done her mouth, I had him remove her boots, then I ground my heel into her toes on both feet. If I'd had a length of barbed wire, I'd have cinched it around her neck too.

Contrary to the handwringers who jerk each other off at thousand-dollar-a-plate human rights dinners, terrorists, enemy combatants and the truly pathological—even females—don't stop trying to kill because of a pair of cuffs and suggestion. Check with the family of Mike Spann or the guards at Guantánamo. You need to incapacitate them or, at the very least, keep them off-balance. Crimson was uncomfortable, but she was still mobile in a hobbling sort of way. More to the point, now a Cub Scout could handle her.

Before she and I left, I made eye contact with each of those on the floor, letting them watch me memorize their faces. "It's going to take us a few minutes to get out of here," I said. "If I see any of you . . ."

I didn't need to complete the sentence. I was pretty sure they believed me. I found the sound board and cranked up Mr. Cave again. Loud.

Lunging Dogs and Cold Hands

Back in the hallway, I heard running feet. One of the first rules of clandestine work is to have a backup escape carefully thought out. Mine was a little sketchy, but so far, no one knew exactly what was happening, so I had the element of surprise. It wouldn't last much longer.

The elevator was still on our floor, and it opened as soon as I pushed the button. I doused the lights, and we got in. Birdy had managed to get on a blouse and a pair of jeans but was shoeless. Crimson made one attempt to sound an alarm by shouting, so I jammed the Sig in her mouth, mashing her lips, breaking a couple of teeth and getting it far enough down her throat to make her gag. With her arms pulled up behind her causing her to bend forward at a nearly ninety-degree angle, she was spitting quite a bit of blood. I hoped Chuck and Lucille were watching.

The pool area was heated with propane lamps, and several people were enjoying each other under their warmth. Drugs and assorted paraphernalia lay on the tables and were strewn across the deck. I've never used drugs recreationally, so I don't have a frame of reference for what they do for sex. But if this stuff was any indication, once you come out of the haze, you've got to be sore as hell.

There had to be another way out, if only in case the elevator failed. Asking Crimson wasn't likely to get me an answer, so I told Birdy to hold her and went looking. I found it behind one of the cabanas. It was a long upward ramp that led under the house. Cutting through the mountain would have been difficult under any circumstances, but only the concrete floor and cage lights were new. Almost certainly, this had been one of the tunnels dug throughout the colony during the Japanese occupation. I was glad the walls couldn't talk.

We came out in a small cottage hidden in the trees beyond the garage. As we entered the woods, I looked back and saw that the door I had used to enter the house was still standing open, but there were men with guns guarding it.

The barbed wire was still silent, and I had just lifted Birdy over the strands when the first shot went past my head. I had intended to hoist Crimson over too, but when I reached for her, she started twisting and kicking. I was fully prepared to drag her over, but she was going to slow us down too much. It was time to shoot her and be done with it. The problem was, I might need the five bullets I had left.

"You're what we call unfinished business." I clipped her on the chin with a right hook that sent her down for the count. As I took Birdy's hand and ran toward the footpath, I immediately regretted not finishing her. Had I still been in Delta, it would have been a close call not to cashier me. I didn't envy the guy who'd taped her for me.

It was then that I heard the barking. Lots of it. On the move.

Birdy said her first words since I'd found her. "Kennels. Big dogs. I saw them tear a man apart."

That would have been the outbuilding I'd seen from the air. I didn't know anything about Tibetan Mastiffs. However, the path didn't seem like a good idea. Pulling Birdy with me, I made a hard left turn and went into the brush. Birdy was a good runner. She also wasn't a complainer even though I was sure her feet were being sliced to ribbons.

The baying was getting louder, and I chanced a look over my shoulder. I couldn't see them yet, but the foliage was moving erratically about twenty-five yards back, and I guessed we had at least a hundred yards to go to get to the road. I didn't have time to do the math, but I was pretty sure we weren't going to make it.

"Car's up the road. Look for tape on the headlight," I shouted, and pushed Birdy ahead. She put on a burst of speed, and I headed off on a right angle away from her. As I ran, I yelled and thrashed to draw the dogs in my direction.

I didn't know how many there were, but they were moving too fast to have handlers with them. That meant whatever course the alpha dog took, the rest would follow. For better or worse, I got my wish.

When I broke onto the path, all of the nighttime strollers had disappeared. I was well into my adrenaline rush, but even if a new supply was on the way, it wasn't going to help me outrun a dog. I allowed myself a look back and corrected the count. Four.

Ahead on the right, a ten-foot, spiked iron fence separated the ridgeline from the path. Since I hadn't seen any similar barrier earlier, I had to assume the drop-off there was severe. I waited until the last possible second, then veered off the path and put the iron bars between myself and the walkway. *Severe* was the appropriate word. Far below, I could see tiny lights. I grabbed on to the fence and moved along it, hand over hand.

One of the mastiffs had gotten onto the same side of the fence as me, and I heard him, pawing at the slope, gaining on the horizontal but losing on the vertical. Then I heard him start to slide. After a few seconds, he must have hit a level spot, because even though it was too dark to see him, his barking told me he was directly below me.

The remaining three dogs were still on the path only

inches away. Over and over, they lunged against the bars in a frenzy, and I had to keep moving my hands to avoid having them torn away. I guessed their weight at nearly two hundred pounds apiece with coats as thick as bears'. And unlike some guard dogs who are trained to occupy their quarry, these wanted to tear me apart. It was probably wiser to shoot them rather than try to outsmart them, but it's difficult for me to punish animals because of asshole owners.

They kept lunging, and I kept moving, as did my escort below. A few yards ahead, I saw the barrier coming to an end. The dogs didn't notice until they were almost there. When they did, they came around it with a vengeance. The lead dog leaped earlier, higher and farther than I expected, and I mistimed my kick. I just grazed its side and felt my leg go numb as it got a piece of my ankle before it clawed at the air and tumbled down the grade.

The other two began slipping and sliding before they could charge, and soon, all four were on the flats below creating an ungodly racket. I swung around the fence and heard the sound of men running in my direction.

Suddenly, a horn sounded, twice. Like a foghorn, but more shrill. It came from the direction of the Silk House, and the running stopped. I heard anxious voices, then the footsteps headed back the way they had come.

The headlights of the Maserati were on, and the piece of duct tape was in place. The passenger and driver doors were open, but Birdy stood several feet in front, staring through the windshield. I grabbed her arm, but she stayed rooted and shook her head. I went to the car. Regina's head lolled back on the seat, her chest ripped open by bullets, blood spilling down her front.

In the ditch next to the car, two men with tattooed faces lay face-up, each shot through the forehead and still clutching their guns.

In the quiet, I heard tires squealing farther down the mountain. Lots of them. The rats were clearing out. I waited for one to come this way, but none did. A few minutes later, all was quiet again. But only for a few seconds. This time, the rush came from up the mountain. The six Mercedes barreled past me traveling much faster than should have been comfortable.

I looked into them. I couldn't be sure, but I thought I saw former LAPD lieutenant Perry Duke in the third car. Just in case, I waved.

I lifted Regina's body gently and placed it in the backseat. I found a blanket in the trunk and covered her, taking a moment to smooth her hair off her brow. I got Birdy in the car without difficulty this time, and she huddled against the door, wide-eyed. I started the Mas and headed down the hill.

A wiser man would have called it a night. Instead, I turned into the Silk House. I waited for Birdy to react, but she sat mute.

The silk moth gate was wide open. Somebody had even clipped one side and torn it halfway off the pillar. The driveway that was full earlier was now empty. The garage was open and bare except for some gardening equipment and an old bicycle. I walked around the house to the kennels. There were two dogs left. Older ones, sharing a cage. They looked at me with curiosity but didn't snarl or bark.

I approached them, and one leaned against the bars, urging me to scratch it. I did, then opened the cage. Both dogs took their time coming out, then stretched and looked around. Suddenly, in the distance, I heard barking. The two mastiffs pricked up their ears, cocked their heads and bolted out of the building.

It was dead quiet inside the house. I'd left Birdy in the car, but she didn't let me get to the door before she was behind me. "I'd rather be in here than out there alone," she said. "What are you going to do?"

I kept it to myself. Things aren't evil, only people. But sometimes, you have to get rid of things so people can begin to heal. And sometimes, you just have to finish what you came to do.

It had to be there somewhere, and I decided to start with the least obvious, yet most obvious place. I couldn't guess the combined weight of the jade tiger and its base, but it was formidable. The tiger's ivory teeth and claws were individually set into the stone, and they looked as sharp as they would have in life. It was a bizarre piece, but then this was the home of someone for whom a snuff film seemed reasonable.

I reached out and touched the tiger's uplifted foot. The jade was smooth and cool, the claws firmly attached. The three remaining paws were secured to a bronze plate that was slightly smaller than the limestone base. Something was nagging at me, trying to push past the still-dominant chemicals of fight or flight. The bronze wasn't right. No artist or purveyor would mount a dark piece of jade on an even darker piece of metal to affix it to white stone. The drama was in the contrast of the green against the lighter base; in the sleek, polished jade in opposition to the rough rock.

I ran my finger along the bronze plate's vertical edge. It was gently scalloped, which was also aesthetically off. Even if the metal had a legitimate purpose, it shouldn't compete with the piece. Three sides were regular and cold. In the rear, however, one depression had three faint ridges in it that were almost invisible to the naked eye. It was also more than warm to the touch.

In the U.S., we're used to uninterrupted electrical current. In Asia, two weeks of continuous juice would trigger a national holiday. Multiple dedicated lines are also unheard of, and microelectronics are the first victims of power anomalies. Whether it was the shorting out of the electrical fence or just a run-of-the-mill deviation, it appeared one of Markus Kingdom's chips was running hot.

I turned to Birdy. "See if you can find a hair dryer and some ice."

It took her a few minutes, but she came back with a pro model Conair and a glass champagne bucket half-full of cubes. I plugged the dryer in, turned it on high, and held it near the depression.

"I don't know what you're doing, but wouldn't it be faster with a lighter? There's a bunch of them lying around."

"No, it's a fingerprint sensor, and they shut down in a fire. But if the temperature is raised internally, sometimes you can reset them. I'm trying to help it along."

"Where did you learn this?" She swept her arm around. "I mean *all* of this?"

I ignored the question and put my finger near the sensor again. The heat coming off it was now much hotter than the dryer. I turned off the Conair, cupped my hands and out of the bucket scooped ice, which I held against the depression. It melted rapidly, and I took another scoop. This time, it took longer to turn to water.

I wiped the depression dry with my sleeve. "Give me your right index finger."

Birdy extended her hand, and I pressed it into the cavity. "Why mine?"

"My hands are cold. If this is going to work, it needs a normal body temperature."

I held her finger in the depression for sixty seconds as timed by Bert's watch, then pulled it away and waited another sixty. "Okay, put your finger back in the slot."

She did, and after a moment, the limestone block suddenly began to move. I saw no track, but it glided over the hardwood soundlessly, revealing a stainless steel plate. The plate then slid under the floor, and light burst from the hole. Birdy and I peered in.

A rolling, mahogany library ladder reached twenty feet to the bottom. Running from just below to beyond my range of vision were neatly organized shelves of DVDs, videotapes and 16mm film cans, the labels under them coded. It was, almost certainly, a pornography and violence collection of epic proportions, probably containing things most imaginations couldn't conceive. Down there would also be the last hours of Lucille Brando's life . . . set to music. And Sherry

Huston's unfinished tape. I preferred not to contemplate what else.

I turned to start down the ladder. "I want to go too," Birdy said.

"That won't be necessary," I said softly. "In the garage, there'll be gasoline for the gardening equipment. Bring as much as you find."

She waited until I got to the bottom, then turned and disappeared.

The room opened into a broad V with separate racks of shelves laid out in a maze filling the additional space. I made my way through them, noticing that many of the containers were very old. I opened one that looked like a nineteenth-century ledger box and found a stack of stereopticon slides. From the moment man invented a way to record images on film, he has been using it to make erotic pictures. This particular unclad drama was entitled *Afternoon with a Horse,* and I didn't need a viewer to see that it offered little new. I tossed the box on the floor.

When I passed the last rack, the lights ended, and it became quite dark. There was a door on the wall at the end, and I assumed it was another entrance to the upstairs. I was wrong. It was a walk-in freezer. I pulled on the heavy latch, and stepped forward, reaching along the inside wall to my right for a light switch. I found it just as I felt a presence against my face.

I jammed my forearm up to defend myself at the same instant the light came on. It took a second for my brain to process what I was seeing. I was nose to nose with a Siberian tiger. Its head was three times the size of mine, and my face was halfway into its wide-open mouth. Fortunately, it was also dead, suspended from the ceiling on hooks and frozen solid.

The carcass swung back and forth in a kind of icy ballet while I got my heart restarted. The freezer was packed out with heavy plastic-wrapped bundles of what I presumed were tiger organs and various other identifiable and not-so-identifiable pieces of yet more tigers, all considerably smaller than the behemoth on hooks.

I was caught off guard by my own disgust. I remembered reading that all pathological behavior is rooted in sex. Serial murder, thrill arson, compulsive theft. I didn't know if anyone ever thought about including the killing of endangered species, but it seemed to apply here. This wasn't just illegal, it was demented.

Birdy had found two ten-gallon jerry cans of gas. I emptied the first into the repository. The second, I fed slowly through the house to the makeshift film studio, where I doused the two bodies liberally, leaving a small amount in the can. When I was ready to leave, I had to shake Birdy out of a trance. Even then, she couldn't tear her eyes off the steel rack.

On our way out, I tore down two of the silk panels, grabbed a butane lighter and went back to the subterranean vault. I crumpled the silk and poured half the remaining gas on it. It flared as soon as the lighter flame touched it, and I kicked it into the hole. The concussion from the whoosh pushed me back a step.

In the doorway, I poured the rest of the gas on the remaining sheet, turned and handed the lighter to Birdy. She bent and flicked it once.

When we reached the bottom of the mountain, a fire engine passed us going up. His lights weren't flashing, and he didn't seem to be in a hurry. I didn't see any others. Apparently, the locals weren't anxious to save the Kingdom place either.

I dialed Brice Fleetwood. Not confident of the privacy of any cell conversation, I told him Regina had joined my father.

He was shaken. "Quite an accomplished young lady," he finally managed.

"Quite. I'd like to see her honored for her service. Personally."

"I'll have someone meet you. Unfortunately, we've done this before."

"Thanks, Brice. I'm also going to need you to arrange a flight back to the States for someone. She seems to have misplaced her passport."

"Happens all the time. The consul is a personal friend."

The young man who took the car in front of Black House was businesslike. "Mr. Fleetwood wishes to know if he can be of any further service?"

"I'd like to know where you'll take her," I said. "Someday, I want to visit."

"The Gallant Garden, sir. Arbor of Heroes. It's not marked, but the caretaker can direct you."

I thanked him, and he drove away.

Showered, fed and dressed in warm bathrobes, Birdy and I stood on the third-floor balcony. She held a cup of coffee, I a glass of wine. We watched the orange spot on the Peak glow and recede, then rise again. "It seems like a long time ago," she said. "No, that's not right. It seems like it happened to someone else."

I didn't tell her that wouldn't stay the case. I put my arm around her and drew her close. Tomorrow, we would each begin the rest of our journey, but there was nothing either of us could do tonight except not be alone.

Life-altering events always affect intimate relationships. Sometimes they are intensified, more often, not. Birdy and I would never be more than friends again. We both knew it. And so, I stayed with her until she went to sleep, then got up and went into the living room.

Even the Dead Can Be Wrong

It was late afternoon when we tethered our rented Chris-Craft cruiser on the opposite side of Vuku from the abandoned submarine refueling installation. Even though the Chris's glory days were a long time past, the choppy, fifty-five-mile run over from the nearest inhabited island of the Tongan archipelago had presented no problem for her, and it had felt good to bang her into the swells. The fishing gear was pretty good too, and we'd stopped twice to put lines in the water just to make sure we weren't being followed.

I couldn't say the same for the chart the rental agent had sold us. Nothing on it conformed to the coastline we encountered, so we systematically probed the meandering inlets until we found a secluded lagoon with a rock overhang that would keep the boat out of sight from the air.

Over his protests, we'd left Jody at the row of seaside shacks that had been our hotel the previous night. If things went bad, somebody had to be healthy enough to fly us the hell out of Dodge, and no one wanted that to be me. Jody had known his role going in, but I admired his pluck.

Eddie, Coggan, Fat Cat, Wal-Mart and I checked our weapons: five AR-15s and five Colt .45s, that they had picked up during a quick stop in Samoa and a night of roast pig and Vailima with Fat Cat's extended family. Separately, I was carrying a Benelli M4 with six extra cartridges Velcroed to the barrel. I like a 12-gauge for close-in work, and choking it gives me as much knockdown as I usually need. The boom is also disorienting to the uninitiated, which can be the difference between your enemy's getting off an aimed shot or wincing as he pulls the trigger.

Special ops guys love Benellis, especially this one, but the simpletons running Sacramento wet their diapers if somebody mentions "pistol grip" on anything but a dildo. As a result, Joe Citizen can't legally shore up his home defenses with one. I suggest the legislature go on a field trip to a major drug deal and see what the gangbangers are carrying. I keep one behind a false panel in the BBJ and another on my boat that's easier to reach. I've had pirates approach me on both vehicles, and just seeing that piece of black steel made them change their minds. As for those who recently spent several days debating a bill that would regulate my tire pressure, I'll take my chances.

"You let me run a few shells through that when this is over?" I looked over at Wal-Mart, whose Mississippi drawl was as thick as his forearms. His massive bald head blocked out the sun and still seemed small on a body wider than a Kenworth's grille.

"I'll do better than that. I'll give it to you."

"No, shit?"

"No shit. I appreciate having you here. My back feels safe."

He took a long, loving look at the M4 like only a country boy could. "Fuckin' ducks better leave early this year. Right along with the animal rights assholes who've been springing my beaver traps."

Eddie broke out the food and bottled water, and we dug into crab sandwiches and Evian while Coggan and Wal-Mart went over the Sony ENG cameras again. Wal-Mart was in charge of the wide-angle, so all he had to do was make sure the tripod didn't get bumped and replace the battery pack when necessary. Coggan would be doing the close-ups, taking special care to get as much coverage as possible of our star, Markus.

We were going to be recording onto flash drives and simultaneously uploading to my London offices. When the participants arrived, every one of my media properties would break into whatever they were covering and go to Kingdom's auction. Wes's audio would go out separately, and Black Group technical people would marry it to the video with less than a ten-second delay. Conservatively, the event would be available to half a billion people as it was happening, and I expected that number to triple almost immediately. I was also willing to bet that they wouldn't get through the bidding for the first animal before somebody called Kingdom and told him he'd gone global. Just in case, I had the cell number for the ship's captain.

The lenses Coggan unpacked from their specially reinforced cases were wider, longer and far heavier than standard commercial barrels, and even someone as strong as Wal-Mart had to be careful of how they unbalanced the unit. "Any chance you're going to tell me where you picked those up?" I asked Coggan.

"Sure, right after you tell me about that kidnapping in Cuba a few years back."

"Didn't happen."

"Neither did these."

I set up a rotating watch, and we each grabbed a comfortable piece of deck and slept until midnight. I'd wanted to scout the island first, but I couldn't risk Kingdom's having posted a lookout.

As it turned out, I needn't have worried. The last people to live on Vuku had gone home to their farms and taxicabs in 1945, and the footpaths they'd left behind had fallen victim to erosion and overgrowth. Nothing without feathers had walked them for decades.

We humped our gear five very rough miles up the low bluffs to a line of a tree-shrouded caves at the highest point on the island. Despite the cool night breeze, every one of us sweated through his clothes, and even I was winded.

Once we were settled into the largest cave, Coggan and Wal-Mart went to work setting up the cameras, and I crawled to the edge of the ridge, where I could scan this side of the island with my field glasses. I was helped by a full moon, which periodically disappeared behind some of the large white clouds the South Pacific is famous for.

The mile-wide, crescent-shaped harbor was two hundred feet down the cliffs and five hundred yards distant. On the left and right sides of the U, the verdant jungle grew to the water's edge, but in the bowl, thirty yards of white sand beach buffered the tree line from the surf. A long, coral reef two miles out to sea formed a natural breakwater, and even from this distance I could hear waves thundering against it.

Not including two rusting submarine hulks in the collapsed navy pens, I counted seventeen derelict ships anchored in an uneven line to my left. The four in the worst shape were WWII leftovers: a pair of LSTs, a mine layer and a destroyer escort. The rest were abandoned freighters of varying ages, creaking and groaning as they rode their chains. Vuku was apparently where the elderly went to die.

At the end of the line and closest to our position sat the *Resurrection Bay II*. At more than nine hundred feet and another seventy up to her deck, she looked like Gulliver among the Lilliputians. Though not in a state of total decay, other than the fresh paint used to change her name, she wore her years of tropical neglect openly. Her twin cranes were minus hooks, her decks piled high with battered containers, some overturned, others crushed. Seaweed and mold crept up her sides, and the forty-foot gash the previous captain had scratched just above her waterline was wide enough that I wouldn't have trusted it in the Central Park Lagoon. I ran my binoculars over her carefully and saw no signs of life.

Fifty yards from the *Bay* sat an eighteenth vessel with a familiar paint scheme. She was clearly anything but a derelict, and her name followed an established theme:

Kingdom of Samudra

This was almost certainly Cheyenne's *Kingdom of Sam*, and it was confirmed when I saw the seam where a section of the hull opened. She was a custom-built four-hundred-foot research vessel with an exceptionally wide beam. Antennas of every description poked at the sky, while lights flooded her capacious afterdeck, revealing red and white helipad markings. The high, sharp, reinforced prow had been built to both run fast and break ice, and the boom extending from her bridge would handle several tons.

I counted four men with automatic rifles patrolling the deck. They wore blue jumpsuits and flak jackets, and the yellow embroidery on their baseball caps read KINGDOM STARR DEFENSE. I had no illusions that they were the only security. And somewhere in the big ship's bowels, nine tigers prowled their cages, sensing the tension, perhaps even aware of us.

Jackie Benveniste had texted me once saying he was having trouble reaching his contact. Now, in the dark recesses of the cave, away from the bats, I checked my cell again. The message was short: an international number and the note, 24/7 Good luck. JB. I didn't recognize the 268 country prefix, but 24/7 or not, I needed the information now. I told Fat Cat I'd be back and left the cave with my Benelli.

I headed back the way we'd come in, and after what I estimated to be a mile, I found a spot where the hillside had collapsed into the sea several hundred feet below. I was well around the island from the harbor, and my phone had a clear 180-degree throw, so I turned it on again and dialed. There was some crackling, then it smoothed out into a sequence of three short rings followed by a long silence, then repeated.

Perhaps thirty rings later, a female voice answered. The language was English and the accent African with south continent inflections.

"This is the Solomon Lubombo home, who is calling?"

"Rail Black. Jackie Benveniste gave me this number."

I heard her cover the receiver and speak to someone. Then, there was rustling, and a halting male voice come on. "This is Solomon Lubombo. Can you please tell me something about Mr. Benveniste."

I've dealt with most types of verification, but this was the first time I'd ever been asked to make up my own questions and answers. I hoped they'd given this guy the right cheat sheet.

"He's Corsican and Jewish."

"Go on."

"Bad knees. Hazard of being a paratrooper."

"Anything else?"

Christ, it wasn't like we'd grown up together. I thought about it. "He likes beer and good-looking women. Me too."

The voice laughed weakly, then coughed for a few seconds. "Our mutual friend said if you didn't mention women, you don't know Jackie."

"May I ask where I'm calling?"

"Mbabane, Swaziland."

"I've flown over but never landed."

"I recommend a short stay, but not in one of our prisons."

"I take it you have some experience."

"Until two this afternoon. Twelve years."

"Congratulations on your release."

"I'll be dead in ninety days. AIDS. Half the country has it, and everybody in prison. The government says there's no sodomy, so I figure it must be the champagne. At least I'll go out sitting in my backyard."

There wasn't much to say to that, so I didn't try.

"I understand you want to know about Rennie Holden."

"If you can, I'd appreciate it."

"Oh, I can. Mr. Holden's the reason rat has been my protein of choice for the last decade. But you'll have to wait a second, my wife needs to give me a shot."

When he came back on, he sounded weaker but still game. "We've got a rhino problem here. Not enough of them. And not enough money to protect the ones we have left. Back in the nineties, we were overrun with poachers, and you could drive all day and not see a large animal. At the same time, there were a lot of unemployed mercenaries on the continent—some waiting for the next revolution, most with nowhere else to go. Our interior ministry came up with the idea of hiring them to shoot poachers. It looked good on paper, but if you hire killers, you've got to expect they're probably going to kill something."

"I thought Rennie Holden made his living as a guide."

"He did, and he was richly commissioned to bring his high-priced clients to Swaziland rather than Tanzania or South Africa. Nobody begrudged him. We didn't have the money to compete with those other countries or the outfitters to handle the hunters if they came. Holden's was a self-contained operation, and since he only dealt with wealthy people, they spent lots of money that he got a piece of. The poachers were cutting into his pocketbook too."

"How did he get into the mercenary mix?"

"That depends on who you ask. He says he was approached by the ministry to oversee the operation. Others say he made a deal with the mercs to get them hired for a piece of their fees, then went to the poachers and offered to guide them past the protection for a share of the rhino sales."

"I'll take Door Number 2."

"That's both of us. There were also rumors that he'd had a wink and a nod from the government for years to shoot poachers. And that that was one of the reasons he had so many important clients to begin with."

"The Most Dangerous Game. Every time it comes up, people dismiss it as a myth. I'm not sure why."

"Because they haven't been to Africa, where men have been hunting other men since the dawn of time. Anyway, with Holden in charge, poaching was suddenly a very safe business and far more lucrative than stopping it. So the mercs became poachers too. The problem was there weren't that many animals to begin with, and one night a few bored soldiers of fortune wandered into a suburb of Mbabane for a little drinking and raping. When that wasn't enough, they killed three men who dared to interfere."

"Family?"

"My brother. My nine-year-old niece didn't make out too well either. I didn't care about the mercenaries. I went after Holden. Got him too. If you meet, you'll notice one of his legs doesn't bend too well."

"And you got twelve years for that?"

"I killed two of his bodyguards first."

"So the trial was a formality."

"No trial at all. I ran a small auto shop, and Holden had dinner with the king. The meeting lasted ten minutes—at the palace. I didn't get to speak."

"Is there anything I can do for you?"

"Unfortunately, no. I do have something else you might be interested in, though. Your biggest enemy is prison is boredom. I occupied my time staying up on Rennie Holden. He lives on a thousand-acre estate now. Drives a Bentley that used to be owned by Adnan Khashoggi. He also belongs to some very exclusive clubs."

"And you can't do that just by guiding people to an occasional cape buffalo."

"Not even a lot of occasional buffaloes."

No you can't. Rennie Holden was still hunting men. Only now, that was all he was hunting. Jake's words came flying back to me. *His partner turned him in because he'd been cheated out of a million dollars. And if that wasn't enough, Markus-baby fucked the guy's wife and left a kid for him to raise.*

I thanked Mr. Lubombo and hung up. I stared at the stars for a long time, getting angrier the longer I stood there. *Rennie Holden was on that goddamn cargo ship.* Smithson, the man Cheyenne Rollins had met in Perth, was there too, and who knew how many others? Coggan's phrase was "broken patterns and nonevident relationships." What was more nonevident than the beautiful, diminutive Lucille Brando hiring killers? This was a *fucking manhunt,* not a rescue. And a ship named *Resurrection Bay* was a tool for aggressors not victims.

The only open question was whether Lucille had gone looking for them or they had come to her. But did it really matter? Either way, this group wouldn't blink at shooting other men. And then there was Holden. A man settling a decades-overdue personal debt with Kingdom. Lucille had dragged me into this, not to be the hero of the moment, but to take control of the tigers after the bloodshed. Because if left to Holden, he'd do what came naturally. Kill them and sell the parts.

I'd gone from being presumed upon to manipulated, and I didn't like the cut of either suit. In case she were listening, I said out loud, "Lucille, you're dead, and I'm sorry about that, but goddamn you. Goddamn you." Then I shut off the phone and headed back to the cave. Part of me, though, had to give her a nod. There was nothing Crimson could have done to her to make her talk.

I led the team back down the mountain at a sharp pace. Even under a full moon, it was too fast, but I was trying to work off some of my fury. Finally, Fat Cat just stopped, and the others did too, gasping for breath. When I realized they weren't behind me, I went back, but the detective waved me on. "I don't know what your problem is, but get it out of your system before one of us ends up paying a price because you have your head up your ass."

That should have pulled me up short, but it didn't. It was irrational, of course, but even professionals lose their cool. It's why there are dead professionals.

When they got to the boat, I'd already stowed my gear. I wasn't any less pissed, but I was on top of it. I filled everybody in on my conversation with Mr. Lubombo. Fat Cat beat me to the bottom line. "And you can't broadcast a massacre. I get it. So now what?"

"What I hate more than anything. Make it up as we go along."

But Fat Cat wasn't quite finished with my attitude. "I just want to clear up one thing. Are you angry because you were handled or because of who did it?"

"I've been dancing on the head of this pin since the night Chuck and Lucille were murdered. I don't like being the last guy invited to the party and expected to clean it up."

Fat Cat wasn't cutting me any slack. "Welcome to the world, Rail. But in case you haven't noticed, the woman's dead. D-E-A-D, dead. So grab your emotions by the balls, stuff your ego in your Rolls, and lead. That's L-E-A-D, lead. We signed on to follow you, remember?"

He was right, and I told him so. Then I placed a call to the Black Group tech center in London and told them they could all head out for a few pints—on the company.

"Thanks, sir, but the team will be disappointed," the supervisor said.

"I'll make it up to everybody at Christmas."

"Those, sir, are the magic words. Good night."

45

Jack Daniel's and Uriah Heep

Eddie had tipped the rental agent to load a few bottles of Jack Daniel's aboard. I don't like booze anywhere near a mission, but this wasn't a crowd that had an alcohol problem, and if he wanted to celebrate on the way home, I couldn't argue. Now, he broke open the box and handed quarts around. "Pour half on the deck," he said. "It'll look and smell like we've been at it all day."

"Pour out Jack?" blurted Wal-Mart. "Not gonna happen," and he searched around until he found a Tupperware container to take his excess. The other three poured enough Old No. 7 sour mash around to get the boat and themselves really stinking, then we baited the hooks and stuck the rods in the deck holders.

"Make sure none of those lines get in the water," said Eddie. "It might get a little wild."

"How about some music?" said Fat Cat. He fooled with the radio, getting mostly static until a loud, clear voice broke through the night. "Hey, assholes. Wake the fuck up. Mo Pidgeon here holding down Subic Bay. Passed out in Lottie's and when I woke up, the fleet was gone. Jesus, I can't tell you how much I miss Captain Shitheel and the United States

Fuckin' Navy. So wherever you assholes are, here's another blast of classic rock while I do a few lines of Manila prime and this little babe here gives me a blow job."

"So much for Armed Forces Radio," I said.

Fat Cat laughed. "Man's been on the air as long as I can remember. Parents used to beat their kids if they caught us listening, except they had it on in the next room. He must have some powerful equipment because it always sounds like he's right next door. Buckle up your Nehru jacket, he plays some really old shit."

Just as Cream blew into "White Room," Eddie brought the Chris to life, headed out of the lagoon and turned up the coast. As we rolled north, the Kinks and Country Joe were each able to get in a song, and I'm sure they could hear us coming all the way to Honolulu.

As Mo Pidgeon introduced Uriah Heep and "July Morning," Eddie turned the corner into the harbor, and yelled, "I always wanted to direct. Roll film." I didn't have time to tell him we were shooting digital before he opened the throttle and accelerated toward the sub pens. The Chris's nose came out of the water and Coggan and Wal-Mart brought their cameras up while Fat Cat sang with Uriah and swigged Jack.

Eddie spun around the first LST, then proceeded to slalom through the rest of the rust buckets without coming off the gas. As we exited from behind the *Resurrection Bay II,* Wal-Mart fired two flares over the *Samudra,* and Fat Cat dialed the music up to ear-bleed.

As I was wondering what Kingdom Starr Defense was thinking, they showed me. Five 150-million-candlepower xenon searchlights hit the Chris, turning it into a tanning bed. Everybody abovedecks was blinded, and I crouched low in the cabin and pulled a blanket over my head to preserve my night vision. In the several acres of bay between the two ships, Eddie zigged, zagged, slowed, sped up and threw the cruiser into turns that had the railings underwater. The men handling the *Samudra*'s lights tried to keep up, but lost us more often than not. Uriah was heading into their final crescendo, when two Zodiacs appeared and flanked the cruiser's wake.

Eddie shouted, "Grab on to something!" and I felt a surge of power as he headed directly at the *Bay*. I braced for the turn but was still tossed across the cabin when it came. At its apex, I rolled to the door, regained my feet, mounted the steps and hurled myself into space, hoping the water was where I'd left it. I landed on my back and disappeared into the murky sea, shocked as always by the cold of the Pacific. I was shocked even more by the burning in my eyes and nose. The *Bay* was sitting in an ocean of fuel.

I quickly checked that my Colt and Maglite were still buttoned into my cargo pockets. They were. Then, seeing only the moon overhead, I allowed myself to drift to the surface. It wasn't much better there. The fumes were strong enough to sear my lungs.

Eddie was still racing around the harbor, firing flares and dodging lights and Zodiacs, but he had taken the action well away from me. I used a smooth breaststroke to cover the twenty yards to the *Bay*'s hull, hoping none of the fireworks landed nearby.

The gash was bigger than I thought, but it was also more treacherous, the peeled-back steel plates rusty and jagged. And then, I felt rather than saw the searchlight coming and dropped back under before I could take a full breath.

The beam stopped directly over me and sat there. Eyes on fire, I kicked a few yards left and started to ascend, but the light moved too. My lungs were beginning to ache, and I grabbed my nose to prevent involuntarily inhalation. Another light appeared, crossing the first. I couldn't go backward, the ship was there, the searchlights had me bracketed, and the moon might as well have been the sun. I was dead.

My chest screaming, I dove and swam as hard as I could directly at the *Samudra*. My vision began to blur as oxygen deprivation set in. Your body will not allow you to hold your breath until you black out, so it was going to breathe for me pretty soon if I didn't do it myself. I broke the surface, trying not to gasp too loudly. I was stunned by how far my adrenaline had taken me. Too far, but at least the fumes weren't as bad. Then, here came Eddie, music and all, followed by the Zodiacs. I took in all the air I could and dove.

This time when I got to the *Bay*'s hull, I didn't waste time assessing. I stripped off my T-shirt, threw it over the rough metal, pulled myself up and leveraged myself inside. I fell several feet and into eighteen inches of fuel-fouled water, and something slithered past my face that I was glad I couldn't see. A moment later, a searchlight swept over the gash with my shirt still hanging there. As it passed, I reached up and pulled it in.

Then I heard gunfire. A lot of it, and the searchlight on the gash disappeared. I stood and saw Eddie firing off another flare, then he pulled alongside the *Samudra* and turned off the music. His challenge was as clear where I stood as if I had been aboard. "Hey, kill those lights, motherfucker!"

The voice that called back was calmer, but not by much. "Shut the fuck up and identify yourself. And turn off those fuckin' cameras."

Guns or no guns, fucks and motherfuckers, nobody can intimidate Eddie. Ask any of the airlines that fired him. "Fuck you. Call a cop."

I saw some of the searchlights go out, but one stayed on the Chris. Then the voice said, "Jesus Christ, is that you, Saleapaga?"

"Get that fuckin' light out of my eyes," Fat Cat roared. "Who's talking?"

"Perry Duke."

"Jesus Christ, the LAPD send you all the way out here just because you shot your baby's mama? Whatever happened to desk duty in South Central?"

"You were never funny, asshole." Duke signaled somebody, and a volley of shots ripped into the water. "What are you doin' out here?"

"In case you forgot, you're in my backyard. My daddy was bringin' me here to fish when I was four."

That stopped Duke for a moment. "Who's with you? More sheriff assholes? Goddamn it, turn off those fuckin' cameras."

"A&E's doing a special. *Samoan with a Badge.* This here's the crew. We just got a call that we've been picked up for a series, and we're celebrating. What do you think of that, asshole? I'm a star."

"What are you doin' with that phone?" Duke shouted.

"Textin' my undersheriff. Tellin' him who I just met on the high seas."

"Don't!"

"Too late. You got a lot of fans. They'll love seein' you in that outfit. How many times did you wash out of SWAT? Five? Six? Must feel kinda like when you used to play dress-up with your sister."

Duke's voice was cold. "I suggest you follow the Zodiacs around to the ladder. And don't give them a reason to blow your asses away."

"You were never too bright, so maybe I should explain something. What we're shootin' is going live to the editin' room. Right now, ten guys in LA are watchin' this and making sure your face is color corrected. So, go fuck yourself, Duke. We're gonna go catch ourselves some fish."

With that, Eddie jammed the throttle forward again, and the Chris headed toward the open sea. Perry Duke didn't move, but neither did the Zodiacs. Round one to the good guys. I had exactly thirty minutes.

I felt my way into the interior of the ship and turned on the Maglite. I was getting light-headed from the fumes, and I didn't understand how anybody could be sitting out here and not know they were on top of a bomb. I followed the stream on the floor to the starboard side fuel storage tanks. Someone had opened a valve on the first tank, and a steady flow of #2 diesel was running across the deck. Numbers two and three were the same.

I tried to put what had happened to my wife and child out of my mind and focus. Whoever had done this probably wasn't expecting to die, so he had an escape route somewhere. And he wasn't going to have a lot of time, so it had to be close to zero hour.

Since the dawn of shipbuilding, there has been one constant. Military, merchant or some other working vessel, except for the captain's quarters, creature comforts are the last consideration. On the water, every cubic inch is either productive or deadweight, sucking energy and money out of the trip. In the early days, a lot of captains got heaved overboard for no other reason than anger at the inequity.

The most likely place to find my quarry was the common area where off-duty deckhands congregate. Every operator blueprints it differently, and some divide the space into several smaller rooms, but it's almost always in the windowless interior of the vessel near the galley. That's where I headed.

Five stories up, I stepped into a tiny linoleum-floored space where a pair of institutional picnic tables grew out of the floor. The smell of fuel hadn't reached here yet. I tried three doors before I found one that opened. It was a dimly lighted exercise room where a rack of free weights sat against one wall, flanked by two treadmills that had seen better days. The rest of the equipment was overturned or broken or both. A good-sized rat was chewing on something green, and he glanced at me, then resumed his meal.

I crossed the space and stood in a dark corner. I heard a voice on the other side of the wall. I couldn't make out what was being said before it stopped. I waited and listened. When it came again, it was emphatic. "No, I'm not going up for a look. Weiss and Boudreaux can see what's going on, and if they're not concerned, neither am I. Besides, it's quiet out there now."

"You'll go, or you'll wish you had. We don't vote, you take orders." The accent was Australian, but through the wall, I couldn't tell if it was Holden or not. There was, however, no mistaking its anger.

"Fuck you. You couldn't work for me for ten minutes."

"We're not building houses here, Capelli. Do as I tell you. Now."

There was murmuring and the sound of a chair being pushed back. "Two weeks sitting in this sweatbox eating shit food, and . . ."

"Go."

I heard footsteps coming in my direction, and I melted against the wall. The man who came through the door was overweight and breathing hard, but his bush clothes looked like they'd been custom-made. As he passed, I stepped behind him, put my forearm around his neck and jerked him hard. He let out a little gasp, struggled, then became dead-weight.

I dragged him back to the stairwell and waited until he got enough blood to his brain to revive. He couldn't see me, but he could sense that I was much bigger than he was, and he began whimpering.

"Please, whoever you are, don't hurt me. I didn't want to come. Really, I didn't."

I grabbed him by the balls and twisted them, simultaneously shoving my Colt down his throat to stifle his cries. He gagged and made a sound like a terrified kitten. "How many?" I spit. "Show me with your fingers."

He managed to hold up five fingers, and I twisted his nut sack again. "Counting you?"

He nodded emphatically.

"Okay, two on deck. Probably in containers. Which ones?"

He couldn't talk around five inches of steel, so I pulled the .45 out halfway. His words were garbled but intelligible. "The ones partly open in the back for ventilation."

"Are the other two in the room where you were?"

He nodded again.

"My best to Rennie." And I smashed the Colt into his temple. He was out immediately.

I retraced my steps, but as I entered the exercise room, something was wrong. The door Capelli had come through was standing wide open. I went through it low, my .45 ready. It was a lounge. Some tattered La-Z-Boys, two TVs, an ancient Pac-Man console and a long table with ten chairs.

There were two cups of steaming coffee on the table. Other than that, the place was empty.

But it was the long wall opposite the table that got my attention. I counted sixteen thirty-six-by-thirty-six color drawings of Asian men, each extremely detailed, down to the pattern on each man's shirt. Some had names under them, others didn't.

Northcutt had been right. Milt O'Keefe's work was way beyond that of any police artist I'd ever seen. The girls returning from Hong Kong had brought back the only photographs they could take—the ones in their mind's eye—and O'Keefe had coaxed their memories to life.

I saw the several neat folds in each one, which confirmed that these were what Lucille had been shipping to Parkinson-Lowe every month. And what Rennie Holden and his shooting team had studied in preparation for the hunt.

"The Animal Kingdom's Most Wanted. All except the boss, but then we all know what he looks like," a voice said.

I turned and saw Holden and another older man standing in the doorway, leveling a pair of .30-06s at me. I'd violated the first rule of special ops. I'd gotten distracted.

"You must be Foster Smithson," I said to the older gentleman.

"Very good. Rennie said you were the wild card. I'm just sorry we had to meet like this. You would have made a welcome addition to the team. Please place your weapon on the table."

From his tone and ease, I now knew who Rennie took orders from. I also knew that, depending on how the rounds in their rifles were jacketed, I was looking at an exit wound the size of a saucer or a Michelin. Either way, most of my insides would be racing the slug to the wall. I very carefully did what I was told.

I wasn't sure I was right, but I didn't have many cards to play. I looked at Smithson. "Does Rennie know he's sitting on top of Hiroshima? He doesn't smoke, does he?"

I'd caught him off guard, but he recovered nicely. "No, none of us do. One of the prerequisites."

Holden had no idea what I meant, but he now knew there was a loop out there he wasn't in. "What the fuck is he talking about?"

I decided to go all the way. "Weiss and Boudreaux are dead too, right?"

Smithson didn't like that, which meant it was true. "Too much talk. What did you do with our chubby friend?" he asked.

"He couldn't keep his eyes open, but that's just fine too, isn't it? You didn't ever intend to kill Kingdom. Why would you? You're in this with him."

Without warning, Smithson suddenly jerked the butt of his rifle up and jammed Rennie Holden in the jaw, hard. Holden reeled backward, dropping his weapon and going to his knees. I started for my Colt, but Smithson recovered quickly, and I thought better of it.

Smithson kicked the second rifle under the table, and Holden got up, shakily. The cool Aussie looked at me with interest. "When did you know?"

"Not until a few minutes ago. Your reaction when Ms. Rollins told you Zhang had survived the sinking of the *Richer Seas* should have been my first indication, but I completely missed it. Even when it came back to me a little while ago, I still put it down as your wanting to get him yourself. Then I met Capelli. You don't set out to kill a man who has his own army with an out-of-shape, wheezy deputy. Weiss and Boudreaux were probably second-stringers too, am I right?"

"They were competent, but they'd never hunted men before."

I nodded. "You had to bring Rennie, but he was so blinded by rage, he was easy to manipulate."

"He's also a fool. A useful one, but a fool nonetheless. He would have wiped out half the power structure in Asia because his wife got knocked up back before time began. Can you imagine anything so ridiculous?"

Holden was finally getting to the party. "You mean to tell me you're in business with Kingdom?"

Smithson scoffed. "Wake up, Rennie. I'm money, Kingdom is money, and our business is more money. Black understands, he's money too. Guys like you are useful to us, then you're not."

While I was pondering Foster Smithson's insight to our moneyed souls, I heard a helicopter approaching. I knew that sound. It was a Chinook.

"No longer any reason for silence," Smithson said, and he turned and shot Rennie Holden in the face. If you haven't seen a high-powered-rifle bullet hit a head, it's not like a handgun wound. Actually, there's no wound at all. The velocity of the round coupled with the slightly pressurized, part liquid, part pulp of the brain causes the head to explode. Literally.

Holden took two steps forward before his body figured out there wasn't anybody calling the shots, and he pitched forward. I didn't waste the opportunity. I lunged at Smithson, but he Lee Harveyed the bolt action and got off another shot while I was still in the air. I heard the crack of the bullet break the sound barrier as it went past my ear.

I got one hand on his shoulder, but all it did was spin him around. He racked another shell and fired again. But this time, he was just taking pot luck, and he came up with borscht. I rolled into his legs, and he went down, but not before he caught me in the forehead with the rifle's stock. While I was trying to find a handhold on him, he slithered away and ran toward the deck.

It was still dark outside, and Smithson had disappeared into the three football fields of containers. I checked until I found an open one. Inside was another .30-06 next to either Boudreaux's or Weiss's body. I didn't think he'd miss it.

Fifty yards across the water, the helipad floodlights were on, and a civilian Chinook in Kingdom Starr colors was dropping onto the deck of the *Samudra*, its twin rotors rippling the harbor halfway to where I stood. I saw a pair of elevator doors open in the deck and a large covered cage ascend. The Chinook was loud, but the blood-chilling scream of the tiger was louder. It penetrated me to the bone.

Before the rotors came to a full stop, the chopper's door opened, and Markus Kingdom stepped out, followed by Zhang. A moment later, Crimson, back in her red and black leather, appeared. The three descended to the deck where they were met by Perry Duke and a man in uniform, who I assumed was the *Samudra*'s captain.

After them came the bidders. I looked carefully at each, recognizing one or two, then I saw Quan. He had the same surly walk as his attitude, and he ignored the offered hand of the captain.

Suddenly, one of the floodlights turned toward the *Bay*, illuminating a section near the stern. I couldn't be sure, but I thought I saw a man's arms waving down there. On the *Samudra*, Kingdom pointed and said something to Duke. It wouldn't be long before a Zodiac arrived, perhaps several. I checked my watch. Eddie and the others would be just rounding the tip of the island, but all that meant was that they were going to be dead before they knew what hit them.

I don't possess the Zen qualities of a professional sniper, but I am very respectful of those who do. Their willingness to operate unsung and far from any support has saved countless lives, mine included. I have no compunction about long-distance killing, but I haven't had to do much. This time, I was looking forward to it.

I lay on the deck, concealed by containers, and looked through the scope. It was a magnificent weapon, probably ten grand worth of expert craftsmanship supporting another two grand of Zeiss. All to push a two-dollar slug on a one-way trajectory to destiny.

I didn't even have to think about it. I centered the crosshairs . . . slowly let out my breath . . . and squeezed the trigger. The bullet caught Crimson under her sternum, lifted her off her feet and threw her backward. When she landed, she looked like all the bones in her body were broken. They weren't, of course, but the rag-doll finale added to the satisfaction.

Zhang was a little more difficult. He was the son of a soldier and used to living outside the law. His instincts took over, and he ran, crouching behind the tiger cage. But he didn't know where the shot had come from, which is never good, and the top of his head was visible. And then he didn't have a top of his head to be concerned with.

I wanted Kingdom next, but he was caught in the scramble to get back on the Chinook, and though most of the Asians probably deserved to die, they weren't my call. Instead, I shot Perry Duke. I hoped his late partner was watching.

The chopper began revving its engines long before everyone was aboard, and I waited for the scrum at the foot of the stairway to clear so I could get a good look at Kingdom. Suddenly, I saw a flash out of the corner of my eye, and a bullet slammed into the container next to me. Wherever Smithson was, he could see me, and that wasn't good.

I rolled until I found new cover and waited for him to show himself. When he didn't, and there were no more shots, I suspected that he was on his way to the outside stairway. If so, he wasn't my problem right now.

Kingdom had finally gotten on the helicopter stairs, and the earlier terror among the bidders had grown to a full panic. I had just placed the crosshairs on his chest when several pairs of hands reached up and dragged him down. As he fell, his foot caught in the metal steps, and he slammed back first onto the deck, his leg twisted at a gruesome angle. I watched through the scope as several men began kicking him, then, suddenly, the crowd's fury grew, and more joined in. The pilot was gesturing frantically out the window that he wanted to go, but the mob wouldn't or couldn't stop. Markus Kingdom was unrecognizable now, and as he gasped for breath, red spray flew out of his mouth.

Finally, the Asians scrambled over him, and, when the last was inside, the chopper began to lift off with the stairway still down. Kingdom's head banged along the deck, until the Chinook was finally airborne. The Baron of Victorville hung upside down, his arms flailing, until the aircraft reached a few hundred feet. Suddenly, several men appeared in the doorway and began pulling at the stairs. A moment later, the man who most deserved to die, obliged us all and dropped slowly through the air until he splashed heavily into the sea.

I ran to the *Bay*'s outside stairway. This side of the ship was bathed only in moonlight, but it was enough to see Foster Smithson trying to start the outboard on a small inflatable he must have had hidden on deck. I made sure I had a clear path to the opposite side railing, then aimed and put a round through the tiny gas tank.

I expected the *whoosh*. What I hadn't thought about was that it would travel under the ship and lift thousands of tons of Norwegian steel skyward, breaking it in half as it ascended. I sprinted across the wildly tilting deck, hit the top of the railing with my right foot and launched myself as far as possible up and out as shrapnel raced flames toward the moon.

It wasn't the prettiest dive I'd ever done, but it was a lot prettier than the one I'd done off Victoria Peak.

The Uncontacted

As it turned out, it wasn't difficult to convince the *Samudra*'s captain that sailing with us wasn't an act of piracy. Like most ships, she was insured by Lloyds, and as a syndicate member, I could purchase a share of her risk. With Kingdom at the bottom of the harbor, his death duly witnessed and attested to by three parties, I had myself declared acting agent for the insurer and took legal possession to protect all interests.

She was such a magnificently built vessel, I immediately put my London office to work to acquire her. We didn't do oceanic research ourselves, but we do lease to those who do. I had no doubt the *Samudra* would quickly pay her way.

We sailed northwest out of Vuku, staying outside the major shipping lanes and well off the coast of the Solomons. The last thing I wanted to run into were pirates with bigger balls than brains. With the heavy firepower Kingdom kept aboard, we had enough artillery and the willingness to use it to thwart any attack, but I didn't need some Third World pussy who'd read too many UN human rights press releases to send out an SOS in hopes of a lawsuit.

At the tip of the hump of Western New Guinea, the Mamberamo River empties at Point D'Urville. Like the Nile, the river flows north, carrying sediment from the Van Rees Mountains of the interior into the Bismarck Sea and turning the water white for miles. Just south of this churning of fresh and salt waters is one of the last great unexplored rain forests of the world, where trees grow so closely together one cannot find space to walk, and where not even my beloved Amazon can match what is unknown about it.

The *Samudra* had no difficulty handling the current, but the river's sandbars ebb and flow daily, making them unchartable—even if there were someone around to notice. Several times the captain was required to perform magic to unground us, often at the expense of hours. I couldn't have cared less. Seeing what God made the way He made it suspends time. And for those who don't believe in God, He suspends time for you too.

Fat Cat, Coggan, Wal-Mart, Eddie and I sat on the bow watching the endless green, the crocodiles, parrots and dinner-plate-sized butterflies and rarely saying anything to one another. That's when you know you're truly among friends. When you don't have to speak to share.

I'd planned go fifty miles, but at the forty-two mark, the river suddenly narrowed into a deep valley of towering trees and hundreds of tiny inlets. Monkeys chattered at us, and we were dive-bombed by a green-and-white bird with the wingspan of a vulture who seemed to be saying, "Far enough."

I told the captain to secure the ship, and we went down into the hold. The tigers had become animated and were prowling their cages with an almost manic energy. I'd slept down here each night, and now I sensed I was no longer welcome. I pressed the buttons to open the wide aft bay, and the door slid back. Another series of controls sent a ramp down into the water, and Wal-Mart and Fat Cat pushed the first cage to the edge. It contained a large female who had seemed to be the most restless in captivity.

I wanted to say something prescient, perhaps historic, but it is the height of hubris to speak when what you are seeing is beyond words. I nodded, and Wal-Mart opened the cage. The big female didn't even pause. She bolted out, down the ramp and splashed into the river. Fat Cat looked at me as if to reassure himself, and I nodded. Of all the mammals in creation, there are probably no better swimmers than tigers.

When the last had been released, we once again went topside. My associates and the crew stood amidships watching the nine striped swimmers race toward their new home. New Guinea has no history of tigers, no myths, no religion built around them and no commerce that requires them. And here, in this final frontier, is the last major collection of uncontacted peoples. The tigers couldn't fare any worse than they had under the contacted ones.

As I looked down at their rippling orange and black muscles, I was reminded of my father. He never released any tigers, but he was a keen observer of life. Our Derbyshire home is filled with books, art and the remnants of his conquests and failures. As a young boy, these mementos had been fascinating. A piton from his scaling of K2. The screw from a sunken liner he'd owned. The deck of cards that had won him a kitchen slave in some sheikdom who he'd brought back to London and now ran Black Group's hotel division.

He had constantly sought out the most difficult challenges and conquered them. He gave great sums to rescue the less fortunate, but his trophy room contained the most-soughtafter of big-game prizes. He was always clear that men were men, and animals were not. There was no doubt he would have done what I had done, but I wondered what he would have said about killing so many men to do it.

There was no answer, so I would have to wrap myself in the cloak of the evils Kingdom had perpetrated. That and that I had been trained to kill, which is exactly what I had done.

I walked forward to the prow of the *Samudra* and saw the female make landfall. She shook herself violently for a few seconds, then turned and looked back at the ship. Those watching cheered, and she swung around and bolted into the jungle.

Several stories below was the gray water, and I reached into my pocket and brought out the gold band Regina had given me. I noticed for the first time that it had several strands of her hair caught in its clasp. I kissed it and tossed the band toward the water as the last of the tigers disappeared into the bush.

"A thousand miles," I said.

Pink Cats and Yellow Stearmans

We gathered on the main deck an hour before dusk. The *Sanrevelle* was parked at almost exactly the same spot where we'd said good-bye to Bert, but this time there was no wind, and the Pacific was as placid as its name. To accommodate the crowd, Mallory had slid the curved wall of glass between the salon and afterdeck all the way open, creating one grand space. I'd also suspended the shoe rule, so the ladies could dress all the way up. Dominick, my deck-refinishing guy, was probably out shopping for a BMW.

Cheyenne was wearing something lacy, white and split high up the side, capped by a fragrant, flowing tiara made of hundreds of miniature rose petals the floral artists at Black Iris had spent the better part of a week weaving. At a natural six feet, extended several more inches in heels, she was a vision.

"She looks like a Renoir, doesn't she?" said Brittany Rixon, who was clutching my left arm. She did, I just didn't know what Pierre-Auguste would have made of the acre of silk and matching shoes Fat Cat was sporting. He claimed the color was coral. Eddie, who'd been with him when he bought it, thought it looked more like salmon. They were both wrong. It was pink, but I wasn't going to be the one to tell him.

I made a survey of the guests. Coggan had flown in from Mississippi with his latest girlfriend, Missy, a grad student who looked a little seasick. They were standing with Liz, Eddie's wife, along with Wal-Mart, who'd somehow located a suit that almost fit. Manarca, not surprisingly, was escorting one of his UCLA angels of mercy. Nurses and cops. Professions that should probably steer clear of each other but can't.

Yale Maywood, in dress blues and polished brass, had brought Mrs. Maywood, who looked like she spent most of her life pretending to be deaf every time her husband launched into a story. Yale, who I had forgiven, had conveyed the chief's regrets about having a prior commitment, and I couldn't have been happier. There's only so much pomposity even a large yacht can hold.

Julius Watson, not in uniform, had graced us with his presence and stood with Jake, who was squiring Vivian DeLamielleure, supposedly the world's highest-paid foot model. All I could say was that if her dogs were half as alluring as the rest of her, they were worth every penny.

And Birdy. The trainer of next year's Derby favorite and Triple Crown contender had been all over the papers lately. But not for her handling of MrSaturdayDance. Her ascension to gossip prominence was because of the romance between Saturday's owner and the best-looking horse whisperer to ever stroll through a paddock. They made a lovely couple, though the thirty years difference in their ages was going to be interesting as time went on. But that's why there's a Vegas.

I caught a glimpse of Astaire Cañada's pretty face. She possessed an air of dignity rarely seen anymore, and I counted meeting her and Fabian as one of the better moments in my life.

The minister was my find. When I feel the need to regroup spiritually, I wander over to Hoag Hospital and sit in the chapel. Usually, it's just me, my thoughts and maybe somebody worrying about a patient, but the last couple of times, a young man in jeans, flip-flops and a clerical collar was there, praying quietly with anybody who asked. He looked more like a surfer than a pastor, and I got curious.

It turned out the thirtysomething Reverend Rudy Hilton had OD'd on Presbyterian politics, left his Oregon church and begun traveling up and down the coast in an old VW van, conducting services on whatever beach he happened to land. He said he met a lot of people who hadn't been near organized religion since they were kids, and the work renewed his spirit as much as theirs. Exactly my kind of guy, and exactly right for this event. His shaggy, curly blonde hair and bare feet didn't get a second look, except from the foot model, who might have been weighing his Madison Avenue prospects—or more likely, how to shake Jake for half an hour.

The rest of the forty or so guests were an assortment of cops, Vegas types, my better-behaved friends and a few fellow boaters from the club. A rough check of ethnicities would have gratified Justice Sotomayor but had forehead veins bulging among the Beijing secret police. Far too many freedom-loving Chinese.

Someone had suggested inviting Suzanne Chang, but I'd stopped the conversation in its tracks. The tragedy that had befallen her family was grievous, but that was the point. When her turn came to be counted, she'd wrapped herself in self-pity and opted out. I don't like contests where no one keeps score or where spectators are invited to the team banquet. After I gave that speech, Astaire looked relieved.

I'd spent the morning at Jake's office. It was the day after Christmas, and the firm was technically closed, but I wanted to wrap up Chuck's and Lucille's affairs before the tax laws changed with the new year. Jake had persuaded the Brandos' estate lawyer, Ernie DeHoff, to give up his golf game at Hillcrest by promising double fees and a chance to meet me. I'd have paid more to have been spared the leering, garlicky grin and nonstop sales pitch. Jake also hauled in a paralegal and his secretary, Stella. I knew they'd show up on my bill as well, and I wondered how generous I was going to be.

My plan was straightforward, but the mechanics were going to take time to sort out; the politics even longer. The good news was that Astaire had taken the reins firmly, and it appeared she intended to make a career of it. To help her, I commandeered a willing Brice and Molly Fleetwood, whose contacts would be invaluable.

After providing for some special people, Chuck and Lucille's property would be liquidated and the proceeds, along with Chuck's ongoing publishing and movie royalties, would be placed into the Brandó Children's Trust. The trust would open its first free clinic in Hu-Wei, then expand into small villages throughout the country.

To secure Beijing's cooperation, everyone agreed that the baby-smuggling business would end—immediately. From this point forward, the trust and the Interior Ministry would work together to place all unwanted children with families in China. Only in extreme cases would adoptive parents outside the country be sought, which Astaire guaranteed would happen the first time a disabled child was involved.

To prove her point, she made two phone calls, and suddenly, the four-year-old with the missing leg that Sherry Huston would have been carrying home to Chuck and Lucille was on a plane to Los Angeles. Astaire was now speaking with community leaders in Chinatowns around the world and assembling a list of eager parents for similar children who would follow.

Until suitable quarters were found, I offered Black House as the trust headquarters. The place sat empty 90 percent of the time, and a few crying infants might get rid of the ghosts.

I was brought back to the present by murmuring behind me, then a smattering of applause that built until it swept the ship. Special Agent in Charge Francesca Huston, wearing a white sundress trimmed in teal, straw hat festooned with teal flowers and teal heels parted the throng. In her left arm, she carried Cheyenne's baby, who was wide-awake and taking in everything. Cheyenne had named her Sherry, and Dr. Hadley Carson at Children's Hospital of Orange County had gotten one of his colleagues to perform surgical magic. Her new smile embraced everyone.

Holding on to Francesca's right hand was the little boy, dressed in a sharp white coat, razor-creased white shorts, white socks and shoes. He looked like he was on his way to his yacht, and he walked on his new prosthetic leg like he'd been born with it. That's the thing about kids. They adapt. With Brittany's help, Bert's old company had fitted him with their best. He'd get a new one every six weeks, and all he had to do was let the technicians shoot some digital footage every now and then and maybe come out to cheer at his Little League games.

Francesca handed Sherry to Cheyenne, and Fat Cat reached down and swept his new son, Davey, into his arms. David Saleapaga II. Hopefully, somewhere, Fat Cat's father was watching.

The man in pink beamed as he placed a meaty paw around Cheyenne's waist. Davey put his hand on Sherry's head, and she immediately reached up and grabbed her brother's wrist. I heard catches in throats, including Brittany's, and saw people dab their eyes. Birdy begged a tissue from a woman next to her. My eyes were a little damp, but I'm allergic to rabbits, so somebody probably had one in their pocket.

United States District Judge Federico Cavalcante stood off to the side. Lords of the courts, federal judges can do just about anything they want, and bureaucrats usually scramble to help or scramble faster to get out of the way. Thanks to Cavalcante's jutting jaw and a compliant immigration official, the newest citizens of the United States were about to watch their parents get married.

The Reverend Rudy began, "We have come together in the presence of God . . ."

I'd been hugged by everybody except Jake, and if he tried, he was going over the side. Emilio's staff had poured each guest a flute of Blanc de Blanc, and as people sipped, the pitch of the conversation rose momentarily, then began to drift as we waited.

Jody's yellow Stearman was just a speck in the eastern sky, but the setting sun glittered off its windshield as he nosed the little biplane down below five hundred feet. The guests who were in the salon came back out and found places along the railing.

I'd asked Jody to make a circle around the *Sanrevelle,* then climb southwestward, and he did exactly that, slowing to what amounted to a crawl. Eddie sat behind him in the open-air cockpit, and they were close enough that I could see the tightness on their faces. Neither had ever done this before.

Jody gave the Stearman a wing waggle, then pulled back on the stick and throttled up. The scene seemed to stand still as they became a silhouette against the massive orange sphere sinking into the sea. Eddie's arm went over the side and turned the canister of ashes upside down. They fanned out and trailed behind the plane for a while, then disappeared. I gave Fabian Cañada a final salute.

A handsome young navy bugler named Pettigrew had driven down from Port Hueneme, and his mournful "Taps" filled the gathering twilight. When the last note had died away, Mallory put Fred Astaire's "One for My Baby" through the *Sanrevelle*'s sound system. Our copy was a little scratchy, but that somehow seemed right, and in unison, everyone lifted their glasses to the sky, held them there for a few seconds, then pulled them down and drank.

"Good night, Fabian," Astaire said quietly. I took her hand and squeezed it.

And then, Sherry gurgled with laughter, and everyone smiled.

"I think she's calling for you, Grandma."

I took her flute and watched her stride purposefully toward her new family. A moment later, Astaire and Sherry, two people who had gone into the unforgiving sea almost seven decades apart—and survived in the arms of strangers—were putting their arms around each other. I had no doubt, each felt safe tonight.

Epilogue

Eddie was in New Orleans with his family—Coggan included this time—so Jody had to find a stand-in right-seater for my trip. He selected a sharp-looking young lady who had just been laid off from Air Canada. Dominique LaChapelle had a couple of thousand hours in 737s, not to mention a nicely tuned French-Canadian accent and a pair of beautiful brown eyes—not that Jody would have been influenced by them. I did notice the way he looked at her, however, and I didn't think he was going to mind if we were on the road a few weeks.

Ms. LaChapelle passed muster with me as well. She answered my questions in a clipped, professional manner that imparted confidence. The last thing you want in a pilot is obsequiousness—or long explanations to yes or no questions.

Mallory was on his way to Rome to meet up with his paramour, Jannicke Thorsen. I'd arranged the trip as a surprise. Well, not personally. Somewhere in my holdings is a chunk of British Airways stock, and though it's not likely to make me richer, I keep it for sentimental reasons. My grandfather was an early shareholder, and he always said it was his proudest startup. Someone at BA investor relations had done the heavy lifting and even sent a Bentley around to take Mallory to the airport. He did what I expected and rode up front.

A month ago, a package had come from Spain. Inside were twelve red grapes and a card:

On New Year's Eve, we gather on Puerta del Sol Square and eat a grape with each chime of the bell atop the Casa de Correos. It's supposed to bring good luck, especially if you're doing it with someone special.
Perhaps you'll join me this year.

Marisol

Mallory had freeze-dried the grapes, and they looked a bit haggard. I hoped I wasn't going to have to answer any questions from Spanish Customs. But maybe they'd understand.

Just before takeoff, I made an overseas call. Lord Rittenhouse answered the phone himself. "Ah, Mr. Black. How are you?"

"Very well, sir, and you?"

"A continuing disappointment to my undertaker. I presume, you're calling about the knighthood ceremony. You should be receiving the details shortly."

"Lord Rittenhouse, I'm deeply grateful for the honor, but I'm going to have to decline. I sincerely hope I haven't put you in an awkward position."

I'd clearly caught him off guard. "Of course not, I was only the messenger. But I'm not sure this has ever happened before, and I expect it will eliminate you from future consideration."

"I've taken that into account."

"Then, if I'm not prying, would you mind telling me why?"

"It's difficult to articulate, but you're more likely to understand than anyone. If I become Lord Black, then my father is really . . . how do I say this . . . I'm not ready to let him go."

There was a long silence, and I thought I heard some roughness in the lord's voice when he spoke. "It is said that a son cannot truly become a man until he has buried his father. You became a man long before you buried yours, and it was a great joy to him."

"Thank you. I still speak with him every day. I'll give him your best."

"I would be honored."

As I rang off, Dominique's lovely voice came over the intercom. "If you're secured, Mr. Black, we're ready to begin our roll."

I sat back, closed my eyes and felt LA drop away.

Acknowledgments

No novel is written alone. All are outgrowths of relationships, experiences and information that come together only when an author sits down with pen and paper or puts fingers to a keyboard. The spark that coalesces this primordial soup of data and ideas is often indeterminable. But sometimes it is anger, and that is never mysterious.

The idea for *Wildcase* began while I was watching the opening ceremonies of the Beijing Olympics. Information about Communist China gained from interaction with Chinese military officers, American intelligence professionals and expatriate mainland nationals during my years as a motion picture executive left me with my teeth on edge as I watched the endless media fawning over a government, which, in political prisons only a few miles off-camera, was concurrently torturing gays, students, journalists, nurses, doctors, businessmen and housewives without mercy or appeal.

The centerpiece of that evening's gut-wrenching chill-fest was the six-foot four-inch, black-booted, goose-stepping Praetorian Guard, carrying flags in that stylish, cross-handed manner made popular by those sensitive gentlemen in 1936 Berlin. Of the hundreds of network sycophants fighting for face-time during those two weeks of Potemkin-land coverage, only one anchor was moved to remark that he found the always-present military exhibition somewhat disturbing. He didn't mention why. Had they been asked, the ghosts of Henan and Tibet would have been less reticent.

And for those who are squeamish about calling out a superpower on human rights and free speech—even one that once systematically starved and executed thirty million of its own citizens—I offer that no regime that ever walked the planet has done more environmental damage, eradicated as many species, destroyed as much history, wiped away as many cultures and remains less repentant about its crimes than Mao's and its descendants.

Mass market fiction is not the place one looks for political commentary, and the Acknowledgments section of this novel will be read by fewer people than will be ticketed this weekend for smoking in New York bars. That is just as well, as I make no pretense of speaking for anyone but myself. At least now, I have. Those ghosts, well, I welcome them over my shoulder.

As always, I would like to thank my family for its support. My wife, Sandra; my sons, Andrew and Trevor; and my brothers-in-law, Scott Ricketts and Lee Tawes. My sister, the talented designer, Marsha Russell, continues to provide me with elements from her work that I appropriate without hesitation or shame. The least I can do is say thanks.

I would like to thank HarperCollins for affording me the opportunity to write this novel and the freedom to write it my way. I am grateful for the continuing support of my editor, Matt Harper, and publisher, Liate Stehlik. Thank you also to Christine Maddalena and Greg Shutack, the always upbeat and enthusiastic HarperCollins publicists who work overtime on my behalf.

My literary agent, Lisa Erbach Vance at Aaron Priest, has become a trusted advisor as well as a representative, and I thank her for her insightful words and encouragement. Likewise my entertainment agents at CAA, Matthew Snyder and Tony Etz, whose counsel I would be diminished without.

To Judge James Zagel, Joe Stinson, Dennis Hackin and my attorney, Jay Coggan, I thank you for reading early versions of the manuscript and offering your thoughts and corrections. The novel and I are better for it.

To producers Mace Neufeld and Stephanie Austin, I thank you for your support and hard work on behalf of my writing.

I also offer my deep appreciation to those who toil in anonymity trying to save the castoff children of China and others who seek to preserve the last of Asia's tigers. I fear for the outcome of both of your callings, but Godspeed.

Thank you also to Michael and Wink Jackson, founders of Zeal Optics in Boulder, Colorado, who permitted Rail Black and his yachting guests to wear some very cool shades.

And finally, I would like to remember a group of very brave men, most of whom have passed on to their next mission: the officers and crew of the aircraft carrier, USS *Sitkoh Bay*. My father served among you, and, like so many others, you performed your service heroically and sent us into a future of hope instead of tyranny. I am honored to be the son of one of you.

9222

New York Times bestseller

JAMES ROLLINS

THE LAST ORACLE
978-0-06-123095-0

What if it were possible to bioengineer the next great prophet—a new Buddha, Muhammad, or even Jesus? Would this be a boon . . . or would it bring about the destruction of humankind?

THE JUDAS STRAIN
978-0-06-076538-5

A horrific plague has arisen from the depths of the Indian Ocean to devastate humankind.

BLACK ORDER
978-0-06-076537-8

Buried in the past, an ancient conspiracy now rises to threaten all life.

ALTAR OF EDEN
978-0-06-123143-8

Baghdad falls . . . and armed men are seen looting the city zoo. Amid a hail of bullets, a concealed underground lab is ransacked—and something horrific is set loose upon the world.

THE DOOMSDAY KEY
978-0-06-123141-4

Three murder victims on three continents are linked by a pagan Druidic cross burned into their flesh, part of an apocalyptic puzzle dating back centuries.